Sophie Pembroke h[...]
and writing romance[...]
Mills & Boon as part[...]
degree at Lancaster U[...], so getting to write
romantic fiction for a living really is a dream
come true! Born in Abu Dhabi, Sophie grew up
in Wales and now lives in a little Hertfordshire
market town with her scientist husband, her
incredibly imaginative and creative daughter and
her adventurous, adorable little boy. In Sophie's
world, happy *is* for ever after, everything stops for
tea, and there's always time for one more page…

Cara Colter shares her home in beautiful
British Columbia, Canada, with her husband of
more than thirty years, an ancient crabby cat and
several horses. She has three grown children and
two grandsons.

SOCIALITE'S NINE-MONTH SECRET

SOPHIE PEMBROKE

ACCIDENTALLY ENGAGED TO THE BILLIONAIRE

CARA COLTER

MILLS & BOON

First published in Great Britain 2024
by Mills & Boon, an imprint of HarperCollins*Publishers* Ltd,
1 London Bridge Street, London, SE1 9GF

www.harpercollins.co.uk

HarperCollins*Publishers*, Macken House, 39/40 Mayor Street Upper, Dublin 1, D01 C9W8, Ireland

Socialite's Nine-Month Secret © 2024 Sophie Pembroke

Accidentally Engaged to the Billionaire © 2024 Cara Colter

ISBN: 978-0-263-32129-6

04/24

This book contains FSC™ certified paper
and other controlled sources to ensure responsible forest management.

For more information visit www.harpercollins.co.uk/green.

Printed and Bound in the UK using 100% Renewable Electricity
at CPI Group (UK) Ltd, Croydon, CR0 4YY

SOCIALITE'S NINE-MONTH SECRET

SOPHIE PEMBROKE

MILLS & BOON

For anyone who feels the need to hide away
from the world for a little while.

I know you'll come out fighting when you're ready.

CHAPTER ONE

AFTER A LONG FLIGHT, a sleepless night in an airport hotel and too many hours in the town car she'd hired to drive her from London to Cornwall, the sight of the first sign for the village of Rumbelow sent relief flooding through Willow's tense body.

She'd made it—near enough, anyway. And, as far as she could tell from social media, without being spotted, which was the most important thing.

Nobody would be looking for supermodel and social-ite Willow Harper in Cornwall, when she was supposed to be in New York. What possible reason could she have to go there?

Even those who remembered the early days of her career, when she'd modelled with her twin sister, didn't know where Rowan had fled to when she'd disappeared six years ago. The family had no link to Cornwall, de-spite hailing from London originally, and Rowan had been *very* circumspect regarding her whereabouts ever since. Willow suspected she was the only person from their old life who knew where she was at all.

And even she hadn't visited, or seen Rowan, in those six years.

Until now.

Because now she needed her help.

The car and its silent driver took the last curve in the road and the small harbour of Rumbelow came into view, the sea glistening in the early spring sunlight. Tiny fishing boats bobbed out on the waves—so different from the mega yachts and sailing club boats she'd grown used to in her society circles in the States.

They drove along the edge of the village, the long black car slowing almost to a stop to make the tight corners safely, and Willow peered out of the tinted windows at the quaintly painted cottages and the cobblestone streets that led away from the road and into the village centre.

It was a pretty enough hiding spot, she had to allow that—for Rowan, and for her.

Rowan's cottage, it seemed, was on the outskirts of the village. They drove around the outside to the other side of the harbour, where the glass and steel outline of what appeared to be an old lifeboat station that someone had converted into living accommodation gleamed in the distance above the waves. Before that, though, was a small stone cottage with a thatched roof, looking down on the beach below, its sand covered in seaweed and stones, and over at the cliffs beyond, now the neat harbour had given way to more natural coastline.

The driver drew the car to a halt and got out in silence, the same way he'd undertaken the entire journey. She heard the trunk of the car open and assumed he was getting out her suitcase. She waited and, soon enough, he opened the door for her and she climbed out.

It was the air that hit her first: salty and tangy and fresh as a steady breeze beat against her skin and tried to mess up her hair. There was no reason for it to feel so different from the coast in the States, really, but it did. If she closed her eyes, she could be back at the seaside with her grandparents, Rowan paddling beside her, waiting for salty chips and sweet, sticky ice cream.

Before her grandparents died. And before that scout told their mother how much money they could make her.

Willow swallowed and shook the thought away. She had nothing to complain about. Her whole world had changed that moment—and look how far it had taken her. She had fame, riches, a life others would kill for.

Right now, though, she also had a secret.

The driver was looking dubiously at Rowan's little stone cottage. Willow supposed she couldn't blame him; it did look a little like it might crumble into the sea at any moment.

'Do you have the keys, miss?' he asked, his voice a little creaky. 'I can take your bags in for you.'

'Uh, actually, I'm just going to wait here for my sister.' Along the cliff path, she could see a figure approaching, perhaps from that lifeboat station, since it seemed the only house further out of the village than Rowan's. 'You can just leave my bags here, it's fine.'

The driver frowned. 'Are you absolutely sure?'

'Very.' Willow swallowed down her irritation and forced a smile. She needed him to go, and fast, before Rowan's neighbour got any closer and started asking questions. She fumbled in her bag for a tip, and thrust a few notes into his hand. 'Thank you for the drive. Please, you should get going. It's a long way back to London.'

He gave her one more sceptical look, then took the money and got back into the car, reversing slowly into a side path to enable himself to turn around without driving off the cliff. The car disappeared towards the town before Rowan's neighbour reached her front gate, and Willow let out a small sigh of relief. She settled on sitting on top of her suitcase while she waited for her sister, her eyes tracking the neighbour as they jogged closer.

He. Definitely a he. With strong muscled legs under his running shorts and a black T-shirt already clinging to his torso. His dark hair hung long enough for him to shake it out of his eyes as he ran, and he was moving at an impressive pace. Willow ran, for fitness, stress relief and because it looked good in paparazzi photos, but she never went fast enough that she ended up unpleasantly red-faced and sweaty in those photos. She saved that sort of effort for the private gym in her Manhattan building.

But this guy was moving fast and *still* looked good. She was almost jealous.

She jerked her gaze away as he approached the gate and, standing quickly, dropped her tan leather jacket over her bags in the hope he wouldn't notice them, pushing them slightly behind the overgrown shrubbery of Rowan's front garden.

'Morning!' he called as he reached the edge of the fence marking her property.

'Uh, yeah,' she said back, somewhat taken by surprise. 'Morning.'

In New York, locals and tourists barely acknowledged other people with a nod, let alone a verbal greeting.

You're not in New York any more, Willow.

For all she knew, Rowan was best friends with her neighbour round the harbour. Maybe they had coffee together every morning. Maybe they were *more* than friends.

In which case, her sister had definitely been holding out on her during their calls, and she was in for a grilling.

The guy slowed to a stop at the gate, one hand on the fence as he looked at her, a small frown line between his eyebrows. 'You lock yourself out or something? I can run back and get my spare key if you need it.'

He had a spare key. Okay, so friends, then.

He also thought she was Rowan, even if the frown suggested he sensed something was amiss.

'Oh, no, I'm fine, thanks. Just…enjoying the morning.'

'Not contemplating joining me for a run at last?' The teasing tone of his voice hinted that this was something he suggested often.

Willow shook her head. 'I don't think I'm dressed for it.'

'No.' And now that frown was back, as he looked her up and down. 'Big plans today? You're looking very… smart.'

She glanced down at herself in case she'd suddenly changed into a ballgown or something. Nope, same wide-leg nude trousers and black sweater, with her chestnut leather boots. It was warm enough that she'd even taken her tan leather jacket off for now.

'No, just…a normal day. Perfectly normal.'

Oh, yeah, that sounded convincing.

And from the way the guy's eyebrows rose, he wasn't convinced either.

Gwyn looked at his neighbour with what he could only think of as amused suspicion.

He and Rowan weren't exactly close friends, but they *were* neighbours, the two furthest out dwellings in the village, and so they'd got to know each other a little. They had spare keys to each other's houses, checked with each other on bin days and WhatsApped snippets from the local village Facebook group for their mutual entertainment.

And he jogged past her cottage every morning and more often than not spotted her on her way in or back from the village centre, or working in her garden, or just pottering about inside the cottage. Sometimes she'd wave. Sometimes he'd invite her to join him and she'd laugh and shake her head. Sometimes he'd stop for a chat, especially if he was on his way back and kind of already done and needing a break before the last burst up the hill and round the harbour to his house.

But never, in all the years they'd been doing this, had he ever seen Rowan in full make-up, her hair brushed and her shoes shined at this time in the morning. Or ever. He'd never seen her wearing clothes so plain and colourless either.

And he'd never seen her hiding a suitcase under her coat, for that matter.

Was she going somewhere and didn't want him—or, by extension, probably the rest of the village—to know about it?

Rumbelow was a small place. And as much as the locals let newcomers live their own lives without asking too many questions, that didn't mean they weren't watching. Or talking about them behind their backs.

Gwyn wasn't a newcomer, exactly—although he suspected Rowan thought he was. After all, he'd bought the most obvious, expensive, fancy modern renovation place in the whole village when he'd moved back from London.

That wasn't *why* he'd bought it, of course—he'd bought it because it was the furthest out of Rumbelow he could be while still being in the village, and because it only had one real neighbour, and because he liked looking out over the sea from the giant glass windows that used to be the doors to the lifeboat shed.

Rowan, as far as he knew, didn't know that Gwyn's family had been in the village for generations, or that his sister and nephew still lived there. She didn't know he'd grown up there, moved away, then come home when everything had fallen apart.

But then he suspected Rowan still thought that nobody in town had clocked that she used to be a kind of famous model, when obviously they had, almost immediately. They were just too polite around here to make a big deal of it, since she so obviously didn't want a big deal being made.

None of which explained why she was sitting there with a suitcase, looking like she was about to head up to London for some big fashion shoot. Maybe she was. Maybe that was what she was hiding—or hoping he wouldn't notice.

Well, if she wanted to keep her secrets, he'd let her. After all, he had no interest in sharing his own.

So he gave her a last smile and said, 'Okay, well, enjoy your day.' Then he pushed off again and began the easy run down the hill back into the village, planning to stop in at his sister's to see if she had any coffee on the go, and maybe some of those cinnamon rolls she made…

Which was when he spotted Rowan walking up the hill towards him, wearing the bright turquoise and pink maxi skirt he often saw her in, her hair in its usual bun on the top of her head and a straw shopping bag swinging at her side as she smiled and waved.

He blinked, almost stumbled and then kept going.

Other people's secrets were none of his business. And neither were their problems.

Although he had to admit he was curious as to what supermodel Willow Harper was doing pretending to be her own sister, right here in Rumbelow.

Willow braced herself as she saw her sister appear around the corner, looking as bright and cheerful as she always did on their video calls these days—a sort of relaxed contentment that Willow couldn't remember seeing in person since they were kids.

It was real, that contentment, she was sure. But she always felt there was just a hint of something missing underneath it too. A feeling that Rowan had settled for contentment rather than reaching for happiness.

Willow stifled a snort. Who was she to talk about happiness as something to be actively pursued? Hadn't she spent the last few years settling for image—style over substance—in all areas of her life?

Not any more, though. I can't do that any longer.

And maybe her new resolution to do better could help her sister find the life she was meant to be living too. Even if she had doubts at how effective her plan would be at *really* fixing everything that was wrong in her own life.

I just need time. Space. To breathe and think and figure things out.

Rowan was the only person in the world that Willow could rely on to give it to her.

She knew the moment that her twin spotted her. It was

obvious in the way her easy gait faltered, and her shoulders stiffened even as her face slackened.

Maybe she should have called ahead, told her she was coming. Or emailed, even. Except…she was never sure how secure those things were. All it would take was one journalist listening in or hacking her email and her secret would be out.

Because Rowan was going to have questions—a lot of questions. Questions Willow needed to answer in person, without being overheard, if she wanted to keep her secrets.

Suddenly Rowan shook her head and hurried towards the gate, fumbling for her keys even as she stepped onto the path.

'What are you *doing* here?' Her whisper was harsh, unwelcoming, as she fiddled with the lock until the door fell open. 'Come on, come in. Before someone sees you.'

Willow did as she was told, following her sister into the tiny, dark cottage. Not quite the homecoming she'd been hoping for, but that probably served her right for showing up with no notice.

'How long have you been here?' The door slammed behind them.

Willow raised her eyebrows. 'In England or on your doorstep?'

'Both.'

Willow placed her large tote bag on the floor beside the telephone table and frowned at the old-fashioned rotary dial phone that sat there. How ridiculously impractical. And convenient for her, actually.

'I arrived in England last night,' she said, straightening up again. 'I stayed at a hotel near Heathrow, then got a car to bring me down here this morning. I'd been standing on your doorstep for about ten minutes when you arrived. I did try to call, but...'

She gave the rotary dial phone another dubious look to back up her little white lie.

'Cell signal can be unreliable here.' Rowan carried her own tatty straw bag down the darkened hall into a decidedly brighter kitchen at the back of the cottage. It looked out over a higgledy-piggledy garden that looked like someone—presumably Rowan—might have been trying to grow vegetables.

This really was another world.

Rowan emptied her bag out onto the battered kitchen table. 'Croissant?'

The morning sickness had mostly passed now, which she took to mean she was probably past twelve weeks, since that was when all the websites she'd read in secret said it would. But mornings had never been Willow's favourite time to eat, and after a long flight and a lengthy car journey her stomach turned at the idea of the flaky pastry. She shook her head and Rowan bit into one with a shrug.

Willow looked away, taking in the kitchen, with its mismatched sage and lavender chairs that matched the pots of lavender growing outside the window. It was a sunny, happy place. It suited Rowan.

Willow had never felt more out of place in her life.

Still, when her sister motioned for her to sit, she did. And then she got down to why she was there.

'I need your help.'

Rowan reached for another croissant. 'That doesn't sound good.'

Willow knew why. This wasn't the way things went. Willow didn't come to Rowan for help; it had always, always been the other way around, ever since they were kids.

Willow had been the strong, capable one. Rowan the one who needed protecting, looking out for.

When Rowan had needed to leave, Willow had been the one to get her out—and the one to stay behind and face the wrath of their mother, and all those contracts Rowan had walked out on.

Rowan hid, Willow stayed and faced the music.

But this time…this time it needed to be the other way round. It was time for Willow to call in that favour.

'What do you need?' Rowan asked cautiously.

Willow glanced towards the kettle. 'I think we might need tea for this.' She would have preferred coffee, but apparently tea was better right now. She'd been trying to limit herself to just one strong coffee in the mornings, and she'd already had that on the way from the airport.

She waited until her sister had got up to find mugs and tea leaves and an actual teapot, complete with knitted cosy, and poured the tea. Then she took a deep breath and said, 'I'm going to have a baby.'

'You're *pregnant*?' Rowan plonked one of the mugs of tea down in front of her, and Willow watched a few drops slosh onto the table top. 'How did that happen?'

'It certainly wasn't planned, I can tell you that.' Willow sighed and reached for her mug, blowing slightly over the surface so steam snaked up towards the ceiling. The *plan,* such as it was, had been very, very different. If it had been *planned* she might have a better idea when exactly it had happened, but her cycle had never been regular enough for that. Still, that many pregnancy tests didn't lie.

'Who's the father? Does he know?' Rowan demanded.

'Ben, of course.' Willow frowned at her sister across the kitchen table. 'What did you think?'

'Sorry. I just…' Rowan trailed off. She'd never met Ben, Willow supposed. She wouldn't know. 'I guess I figured that if the father was your long-term boyfriend you'd be talking to him instead of me.'

That made Willow wince and look away towards the window. Talking to Ben was right at the bottom of her list of things she wanted to do right now.

How on earth was she going to explain her relationship with Ben to Rowan? Rowan believed in true love and authenticity and finding your person.

She wasn't going to understand what Willow had with Ben.

'Things with Ben and me…it's not what I'd call a stable relationship environment. Or anything a kid should be involved in.' Willow took care to keep her words flat, unemotional. But Rowan's expression told her she was reading plenty into them, all the same.

'Does he hurt you? Physically or emotionally? Because you do *not* have to go back to him—'

'It's not like that.' Willow sighed. 'He's… I mean, we're…'

'You're really convincing me here, Will.'

Willow huffed a laugh and looked down at her tea again. Fine. It was going to have to be the truth, then. However shameful it felt in the face of Rowan's fairy tale cottage by the sea life.

'I know. I'm sorry. It's just…the world thinks we're

some fairy tale romance, right? The supermodel and the CEO, living our perfect glamorous life together, madly in love?'

'And it's not really like that?' Rowan asked softly.

It was, she supposed, in parts. They *were* a supermodel and a CEO, and their life was pretty glamorous, certainly from the outside.

It was just the *in love* part that tripped the whole thing up.

'You know, some days I'm not sure we even *like* each other,' Willow admitted. 'Right from the start...we were together because it was good for our images, our careers. We look good next to each other, and the papers like to talk about us a lot, and that was kind of what we both needed. We could fake the rest.'

Her mind flashed back to the night they'd met, at some party held by a mutual acquaintance. The way they'd sized each other up, figuring out what the other could offer them in a world where everything was a commodity or a status symbol. Even love.

'You *faked* being in love with your boyfriend?' Rowan made it sound like a bad rom com movie.

'Not...intentionally.' Willow sighed again. She'd known Rowan wasn't going to get it. She was barely sure that *she* understood how it had all happened.

But Rowan was obviously determined to try. 'Okay, tell me the whole story.'

CHAPTER TWO

THERE WAS NO sign of Rowan or the woman Gwyn assumed must be her sister when he jogged past the cottage towards home at the end of his run. That in itself was suspicious. Normally Rowan would be in the garden on a day like today; from the road, he could see all the way around the cottage into the back. But there was no sign of her, and the kitchen blinds had been tilted half closed too.

A clandestine visit, then.

Rowan had never mentioned her twin sister, but the identical part of their twin status was definitely no longer in doubt. If he hadn't seen the *real* Rowan just moments later, he'd have probably assumed she was just dressed up for a secret event and left it at that.

As it was, his mind kept ticking over the differences as he ran. He didn't know Rowan well enough to have been able to tell that the woman on the doorstep wasn't her—they were friends, but in a very loose, wave in the street sort of way. He wasn't even sure if *she* considered them friends.

But that was as friendly as Gwyn got these days. He didn't want to let new people in, and she didn't seem keen on the idea either, so that was fine.

Still, now he thought about it…

She'd held herself differently, maybe that was the big one. More...defensive? No. Assertive. As if she held the power here. Rowan never stood that way.

And he'd felt a sort of nervous tension coiled inside her as she spoke, but there was still a hint of something behind her eyes. A spark, as she looked him over.

He'd never felt *that* when talking about the latest bin collection shambles with Rowan.

Still, she'd obviously wanted him to believe she was her sister. Why? Why was she here at all, for that matter? She must need or want something from Rowan.

He wondered what.

He didn't spend *too* much time wondering though; other people's lives weren't his business—which meant they couldn't be his problem either. And that was the way he liked it.

But when he reached home he saw one of the few people whose lives *were* his business—and often his problem—waiting for him.

Gwyn slowed to a halt on the steps down to the deck that surrounded this half of his ex-lifeboat station home, resting his hands on his thighs as he caught his breath. 'Sean. Everything okay?'

It wasn't that his nephew never came to see him unless there was something wrong, but...actually, yes, it was exactly that.

But Sean just shoved his hands deeper into the pockets of his jeans and nodded. 'Yeah, all good. I just...there was something I wanted to talk to you about.'

Oh, that was worse than there being a problem to solve. Sean wanted his *advice*. Didn't he know how bad Gwyn was at giving that?

He moved past Sean to unlock the side door and let them in. 'Have you spoken to your mother about it?'

Gwyn's sister, Abigail, was the best at knowing what to do and giving advice. Why Sean had decided to come to him instead was a mystery.

'Yeah, a bit.' Sean eyed him cautiously, still hovering in the doorway with his hands in his pockets. 'She said that you'd be the one to ask, except you wouldn't want to talk about it.'

Gwyn's shoulders tensed involuntarily. That didn't bode well at all. Although, in fairness, there were a lot of things he didn't want to talk about.

'We're going to need coffee for this, I reckon,' he said, and moved towards the kitchen.

When he'd decided to move home to Rumbelow—although *decided* was a bit strong, wasn't it? Given that he'd mostly stumbled back in a panic and crashed on his sister's sofa for the first six months. But when he'd decided to *stay*, and buy his own place, discovering that the old lifeboat station was up for sale had felt like a sign.

Now, standing in his kitchen, looking out at the waves as he pressed buttons on the coffee machine on autopilot, he had that feeling again. This was where he was meant to be. Close enough to be on hand if his sister and Sean needed him, far enough away from everyone else that he couldn't get drawn into village politics or other people's problems. And at a moment's notice, he could always jump off the deck down the steps at the back of the house and into the sea—or at least take out the little boat he kept tied up there.

It was perfect.

What *wasn't* perfect was whatever problem had brought Sean to his door.

He wanted a shower, and then he wanted peace and quiet to mull over what was going on with Rowan and her sister without having to worry that it would affect his life in any way. But what he *had* was a nephew who needed him, and coffee.

He sighed, and turned back to hand Sean his mug.

'Okay. What's going on?'

'It's Kayla,' Sean said.

'I could have guessed that.' Kayla was Sean's girlfriend of the last six months or so, and probably the only thing Uncle Gwyn might be more qualified to talk about than Sean's mum. Okay, not *qualified*. Comfortable, maybe.

He waited silently for his nephew to say more, but his mind was already working overtime. Was Kayla pregnant? Did Sean plan to propose? Was *she* pushing for him to propose? Had one of them cheated? Was she leaving the village for some reason? Or was there another argument he didn't know about, something causing tension between them?

'She thinks we should head to London and try and make it on the music scene there,' Sean said finally.

Gwyn's chest tightened. Of course she did. Of course she would.

He knew how serious Sean and Kayla were about their music. That was how they'd got together in the first place, performing together at the local pub's open mic night after weeks of watching each other up on stage. They were a great duo, and they both had real talent. Gwyn should be encouraging them.

But instead he said, 'You're not ready.'

Sean nodded dutifully. 'That's what I said. We need more songs first; we've got a few really great ones, but the rest are covers, and I want to go there with our strongest game.'

'Right,' Gwyn said, even though that wasn't what he'd meant at all.

'She figures we'll get inspired just by being there, though, being part of the scene,' Sean went on. 'Except we don't have the money for that. We'd be working all the time just to pay rent.'

'Exactly.' He hadn't meant that either. But Sean seemed to be talking himself out of the idea all on his own, which worked for him.

'So we shouldn't go yet, right?' Sean looked up at him with an uncertain gaze, the vulnerability in his face clear.

He trusted his uncle to tell him the truth. To offer advice in his best interests.

To put aside his own past to consider this situation.

It was only the last one Gwyn couldn't do.

He sighed. 'Look, I think you're right. London is tough, the music industry is tougher, and if you don't think you're ready for it, then you're not. Take the time and do it right.'

Or never. Never would work for Gwyn too.

He'd seen what the music industry could do to talented young men from Cornwall. He'd lived it. And his best friend hadn't survived it.

He and Darrell had been just like Sean and Kayla—well, musically, anyway. They'd been young and talented and determined to make it big, and they'd moved to London in search of fame and fortune. And they'd got lucky—after a lot of hard work. They'd got that coveted record deal eventually.

Yes, they'd been a success—there'd been albums and tours and billboards, for a time, anyway.

But there'd also been drugs and depression and death. And a life Gwyn could have had here in Rumbelow that had slipped through his fingers when he'd left, and he'd never been able to get back.

Was any of it worth it? Not in Gwyn's book.

Fame brought misery, not just fortune. And he wouldn't wish it on anyone. Especially not one of the only two people in the world he still cared about.

Gwyn didn't like to mess with other people's lives. He didn't want to get involved. But in this case…

'You're doing the right thing, Sean,' he said. 'Stay here in Rumbelow.'

He had to keep his nephew safe. He couldn't let him walk the same path he had.

That was the only thing that mattered.

Telling Rowan the whole story took longer than Willow had expected—and required several cups of tea. But the basics—the unvarnished, unflattering, unimpressive basics—didn't change, no matter how she explained it.

She and Ben had met at that society party and realised they were a good fit—not personally, exactly, but in the eyes of all the people around them. They were the sort of partner the other needed by their side at functions and in paparazzi photos.

For her part, Ben was rich enough that she could be sure he wasn't just after her money, and he was successful enough that he wasn't intimidated by her fame—which had definitely been an issue in the past. They also had a lot of friends—or, well, acquaintances—in common, so it was inevitable they'd end up at a lot of the same events.

As far as she understood Ben's motives, the fact that she was universally acknowledged as being beautiful seemed to be enough for him.

So they went out on a date and got photographed by the paparazzi. So they went out on another one, and people started talking about them. And she liked that. She liked being seen with a popular, rich, intelligent man. It gave her a sort of cachet that just being beautiful had never achieved. As if people saw the way Ben looked at her and thought, *There must be something more to her.*

Except, she realised too late, all Ben *ever* saw was her looks.

She sighed and finished the story. 'And now it's two years later, and we've never really had a conversation about our future, or our feelings, or if we even like each other beyond spending time in the public eye together and having someone there to have sex with whenever we want to scratch that itch.'

'Do you want to?' Rowan asked, her brows knitted together as she tried to make sense of the mess Willow had made of her love life. 'I mean, do you want to tell him about the baby? See if the two of you can be a real family together?'

Willow knew why she was asking the question. It was something neither of them had ever known. Their father had been out of the picture almost before they were born, and their mother hadn't exactly been mum of the year. She'd always been more interested in how much money they could make her than who they were inside.

Even Willow knew that. Rowan had been the one who

couldn't take it, who'd run away because she needed more. Who'd never spoken to their mother since.

Willow... Willow had understood their mother better, she thought. And once she was a grown-up, and her mum had remarried and moved away, it seemed she'd found someone else to fulfil that role—of seeing Willow as a commodity, rather than a person.

God, how had it taken her so long to realise that?

'I...' Willow looked up and met Rowan's gaze, swallowing hard. 'It sounds awful, but I don't think I do. This is the man I spent the last two years of my life with, sort of. But I know—like, deep down, heart knowledge—that he'd be the wrong partner for me in this. That we wouldn't be happy—and neither would our kid.'

Just saying it out loud made it feel more real.

She might have screwed up in her relationship with Ben. She might have screwed up by getting pregnant in the first place.

But she didn't have to *keep* screwing up.

'You still need to tell him, though,' Rowan pointed out. 'Especially if... Wait. I skipped ahead a step. Do you know what you want to do? Do you want to keep the baby?'

That at least was an easy question.

The timing was terrible, the circumstances anything but ideal, the father not who she should have chosen... but she wanted this baby.

It was strange. Being a mother wasn't something she'd ever really spent much time thinking about, the same way she'd never really imagined her wedding the way some other girls seemed to. She'd assumed the wedding thing was because she got to wear incredible dresses every day in her job, so what was one more? The baby thing… It was just impossible to picture it in her life as she lived it.

But now it was here, growing inside her, none of that impossibility mattered. Because, one way or another, she was going to make it possible.

She was fortunate, she knew that. She had the money and the resources to make this far easier than most unplanned pregnancies turned out. But she also had an unexpected extra asset—a fierce, inexplicable love and fire that had shown up the moment the test turned positive that made her determined to do whatever it took to make sure this child had the best life she could give it.

'I do. And it might be crazy, because what about my career and my figure and my life, and I don't have any support in New York, but I guess I can hire that? I don't know. All I know is that I want to be a mum—a better one than ours was. I want to raise this baby right. And yes, I *know* I have to tell Ben. I just… I need to figure some things out first, about how this is all going to work.'

'I can get that.' Rowan smiled, as if she understood at last. But Willow knew she didn't really. Not yet.

She picked her words as carefully as she could. 'I just know if I talk to Ben before I've made some decisions about everything…he'll take over. He'll want things his way and I won't be sure enough of anything to fight him on it.'

Ben had what other men described as a 'forceful personality', the sort of trait that was useful in the boardroom, she supposed, but terrible in a supposedly equal relationship. He would make a split-second decision based on the information at hand, and that was it—it was done.

Usually, Willow was happy enough to go along with

what he wanted, when it came to where to eat for dinner, or which party to go to, or where to holiday to best be seen together. But this…their child wasn't a PR stunt. And she was half afraid that if she told him, he'd have her halfway down the aisle before she'd finished the word *pregnant*.

She didn't want to marry Ben. That much she was one hundred per cent sure of.

Which meant she had to figure out what she *did* want, so she could give him that information straight, with no wiggle room for him to demand his own way. She'd discuss and debate with him, fine. But she wouldn't let herself be talked into something she didn't think was right.

So that was why she was here. To figure out what was right, before she talked to Ben.

Rowan reached across the table and grabbed her hand. 'You can stay here as long as you like,' she said, her voice fierce. 'We'll figure this all out so you can go back with a plan and do this the way you need to.'

Willow's face relaxed into a small smile. 'Thank you. That will really help.'

'Of course. You're my sister. I'll always be here for you.'

She hoped that was true. Because Willow wasn't done asking for what she needed yet. And even though she had a feeling that what she needed from her sister would end up being good for *both* of them, she was pretty sure Rowan wouldn't see it that way. At least, not to start with.

Rowan stood up and started towards the kettle again, but Willow stopped her with a gentle hand on her arm. 'Actually, there was one more thing I needed. It's a lot to ask, but…'

'Anything.'

'I need you to go to New York and pretend to be me. So Ben doesn't get suspicious. I need you to be Willow Harper, supermodel, for a few weeks.'

Gwyn was late going for his run the following day. And, actually, it was less of a run and more of a stroll into the village in a search for breakfast and coffee. Lots of coffee.

He'd slept badly after Sean's visit, memories of his own life in London, his own experiences of fame, swirling around in his head. He'd tried to drown them out with a whisky or two, drunk straight from his best cut-glass crystal, sitting out on his balcony watching the ocean. Usually, the sea made him feel relaxed, the relentless motion of the waves reminding him that the world was constantly in flux and all things would pass.

Last night, it just made him feel queasy, so he'd called time and headed to bed, where his dreams had been haunted by Darrell, asking why he hadn't saved him, why he hadn't been there. Then he'd merged into his sister, Abigail, asking him the same thing. *'Where were you, Gwyn? I needed you.'*

And finally, perhaps not worst of all, but always last somehow, the gentle ghost of Rachel—not dead, but still gone—smiling sadly at him as she said, *'You weren't here. I had to deal with it and move on.'*

He'd given up on sleep early and tried to work for a couple of hours, before falling asleep at his desk and crawling back into bed to see if it would stick for a while.

When he'd finally dragged himself out again to shower, dress and head into the village, his day was already behind schedule. Not that he really needed to stick to one that much these days.

His time as a music star had made him richer than he'd ever imagined, and the money kept rolling in as his songs were played on radios and adverts and films and TV. He still worked, keeping his hand in the industry, but writing songs for other people instead of himself. Without Darrell at his side, he couldn't imagine performing again, but the music was still inside him and he needed to get it out somehow.

The early spring sunshine was weak but still warming as he walked along the cliff path towards the town. His house, sitting just past the harbour, had a path down across the beach in low tide, or around the boats in high, but he usually preferred to climb the steps at the back of the house up to the clifftop and walk down that way. Less chance of bumping into people, except Rowan.

The locals at Rumbelow had welcomed him home without a fuss when he'd returned from London. They'd all known him since birth, remembered his parents before they passed, knew his sister well, and had stories of the scrapes he'd got into as a child. But they'd known Darrell the same way, and they all felt his loss too. So nobody had pushed, nobody had asked questions, and if they talked about what had happened, they did it behind his back, which at least meant he didn't have to hear it.

They'd just accepted him back and never blamed him—but they'd never really trusted him again either. Gwyn knew he wasn't one of them any more.

Another reason to stay out at his cliff house.

Once he'd found breakfast and coffee.

The village was busy at mid-morning, full of shoppers picking up pastries and freshly baked bread, people meeting for coffee, early tourists making the most of the sunshine before the promised rain later. The fishermen, of course, had been out at sea for hours already, but soon they'd be returning with the fresh catch, ready for the local pubs and restaurants to cook it for lunch.

In the winter the village hibernated, shrinking down to just the locals—or at least the people who lived there all year round. The holiday homes stood empty, the local caravan parks and camping sites closed for the season, and the weather drew in, dissuading day-trippers from visiting too.

Winter was the time to stay in, stay warm, and wait it out. But now, in the spring, the village was coming to life again. By the middle of summer he wouldn't be able to get a table at his favourite café for all the tourists queuing out of the door, but right now there was a seat at the window counter just waiting for him, and the waitress, Michelle, nodded to him as he took it. In no time at all, he had both a coffee and the bacon sandwich he'd been craving. The sandwich went down fast, but he took some time savouring the coffee. It was even better than the stuff from his high-end machine back at the house.

As he sat there, looking out over the village square, he spotted someone who looked both familiar and out of place at the same time, and smiled. Rowan.

Or maybe not.

Usually, his neighbour favoured bright and colourful clothes, or at least relaxed and comfortable ones. Today, she appeared to be wearing designer jeans, heeled boots, a white sweater and a tan leather jacket—the same one he'd seen tossed over a suitcase the day before. The clothes themselves didn't look overly ostentatious, but somehow the sleek and groomed outfit still gave the impression of money. As did her perfectly styled hair, make-up and designer sunglasses.

The fact she looked completely lost was a bit of a give-away too.

He ducked his head as she turned towards the café so she didn't see him, then smiled as he watched her feet move towards the door and heard the bell tinkle. Glancing up from behind his menu, he saw her scan the room then head straight for the counter.

'Rowan, take a seat, honey, and I'll bring your tea right over,' Michelle called to her. 'You want a *pain au chocolat* with that?'

Not-Rowan's eyes widened. 'Oh, I was just going to get a takeaway coffee...' she started, but Michelle had moved on and wasn't listening—which meant she didn't hear the transatlantic twang to her voice either.

Yep. Definitely not Rowan. But she hadn't corrected Michelle either, which meant she probably wanted people to think she was.

She stood uncertainly by the counter for another moment, which made Gwyn smile. She didn't look like the sort of woman who was *ever* usually uncertain.

In fact, if he was correct, this woman was used to people scampering around, catering to her every whim. Because if he was right—and by now he was pretty certain he was—this woman was Rowan's sister, supermodel Willow Harper.

Which begged the question, what the hell was she doing in Rumbelow? And why was she pretending to be Rowan?

There was only one way to find out, really.

He turned to Willow and raised a hand, beckoning her over. He figured, if she was trying to pretend to be her sister, she'd have to acknowledge her neighbour.

The indecision was clear on her face, and Gwyn hid a smile at the sight. Really, what *was* she playing at? As much as he tried to stay out of other people's issues, he had to admit he was intrigued.

Finally, she came and took the stool beside him at the window. 'Hi...uh... Gwyn.'

'Hello, *Rowan*.' If she noticed the extra emphasis he put on the name, she didn't mention it. She was still looking hopefully towards the waitress.

If he was right, she was going to be disappointed.

'It's a lovely morning out there, isn't it?' he said, jerking his head towards the window. 'Spring has definitely arrived.'

When in doubt, talk about the weather. It was the British way, after all.

'Yes. Lovely.' She gave him a tight smile.

'How's that herb garden coming on?' Gwyn had no real interest in gardening, but he knew Rowan had been sweating over trying to keep herbs alive recently because she'd complained to him about it often enough.

'Fantastic,' she responded. 'Growing like, um, weeds.'

That seemed unlikely. More proof this wasn't really Rowan.

Awkward silence stretched between them until Michelle bustled over with Rowan's usual tea tray. She plonked it down on the counter in front of her and Gwyn watched her pull a face at it.

'More of a coffee girl these days, huh?' he said.

'Oh, no, you know me. I love my tea,' she said, entirely unconvincingly.

'Of course you do.' Gwyn swallowed the last of his own coffee, then pulled out his wallet. Leaving enough to cover both orders, he got to his feet and smiled down at her.

'Come on, *Rowan*. If you're after coffee, I've got a great machine at my place.' He lowered his voice. 'And maybe once we're in private you can explain to me exactly why you're here in Rumbelow pretending to be my neighbour.'

CHAPTER THREE

FOR A SPLIT second Willow considered continuing the charade, but it was clear Gwyn wasn't going to buy it. When she'd asked Rowan about her neighbour the night before, she'd said he was nice enough but they weren't really close. But apparently he thought there was more to their friendship than she did—that or he was just incurably nosy. Either way, he was a problem. One she had to solve if she didn't want this whole scheme to be over before it even started.

So she nodded and stood up, letting him hold the door open for her as she stepped out into the spring sunlight.

If he wasn't going to buy their story, then she needed a better one. And she figured she had the length of the walk back to the lifeboat station to come up with one.

She really wished she'd had her one morning coffee already. It could only have helped.

The walk up the hill out of the village wasn't a long one, but it took long enough for Willow to mentally run through all her options.

Option One: call the whole thing off. Rowan would be at the airport by now, but her flight wouldn't have left. She could call her, tell her the jig was up and get her to head home. Give her back her passport and go back to hiding out in her cottage.

Except Willow didn't want to call her back. Convincing her to go in the first place had been hard enough. If she showed any sign of weakness Rowan would be back in a flash. And, as much as she was doing this for her own reasons, a little part of it was for Rowan too. Her twin had spent too many years isolated and alone here. It was time for her to get back out into the world again.

And Willow needed that same space and isolation to think, here in Rumbelow, away from Ben. Which meant Ben couldn't have any reason to think she wasn't in New York. Even though they were technically split up right now, she knew he'd be keeping tabs on her—and she was an easy person to keep tabs on, usually. She didn't have any shows or shoots planned for the next few weeks—much to Rowan's relief. But in a normal week she'd definitely get papped by a passing photographer and end up with her picture in the gossip mags or on the internet. All Rowan would have to do was take a walk through Central Park once a week, or maybe go shopping, and they'd be covered. Ben would believe she was still in New York, and he'd leave her be.

He'd be waiting for her to call and beg him to come back. Not that she'd ever done that before, but in his head she was sure that was what her texting to ask if he was free for a party or a premiere would amount to. Or her saying yes when he did the same. Either way, he'd be expecting her to be at his beck and call.

Rowan would probably do a better job of saying no to him than she ever had, anyway.

She didn't know how he got under her skin the way

he did, but it was a talent he'd honed over their years together. With everyone else she felt confident, together and capable of anything. But with Ben...

But she didn't have to deal with Ben right now. Right now, she needed to handle Gwyn. And he *had* to be easier to manage than Ben, right?

The salt air floating in from the sea helped to clear her mind, and she moved onto Option Two.

Tell Gwyn the truth. Come clean about who she was and hope that he'd help her. After all, Rowan said he was a good guy, and he'd obviously already figured most of it out. Maybe he'd be willing to help her keep her cover for the rest of the village.

Apparently she was going to need some help if she wanted to pass as her sister. Being literally identical didn't seem to be enough.

If nothing else, she was going to have to learn to love tea again.

There was an Option Three, she supposed—stay here in Rumbelow as Willow, not Rowan, and hope nobody said anything. But it felt like a bit too much to ask for an entire village to keep a secret. Besides, it was spring, and tourists were starting to arrive, from what she'd seen that morning. Someone would be sure to say something.

The two things she had In her favour were the fact that nobody expected to see a world-famous supermodel in a tiny Cornish village, and the fact that nobody really looked the same off camera as they did on. Without the photo retouching, the filters, the make-up and hairstyling, not to mention the incredible outfits, even Willow barely looked like Willow Harper.

She just needed to do a better job of looking like Rowan.

As they turned the next bend in the path and the village fell away, Rowan's cottage came into view. Gwyn paused for a second as they approached.

'Do we need to stop and get her too?'

Willow didn't bother pretending she didn't know who he meant. It was already clear the jig was up and Option Four—tell him he was wrong and try to style the whole thing out—wasn't going to work.

She shook her head. 'She's already gone.'

Gwyn nodded and kept walking. 'You know I'm going to be asking where, very soon.' His voice was tight, and she realised he was genuinely concerned for her sister, and whatever scheme Willow had got her caught up in.

Which, now she thought about it, was fair enough.

'When we get inside,' she replied. She didn't think it was likely anyone was hanging out on the cliffs listening in, but she wasn't going to chance it. Besides, she still needed to find the right words to explain everything, without making herself sound like she'd lost her grip on reality.

Explaining the plan to Rowan had been one thing. She'd been concerned, maybe confused, but Willow had always known her sister would come through for her in the end.

Trying to explain it to someone else…she wasn't sure quite how sane it would sound.

The cliff path turned again, one last bend leading them to a steep staircase attached to the rock. Gwyn hopped down them nimbly, with the obvious practice of having done this every day for who knew how long. Willow took them rather more gingerly. The last thing she needed now was to fall and break her leg.

Or worse. Hurt the baby.

She swallowed, and focused harder on where she placed her feet.

She wasn't used to it yet, the feeling of being more than just herself. Of having to worry about someone who couldn't take care of themselves. Who was so entirely reliant on her own body to even exist.

And that feeling was here to stay, she knew. Right now, all she had to do was eat right, rest, take the vitamins the internet said she needed, and not fall over. In just over six months' time, she was going to need to do a heck of a lot more.

Gwyn swept ahead to open what she realised must be the back door to the place, which led them into a wide, wooden-floored open-plan kitchen, dining and living space.

Willow wasn't looking at their, though. She was captivated by the view.

Huge frameless windows opened out straight onto the ocean, the glass almost disappearing until it felt as if she hovered over the waves. Without realising she was doing it, Willow moved straight to the edge, one hand resting against the glass as the sun shimmered on the water below.

There was no sign of any doors off the downstairs space, but a compact spiral staircase led up to a mezzanine floor above, where she assumed the sleeping and bathing areas must be. The upper floor came not quite to the window, but close enough to make the most of the view.

Imagine waking up to this every morning.

Her own Manhattan penthouse had its own charms, and a view out over the city and Central Park was certainly one of them. But this…this was magical.

How had she stayed away from England for so long?

'I can see why Rowan came here,' she murmured.

Behind her, coffee cups clinked and she heard the welcome sound of a coffee machine whirring, pouring hot, dark caffeine into the china. Moments later, Gwyn appeared at her side, holding out a cup towards her.

'Does that mean you're ready to tell me who you really are, and why you're pretending to be my neighbour?' He held the cup just out of reach until she nodded.

'But we'd better sit down,' she said, taking the coffee. 'It's a bit of a story.'

Gwyn tried to keep his expression blank as he listened to her story. Some of it he'd already figured out for himself—that she was Willow, Rowan's twin, and that she needed to lie low for a while so was hiding out in Rumbelow.

Other parts of the story took him rather more by surprise.

'Wait. You convinced *Rowan* to go to New York and pretend to be *you*?' He hoped to God she was doing a better job of it than Willow was here in Rumbelow. But still, the idea of his reclusive, homebody neighbour jetting off to New York to live the high life was sort of unbelievable. Rowan didn't even like having to go into the next *town* to go shopping. She ordered everything she could on the internet—he knew because he ended up with her parcels when she wasn't home. But even then he knew she was never further away than the village or the beach.

Rowan didn't go places.

Until now, apparently.

Willow pulled a face. 'It took some doing. But... I think it'll be good for her. She was stagnating here in Cornwall.'

'Stagnating,' Gwyn repeated. 'Is that what you think?'

She seemed to realise too late that she might have offended him. 'Oh, I mean, it's a gorgeous place, and I can absolutely see why anyone would want to live here. Well, not me. But Rowan, for sure. It's just, when she came here...she was running away. This was her hiding place. And it's just that it's been six years. She has to come out of hiding eventually, doesn't she?'

'I don't know,' Gwyn admitted. 'I don't know what she was hiding from.' Some things you had to hide from for ever, he supposed.

Willow tipped her head to the side. 'I thought you two were friends.'

'We are,' he said with a shrug. 'I guess. Just not the "confess our darkest secrets over bottles of wine" friends. More, "Can you take the bins out for me while I'm away?" friends. Except she's never away, so that one's just me.' Maybe they weren't friends. Maybe they were just convenient acquaintances.

'Hmm.' She seemed to be re-evaluating how much she could trust him. 'But you knew I wasn't Rowan, so you must know her pretty well. No one else noticed.'

He couldn't help but scoff at that. 'They would have done. Rowan always thought no one knew who she was either, but they did. They just didn't want to bring it up and embarrass her.' Not when she was so clearly trying to go incognito. And after a while she was just part of the village, anyway.

'Oh.' Willow's eyes were wide as she digested that information. 'So, what gave me away?'

'You mean, apart from ordering coffee instead of tea? I don't know... Your clothes, your accent, your everything. Plus, don't forget, I saw both of you at the same time yesterday. That was a pretty big giveaway.'

She winced. 'Yeah. So...are you going to tell everyone who I am?'

'Why would I?' Gwyn sat back in his chair and folded his arms over his chest as he studied her. She was tense, sitting right on the edge of her seat, her back perfectly straight. Maybe that was just model posture, but maybe not.

If he had to bet on it, he'd say she was scared—of something or someone. But what? Or who?

'I don't like to get involved in other people's business,' he said slowly, and she huffed a laugh before looking away. 'Yeah, okay, I can see how it might not seem like that. But usually, I stay as far away from other people's issues as I can—ask anyone. Maybe *that's* why Rowan and I aren't "sharing" friends.'

'Then why are you so worked up about me being here, pretending to be her for a few weeks?'

It was a fair question, and one Gwyn wasn't entirely sure he had a good answer to.

'I just hate to see anybody doing something so badly,' he said, mostly to buy himself time.

She snorted. 'Fine. You want to coach me on how to be my sister?'

'No. I want you to tell me why you're even trying.' The words came out without thought, without intention for sure. He didn't care what her problems were, and he sure as hell didn't want to get involved.

Except…he'd saved her from embarrassed explanations in the café, and he'd brought her home for coffee. So maybe he cared a little bit, despite himself.

Somehow, he suspected this was his nephew's fault, or maybe his sister's. They kept trying to get him more involved in things, to the point of even asking him for *advice*. Yeah, this was probably their fault.

Willow's eyes had narrowed and she was studying him carefully, obviously deciding what to tell him. Which meant whatever she was planning wasn't the truth. Well, he didn't have the time or energy for lies.

'Don't bother trying to sell me on some "it's all for her own good" scheme,' he said casually. 'We both know you wouldn't be here if you weren't running or hiding from something. So, if you want me to help you, tell me what it is. If you don't…' he shrugged '…finish your coffee and we'll talk about the weather. It's no skin off my nose. Just don't bother lying to me. Okay?'

Willow gave a slow nod, sighed, then put her coffee cup down on the small table between them.

'It goes without saying that this has to stay just between the two of us, right?' She sounded suddenly far more serious, and more weary, than she had before.

Gwyn nodded. 'Trust me, I don't tell my own family what's going on with me. I'm not about to start gossiping about you.'

'Good. Because…you're right. I *am* hiding out here. And I asked Rowan to go to New York and be seen there so that people—one person, really—would think I was still in the city. Because I need to take some time away to think and decide what to do next. Because, you see…' she swallowed so hard he saw her throat move '… I'm pregnant.'

Gwyn looked so astonished she felt obliged to add, 'It's not yours, don't worry,' in her driest voice.

He chuckled at that, which made her feel a little better.

Here she was, outing her biggest secret to a virtual stranger, and he just looked horrified. Why? Did he think she was going to be a terrible mother? Well, yes, he probably *did* think that since the only thing he knew about her was that she'd conned her own sister into leaving the safety of this village to fly to New York and assume a fake identity, and she was drinking strong coffee while pregnant and hiding from the father of her child.

She dropped the cup into the saucer. At least the caffeine thing she could do something about. The websites said *some* coffee was fine, and she'd been trying to stick to that, but right now she couldn't remember how much counted as some and this stuff was really strong, and really she needed to *know* these things. Mothers knew things, didn't they?

She wished she hadn't sent Rowan away. She really didn't want to be alone in this.

But she had. So all she had now was… Gwyn. Who was still looking at her as if she might be playing a practical joke on him.

Then his expression hardened. 'So you've come here to—what? Get rid of it without the father knowing? Pretend it's Rowan's baby and give it up for adoption? What?'

'No!' Okay, she might not have made the best first impression here, but that was quite a leap in logic, wasn't it? Willow suspected he had his own reasons for jumping to such conclusions, but for now she just needed to focus on setting the story straight. The last thing she needed was him going to the papers with his assumptions. 'Oh, God.' She slumped down in her chair. 'That's exactly what the gossip sites are going to assume if they find out I'm here, pretending to be my sister, aren't they?' Those sites always assumed the worst, especially about her.

The more famous you were, the further you had to fall. And they just loved pulling people down.

'I'd imagine so,' Gwyn said, still watching her carefully, presumably waiting for a real explanation. 'You know how those sites are.'

And so did he, she realised from the bitterness in his voice. How? When had he been on the wrong side of their sharp tongues?

A question for another time. But definitely another layer to explore.

She was just as guilty of making assumptions about him as he was about her. She'd assumed Rowan's neighbour would be a local boy—made good, somehow, to afford this house, but still part of the community, never wanting to be anywhere else, everybody's best friend.

But the more she got to know him, the more she wondered if there was another story here she was missing. One she maybe should already know.

Right now, though, she had to challenge his assumptions about *her*.

'I came here because I needed time and space to think,' she explained. 'Not about the baby, exactly—I know I want to keep it and I'm in the fortunate position where I can afford to look after us both whatever happens next. But about the baby's father.'

'You don't want to tell him?' Gwyn guessed.

'I know I need to,' she said. 'And I wouldn't keep that information from someone, not long-term. I just… I don't think we should raise the child together.'

Now Gwyn's posture changed—from the defensive arms across the chest pose he'd been in since she'd first mentioned the pregnancy, to leaning forward, his wrists resting on his knees. 'Is this… Are you scared of him?'

It wasn't quite the same question Rowan had asked, and for some reason it gave her pause. *Was* she scared of Ben?

Yes. Yes, she was.

Just not in the way Gwyn probably meant.

'I don't think he'll hurt me, if that's what you mean,' she said slowly. 'Or the baby. That's not the sort of man he is.'

'Then what sort of man is he?' Gwyn didn't seem to have relaxed any at her words. As if he knew as well as she did that violence wasn't all of it.

'He's used to getting his own way. And he…he expects to make all the decisions.'

'You're worried he's going to offer to "do the right thing by you",' Gwyn said. 'And you don't want to.'

The right thing. What even *was* that anyway? Oh, she knew what Gwyn meant—and what Ben probably would too. That they'd get married and give the kid two stable parents and she'd probably have to give up work and push swings or bake cookies or something.

The right thing, in Ben's eyes, would be a child born

legitimately inside wedlock who could inherit the family business after him, and who he could pressurise and torment and belittle the same way his father had him.

And there was no way in hell that Willow was letting that happen.

She sighed and rubbed a hand across her forehead. 'It's complicated. His family…they have a lot of expectations. And yes, he probably would expect that we'd get married. And no, one thing this whole situation has made abundantly clear to me is that I don't want to marry him.'

She could hear Ben's voice in her head now, telling her that most women would be begging him for a ring, under the circumstances. She knew some of his past girlfriends had even tried to get pregnant to trap him into marriage—at least, according to him.

But she wasn't most women.

'So, what *do* you want?' Gwyn asked.

Willow looked up and met his steady gaze with her own troubled one. 'I guess that's what I'm here in Rumbelow to figure out.'

Gwyn held her gaze for a long moment before sitting back and nodding to himself.

He was sure she wasn't telling him everything—hardly anybody ever did, and it wasn't as if they were best friends. He barely knew this woman. But as much as his usual instincts were telling him to run—to send her on her way with good wishes and then stay the hell out of her way for the rest of her visit to Rumbelow—there was another part of him that wanted something else.

It wanted to *fix* things for her.

He tried to fight down that part, silently reminding

himself of every other time he'd tried to fix things for someone, and how every single time things had fallen apart until they were worse than before.

It wasn't just trying to save Darrell from himself in London. Or not being there in Rumbelow to save Abigail when she'd needed him, even if he knew she'd never have let him. It wasn't even everything that had happened in between with Rachel, not really—even if the baby talk had instantly brought her to mind.

It was all of those things put together, he supposed. All of them telling him that he was safer—that *everyone* was better off—if he let people live their own lives. Make their own mistakes.

Because even when he tried to intervene, to help, he only made things worse. And if he didn't let himself get involved, he wouldn't hate himself when it all inevitably went to hell.

He could already see exactly how this whole thing with Willow was going to play out, like a movie trailer in his head that gave away the whole plot in sixty seconds.

He'd go against his better instincts, give in to those big blue eyes and that lost and lonely smile, and help Willow—especially since she was all alone here in the village, vulnerable, and very likely to give herself away in about thirty seconds if he didn't. He'd challenge *anyone* not to help her.

So he'd show her around, get to know her, probably ferry her to doctors' appointments, that sort of thing. He'd listen to her worries, try to offer helpful advice or at least show her she had more options than she thought. He'd probably introduce her to Abigail, since his sister was definitely better at that sort of thing than he was.

And he'd grow to like her, he was sure. She seemed a likeable person, against the odds. He'd assumed famous supermodels would be, well, less approachable at least. Living in a different sphere of reality, perhaps. But she just seemed like a normal person, grappling with the problems of life.

He wouldn't fall in love with her—at least he didn't have to worry about that. Love wasn't really a word in his vocabulary any more—not romantic love, anyway. If he was sensible, he wouldn't let himself grow too close at all, knowing she wouldn't be staying—she'd be gone before the summer, he would bet.

Still, life would tick along and he'd help her out and feel as if he was a useful, valuable human being again for a change.

And then it would all fall apart—because it always did.

Maybe she'd go back to the boyfriend, get married, even though she knew it was the wrong thing for her.

Maybe she'd decide she wasn't cut out to be a mother and give the baby up for adoption—or farm it out to a nanny so she didn't have to be involved.

Maybe she'd realise her real life was waiting somewhere else and leave without a backward glance or a second thought.

Or maybe there was something even worse waiting around the corner for her, or for him. Heaven only knew how many times the universe had blindsided him with worse things than even his nightmares gave him.

Something would happen, and he'd be left picking up the pieces. And someone would say to him, not for the first or second or even third time in his life, *You shouldn't have got involved.*

He *tried* not to get involved. He knew how it ended.

But he looked up at Willow again, watched her worrying at her bottom lip with her teeth, twirling her blonde ponytail around one hand, and he knew that wasn't going to matter.

He sighed. 'I don't suppose you've got a doctor sorted out over here yet, have you? I've got a mate over in the next town who's a midwife. Might be more discreet than going to Dr Fenton here in Rumbelow.' Especially since Dr Fenton was a hundred years old and a notorious gossip, despite all his protestations of patient confidentiality. 'I can make a call.'

Willow smiled. 'That would be wonderful. Thank you.'

CHAPTER FOUR

IT WAS POSSIBLE that Willow hadn't thought this plan all the way through before she'd put her sister on a plane to New York.

For instance, being pregnant meant things like doctors' visits and hospital scans and not eating some things and eating others, and basically it felt like it might actually be a full-time job, just growing another human. Which she supposed made sense, when she thought of it that way.

Gwyn laughed when she mentioned it to him the following week as they drove out of the village together— the long way round, to avoid any gossip if they were seen driving through the village square together, heading off on an adventure.

'You'd be amazed what people will gossip about around here,' he'd told her as his car took the path away from Rumbelow.

'I thought Rowan said one of things she liked most about this place was that people *didn't* talk about her,' Willow had replied, confused.

'Not to her face, no,' Gwyn had said.

'Ah.' After that, she'd watched the sea fall away behind the cliffs as they turned inland towards the next town, and Gwyn's midwife friend.

It was fortunate that she'd never given up her British citizenship—it had made registering for medical care in the UK far easier than she'd expected. She'd considered just using Rowan's doctor and assuming her identity for this too, but that felt like a step too far, even for her.

She'd planned—as much as she'd planned anything—to go private. But private care this deep into Cornwall appeared to be more remote than she'd imagined, and even the nearest hospital was a serious drive away. And Gwyn's midwife friend had, against the odds, been able to fit her in without too much of a wait. So, in the end, this had just been easier.

Except, of course, she didn't have a car. It would have been kind of conspicuous to call for one of her drivers to pick her up, and according to Gwyn the local taxi driver—singular—gossiped worse than the doctor, so in the end she'd had to accept his offer to take her.

'I guess it's not the kind of job you're used to,' Gwyn said, referring to her earlier comment. 'Growing a baby, I mean.'

'Not exactly,' Willow replied drily. 'My job usually involves staying slim and—if possible—slimmer. Not growing at all.'

He glanced over at her then, his eyes only leaving the road for a second, but long enough for her to see something unexpected flash in them.

'You know, a lot of men find a pregnant woman very sexy.'

'And you're one of them, I suppose?' At least it would explain why he was being so helpful. Otherwise, she was building up a debt she was rather afraid her sister was going to have to pay when she got back.

But Gwyn shrugged. 'I've never really been around enough of them to find out. Except my sister, and she *really* doesn't count.'

'No, I can't imagine she would.' Willow pulled a face. 'But my job isn't to be sexy anyway, not really. It's to make the clothes look good.'

'You make yourself sound like a glorified coat hanger,' Gwyn pointed out.

She shrugged. 'Maybe. The point is, the clothes aren't made to fit a pregnant body. So I'm not going to be working for a little while. Which means I might as well concentrate on doing *this*.' She waved a hand around the centre of her body.

She knew she sounded nonchalant, even dismissive, about the whole thing. But that was how she dealt with it. Inside, maybe somewhere around where her baby sat, she was fizzing—with excitement and fear and anticipation and apprehension. She *wanted* this baby, more than she'd thought was possible before she'd found out she was having it.

But she also had no idea how to be a mother—especially a single mother—without screwing up. Her own hadn't exactly been a shining example.

The rest of the winding drive through the Cornish countryside passed in silence. Willow stared out of the window, ostensibly enjoying the views, but by the time Gwyn pulled into the car park at the doctor's surgery she couldn't have told him any of the things she'd seen. Her mind was elsewhere, on tiny fingers clutching hers, with no one else in the world to depend on.

'You okay about this?' Gwyn asked, and she realised

suddenly that the engine was off and he was waiting for her to unfasten her seatbelt.

She took a breath. 'I think I have to be, don't I?'

That was the thing about babies. Doubts didn't stop them coming.

Not doubts. I want this. Just... Worry. Fear.

But Willow Harper had never let being afraid stop her before. So she pressed the button to release her seatbelt and opened the car door just before Gwyn darted around to do it for her.

Inside, the waiting room was busy. Willow hung back behind Gwyn as he headed to the desk to tell the receptionist they'd arrived. She really didn't want to be noticed or recognised here and she'd dressed accordingly—in a faded pair of jeans with a striped T-shirt and an oversized cardigan of her sister's, along with baseball shoes. With her hair up, her shoulders hunched and her face dipped, the odds were she'd look just like a thousand women. At least that was the hope. Gwyn hadn't looked convinced when she'd explained about her disguise.

Now, Willow scanned the room from under the brim of the baseball cap she'd found in the depths of Rowan's wardrobe, but luckily everyone seemed preoccupied enough with whatever reason *they* had for being there that day to pay too much attention to the new couple who'd just arrived.

Couple. Oh.

Everyone here was going to think they were a couple, weren't they? If they realised she was here to see the midwife, they'd assume Gwyn was the father. Even his friend would probably think the same, unless he'd explained.

Even if he *had* explained they might suspect. She wondered if that had occurred to him yet.

There were forms to fill in, of course—lots of them. Willow hesitated only for a moment before putting her real name down rather than her twin's. Gwyn noticed, though, she was sure. She could tell by the way he watched her hawkishly until she wrote, then turned away, looking satisfied, and stretched his legs out in front of him.

'It shouldn't be too long,' he said, although Willow had no idea how he could possibly know that.

In the end, he was right, though. Her name was called just a few minutes later.

'Do you want me to come in with you?' he asked.

She did, she realised. She didn't want to be doing this alone.

But coping alone was something she was going to have to get used to, if she didn't want Ben to be a regular part of her life any more.

Maybe that was what she was really doing here in Cornwall. Testing the water to see if she could make it on her own.

Which meant not leaning on her sister's friendly neighbour any more than was strictly necessary. However appealing that idea might be.

'No,' she said finally, after too long of a pause to be convincing. 'You stay here. Otherwise, no one will ever believe you're not the father.'

He huffed a laugh at that. 'Fair point.' He sat back with his arms folded as she turned away, paperwork in hand, and walked towards the midwife's room.

But she felt his gaze on her the whole way.

* * *

Gwyn didn't really know what to expect from Willow's visit to the midwife—and he got the impression that she didn't either. She'd been nervous and distracted in the car, then fidgeting with the pen in the waiting room as she'd filled in the forms, but she'd told him not to go in with her so he hadn't.

'Otherwise, no one will ever believe you're not the father.'

It hadn't occurred to him that people would jump to that conclusion, not least because she'd only been in the country a few days and he hadn't met her before. But if people thought she was Rowan, they wouldn't know that. They'd think they were friends—maybe friends with benefits.

Of course that was the conclusion people were going to jump to—especially back in Rumbelow—once the news of the pregnancy got out.

Another reason he shouldn't have got involved.

He settled back into his uncomfortable plastic waiting room chair and waited.

Too late now.

In the end, she was much quicker than he'd expected.

'It was mostly just about getting set up and registered,' Willow explained as she hurried past him out of the building. 'She's given me some information, and taken some details from me, that sort of thing. I'm to make another appointment according to the schedule in the file, and get booked in for a scan at the hospital.' She waved a green folder vaguely.

'Don't you want to do that now?' Gwyn asked as the door swung shut behind them. 'I mean, the reception desk is right in there, and getting through on the phone can be a nightmare...'

But Willow shook her head firmly, already striding towards the car.

Gwyn hesitated for a moment, then followed. But he didn't unlock the car, not quite yet.

She looked rattled, that was the only word for it. And if they got back in the car and he started driving they'd never talk about it—or she'd have some sort of massive breakdown in the middle of the road and he'd have to pull over and deal with it there.

Playing the odds, he'd rather deal with it now.

'What happened?' he asked as he approached where she stood, leaning against the passenger side door.

'I told you. Just forms and information and setting things up. There's not much they really need to do at this point, apart from schedule my probably very over-due twelve-week scan—the dates are a little...uncertain. Anyway. It's just...it's just all up to me.'

Her voice cracked on the last few words, and under-standing rushed in.

'You're feeling overwhelmed.'

She arched an eyebrow at him. 'You don't think I *should* be? I'm entirely responsible for growing another human here, Gwyn.'

'And you just realised that if you don't go back to your boyfriend soon and come clean, you're going to be doing that all alone,' he guessed. Yeah, he could see how that would send a person spiralling.

He barely liked being responsible for himself, these days. Being responsible for other people... Just the idea made him shudder, given how badly he'd failed at it in the past.

Which was why he couldn't offer to make this any easier for Willow. If she was doing this, she was doing it alone—he certainly wasn't going to promise to be there for her, not on a few days' acquaintance and a passing friendship with her sister. It wasn't his baby, she wasn't his girlfriend—he was just a neighbour with a car and a friend who happened to be a midwife. That was all.

And he wasn't going to let it be any more, no matter how his gut told him to step in, to help, to comfort her.

He knew what lay that way, and he wasn't starting on that path.

'It's just…' Willow took a long, shuddering breath. 'It's just a lot. And my scan probably won't be for another couple of weeks, so until then all I've got is the internet for support.'

'There are probably…' he waved his hand around vaguely '…books, or something? You could order?'

'Yeah. Books.' She gave him a wobbly smile. 'That's a good idea.'

But he knew it wasn't enough. This woman needed more than a bookshop. She needed support. And she'd sent away the one person who'd be best at giving that to her.

Which meant she needed a replacement. She needed a friend.

'Thank you for bringing me today,' she said. 'I know it was an inconvenience. I'll sort something else out for the scan appointment, don't worry.'

Gwyn's jaw tightened with the effort of not promising to take her.

I'm not getting involved, remember? At least, not more *involved.*

'But I'm really glad I didn't have to do today alone.' This time, her smile was a little stronger—which was why it took him so much by surprise when she lurched forward and hugged him.

He hadn't expected her to fit so well into his arms. He was a tall man, and he wasn't used to women being the same height as him—at least, not when he was holding them. But her chin sat neatly on his shoulder, the fresh floral scent of her hair filling his lungs as he rested his cheek against it. She didn't cling on, didn't use him for support, just held him close—and Gwyn felt something dangerous twinging inside his chest.

Not getting involved, he reminded himself.

Willow pulled back and smiled at him again. 'Thanks.' She tucked a loose bit of hair behind her ear and glanced down at the ground. 'I'm not usually much of a hugger but, well, I needed that. Hormones, I guess.'

'Hormones. Right.' That made sense. It wasn't about him, she just needed a warm body to hug.

Which didn't change how stupidly glad he was that he'd been the warm body in closest proximity.

Gwyn gave himself a mental pep talk as they got into the car and he pulled out of the car park, back onto the country roads that would lead them home. He'd done a good deed for his temporary neighbour, bringing her here. He'd got a hug of thanks, and now he was done. That was all.

Okay, maybe he'd use his Amazon Prime account to send her a copy of whatever that pregnancy book was that always showed up in movies, because he suspected she wouldn't bother, and maybe it would help.

But that was definitely it. No more getting involved after that.

The familiar twists and turns of the roads grounded him, although he took them a little slower than usual with Willow in the car beside him. She seemed lost in thought too, staring back out of the window again. He wondered briefly what she was thinking about—then pushed the thought aside. Her thoughts were none of his business.

Probably the baby, though. Or what she was going to do next. The father sounded like a piece of work, from the little she'd told him. Any guy who would make a woman want to travel thousands of miles just to be sure she could figure out her own wants and needs without him trying to pressure her couldn't exactly be perfect marriage material.

Not that he could really talk, after Rachel.

And he was getting involved again.

Despite his slower speed, they made good time and before long he was pulling up in front of Rowan's little cottage to let her out.

'I suppose I'd better go figure out what there is left to eat in here,' Willow said as she climbed out of the car. 'I think I might have finished off all of Rowan's supplies, but I've got a grocery order coming tomorrow, I hope.'

One thing the tourist trade had brought to their remote area—regular supermarket deliveries. Something to be thankful for, Gwyn supposed.

But it wouldn't solve her food problem tonight. Her appointment had been late afternoon, and by now most of the shops in town would be shut. She could probably get takeaway, or put something together from whatever was in the back of Rowan's cupboards. Or…

Gwyn sighed.

He wasn't getting involved. He *wasn't*.

But he wasn't about to watch a pregnant woman starve either.

'I was going to grab dinner at the Star and Dragon in town,' he said. 'It's folk night—usually a good night. You're welcome to join me if you like.'

She gave him a wary look. 'As Rowan? Is that… Does she normally go there?'

Gwyn shrugged. 'I've never seen her there. She, uh, mostly keeps to herself, I think. I don't think anyone in the village really knows her that well.'

'But the woman in the café…she knew her regular order. She brought it over, even when I tried to order something else.'

'Yeah, well, that's just good business,' Gwyn explained. 'I mean, yes, people know her in the café and in the local shops, but only…superficially.' The same way he knew her, he supposed.

'Sometimes it feels like that's the only way anyone knows anyone else in New York,' Willow said with a sad smile. 'So you don't think anyone would notice I wasn't Rowan, if I went?'

He looked her over. Even dressed down to be incognito, she'd stand out anywhere. 'We'll stay in the corner,' he promised. 'So, you coming?'

She took a breath as if she were steeling herself, and he could actually see her resolve hardening. 'Just give me twenty minutes to get ready.'

It was closer to half an hour before Willow was ready to go, but since it took Gwyn even longer to get home,

showered, changed—and pick up what looked like a guitar case—she didn't feel bad about it. Not as bad as she
felt about admiring how good he looked with his damp
hair curling at his neck, above an open-necked white shirt
and blue jeans, and a cognac leather jacket almost the
same colour as the one she'd stashed in Rowan's closet
on arrival.

Rowan didn't wear such things. Which was why she'd
raided her sister's wardrobe to put together an outfit for
tonight.

When they'd been modelling, Rowan had always been
the one to object to the more outlandish clothes, the ones
people would never wear in the real world—but Willow
had always suspected that secretly she loved them. It
made it all feel more like dress-up, make-believe.

That was sort of how she'd felt, standing in front of
the rail of Rowan's clothes, looking at all the colours
and textures.

Willow had always been more of a neutral, classics
girl. Simple basics showed off her beauty best, according
to Ben, and countless other designers. But Rowan had
stopped caring about that once she'd left the modelling
world, it seemed. She wore the colours and the designs
that appealed to her, that made her happy.

A memory surfaced, from a long London summer
years ago, when Rowan had been almost housebound
by her own anxiety. She'd taught herself to make her own
clothes—all so different from the outfits they modelled
on the catwalk. These clothes weren't about making a
statement, or being controversial, or even showing off
as much skin as possible.

Rowan's clothes had been about comfort and love.

She'd picked colours that vibrated happiness, styles and fabrics that swept around her like a protective cloak. They'd been amazing.

It was something she did, Willow had realised from her explorations of the cottage. She'd found a tiny sewing room in the back with an empty dress form, baskets full of material and pattern paper and her trusty sewing machine in the middle on a sturdy table. From the designs pinned up on the walls, she'd been making clothes for more than just herself too.

Willow didn't have that talent. But she *did* know how to put together an outfit. So she'd raided Rowan's wardrobe and settled on a long printed skirt in a Mediterranean blue, she suspected was one of her sister's creations, worn with a fitted sweater and her own boots. She considered for a moment before pulling out her own leather jacket too. If people didn't know Rowan all that well, they might not know it wasn't her style either.

'Passably Rowanish,' Gwyn said now, as he stood in the doorway. 'Come on. We'll walk in. The night's mild enough.'

And it wasn't raining, which Willow always thought an unexpected but welcome bonus when at the British seaside.

They walked side by side down the hill towards the lights of the village ahead, and Willow found herself uncomfortably aware of the man beside her. Not just how good he looked in that jacket, or how much she wanted to touch that curl at his neck. The way his scent mingled with the salt of the sea, making it warmer, spicier. The way he laughed, warm but not mocking, when she made a comment about folk music and dancing to it in primary school.

'You might be surprised,' he told her. 'I suspect we're talking about a different sort of folk song.'

She hoped so. Those songs—all plinky strings and fake Ye Olde English—hadn't really been her sort of thing.

She took a deep breath, and got another lungful of that scent that was half Gwyn, half seaside. Why was she suddenly so aware of him? It couldn't just be damp hair and a jacket, could it?

Hormones, maybe. Pregnancy hormones were notoriously unpredictable, according to the websites she'd found. What else could have her lusting after her sister's grumpy neighbour on just a couple of days' acquaintance?

Hormones were responsible for that hug outside the doctor's surgery too. That damn hug. *That* was probably why she was so focused on his physical presence all of a sudden.

How long had it been since she'd been that close to another person? Probably the night her baby was conceived, actually. And even then…that had been sex, not closeness.

It felt wrong that she was only just now realising how different those two things were.

Damn, I have to learn a lot more about the world before I can be a mother.

But that hug…it had felt like closeness. It had felt—not intimate, exactly, but supportive. As if Gwyn had been sharing his strength and support with her, even though she'd been the one to throw herself into his arms.

It had almost felt like trust.

For someone she'd only known a few days, that was a lot.

The lights of the village grew brighter as they reached the high street, meandering along to the square at the centre. And as they approached the Star and Dragon, Willow could already hear the strains of guitars and harmonising voices.

Gwyn was right; it didn't sound anything like the traditional folk music they'd danced to at primary school.

'Come on.' Gwyn picked up the pace a little as they crossed the square. 'Let's hope we can still get a table.'

Nobody even looked up as they crossed the threshold into the pub, the door swinging shut behind them. The crowd's focus was entirely on the two people on the stage—a young man with a guitar and a woman playing another, smaller stringed instrument. They both leaned in to sing into microphones, harmonising beautifully even as they played complex chords and melodies on both instruments.

Willow wouldn't claim to be an expert on music, but she knew about captivating a room—and these two had this room's attention all sewn up.

'They're good,' she murmured as Gwyn led her towards a free table at the back, near the bar.

'They are,' he agreed. 'That's my nephew Sean and his girlfriend Kayla.'

Willow glanced down at the guitar case he'd brought with him. 'I guess you're where he gets the talent from, then?'

'Mostly he's just worked damn hard at it.' Gwyn

handed her a menu. 'What do you fancy? I can recommend the lasagne.'

The menu was standard pub fare—the lasagne came with chips—and Willow tried to remember the last time she'd ordered food like this anywhere. If she was out with Ben, they were usually in the sort of restaurants that required a tie. At home, she had a food delivery service that provided freshly prepared meals with the correct balance of all macros and micronutrients to keep her in shape.

For the first few weeks of her pregnancy, she'd mostly been concentrating on keeping food down. But as the weeks had passed, the nausea had receded, even as the fear had increased—and now, she suddenly realised, she was starving.

And she was eating for two.

She handed the menu back. 'Lasagne sounds great. With chips.'

He looked amused and as he brushed past her to get to the bar and order, he dipped his head until his mouth was right by her ear. 'Very good. Just what Rowan would have ordered.'

It wasn't until he'd gone that she remembered he'd told her Rowan never came here, so he was probably joking.

So she settled back against the wood panelling of the wall, let the music surround her and tried to fit in.

CHAPTER FIVE

IT WAS, Gwyn had to admit, pretty surreal standing at the familiar bar of the Star and Dragon, listening to the same conversations he heard here every week, with the soundtrack of Sean and Kayla's music, knowing that just over there sat Willow Freaking Harper, waiting for her lasagne.

His life had had odd moments before, but this was probably taking the biscuit.

It was good that there was a queue at the bar because he needed a few moments to make sense of it all in his head, anyway. He'd tried to process it in the shower before going to meet her, but his body kept remembering the feel of hers against him as she hugged him, and that wasn't helping at all, so he'd given up for the time being.

Yes, she was beautiful. But she was also pretending to be his friendly neighbour—who he'd definitely never had those sorts of thoughts about—and she would be leaving to go back to New York in a few short weeks.

Oh, yeah, and she was pregnant with another man's child.

So, really, he needed to get his mind out of any gutters.

To distract him, he focused in on the harmonies swirling around him. Sean and Kayla had moved on to another, more melancholy song—one about the sea and the tides and the passing of time and loss. It made his chest feel tight, but he had to admit the duo had nailed it. Sean had always been talented, but since meeting Kayla they'd taken things to another level.

They should be playing bigger gigs than the local folk night. They should be out there, making music.

He knew it, had known it for a while. But he pushed the thought away all the same.

At least here they were safe. Out there... Gwyn knew how tough it was. And how big the risks were if you wanted the real payoffs.

Not to mention everything you had to leave behind.

'Hello, stranger.' His sister Abigail hoisted herself up onto the bar stool beside him. 'I thought you weren't going to show tonight, and then your nephew would have been very disappointed. They're playing some new songs tonight.' She dropped her voice to a whisper. 'He's hoping to impress you.'

'He always impresses me,' Gwyn admitted. 'They're good, the pair of them. They're good together.'

'Remind you of anybody?' Abigail asked, too innocently.

'No.' Gwyn shut down the line of conversation with one syllable and a look, the way he always did when anyone tried to talk about Darrell. He'd have thought people would have learned by now.

Abigail sighed, and shifted her attention somewhere over his left shoulder. 'Is that your neighbour? The secret model?'

'Ex-model,' Gwyn corrected her. He knew Rowan was sensitive about her history, so people generally didn't

bring it up in front of her—even if they discussed it behind her back. And since Willow was still determined
to pretend to be Rowan, he might as well keep up the
charade.

'Whatever.' Abigail waved her hand. 'You brought
her here? I didn't know you two were going-out-together
friends.'

Gwyn shrugged. 'We were chatting, and she was out
of groceries, so I invited her to join me for dinner.' As the
bartender finally reached him, he leant across to order
their lasagnes, a pint for him and a lime and soda for
Willow, as she'd requested.

When he leant back again, his sister was watching him
even more sceptically. 'You know, that sounds surprisingly like a date.'

'It really doesn't.'

'Because you *don't* date,' Abigail replied with a nod.
'Does *she* know that?'

'She doesn't need to. Because this isn't a date.' He was
almost certain that *Willow* didn't think it was a date. But
then Willow had rather more information about the situation than his sister did. Like who she really was.

'Hmm.' Abigail still didn't look convinced. 'So, are
you going to play for us tonight then? Grace us with your
guitar up on the stage? Impress your not-a-date with your
substantial…talent?'

He rolled his eyes as she elbowed him in the ribs. 'I
brought my guitar. So…we'll see.'

He'd picked up his instrument out of habit rather than
an actual intention to play. Sometimes he did, sometimes
he didn't, but he always felt better knowing he had his
own guitar at his side.

He never played the old songs, though—Blackbird's songs, the ones people knew him for. He and Darrell had developed a reasonable following before his friend's death, and had a couple of breakout hits that people knew. But Gwyn couldn't—wouldn't—play them alone.

Instead, he'd moved away from the more rock styling they'd played together and over to a gentler, more folk-rock style, much like what Sean and Kayla were performing up on the stage. It seemed to fit his surroundings—and his mood—far better these days.

'It would be good to hear you play again.' Abigail's voice was softer now, and he almost missed the yearning in it. 'It's been a while.'

It had, Gwyn realised as he headed back to the table where Willow was waiting. It was probably the time of year. This season always reminded him of that terrible year when he'd lost Darrell, then returned to Rumbelow to find Abigail in trouble and Rachel—

Well. It held bad memories, was the point. He tended to get a little introverted around this time of year.

At least Willow arriving had distracted him from the usual doom spiral of his own thoughts.

She smiled up at him as he sat down beside her. 'Adoring fan?' When he looked confused, she nodded towards the bar where Abigail was still sitting, watching Sean play.

'My big sister, Abigail,' he explained. 'Sean's mum.'

Willow's eyebrows rose. 'She looks too young to have an almost grown-up son.'

'She had Sean young—she was only eighteen when she got married.' Willow didn't need the whole story, he figured. He didn't particularly want to tell it either.

'So she's, what? Thirty-something now?'

'Thirty-five,' he confirmed. 'There's a six-year age gap between us.'

Willow glanced back at Abigail. 'Well, she looks great.'

'I'll tell her you said so.' He wouldn't, he knew. Mostly because it would be weird telling his sister that.

Their lasagnes arrived just as Sean and Kayla stepped down from the stage. Folk night always took a similar format; someone would be booked to play for the first half of the evening, often Sean and Kayla these days, then the second half would be an open mic sort of affair, or floor night, as Ray, who ran it, called it.

There were a good number of musicians in the village and more travelled in from the surrounding area, so they were never short of performers. Tonight, they had a group of fishermen from two villages over, singing sea shanties, followed by three siblings on fiddle, cello and acoustic guitar.

At their secluded table they were still able to talk over the music, so they chatted while they ate—staying away from any contentious or deep topics, or anything that might give away Willow's identity to someone eavesdropping nearby. It made for a light, inconsequential, but surprisingly relaxing conversation. Gwyn hadn't expected her to be so easy to talk to.

Too easy, almost. More than once he found himself on the verge of saying something that he didn't mean to. Something about his past, and the people in it, that would lead to explanations and stories he didn't want to tell.

Not to mention the pity. There was always pity in people's eyes as they heard those stories for the first time. And he really didn't want to see it in hers.

He'd almost convinced himself that they'd get out of there and home without incident, when Sean and Kayla arrived beside the table.

'Are you going to play tonight, Gwyn?' Kayla asked. She was a sweet thing—petite and delicate, with a short, dark pixie cut and an infectious smile.

Willow turned to him with a smile that did things to his insides that Kayla's didn't. Things he was trying to ignore. 'Are you?'

'Go on, Uncle Gwyn.' Sean pulled up a chair from the next table and sat down, tugging Kayla onto his lap. 'You haven't played in weeks.'

'Months,' Kayla corrected.

'I've *never* heard you play,' Willow added. Which was true for her sister too, luckily. He suspected Rowan might have been to folk night once or twice without him really noticing, but he didn't play that often.

Up on the stage, Ray was waiting, microphone in hand, looking intently in their direction. Apparently, this was a stitch-up.

Gwyn sighed, and reached for his guitar case.

The pub fell silent as Gwyn took the stage, as if this was what they'd all been waiting for all night. Maybe it was.

Kayla slipped from Sean's lap into Gwyn's abandoned chair, resting her chin on her hand and her elbow on the table as she watched. Sean seemed equally rapt, waiting for his uncle to play.

Willow got the distinct impression she was missing something here.

Up on the stage, Gwyn settled himself onto a stool, his guitar across one knee, and plucked at a few strings, twisting pegs to get a better tuning. Then, into the waiting hush, he started to play.

And suddenly Willow knew *exactly* what she'd been missing, and wondered how it had been absent from her life for so long.

It wasn't just that he was *good*. He was captivating. Each note—not just strummed but plucked, making it sound like a hundred instruments were playing at once—rose up into the air and hung there like a perfume, changing the very feel of the pub. This wasn't an open mic night any more. It was a secret performance by a master, and everyone in the room felt it.

By the time he started to sing, Willow was already enraptured. His voice was low and warm, deeper somehow than his speaking voice, and she felt it behind her ribcage, vibrating through her bones. He sang of love and loss, of hope and disappointment—and most of all of carrying on, alone.

She didn't think she'd ever heard anything more beautiful, or more heartbreaking.

'He's good,' Willow murmured, making Kayla scoff.

'He's *great*,' she corrected.

'Sometimes I wonder if she's just dating me for my uncle,' Sean joked.

Kayla leaned into him and planted a soppy kiss on his cheek. 'Nah. Too much baggage for me.'

Willow didn't know what Gwyn's baggage was, but as she listened to him sing she knew she was hearing the effects of it. Whatever had happened in his past, it had changed him. And she got the feeling he still hadn't moved past it.

'What kind of baggage?' she asked.

Sean and Kayla exchanged a look. 'He never told you? About, well. Darrell, I guess.' Sean looked uncomfortable just saying the name.

'It's not a secret,' Kayla said quickly. 'I mean, it's all over the internet. It was in the news at the time. I'm surprised you don't already know.'

'I was probably still in the States,' Willow hedged, hoping that the timelines worked out for Rowan as well as her.

'Yeah, maybe it wasn't as big a story over there,' Sean allowed.

Willow swallowed a sigh of relief. 'Will you tell me? I mean, I could Google, but we all know how accurate that can be. And, well, I don't really like to ask Gwyn…'

'God, no.' Kayla's eyes went wide. 'He won't talk about it anyway. I mentioned it *once* and we didn't see him here for, like, a month.'

'That's what I'm worried about,' Willow said. 'We're just starting to hang out a little more now, and I don't want to put my foot in it.' All true, even if she hadn't explained the reasoning behind it. Those were *her* secrets, after all.

Okay, maybe it was rude to try and get Gwyn's secrets out of his nephew and his girlfriend. But it wasn't as if Gwyn didn't already know all of hers. She was just evening up the score.

Kayla looked to Sean, who shrugged. 'I guess there's no reason not to tell you,' he said. 'Maybe you can even convince him that it's time to move on.'

'Or to let *us* move on,' Kayla muttered, which Willow didn't quite understand, but hoped would make sense before long.

'Uncle Gwyn used to be in a band with his best friend, Darrell,' Sean said. 'They played around here a lot and made a name for themselves, then they moved up to London and started playing bigger gigs. They were spotted by some talent scout and, before they knew it, they were supporting some huge band or another on a European tour.'

'Wow. What were they called? Would I have heard of them?' Willow asked.

'Blackbird,' Kayla supplied. 'They had a couple of big hits on their own too. You'd probably know them if you heard them.'

Well, Willow knew what she *would* be tracking down on the internet when she got back to Rowan's cottage. If the songs he was playing tonight were any indication, she wanted to hear more.

But she also knew that this story wasn't going to have a happy ending. Gwyn's songs told her that much.

'What happened?' she asked. 'Where's Darrell now?' Had his best friend betrayed him? Run off with his girlfriend, maybe? Taken a solo contract and left Gwyn behind? Embezzled their money? Any of them sounded perfectly plausible.

But the serious look on Sean's face told her it was worse than that.

'He…he died. He got into drugs, hard and heavy, when they were touring and, well. Uncle Gwyn tried to help him, even got him into rehab, but it never stuck. And the last time…'

'He checked himself out and went straight to his dealer,' Kayla finished. 'Gwyn found his body the next day.'

'Oh, God.' Willow had seen a lot on the modelling circuit, and there were always recreational drugs around at the parties Ben dragged her to—not that she'd ever indulged, it wasn't her scene. But she'd never seen the way they could ravage a life like Gwyn had. 'That was when he came home to Rumbelow?'

Sean nodded. 'Seven years ago now. He was only, like, five years older than I am now, and he'd already quit the business. It's crazy.'

'He still writes though,' Kayla added. 'Music for other people—and some for himself, like this. But he never plays, except for at folk night here. And he never goes to any industry awards or events or anything, no matter how many times they invite him.'

From the tone of Kayla's voice, Willow surmised that the teenager was both baffled by and a little envious of this. Having been to enough similar sort of events herself, Willow could see both sides. They were always glamorous and fun, but they meant putting yourself on display—which was why Rowan had hated them, and modelling generally.

For Gwyn, knowing—or at least believing—that everyone looking at him would be seeing the ghost of his dead friend, she could understand such occasions would be unbearable.

'At least he still plays here,' she said softly, as the song Gwyn was singing drifted to a close. 'It would have been a travesty if he'd stopped playing altogether.'

'Agreed,' Sean said.

'What's agreed?' Gwyn's sister, Abigail, leant against

the wall beside their table. 'Sean, Ray wants to know if you and Kayla will go back on after Gwyn finishes, to close the night?'

'Go on *after* Uncle Gwyn?' Sean shook his head. 'No, thanks.'

Kayla rolled her eyes. 'Of course we will,' she told Abigail, then turned to Sean. 'I know he's amazing, but he's also the old guard. You can't be intimidated by him all your life.'

'I'm not intimidated by him,' Sean objected. 'I *respect* him. That's different.'

'And that's fine, but when you start making life decisions based solely on what he thinks is a good idea—'

'I'm not—' Sean broke off as Gwyn, guitar back in its case, joined them at the table.

'You two up again now?' He motioned to his seat, and Kayla jumped up.

'We are.' Kayla grabbed Sean's hand and dragged him back towards the stage, Abigail trailing behind to watch.

Leaving Willow alone with Gwyn, and the twinge of guilt she felt for talking about him behind his back.

Gwyn hadn't caught much of the conversation between Willow and his family, but he'd heard enough.

He supposed it was only fair; he knew her secrets, so of course she wanted to know his. He'd just been enjoying spending time with her without seeing that look in her eye. The pitying look everyone gave him once they knew his story.

And if she'd got it from Sean and Kayla, she didn't even know the half of it.

'Making friends?' he asked mildly as he picked up his pint.

Willow winced. 'You heard what we were talking about?'

'Me, I'm guessing?' He was fairly sure he was the biggest bone of contention between his nephew and his girlfriend, given that Kayla wanted them to move to London and Sean was only saying no on his say-so.

'They were telling me why you don't play music much any more. Or participate in the industry.' At least she wasn't trying to hide it. He got the feeling that Willow was usually upfront about things. Apart from her pregnancy, it seemed.

'All my dirty secrets, huh?'

She gave him a speculative look, as if she were seeing new angles to him she hadn't considered before. Perhaps she was. So far, their friendship had been weighted towards her problems. Maybe it was only just occurring to her that he might have some too.

'I don't think all of them,' she said after a pause. Then she shifted in her chair, turning back to look at Sean and Kayla on the stage. They were playing an old favourite, and plenty of people were clapping or singing along.

They really were too good to be stuck playing here.

'What did Kayla mean? When she said Sean was making life decisions based on what you thought?' Willow asked.

Oh, but he did *not* want to have this conversation tonight. Because that one question just led to a world of hurt he didn't want to revisit. Ever.

But Willow was waiting for an answer.

'She wants them to move to London. Look for streets paved with gold, fame and fortune, that sort of thing.'

'And you don't want them to go?' Willow guessed.

'I think they're not ready. They're too young, too raw. The industry would chew them up and spit them out.' He knew he was right about this. And yeah, maybe he had his own reasons for not wanting them to go, but that didn't mean he was wrong. 'Abigail agrees.'

'I'm sure she does.' Willow's voice was mild, but he heard something else behind it.

'Want to say what you really mean?' He knew he sounded testy, but it was difficult to care. Just playing tonight had already got his emotions swirling, the way it always did. He loved to play—to perform. It was part of who he was. He knew he couldn't give it up entirely. But even just doing a few songs at folk night was usually enough to send him back to the bar for something stronger than beer. And more than one of them.

Tonight, though, he had to get Willow home safely, and that meant staying sober. It also made it a lot harder to avoid this conversation, and the feelings he'd been pushing down about it.

'Just that…if I was a mother, I'm sure I wouldn't want my seventeen-year-old son running off to London with his girlfriend chasing an almost impossible dream either.' Her eyes widened as her own words obviously sank in. 'Oh, God. Not if. When.'

'Yeah. So you see my point.' He took another long glug of his pint and wondered if one whisky would be so bad. 'I'm just looking out for them.'

'Right. I mean, it's hard to crush the dreams of someone we love, but it's a competitive field. They might not be good enough.' She was watching him over the rim of her glass as she said it, and he knew that the righteous anger that rose up in him was exactly what she was trying to provoke.

Knowing that didn't stop him from reacting, though. 'Are your ears missing? Did you not hear them tonight? Of course they're good enough. They're incredible.'

'So why don't you want them to go?'

He didn't answer. How could he?

Willow sighed. 'Look. As someone who was on the public stage long before I finished school—and instead of finishing school actually—I get that it's problematic. There are definitely issues about being in that world too young, too naive and too inexperienced. It's not for everybody, that's for sure. Look at my sister! If our mother hadn't forced us to be the most famous, recognisable and lucrative versions of ourselves we could be, Rowan probably wouldn't have spent the last six years hiding out here. But the flip side of that is…if it's what they want, what they're made for, they're going to do it anyway. You have to let them make their own mistakes.'

'Even if it kills them?' The words shot out before he could stop them, and he was relieved when he looked around to see that everyone else in the pub was paying rapt attention only to Sean and Kayla on the stage.

'I understand why you're worried about that,' Willow said cautiously. 'And I won't say I didn't worry about it for Rowan at one point. That's why I helped her get out. She knew she wasn't alone. And maybe…maybe that's what they need too.'

She had a point, not that he was about to admit that. When he and Darrell had left, it had just been the two of them, out in the big wide world. Neither of them had been close to their parents, and Abigail… Well. She'd had her own problems back then.

He'd had Rachel, though, back in Rumbelow. Or he'd thought he did.

Turned out he'd had no one, same as Darrell. Maybe he was just lucky he hadn't ended up following the same path.

'They're seventeen,' he said bluntly. 'What they need is to stay home, finish their education, and figure out that there are no golden streets out there. You pay for everything you get in this life, and sometimes the price is far higher than the reward.'

'Is that what you learned?'

Gwyn drained the last of his pint and slammed the glass down on the table. 'Yep. Come on. Let's get you home.' And him back to his home, and the bottle of whisky he kept on the top shelf for the rare nights like this.

Before he had to talk about this with her any more.

CHAPTER SIX

IT WAS OVER a week before Willow spoke to Gwyn again.

Oh, she still saw him every day, jogging past her window, but even when she raised a hand to wave, he either didn't see her or ignored her.

She was guessing the latter.

Whether it was the conversation about his nephew at folk night, the fact that she now knew his secrets rather than him hoarding hers, or even the hug outside the doctor's clinic that had driven him away, she wasn't sure. But she was pretty much certain that he was avoiding her.

Maybe that was for the best. They'd only known each other a little over a week and had found themselves spilling secrets best kept hidden, and growing closer than was strictly advisable, given that she was pregnant and in hiding from the father, and he was potentially her sister's only friend in her hideaway town. Not to mention that she'd be leaving soon.

No point spending time getting closer, under those circumstances.

But that didn't mean she could completely ignore the little pang in her chest every time he ran past without seeing her.

Still, she tried.

Her grocery shop was delivered, and she busied herself putting that away—and reorganising Rowan's kitchen cupboards while she was at it. She hunted through the cottage for clues as to her sister's state of mind, and what she'd been up to for the last six years that hadn't made it into their regular video chats. She admired the dress designs stuck up on the walls, and wondered at all the talent Rowan was hiding away here in the little Cornish village.

When that grew boring, she took to the beach. It was still too early in the year for it to be packed with tourists, although there were a few surfers out, and the usual dog walkers. She needed to stay active, but she wasn't sure exactly what was safe to do, or what would bring the nausea back, so she stuck to walking for now.

And while she walked, she thought. Mostly in circles, but she had to start somewhere.

She thought about Ben. About the kind of mother she wanted to be. She tried to picture her life in a year, in three years, in ten. She used every goal and visualisation trick she'd ever learned from any guru or therapist.

And she ended up right where she'd started. Hiding out pretending to be her sister, unable to fully picture a life in which she was a mother and doing it right.

Or one in which she was able to stand up to Ben and tell him what she wanted.

That was the most frustrating part. Nobody who knew her would call Willow Harper a pushover, or weak, or needy—but Ben made her feel like all three. When he was in a room, it felt as if he sucked all the air—or power—out if it. As if nothing she could do or say mattered when he was there.

When they'd first met, he'd loved that she was beautiful, and a model, and in demand. It was what had attracted him to her—she knew that, because he'd told her as much.

But as their relationship—such as it was—had developed, he'd started complaining about her showing too much skin in campaigns, or wearing 'inappropriate' dresses to events. Where before he'd wanted everyone to admire her, lately he seemed to have decided that he wanted her all to himself. He even complained if she spoke too long to anyone else at parties—especially other men, even if they'd been friends for years.

The last six months or so, she'd got the feeling she couldn't do anything right. That just who she *was* wasn't enough. But at the same time, Ben had been getting closer, clingier. Intimating that it was time to take their relationship/business arrangement to the next level. He'd been using words like 'logical conclusion' and 'plays well on paper', none of which was entirely convincing, or at all romantic.

But maybe she shouldn't be looking for romantic. She was pregnant. She was going to be a mother. Maybe she needed to be looking at the practical side of things instead.

When that day's walk reached its usual inconclusive conclusion, she sighed and decided that coffee would help. Even decaf.

She trudged up the path from the beach into the village rather than turning back towards the steep steps that led up to her cottage. This way, she could have a sit and ruminate some more before she walked the shallower but longer path home. Maybe she'd even bump into Gwyn on one of his runs.

And she was back to thinking about Gwyn again. Great.

She pushed him from her mind and focused on her surroundings instead. Rowan said she found this place grounding, settling. Maybe that was what she needed to find here too.

Spring had definitely arrived in Rumbelow, and the sun actually felt warm at last. Blue skies shone overhead, decorated with wispy white clouds bouncing past on a fresh, but not cold, breeze. Box planters on the sides of the road were blooming with spring bulbs—tulips and daffodils and other flowers she couldn't even identify brightened up the pathways everywhere she walked. Shops had windows and doors open for the first time since she'd arrived, and the scent of baking bread was enticing.

Babies needed carbs, right? Just because *she* didn't usually eat them…right now, she wasn't just eating for her. Finding somewhere to serve her a decaf coffee and some hot buttered toast was basically a moral obligation at this point. Ooh, and maybe some eggs. Or even a sausage sandwich…

She skipped the café where she'd bumped into Gwyn the other morning, more because it was Rowan's local than because she was worried she might see him again and it would be awkward. Rumbelow had a surplus of lovely-looking independent cafés to enjoy, and it seemed wrong to stick to just one of them. Plus, she didn't fancy getting served tea she didn't want again.

With her depressingly decaf coffee and a sausage bap, she took a small table for two in the corner and watched the world go by for a while.

Until Gwyn's sister walked in and waved as she headed for the queue.

Willow stared down at her almost empty coffee cup and debated her options. She could drain it and run, before Abigail was able to get her own drink and join her. Or she could stay here and connect with Gwyn's sister—and maybe learn a little more about the man himself.

Put like that, it was an easy decision.

When Abigail made a beeline for her table with two coffee cups in hand, Willow knew it was the right one. This was a woman who understood early morning needs.

'Decaf, yeah?' she said, taking a seat. 'That's what Shelley at the counter said you were drinking.'

'Yeah, thanks.' Willow tried a friendly smile. It didn't feel so bad. 'It felt like a coffee sort of morning, but I don't want to get all jangly, you know?' No need to explain about caffeine being bad for the baby no one but Gwyn knew about yet.

'I'm glad I caught you, actually.' Abigail blew across the surface of her coffee, holding the cup gently between two hands. 'I've been meaning to talk to you.'

Willow's smile froze just a little bit. In her experience, those words meant what was about to follow could really go either way—but it was usually one extreme or another.

Gwyn's sister was shorter than he was by a whole head, and curvier by far, but she had the same dark hair and eyes. When she pinned her with her—not unfriendly but certainly determined—gaze across the café table, Willow knew that she probably should have run.

'Oh?' she said, trying to portray mild curiosity rather than fear. She took a sip from her fresh coffee and pretended it had caffeine in it.

'Yes. I wanted to say how glad I am that you and Gwyn have become...closer lately.'

'Closer friends,' Willow said quickly. 'Just...closer *friends*.'

Abigail's smile was far too knowing. Even if what she thought she knew was wildly inaccurate. 'Of course. It's just that Gwyn hasn't had so many friends around here since he came home. He doesn't tend to let people in and, well, it's just nice to see him opening up a little.'

'He's been a very good friend to me,' Willow said sincerely. Maybe with just a little extra emphasis on the word *friend,* just in case.

'I'm sure you have to him too.' Abigail smiled brightly over her coffee cup. 'That's why I wanted to ask you to join us for Sunday dinner tomorrow. If you're not too busy?'

Every conceivable excuse to get out of it flew from Willow's mind, leaving it utterly blank. 'Um... I...' She hesitated, then sighed. Really, a home-cooked meal sounded glorious. She wasn't much of a cook herself, and cooking for one was boring, so her grocery delivery had mostly been easy to assemble, simple meals. Besides, it had been a long time since she'd had a proper English Sunday roast. Gwyn might not like it, but at least he wouldn't be able to avoid her any longer.

'That would be lovely,' she said, more firmly. 'What can I bring?'

* * *

'You invited *who*?' Obviously, Gwyn had to be imagining things, because there was no way that his sister could possibly have said what he thought she'd said.

'I invited Rowan over for Sunday lunch this afternoon,' Abigail repeated calmly, as if the words meant nothing.

Of course, if she had *really* invited Rowan, they wouldn't, much. He could have been pleasant and friendly and then she'd have gone away again and he could have relaxed with his family. It would have been fine.

But Rowan was in New York, pretending to be Willow. Which meant that Abigail had *actually* invited world-famous supermodel Willow Harper for roast beef and Yorkshire puddings.

The same Willow he was actively trying to avoid right now.

Looked like that plan was out of the window.

He ran a hand through his hair and sighed. 'I thought it was going to be just us. I *thought* we were going to talk to Sean and Kayla again about, well, you know.'

'We can't talk about London—the capital city of our country—with another person in the house?' Abigail's eyebrows were raised ludicrously high.

'You're being annoyingly disingenuous,' he told her. 'Stop it.'

His sister flashed him a smile. 'Honestly, Gwyn, I didn't think it was a problem. Sean and Kayla adored her the other night, and everyone knows the two of you have been spending time together lately—'

'No, we haven't.' Not that week, anyway. Not since the folk night.

Abigail's expression was quintessential Long-Suffering Big Sister. 'Gwyn, you brought her to folk night. And just because you drove out the long way, don't think nobody spotted you and her sneaking out together in your car last week either.'

Damn. As long as whichever busybody who'd seen them hadn't followed them to the midwife's appointment, they were probably okay, though.

Gwyn really wasn't sure how long Willow was going to be able to keep her identity—or her secret—between just the two of them. But he was pretty sure spending time with his sister and nephew would bring that timescale down considerably.

Abigail put her hand on his arm. 'Nobody's teasing you, Gwyn, or judging you either. Nobody who has noticed thinks this is a bad thing. People around here care about you, and they want you to be happy. If Rowan makes you happy, there's no reason to hide that, is there? You're *allowed* to be happy again, you know. Even after everything.'

Did he know that? Gwyn wasn't sure.

It was that 'everything' that was the problem. So much had happened, there'd already been so much loss, he wasn't sure he even knew how to *feel* happiness any more, let alone believe he deserved it.

Contentment was enough for him these days. And since that was a hell of a lot more than he'd ever expected to feel again when he'd first moved home, he saw no reason to rock that boat.

Besides, in his experience, when you rode a happiness high, it only meant you had further to fall.

The doorbell rang, and Gwyn cast a last glare at his sister before going to answer it.

Willow stood on the doorstep, a bunch of flowers and a bottle of wine in her hands, and an apprehensive look on her face.

'You didn't have to say yes,' he told her.

Willow shrugged. 'I have a weakness for roast beef.'

Abigail did make an excellent Sunday roast; he had to admit that much.

Gwyn stood aside to let her in and took the wine and flowers as she slipped her jacket from her shoulders. Underneath, she wore a simple black sweater and jeans, with a gold necklace and earrings, and he knew in a moment that Rowan would never be seen in something so plain.

Hopefully, his sister *didn't* know that.

'Am I underdressed for the occasion?' Damn. She'd caught him staring.

'You look fine,' he replied. And it was true. If fine also meant untouchable, beautiful, and the sort of woman it was hard to look at for too long without being blinded by the glow.

Yes, she was the most beautiful woman he'd ever seen, and his fingers itched to stroke along her cheek, her jaw and down her neck, just to feel her respond. That didn't mean he had to *tell* her that.

'Rowan! You're here!' Abigail emerged from the kitchen, looking slightly flustered and red in the face, her floral apron wrapped twice around her waist. 'Ooh, are those for me?' She held out a hand and Gwyn thrust the flowers into it. 'Nobody ever brings me flowers. Thank you! Come on through to the kitchen and we'll open that bottle of wine.'

Abigail turned to bustle back kitchenwards, and Gwyn gave Willow a knowing look.

Problem number one: bringing wine and then having to explain why she couldn't drink any, without letting on that she was pregnant, and lying about her identity.

She really hadn't thought this through, had she?

'I'm glad you like the flowers,' Willow said smoothly as she followed Abigail, leaving Gwyn to trail behind after completely ignoring his look. She swung a bag off her shoulder and pulled out another bottle. 'Actually, I brought some non-alcoholic stuff for myself, if you don't mind. I'm not drinking at the moment. Antibiotics.'

Of course. The classic antibiotics excuse. No one could question that. Why hadn't *he* thought of it?

Because he was in a complete mess about her being here in the first place, he admitted to himself finally.

He sank into a wooden chair at the kitchen table as the thought settled into his brain.

Watching her joking and laughing with Abigail made it feel like she was part of his life—in a way he didn't let himself experience any more. He didn't bring women home, he didn't make new friends, he didn't let new people into his life.

The people he already had to care for were more than enough trouble as it was.

Abigail. Sean. Himself, because that was sort of essential.

That was it. That was the list of people he cared about and looked after. Not because he hated everyone else, but because he already knew that three people was more than he could hope to keep safe.

He'd failed enough people in his life to not want to risk letting down any more. Abigail and Sean—they were already there, his family, and he loved them despite himself. The two of them, he'd accepted, he'd always do his best for—even if he knew he'd never let them see quite how much he worried about ruining things with them or for them. Abigail had already forgiven him for abandoning her once, for letting her get hurt. He never wanted to have to ask for that forgiveness again.

But he couldn't let more people in. No matter how appealing it was to play the knight in shining armour for Willow. She didn't actually *need* him to do it, he knew—and that helped, a bit. She had the strength, the brains and the money to be able to cope in this world perfectly well on her own.

Knowing that didn't seem to make it any easier for him to resolve to walk away and leave her to fix her own problems, though. Especially since she was currently taste-testing gravy in his sister's kitchen.

He *couldn't* let Willow in. He didn't have the capacity to worry about saving her as well as Abigail and Sean. Because she might not need him, exactly, but that didn't mean he couldn't help. Make a difference.

And that was all it could be, of course—helping her in her time of need. Because once that time of need was over, she'd be back to America in a flash. Maybe even back with the loser boyfriend/father of her child she'd run away from in the first place.

Gwyn had made a conscious effort not to Google her and find out who that man might be. He told himself that was because it was none of his business. And if part of his brain whispered that it was because he didn't want to see her with another man…well, he was ignoring that stupid part right now.

What did it matter to him who Willow dated? She

was barely even a friend—and that only against his better judgement. Why would he feel *anything* at the idea of her dating someone, being with someone, having a baby with someone who wasn't him?

He swore silently inside his head. Denial really wasn't going as well as he'd hoped it would.

'Why are you looking so down in the dumps over there?' Abigail asked over her shoulder, wooden spoon still in one hand.

Gwyn looked up to see Willow watching him curiously too. Her blue eyes were a little too knowing, for all the curiosity, though. As if she suspected the truth and was just waiting for him to admit it.

He'd already let her in, far more than he'd intended to when they'd met.

And a large part of him—one inconveniently located in his heart, he suspected—wanted to let her in even more.

To Willow's surprise, Sunday lunch with Gwyn's family was…lovely.

She'd been nervous about it ever since Abigail had invited her, second-guessing her decision to say yes, and that uncertainty had solidified in her stomach when she'd seen Gwyn's expression as he'd answered the door.

He didn't want her there, that much was patently obvious. And when Abigail had offered her a glass of wine she could see exactly why.

This was too much of a risk. Spending time with other people—kind, nice people who would expect her to be open and chatty and honest about her own life and things like, well, her identity—only increased the chances that someone would notice she wasn't who she said she was.

She'd almost turned around and left right then. But the look on Gwyn's face—as if he was just waiting for her to turn tail and run—had made her forge on, if only for the satisfaction of proving him wrong. And after Abigail bought her excuse about antibiotics, everything else ran surprisingly smoothly.

'That was delicious,' she told her hostess, pushing away her empty plate, with only a drizzle of gravy remaining to show that it had ever been piled high with roast beef, Yorkshire puddings, roast potatoes, vegetables and gravy. 'It was so kind of you to invite me.'

'Oh, we're not done yet,' Sean said. 'You haven't seen pudding. I mean, Mum's a great cook, but her desserts are to die for.'

Sean and Kayla hadn't seemed surprised to see Willow joining them at the Sunday dinner table, so she assumed Abigail had warned them they'd have company. More unusually, though, the addition of a stranger hadn't seemed to inhibit family conversation and discussion one bit. Friendly debate, rivalry and mocking had continued apace—almost as if Willow belonged there all along.

'Rowan never came for dinner at your sister's, did she?' she asked later, after they'd said their goodbyes and were heading back up the hill towards the cottage and Gwyn's lifeboat station—rather more slowly than she'd walked down. Abigail's desserts were, indeed, spectacular—and very filling.

'God, no,' Gwyn said. 'Abigail hardly ever invites anyone any more. When I first moved home, she was forever asking single friends and acquaintances along, trying to set me up with them. I put my foot down in the end, told her I wouldn't come at all unless she stopped inviting other people. It's family Sunday lunch, after all. It's only meant for family.'

Willow winced. 'I'm sorry. I didn't realise you felt so strongly about it.' That must have been why he'd looked so grumpy when she arrived.

But Gwyn flashed her a grin. 'Nah. I just said that to stop her matchmaking. It was…it was nice to have you there today.'

The unexpected compliment filled her with a warmth that the cool spring air didn't. 'It was nice to be invited. Your sister's a fantastic cook.'

'She is. So, you were just there for the food, then?'

'The company wasn't so bad either,' she admitted. 'Once you stopped sulking about me being there.'

'I wasn't sulking,' Gwyn said, even though he clearly had been. 'I just…' He sighed. 'I don't want them getting the wrong idea. About me and you.'

Ah. Of course. Suddenly the whole afternoon made a lot more sense.

'You're worried they might think we're more than friends?' she asked.

'Oh, I'm not worried they might,' he replied. 'I know they already do.'

Willow winced. 'Did Abigail say something to you?'

'She didn't have to. I could tell by the self-satisfied gleam in her eye. Like she had something to do with facilitating this imaginary relationship in the first place.'

He sounded more exasperated than angry, which Willow took as a good sign.

They walked in silence for a few more minutes, slowly winding their way along the climbing cliff path that led to Rowan's cottage. Willow had enough leftovers in her bag—thrust upon her by Abigail as they'd tried to leave—that she wouldn't have to go shopping for at least another day or so. Maybe she could just hibernate in the cottage until she figured out what to do next. That would solve the problem of people thinking she was dating Gwyn, at least.

Not any of her other problems, but then they were rather bigger things to deal with.

'It's not like I'm embarrassed or anything,' Gwyn said suddenly. 'Obviously, any guy would be thrilled to have people think he was dating you, or Rowan, for that matter.'

'If it's so obvious, then why are you pulling that face?' Willow couldn't help but ask. He looked physically pained at the idea of anyone thinking he was dating her, despite his words. 'Is it because I'm pregnant?'

Gwyn scoffed at that idea. 'No. It's not that—it's not you. It's—'

'Oh, not the "it's not you, it's me" speech!' Willow rolled her eyes dramatically. 'Didn't that go out *decades* ago?' She was teasing him, mostly. He couldn't exactly give her that breakup speech if they weren't dating—weren't *anything*—to begin with. But she meant it a little bit too. Obviously, there was something about her that made the idea of people thinking they were dating utterly repellent to him.

'It *is* me,' Gwyn said firmly. 'I don't date. I don't *want* to date. And I *definitely* don't want my family to get the idea that the situation around me dating is going to change any time soon. Or ever.'

'Oh.' Well, that really *was* him, not her. She supposed that was something. 'Why not?'

'Why not let them get the wrong idea?'

'No, of course not. I understand that. I meant…and this is not to be taken as a suggestion or an offer or anything more than a friendly question, okay?' She waited for his nod of agreement before she continued. 'Why don't you date?'

CHAPTER SEVEN

SHE LIKELY HADN'T meant her question to be such a stumper, but it still took Gwyn a good few moments to piece together an answer. Not because he didn't *know* the answer, but because he wasn't quite sure how much of it he wanted to share with her right now.

He could just say *bad experiences* and leave it at that. Or claim he was focusing on other areas of his life at present. Or invent some lost love he'd never got over—even if that one wasn't *entirely* invention.

Or, he supposed, he could tell her the truth.

'My last serious relationship…it ended badly. Very badly.' Maybe she'd just take that and leave it there, if he was lucky.

Except he'd never been that lucky.

'Can I ask what happened?' She didn't look at him as she asked the question, instead looking out over the cliffs to the sea. It gave him the space to consider his answer, which he appreciated.

He could lie. She'd never know the difference.

But he didn't.

'Sean and Kayla…they told you what happened with Darrell when we moved to London, right?'

Willow nodded. 'Sounds like you were on the verge of being the next big thing when he died.'

'Yeah. We were.' That had been something else to throw into the mix of grief and misery and guilt and loss he'd felt in the aftermath of finding Darrell's body. The loss of the future they were supposed to have together.

But that wasn't the only future he'd lost.

He took a deep breath. 'I'm guessing they didn't tell you about Rachel?'

'Rachel?' Her eyebrows jumped as she looked at him again. 'No. They didn't.'

'I'm pretty sure they don't even know the whole story,' he admitted. 'Almost nobody does, except Abigail and, well, Rachel herself. So I'd appreciate it if you didn't spread it around.'

'I wouldn't.' Willow focused her gaze on him, her blue eyes bright, wide and honest even in the falling gloom of the evening. 'You don't have to tell me, though, if you're worried.'

'I'm not.' It was true, as far as it went. He wasn't concerned that Willow would gossip about him—he held enough of her secrets to make keeping his a no-brainer.

If he was worried at all, it was only about how she'd react. How she'd look at him, after she knew.

'Okay,' she said. 'Then tell me. What happened with Rachel?'

Gwyn shoved his hands in his pockets as they walked, and tried to find the right way to start the story.

'Rachel and I...we were high school sweethearts. You know, the whole ridiculous made for each other thing. We thought—I thought—we were endgame.'

'But she didn't?' Willow guessed.

'She said she did.' It still hurt, remembering, even after all these years. 'She was still studying when Darrell and I moved to London, so she didn't come with us. Looking back, it's fairly obvious she didn't want to. That wasn't the kind of future she saw for herself. I guess...she liked having a boyfriend in a band when we were in school, but she always figured I'd give it up and get a real job eventually. I just didn't see that at the time.'

'So you went to London thinking she'd be waiting patiently at home for you...?'

'And she was, for a bit,' Gwyn replied. He knew already which way Willow's mind had gone, making Rachel the villain. And she wasn't entirely wrong. She just wasn't totally right either. 'I kept thinking she'd join us in London eventually, even when she got a job here after she finished studying. Which probably should have been a clue.'

Up ahead, Rowan's cottage gleamed pearly-white in the moonlight, the outside lamp glowing faintly. They were nearly home. Time to rip off the sticking plaster and tell the worst part of the story.

'Then she found out she was pregnant.' He felt Willow's grip on his arm tighten at the words. 'And she didn't tell me.'

'The baby was yours?' Willow asked. 'Sorry, not to cast aspersions or anything, but I don't know this woman.'

Turned out, neither had he. Not as well as he'd thought.

'It was mine,' he said tightly.

Willow was silent for a long moment. He wondered what she was thinking. If she thought he was judging her for not telling the father of her child yet. She didn't know that he'd completely understood Rachel's reasons. That was what made it even worse.

'Did she…did she keep it?' The tentativeness in her voice told him she'd jumped to the wrong conclusion, maybe inevitably. He'd never mentioned being a father or having a child, of course. Because he wasn't and he didn't.

Couldn't imagine he ever would, now.

'She found someone who could give her what she wanted,' he said, because he had to start there and work up to the rest. 'I don't know if it started before she knew about the baby or after, but it was certainly before she told me she was pregnant. The timings…the baby had to be mine. But she never had any intention of letting me raise it with her. I wasn't… I wasn't the sort of guy she imagined settling down with, apparently.'

The worst thing was, he couldn't even disagree with her.

Even before everything that happened with Darrell, he'd hardly been husband material, let alone *father* material. He'd been focused on his music career, and if that had gone as well as they'd hoped he'd have been touring most of the year. Yeah, other musicians did it, but he didn't think he could have—trying to concentrate on the music when worrying about a wife and a kid at home. He didn't have it in him.

And then, after Darrell…he'd known he couldn't risk it. Couldn't risk letting down someone else the way he'd let down his best friend—especially not letting down his own child. He couldn't save, protect or take care of anyone, and he wouldn't subject a kid to that.

He couldn't let more people in because he was already

at maximum capacity for caring, and he couldn't take the consequences if he tried for more and failed. It was as simple as that. He wasn't built for relationships.

He didn't know if Willow would understand that, though. So instead, he said, 'She miscarried, just before the twelve weeks scan. After that...she didn't want to see me. She moved away with her new man and the last I heard they were happily married with three kids. She got what she wanted in the end.' And he was happy for her, really he was.

'But *you* didn't,' Willow said softly.

Gwyn shook his head. 'I never really saw myself as father material anyway.'

But the look Willow gave him told him she saw the deeper truth: he'd wanted to be. Just for that split second when she'd told him about the baby...he'd wanted to be good enough to have that.

But with Darrell's body still fresh in his mind, he'd known he never could be.

And now...now he couldn't afford to care that much. About anybody.

He'd worked so hard to try and keep Darrell safe and with them—and he'd let down Rachel because of it. Not just Rachel—Abigail and Sean too, not that they saw it that way.

He did.

He'd spread himself too thin, that was the problem. He had to prioritise. He couldn't afford another distraction—however needy, deserving, blonde or beautiful.

Even if she felt like a friend already. Someone who could understand him down to his bones.

So he pulled his arm away from hers as they reached her cottage. 'Here we are. Home safe.'

'Thank you.' Willow gave him a wry smile. 'Although I hardly think that Rumbelow is the sort of place where I need a bodyguard to get home on a Sunday evening.'

'Perhaps not. But we're a full-service sort of village.' The temptation to linger, to joke and banter—to accept the invitation for a last coffee that he was almost certain was about to be forthcoming—was huge. So he forced himself to turn away—to reach for the gate and open it, to *leave*.

Until a soft touch on his arm stopped him.

He huffed out a short, resigned sigh and turned back. 'You okay?'

Willow chewed on her lower lip, and he couldn't help but stare at her mouth. To imagine claiming it with his own. To picture taking her inside that cottage and kissing her again. With intent.

Because she'd felt like she belonged, this afternoon at family lunch. Just for those few hours, having her there had felt like what his life could have been, should have been.

But it was too late now.

'I was going to ask…but I will completely understand if you don't want to…' Willow paused, took a deep breath and started again. 'I've got my first scan at the hospital on Wednesday.'

'And you need me to take you?' Of course. Everyone needed something, and nobody ever seemed to understand that he didn't feel equipped to give it.

Willow shook her head. 'No. I can take a cab. I'm perfectly capable of going alone. But I wondered... I wondered if you might *want* to come with me.'

'Why?'

Her smile was soft and gentle. 'Because you've been there for me since the moment I arrived here. I figured... you might want to see what it was all for.'

Gwyn wasn't prepared for the surge of emotions that flooded his senses. He tightened his jaw against them and gave a sharp nod. 'Wednesday, then.' Then he turned and walked away, towards his own sanctuary in the lifeboat station.

It was that or kiss her. And that would be a step too far down the road to certain disaster.

Wednesday came almost too quickly and too slowly at the same time.

On the one hand, Willow was terrified—about seeing her baby on the ultrasound screen and everything becoming real at last, and having to make a lot of decisions very quickly. On the other, she was impatient—to see her child, yes. And, if she was completely honest with herself, to see Gwyn.

He'd been avoiding her again since Sunday—since they'd shared that strange moment on her doorstep where he gave up some more of his secrets, mostly willingly, and when, just for a moment, she almost imagined he was about to kiss her.

Which was ridiculous, of course.

Gwyn had been nothing but a supportive friend to her, and that was only because of his friendship with her sister, she was sure. Not to mention the fact that she was pregnant with another man's child, and due to fly back to New York any time now.

Of course he hadn't been about to kiss her.

Even if, in the moment, she'd really wanted him to.

With a sigh, she threw herself back into the kitchen chair to finish the dregs of her tea and wait for Gwyn to pick her up.

It had to be the hormones again, didn't it? Because as gorgeous as Gwyn was—she was pregnant, not blind—she was under no illusions that starting something romantic between them would be a disaster. For both of them. Quite aside from her current, rather complicated, situation, he obviously had a lot of past trauma he still needed to work through, and she had no intention of trying to fix anybody. Not when she was still pretty broken herself, if she was honest.

Her relationship with Ben, such as it was, had been exposed in the aftermath of her pregnancy test as nothing more than a sham. A show for the cameras. It wasn't real love, or support, or respect, or any of those other things she knew a relationship needed to be.

Ironically, she was pretty sure that Gwyn *could* give those things—if not to her, then to someone—but he was too scared now to let himself.

She sighed again into her teacup. Maybe that was why they got along so well. They were both a mess, in their own particular way, and neither of them expected the other to be anything but.

Willow looked around the cottage her sister had run away to all those years ago, and understood fully, maybe for the first time, the impulse that had led Rowan to hole up here. It wasn't just the beautiful views, the picturesque village or even the remote location.

It was the safety.

Here, halfway up a cliff, with her nearest neighbour a grumpy ex-musician in hiding, Rowan knew that she was safe from anyone who cared about who she had been before. Here, she could hide out, build a chrysalis around herself and wait until she was ready to emerge as a butterfly. As the person she wanted to be—away from the cameras and their mother's influence.

The only thing with Rowan was, given the chance, Willow suspected she'd have stayed wrapped up in that chrysalis for ever, just to avoid finding out what life looked like on the other side.

Which was just one of the reasons Willow had given her that push, out to New York, to find out what colour her wings were.

Willow, of course, didn't have the option of staying hidden for ever.

She had a baby inside her who'd be coming out in a matter of months, however scared she was, however uncertain about what life looked like on the other side. So she'd just have to woman up and find out.

And as if she'd needed a reminder of that, her jeans wouldn't fasten up this morning, and the maternity bras she'd ordered were already digging in. She'd had to place an emergency order for the next size up—and steal Rowan's jeans from the wardrobe, glad that her sister preferred to wear her clothes looser these days. The difference was hopefully barely noticeable to anyone else, but a godsend to her expanding middle.

She heard Gwyn's car crunch to a halt outside her gate

and got to her feet, grabbing her bag and heading out to meet him before he made it to the door. He had his hand already raised to knock as she opened it.

'You ready?' He didn't meet her gaze exactly, ducking his head at first then looking over her shoulder, as if he was avoiding any unnecessary contact with her. When he took her bag, his fingers didn't brush hers. And when he opened the car door for her, he stepped back as far as he could before she climbed in.

Neither of them spoke until they were on the main road, speeding away from Rumbelow.

'So, what happens at this scan, then?' Gwyn asked. 'Will they tell you if it's a boy or a girl?'

'I'm not sure,' Willow admitted. 'I think usually at twelve week scans it's too early to tell. But I'm a little late having mine, so you never know.' At least three weeks late, if she was totally honest. She was pretty sure she'd been around twelve weeks already when she'd arrived in Britain, and it had taken a little while to get an appointment for the scan.

'So this is just to…check everything is okay?' There was an apprehension in Gwyn's voice that made her think of the story he'd told her the other day. Of the girl he'd left behind, and the baby they'd lost.

She shouldn't have asked him to come. This wasn't fair.

'You can wait in the car when we get there, you know,' she said. 'I don't need you to come in with me.'

'Maybe I want to.' He didn't look at her as he said it, though.

'Why?' She realised the answer as soon as she asked the question. 'Never mind.'

He was coming in with her in case there was a problem. He didn't want her to be alone if the scan showed up something...bad.

She reached out and squeezed his hand where it sat on the gear stick. 'Thank you.'

The hospital was bigger and whiter than the doctor's surgery where she'd visited the midwife. Given the distance they'd had to drive to get there, Willow suspected it must service a large proportion of the county of Cornwall.

Gwyn parked the car after circling the car park for a short while, then they headed in together.

Willow had never spent much time in hospitals in her life, but it seemed that Gwyn had a better idea of where they needed to be, so she followed him.

'You know your way around this place pretty well,' she said as she trotted after him.

'There are signs.' He pointed his chin up towards the overhead signs, his jaw still tight and his face closed off.

'Right. Of course.'

Luckily, they didn't have to spend too long in the sterile waiting room, once they found it. Just long enough for her to flip through all the pregnancy and baby magazines on the table, and for him to stare stonily at the wall. Willow sneaked glances at the other couples going into the ultrasound room—mostly looking excitedly nervous—and the ones coming out again, looking slightly stunned.

It's just a scan. Just a picture. As long as everything is okay, this will be over and done with and I can keep moving on. It's just a scan.

Except it wasn't, not really.

It was concrete proof—in a way that the sickness or

her aching boobs or even the eight positive tests she'd taken hadn't been—that she was growing a new life inside her.

She reached over and grabbed Gwyn's hand, just as the nurse called her name.

'And this must be dad,' the ultrasound technician said as she motioned for Willow to get comfortable in the chair.

'Not exactly,' Gwyn said drily. 'I'm just here for moral support.'

'He's a friend,' Willow explained. 'The father is…overseas at the moment. On business.'

'Right.' The technician looked between them with a slightly knowing smile, but didn't say anything more. Willow supposed she must see all sorts of couples and parental setups in her job. It wouldn't do if she passed judgement on them all.

Besides, it wasn't as if Willow had anything to apologise for here. She hadn't searched the internet for evidence of what Ben was up to in her absence, but she would place money that it was more scandalous than hospital appointments with a friend, or folk nights and Sunday dinners.

The technician got Willow to raise her top and lower the waistband of her leggings, at which point Gwyn started pointedly studying the posters on the walls about smoking and drinking during pregnancy, amongst other things.

'Let's see what we've got in here, shall we?'

The gel was cold on her belly and her core muscles tightened even more—and every muscle she possessed already felt taut with expectation and fear. Willow swallowed and reached out, groping blindly for something, anything to hold on to for reassurance.

She felt Gwyn's fingers tighten around hers in response, and smiled.

Gwyn hated hospitals. He'd hated hospitals for far longer than he could justify from the disasters of the last decade of his life. He'd hated them when he'd visited his grandparents in the last years of their respective lives. He'd hated them when he'd visited Abigail after she had Sean. And he'd hated them more recently too, for more obvious reasons.

Maybe it was the smell as much as the memory. The whiff of death that filled the place. And the people sitting around, tense, waiting for bad news, knowing that life as they knew it could be about to change in just a fraction of a second, in just one or two words.

He definitely knew how that felt.

But Willow had asked him to be there, and it wasn't as if she had anybody else right now, and so…here he was.

He'd reasoned it out to himself as he'd lain awake in bed the night before.

He'd promised himself he wouldn't let anyone else in, that he wouldn't open himself up to letting down and losing another person—Abigail and Sean were enough. But Willow wasn't staying; she wouldn't be here long enough for him to let her down, and losing her was inevitable anyway, so he wouldn't let himself get too close. He'd steel himself against her leaving, and keep her at a distance…but he could still help her.

Willow and the baby were temporary. They were never going to be his responsibility long-term. So this was fine.

That was what he'd told himself over and over in the dark. What he'd repeated in his mind on the drive to the hospital. The thought that had kept him going as he'd gritted his teeth and followed those damn signs to the right department, and sat waiting.

But now, as he watched the image on the screen start to form and Willow squeezed his hand tightly, he wondered who he thought he was kidding.

He wasn't here because he thought it was safe. He was there because he couldn't imagine being anywhere else.

This is dangerous. This is the worst idea since your last terrible one, Gwyn. You need to get out, before this goes bad.

But he didn't. He ignored the sensible voice in his head and leaned closer, peering at the fuzzy picture on the screen.

'Here we go,' the technician said. 'Can you see the head, here?' She pointed to a white mass somewhere around the middle of the screen. 'Then this is the spine, down to the legs.'

In truth, it wasn't exactly a clear picture. Nothing you could really identify as an actual child.

But Willow's fingers squeezed his again, and his heart knew that was her baby on the screen, and that if he hadn't been here with her, if he'd left her to experience this alone, he would have always regretted it.

The technician checked everything looked okay, and confirmed the dating and due date.

'You're around seventeen weeks now, by the look of things,' she said. 'A little late for this scan, but it does mean we might even be able to see the sex, if you want?'

Willow nodded, then glanced up at him. 'I think so.'

He smiled, and shrugged—it wasn't his decision in the slightest. That said… 'I think any certainty you can add to this situation can only help.'

Willow's response was a watery chuckle, and the technician stayed professional enough not to respond at all, except to say, 'Okay then, let's take a look…'

CHAPTER EIGHT

TWENTY MINUTES LATER, they were back in the car park. Gwyn had given Willow the keys and told her to wait in the car while he sorted out paying for parking. She probably should have given him her credit card to pay, but she was too busy staring at the blurry, black and white printout the technician had given her to even think of it.

The driver's side door opened and Gwyn slipped in, closing it softly behind him. 'You okay?'

She nodded and said, 'Fine,' without considering whether it was true. It was just what you said when people asked, wasn't it?

Gwyn reached out and took the photo from her hand, holding it up between them so she automatically looked up at him. 'Let's try that again. You okay?'

This time, she took a moment, and a breath, before answering. 'Honestly? I'm a little overwhelmed.'

'Understandable.' Gwyn turned the scan photo to study it himself. 'I mean, that's an actual person in there. That's pretty overwhelming.'

'Yeah.' Although, really, the living being *inside* her wasn't the problem.

It was what was going to happen when it was time for them to come out.

'I'm sorry they couldn't tell you if it was a boy or a girl,' Gwyn said.

Willow shrugged. 'At least she confirmed there's only one of them.' One baby was more than enough to be fretting about. Twins…that would have been a whole different level.

'You were worried it might be twins?'

'They do run in the family,' Willow pointed out.

'True.' Gwyn gave her back the photo and fastened his seatbelt before starting the engine.

His shirtsleeves were rolled up—it had been warm in the hospital—and Willow found herself mesmerised by his bare forearms as he shifted the car into reverse, put one hand on the back of her seat and smoothly manoeuvred them out of the tight parking space.

She'd be lying if she denied that one of the reasons she'd been glad Gwyn had agreed to take her to her appointment was that it gave her another opportunity to watch him drive. It was surprisingly sexy watching someone as attractive as Gwyn do anything well, and he really was a very good driver.

Of course, she'd also be lying if she pretended that was the *only* reason she'd been glad to have him there.

Willow wasn't afraid of doing this alone. In lots of ways, she'd been on her own since Rowan had left six years ago, and she'd been doing fine.

Okay, maybe not fine.

Her professional life had flourished, and she'd gone on to bigger and better campaigns, being recognised in the street and making more money than she could have dreamed of. She'd managed to put boundaries around her relationship with her mother, wrestling control of her own future from her in return for a *very* generous monthly stipend that Willow could now easily afford, and which kept her mother safely out of her business on the other side of the country.

She'd bought her Manhattan penthouse. She'd featured in magazines, on billboards, on runways, all over the world. She had the fame, money and career she'd always dreamed of. And most of that had happened since Rowan had left and she had to face the world alone.

But now, staring at that black and white image as the English countryside rushed past the windows, she wondered if she'd lost something else.

Someone to enjoy it all with, perhaps.

Oh, she had friends, and colleagues and acquaintances—she was close to her assistant, or had been, until she'd had to quit to look after her sick father, just before Willow had peed on that first stick. At the time, she'd thought that was a blessing—hiding the pregnancy symptoms from her would have been impossible. Now, she realised she'd lost one of the few pillars of personal support she had.

And she'd *paid* her to be in her life.

There was Ben, but he just didn't count, no matter how she looked at it. He was business as much as pleasure and, the last year or so, even the pleasure had been fleeting. He called when he needed her to appear with him, and she called when she had an itch to scratch because, honestly, they *were* in a relationship, however misguided, and she'd never been one for anonymous sex.

Finding anyone else was hard, anyway. Her fame made her a target for people who wanted to use her, and she couldn't get away with promiscuity the way Ben could, just by virtue of being a man. At least Ben was upfront about what he was using her for. That had always seemed the lesser of two evils.

There was her mother, but…just no.

And there was Rowan. Her twin sister. The one person she knew would support her through anything. So she'd run to her and…instantly sent her away.

She knew all the reasons she'd done it, of course—had spent hours running through them in her head even before she'd landed in the UK. And she still believed it was probably the best solution to all their problems.

But it did leave her on her own again.

Alone. Except for Gwyn.

Gwyn, who clearly didn't want to get involved in all this but had anyway because he obviously saw how much she needed someone, anyone.

How much of her growing feelings for him—the ones she was still trying desperately to pretend she didn't have, but failing more often than she succeeded—were just down to him being the only person in her corner when she needed him?

Maybe she was just feeling gratitude, and her hormones had confused it into lust.

That would explain a lot.

Gwyn pulled the car to a smooth stop outside her cottage and she jumped anyway, surprised they'd made it home so fast.

'You okay?' Gwyn asked again, his brow furrowed with concern as she fumbled to unfasten her seatbelt.

'Yeah. Just tired.' That was more convincing than fine, wasn't it?

From Gwyn's nod, it was. 'It's been a long day. Come on, let's get you inside.'

On another day, she might have asked him to stay for a cup of tea, or something. Today, she needed to be alone. She said her thankyous, took her bag and shut the door in his face—ignoring his obvious confusion as she did so.

She needed to think.

After an afternoon spent sitting at Rowan's kitchen table, thinking, Willow took a long, warm bath and went to bed for an early night. But sleep was a long time coming.

In fact, sleep continued to be elusive for the next few days, until the night she finally crashed out into a peaceful oblivion—only to be woken at the crack of dawn by her ringing phone.

She glanced blearily at the screen in the half light, and pressed answer. 'Rowan? What's the matter?'

Rowan's answer was a stream of words without pause, most of which didn't make any sense until Willow's tired brain managed to pick through them and choose only the ones that really mattered.

Eli. Truth. Ben. Needed to tell him.

Oh, this didn't sound good.

'Wait a minute,' she said, once Rowan was done. 'Are you sleeping with Ben's brother?' That was the only Eli Willow knew and, frankly, this sounded like a disastrous idea.

'No! We're just friends,' Rowan insisted. Willow was sure that while that might be *technically* true, it wasn't all either of them wanted.

Like me and Gwyn, maybe? No. Focus.

Rowan was still talking. 'I couldn't do anything more when I was still lying to him about something as basic as my actual name.'

'But you wanted to, right?' Willow guessed, trying not to project her feelings about Gwyn onto her sister and Eli. 'That's why you felt you had to tell him the truth. I can get that.' She sighed. At least she hadn't had to lie to Gwyn, because he'd known the truth from the start. But she was still lying to his family, and everyone else in Rumbelow.

Maybe this hadn't been such a good idea, after all.

'Is everything okay? With the baby? The cottage?' Rowan asked. 'Ben hasn't been in touch, has he? Because honestly, the more I hear about that guy, the more I think you had the right idea, hiding out in Rumbelow.'

At least one of them did.

'Even if it meant you had to make "friends" under false pretences?' Teasing was lots easier than dealing with this right now.

'Even then,' Rowan promised. 'Seriously, Will. Is everything okay?'

'Everything's fine,' Willow replied, hoping she sounded convincing. 'There's just…stuff. But I had my scan and we got to hear the baby's heartbeat and see it wriggling about and everything! Not enough for us to tell if it's a boy or a girl though. It had its legs crossed.'

'I want photos!' Rowan paused, and Willow could almost hear her frowning. 'Wait. We?'

Ah. Rookie error there. 'Me and the ultrasound technician.'

Rowan's pause was suspicious. 'Right. Well, send me photos.'

'I will,' Willow promised, pleased to have dodged that bullet. 'If *you* talk to Eli. Tell him whatever you need to, just make sure he doesn't tell Ben where I am or what's going on.'

She already knew what her sister was going to say before she said it.

'I'm going to tell him the truth, Will,' Rowan replied.

The tables had been turned, and Gwyn really didn't like it.

Yes, he'd been avoiding Willow, a bit. But now she was avoiding him and, well, that wasn't on. Not when he'd finally decided that it was okay to let her in, just a little, just for a while.

It wasn't that he was attracted to her. Okay, that was a lie. It wasn't *just* that he was attracted to her. Because of course she was one of the most beautiful women in the world, that was sort of a given for a straight guy, right?

But more than that, he *liked* her. He liked spending time with her. Liked the way she raised those perfectly arched eyebrows and asked him questions that got him talking about things he thought he'd packed away years ago, somewhere deep in his psyche. Not that he *wanted* to talk about them. But it just felt…good for someone else to know everything that had happened, and why he was the way he was now.

Someone other than his sister, who could only ever look at him with excruciating pity when the subject came up.

Willow didn't pity him. She showed compassion and understanding, but not pity—maybe because she hadn't been there to witness first-hand how comprehensively he'd fallen apart.

Whatever it was, he wanted more of it. He knew it

couldn't be more than friendship—she'd be leaving soon, and she was pregnant with another man's child, and that wasn't a mess he really wanted to be stuck in the middle of. No matter how tempting it might be—and no matter how certain he was he'd be better for her than the *actual* father of her child.

That wasn't the point. He wasn't looking for anything romantic—with anyone. Certainly not with someone who was starting a family and needed a reliable father figure to lean on.

Gwyn already knew he wasn't that man.

But friendship—short-term, without commitment or expectation, just helping a woman out because she deserved it rather than because she needed it, or him—that he could do.

Would do, even, if she wasn't avoiding him.

Which brought him back to his original problem.

Tonight was folk night again at the Star and Dragon, and he *knew* Willow had enjoyed it more than she'd expected when she'd joined him last time. If anything was going to tempt her out of isolation, it would be good music and excellent lasagne.

So he put his guitar in its case and headed down the hill to knock on her cottage door.

'Folk night? Again?' Willow looked confused at the idea when she answered.

'It's a weekly affair,' Gwyn said. 'And it's been a week. A few, actually.' Between him avoiding her and her avoiding him, they'd missed some.

'I realise that. I just... Aren't you worried? About showing up there with me twice, I mean?'

'Worried about what, exactly?' He suspected he knew,

but he wanted to hear her say it. If only because hearing it out loud would probably remind her how silly it was.

'Worried that people will think we're, you know. Together. And then when I leave, or when news gets out about the baby...'

Gwyn raised his eyebrows. 'Since when have you—or I, for that matter—cared what people around here think?'

Willow shook her head. 'I don't want to run back to New York and leave you here to deal with the gossip.'

Something about the way she said it gave him pause. 'Are you planning on going back soon?'

Wouldn't it be typical that, just when he'd decided to let her into his life, she'd decided to leave it?

But Willow shook her head, blonde hair shaking in front of her face. 'No. Not yet. At least, I hope not. I...' She looked up and smiled. 'Let me grab my coat and I'll tell you about it on the way to the pub.'

'Okay.' Gwyn grinned at her retreating back as she headed for the coat closet under the stairs, then caught himself and schooled his expression. It never did to be *too* enthusiastic about things.

'So, Rowan is confessing all over there in the States?' Gwyn summarised, after she'd recounted her recent phone call with her sister.

'Looks like,' Willow said glumly. 'To Eli, anyway. Once she can persuade him to listen to her.'

'And is he likely to tell his brother?' Because from what Willow had now told him about her ex, once Ben found out that she was pregnant and hiding out in Cornwall, Gwyn couldn't believe they wouldn't see his private plane landing nearby very soon.

'I don't know.' Frustration leaked out of Willow's voice. 'I just don't know him well enough to tell.'

So she was in limbo, waiting to see if the axe was going to fall. Gwyn knew how that felt, and it was never fun. The best he could do was try to distract her this evening.

'Come on.' He looped her arm through his as they continued down the hill. 'I'll buy you a lime and soda and a lasagne to take your mind off it.'

'With garlic bread?' she asked hopefully.

Gwyn smiled. 'Definitely with garlic bread.'

As far as he was concerned, the evening was going entirely to plan. Thirty minutes later they were ensconced at what he'd already begun to think of as *their* table in the back, enjoying the music, the ambience and the lasagne. Sean and Kayla were up on stage again, and he was already running through his own possible set in his mind. He even had a new song he'd been working on he thought might be ready to debut. He wanted to hear what Willow thought of it.

'Another?' He raised his empty pint glass and nodded at Willow's similarly finished lime and soda. She nodded, her mouth full of lasagne, and so he headed to the bar.

Which was where his carefully constructed fantasy about the evening fell apart.

It took him a half a second to realise why the woman at the bar looked familiar. A moment longer to realise that she'd seen him too, and that the man at her side must be her husband. The man she'd left him for.

'Rachel.' He forced a polite smile. 'It's good to see you.'

A lie. It wasn't good. It tore at his insides still and to

this day. Not because he still loved her, but because seeing her reminded him of all the reasons he'd never moved on. Why he and Willow could only ever be friends.

'And you.' Her smile looked fake too, but that might be because her husband was looking between the two of them in a way that suggested he was jumping to conclusions.

Gwyn held out a hand. 'I'm Gwyn. I used to know Rachel a long time ago.'

'Mark.' Rachel's husband shook his hand. 'And yes, I've heard of you. Are you playing tonight, then?'

'Oh, probably not.' He hoped they didn't look behind him to where his guitar was propped up beside Willow. Any intention he had of playing had now left the building.

'You're not playing?' Kayla and Sean had finished their first set and joined him at the bar, Kayla looking disappointed as she spoke. 'I thought Sean said you had a new song.'

'It's not ready yet,' Gwyn lied.

'That's a shame,' another voice said, and he felt his eyes close with the effort of not wincing. 'I was looking forward to hearing it. Hi, I'm Rowan.'

When he opened his eyes again, Willow was shaking hands with Rachel and Mark in turn, as if this was a perfectly normal situation.

As if his whole heart and history weren't sitting on the bar, about to be pounded with a mallet.

He knew that Willow had made the connection between his past and the woman in front of her the moment Mark made introductions. He felt her whole body press against his side, and she reached for his hand. To

the other side he saw Kayla nudge Sean and look pointedly at their joined hands.

Oh, this whole night was getting out of control now.

'We've got a table over there, if you'd like to join us?'
Willow said, and Gwyn's heart stopped just for a moment.

'Oh, no. Thank you, though,' Rachel said. 'We're here
with friends.'

She pointed across the bar to a table of four people
Gwyn vaguely recognised, all watching the drama unfolding at the bar with intense interest, until he looked
over and they all quickly glanced away.

It was a very British drama, Gwyn supposed. One
only really noticeable by the heaviness of the tension all
around them. But people knew him. They knew Rowan.
And enough of them knew Rachel to understand why he
just wanted to drink himself under the bar right now, or
at least get the hell out of there.

But he wouldn't. Because he had to make sure Willow got home safely.

Just another reason he shouldn't have let himself feel
responsible for her, he supposed.

'I knew they'd say no,' Willow whispered as they made
their way back to their table a moment later, after some
more awkward goodbyes. 'I'd seen them greeting friends
over there on their way in. Of course, I didn't know who
she was then...'

Five minutes earlier, she'd been watching Gwyn at
the bar, admiring the line of his body as he leant on his
elbows, waiting for her drink. Then she'd seen the attractive brunette approach and greet him, the man at
her side looking far less happy about the situation. She'd

speculated, of course—old friend, fan of his music, family friend...

She'd only figured it out when Abigail had stopped by the table, spotted Gwyn at the bar, and cursed—then sent Sean and Kayla over there as some sort of buffer.

'I daren't go over there myself. I honestly don't know what I might do.' Abigail had dropped into Gwyn's empty chair. 'I can't believe she'd have the nerve to come here again, after everything she did.'

'That's Rachel, then?' Willow had guessed.

Abigail had looked surprised. 'He told you about her? Well, good. Hopefully, that means he's moving on at last. But yes, that's her.'

After that, it had been inevitable that Willow would go up and give Gwyn some moral support. What else was a friend supposed to do?

'You realise she thinks we're here together,' Gwyn muttered under his breath as they reached their table. Abigail, thankfully, had gone, and they were alone—or as alone as they could be in a busy pub.

'Is that a problem?' Willow arched her eyebrows. 'I wouldn't have thought you'd be too worried who your *married* ex-girlfriend thinks you're dating.'

He flashed her an irritated look. 'I would have thought you *did* care who everyone in this village thinks *you're* dating. You know what gossip is like around here.'

Willow didn't point out that she'd only been there a couple of weeks so how could she know, because she *did* know. Even if Rowan believed that she lived in a bubble of privacy here, Willow knew that wasn't the case.

People *always* talked. And after tonight they'd be talking about *them*.

Not that she was about to admit to making a mistake or anything, though.

'I just thought I'd better get over there and support you before you started sobbing into the bar,' she said grumpily. 'I mean, that was the woman who broke your heart so badly you never recovered, wasn't it?'

Gwyn gave her an incredulous look. '*That's* what you got from that story?'

'It's what I got from your sister's swearing and concern the moment she saw her near you,' Willow replied.

He groaned. 'I take it that Abigail sent Sean and Kayla over, then?'

'She did.' Willow risked a small smile. 'I came on my own initiative.'

'Of course you did.' This time, when he looked across the table at her, the irritation in his expression had gone, replaced with a sort of exasperated fondness, if she was reading him right.

'I just didn't want to leave you alone with her,' she said softly.

'Thank you.' He reached across the table and squeezed her hand. 'I appreciate the show of support. But...' He looked up and glanced around the pub. Willow followed suit and quickly took his point.

Everywhere she turned, someone was just looking away from them, not wanting to be caught staring.

'Everyone in this pub thinks we're together now,' she finished for him.

She wasn't quite sure how she felt about that. On the one hand, she was already faking her whole existence— what was one more element of it?

On the other...if people were going to believe she was

sleeping with Gwyn, it seemed incredibly unfair that she wasn't actually going to get to experience it.

She stamped that thought down.

'I'm sorry,' she said. 'I really did just want to support you. You looked...' Broken, she finished in her head. He'd looked broken. And just for a moment, she'd wondered if she *could* be the right person to put him back together again, after all. 'But I get that you don't want everyone in your home village thinking you're dating Rowan. Or even me, for that matter.'

Gwyn huffed a laugh. 'Are you kidding me? Do you really think there's a straight man on earth who wouldn't be just a little bit smug if people thought he was dating one of the Harper twins, even if it wasn't true?'

Willow looked away. Was that how Ben saw her? she wondered. She had a horrible feeling that it was. That Gwyn had just articulated *exactly* why the father of her child was with her in the first place.

Was she any better, though? She wasn't in love with Ben, so it had to be something else keeping her with him. Convenience, if nothing else.

God, how had she got herself into this mess?

Cool fingers touched her chin, bringing her gaze back to Gwyn's. 'That's not why I'm here with you. You know that, right?'

'Why are you?' she asked, feeling strangely vulnerable as he held both her face and her gaze.

He hesitated for a second, and she instantly regretted asking it. That was the question she should be asking Ben—why he was with her, at least until they'd broken up, and was there a chance of a happy future for them?

'I'm here with you because I don't seem able to stay away,' he admitted.

Willow stared at him, then looked away to gather her thoughts before she replied. Because the truth was she couldn't stay away from him either—if she could, she'd have said no when he'd shown up to invite her to the Star and Dragon that night. She'd have left him alone at the bar with his ex and her husband. She wouldn't have invited him to the baby scan in the first place.

Gwyn dropped his hand from her face as she moved, and she reached out across the table to grab it, squeezing his fingers between her own, trying to convey that she wasn't pulling away—just pulling herself together.

'I got another message from Rowan while you were at the bar, telling me not to look online for Ben,' she said. Her sister had also informed her that she'd told Ben's brother Eli the truth about who she was and why she was there, but that Eli had promised to keep their secret—for now.

'So you instantly looked him up?' Gwyn guessed.

'Of course,' she replied. 'He's out on some superyacht with a woman probably fifteen years his junior, proving he doesn't need me.'

'I'm sorry. That's got to hurt.' Despite everything, Gwyn did sound genuinely sorry.

'It doesn't,' Willow admitted. 'It doesn't hurt at all. Which, if I needed further evidence that we're not meant to be together, would probably do it.' She sighed. 'It doesn't make anything much easier though because… the man's practically a child himself. He's doing this for the people watching—the media, the cameras, the gossip

sites. The exact same reason he was dating me. And…
that's not the life I want for my child.'

'Are you reconsidering whether you tell him about the
baby at all?' There was no judgement in Gwyn's voice,
even though she knew he had to have serious feelings
about it, given his past.

'No,' she reassured him. 'Even if I wanted to—which
I don't—his brother knows now, and he's not going to
keep that secret for ever. It wouldn't be fair to ask him
to either.'

'So…what's changed?' Gwyn asked. 'You said when
you told me about the baby in the first place that you
didn't think you should raise it with Ben. What's different now?'

It was a good question, one she weighed up in her head
for a moment or two before she answered. 'Certainty,
I suppose.' She sighed. 'Maybe there was a part of me
hoping that this time he'd grow up, learn a lesson, realise
that he wanted me more than he wanted whatever he's
out there getting right now. And I'd realise that I did love
him after all, and we could all live happily ever after.'

'But that didn't happen,' Gwyn finished for her.

She gave him a soft smile. He didn't even realise how
much of this was because of him.

'No, it didn't,' she said. '*You* happened instead.'

CHAPTER NINE

'ME?' GWYN BLINKED, unsure what to make of this sudden conversational U-turn.

They'd been talking about everyone thinking they were together, then about Ben, and now…he wasn't sure. He'd only had two pints, but that was enough to render Willow's conversational meanderings indecipherable.

But he knew it was important. Whatever she was trying to say…it mattered. And he was going to listen carefully until he got it.

'I don't… What do *I* have to do with it?' He wasn't going to make any assumptions either. That was definitely a sure-fire way to get them both into trouble.

Her smile was gentle. With her blonde hair falling around her shoulders, and the way she leaned across the table towards him, he couldn't blame everyone around them for thinking they were on a date.

He wasn't one hundred per cent sure himself, right now.

'You found me a midwife and made me an appointment and took me there. You drove me to my scan and held my hand when I was nervous. You hugged me when I was overwhelmed. You shared your past with me, even when it was hard. You brought me here to help me get to know the village. You even let me join your family for Sunday dinner, and get to know your sister and nephew.' She was still smiling, so he figured that was a good thing. And when she laid it out like that…maybe he had let her into his life rather a lot more than he'd realised.

'Do you know,' she went on, 'I've never even met Ben's brother, Eli? Rowan seems to have met him her first day in New York, but Ben never, ever introduced us. He never let me into any part of his life that wasn't for show. I don't think I even fully realised it until I came here and things with you were so…different.'

Did that mean she was getting ideas? Thinking he was going to step into Ben's shoes and help her raise this kid? Because the only reason he'd let himself get as close as he had was because he knew she was leaving soon.

Even if the idea of her going, of never seeing the baby born or seeing Willow be a mother, had started to cause a steady ache in the centre of his chest.

'Willow, I—'

She held up a hand to stop him. 'I'm not asking you for anything here, Gwyn. Don't worry. I know you're not interested in me that way—I mean, why would you be? I'm pregnant and hormonal and, if these jeans are any indication because they're *already* only held together by a hairband around the button, I'm going to get huge over the next few months. And I'm leaving soon, we both know that.'

He nodded, trying very hard to concentrate on her words and not the picture in his head of her, round with baby and smiling at him, one hand on her bump, the other reaching for him…

'I'm just saying that you, as a friend, showed me what

I should expect from a partner. And I know for sure now that Ben doesn't have it in him.'

'Good.' The word came out as a fierce sort of half growl that surprised even Gwyn. But the idea of Willow going back to Ben after this set something on fire inside him, even if he wasn't willing to name the feeling just yet. 'He doesn't deserve you.'

Neither did he, of course, but that was beside the point. Willow didn't *need* any man at her side anyway. If she chose to have someone there…that person should just be grateful to be chosen.

'I think we both deserve more,' Willow said, which was more diplomatic than Gwyn would have managed, but also very true. 'We don't love each other. And I think… I think I have to give all my love to my kid now, anyway. For now, at least. Because if it's only going to have one parent, I need to be the best mum I can possibly be, right? Better than my own, at least.'

'Sounds like you've made your mind up what to do, then.' Gwyn took a sip of his pint to hide how uncertain he felt about that. If she'd decided her path she'd be leaving soon, and he was willing to at least admit to himself that he'd miss her company. But already he cared about her enough to want her to go, if that was the right thing for her.

She gave him a lopsided smile. 'I still need to figure out exactly what I want that to look like, but being here, clearing my head…it's helped a lot in enabling me to picture it.'

'That's good.' And it was good. He just had to keep telling himself that—and ignore the pain in his chest that just kept increasing. 'I guess you'll be heading home to

New York soon, and I'll get my old, less outgoing neighbour back. And I mean "outgoing" literally, of course, since Rowan hates going out anywhere.'

That made her laugh, which was his intention, but her expression turned quickly pensive as she studied him across the table. 'Soon, I suppose. But not just yet. I'm not quite done with Rumbelow and all it has to offer yet.'

Gwyn couldn't put his finger on what exactly had changed, but with her words the whole night felt different. Sean and Kayla were back on stage, striking up a new song, one with a low and sensuous melody. The air seemed to buzz, thick with…something. Anticipation? Heat?

It was definitely heat. He could feel it in Willow's gaze, not to mention inside his own body. Filling him up from his belly outwards. Or maybe slightly lower than his belly, if he was honest.

He tightened his fingers around his pint glass. 'You have plans for the rest of your stay?'

There was a vulnerability behind her gaze now too. One that made him want to reassure her. 'Well, that depends a lot on you.'

Couldn't she tell? Didn't she know she'd held him in her thrall almost since the moment she'd arrived in the village?

His mind flashed back to her earlier words and he realised—she didn't. The woman voted most beautiful in the world more than once wasn't sure if he desired her. Even as he was sitting here aching with wanting her.

He placed his pint down on the table and reached for her hand, tracing patterns on the back of it as he stared into her eyes.

'You said something before, and I should have corrected you at the time,' he said, low and serious. 'You said…you said you knew I couldn't be interested in you, all pregnant and hormonal. And you were right in a way—I'm not looking for any kind of relationship, you know that. But the idea that I'm not attracted to you… Willow, pregnant or not, you're the most beautiful woman I've ever seen in real life. But that's not why I want you so damn badly.'

Her breath hitched and he watched her eyes widen even further. 'Why, then?'

'Because you're *you*. Because you're trying so damn hard to do the right thing by your baby, whatever that turns out to be. Because you *listen*—not just to my sob stories, but to everyone. Because you give off the kind of energy that is just irresistible. And because…when I'm near you every inch of my body aches to touch every inch of yours.'

She held his gaze for a long, long moment. Then she pushed away her still half full glass and got to her feet.

'Let's get out of here,' she said.

Gwyn downed the rest of his pint and followed.

Outside, the night was dark and a chill was blowing in from the sea, cold enough to make Willow pause and wonder what the hell she was doing, dragging Gwyn up the hill behind her towards her cottage.

Not cold enough to make her stop, though.

They'd got as far as the street outside the pub when he realised he'd forgotten his guitar and had to go back for it. She was taking that as a good sign—a sign that he was as blindsided by this as she was. She could *feel* the want and the need pulsing in her veins in a way she never had before. Certainly not with Ben.

Not thinking about him tonight.

In fact, thinking altogether was off the agenda for tonight. Tonight, she just wanted to feel. To be herself, rather than a mother-to-be. To forget every reason she had not to be doing this.

One last selfish indulgence, before her whole life changed and she had to adjust and adapt to always putting someone else first.

They didn't speak until they were outside the gate to her cottage, all energy going into just getting there—fast. Willow was breathing hard as she swung the gate open, only to find Gwyn hovering outside the edge of the cottage boundary.

'Are you sure about this?' he asked.

She liked that he didn't pretend to not know what they were there for, or to hedge his bets in case he got shot down at the last moment. She liked that he asked too.

'I'm leaving soon,' she said bluntly. 'And you don't want anything more than short-term fun anyway, right?' He nodded. 'So let's make the most of the time I have left here. Before everything changes.'

He didn't hesitate again.

Inside, the cottage felt smaller with two of them in it. Maybe they should have gone to his spacious home, but it was further away and, really, who could spare the time?

He dropped his guitar case by the front door, and she'd stripped his jacket from his shoulders before it hit the floor.

She surged up before she could change her mind, her mouth meeting his as he wrapped strong arms around her waist, hauling her closer. The heat that had been building between them all evening—longer, since the hug in the doctor's car park, since the day they'd met—exploded into a supernova. Every inch of her skin vibrated with the feel of him. His hand in her hair, the other at the small of her back, keeping her close. The hard ridge that pressed against her belly. His lips, moving across her jaw, down her throat to her collarbone and making her shiver.

'Bedroom,' she whispered, close to his ear, and he nodded.

They stumbled there together, shedding clothes between them as they went, leaving a trail from the front door to the bed. For once, Willow didn't care about the mess.

She fell backwards onto the bed with barely a jolt and he was right there above her, on top of her, his hands then his mouth at her breasts, then working their way down her body, over her slightly rounded stomach, until he knelt between her parted thighs, his mouth making her writhe and scream as the world seemed to contract then expand to contain so much more than it had before.

'Okay?' Gwyn murmured, and when had he got back up here, lying beside her on the bed?

She reached out and pulled him closer again. 'More than.'

'Good. In that case…' He hauled her up until she sat astride him, and the desperate want of him started to curl in her belly again.

'Do we need anything?' She was already pregnant, and she knew she was clean—had been tested the moment she knew she was pregnant, just in case.

'I haven't been with anyone since my last tests,' he

told her, and she trusted him. More than anyone else right now.

'Me neither.'

She lifted her thighs, reaching under her to position him, before sinking down onto him, her eyes closing with the sensation of being so filled, so complete.

God, she'd needed this.

Beneath her, Gwyn moaned, his hands grabbing her hips to steady her as she started to move, picking up the pace with every flick of her hips, until the friction between them, the rise and the fall, the push and the pull, threatened to drive her mad.

When she lost the rhythm, consumed with sensation, he held on tight and moved her for them, thrusting up into her until she fisted her hands in the sheets beneath them, threw back her head and moaned so loud the fish in the sea must have heard it. At the sound, she felt Gwyn tense beneath her too, and curse softly, before lowering her down to rest her head against his shoulder.

'We really should have done that before now,' she murmured.

He chuckled, the sound vibrating through her. 'Trust me. We're definitely going to be doing it again soon. To make up for lost time.'

The morning sun streamed through an unfamiliar window, and Gwyn blinked at the light, shifting against the sheets—until he realised he wasn't alone, and the events of the past evening took shape in his memory.

He smiled.

A proper, purely happy and satisfied smile.

When was the last time he'd smiled one of those? He couldn't remember.

He pressed a kiss to the top of the blonde head that rested on his shoulder, and contemplated waking her up. But Willow looked so peaceful, sleeping in his arms, that he couldn't bring himself to.

Instead, he checked in with himself, searching for regret, anxiety, any of the usual feelings he'd have around now if he'd let himself get a fraction as close to someone as he'd grown close to Willow.

It wasn't there.

It was because he knew she was leaving, he decided. This couldn't last, because she'd be going home to New York soon. That made it safe. That meant he could enjoy it while it lasted—then go back to his usual existence.

Oh. There was that black cloud. Damn. And it had been going so well.

Willow stirred beside him, making a frankly adorable little noise as she woke. She blinked up at him and smiled, bright and sunny, for a moment. Then she bit down on her lip.

'Do we need to talk about this?' she asked, her voice husky with sleep.

Gwyn shook his head. 'Let's just enjoy it while we can,' he replied, and kissed her down into the mattress again.

Eventually, though, they had to get out of bed. Gwyn made them breakfast, pottering around Rowan's kitchen in a way that felt both right and weird at the same time. He glanced back at Willow, sitting at the kitchen table with a cup of decaf coffee between her hands. That part felt right.

It was the strange disconnect, he supposed, of being in Rowan's space with a woman who *looked* like Rowan but wasn't. Not at all. He'd never felt about Rowan the way he felt about Willow.

Not that he intended to examine those feelings too closely. What was the point, when he knew she'd be leaving soon and it would all be moot anyway? No, the built-in expiry date was the only reason this was possible, so he wasn't going to fret about it. At all.

At least, not intentionally.

He'd had a moment, somewhere in the middle of their second time round last night, where he'd belatedly worried about the baby, then remembered the pamphlets he'd read at the hospital that told him sex was perfectly safe for most pregnant women. He hadn't realised he'd tucked away that piece of information at the time, but he was glad now that he had.

Willow was still barely showing at the moment, but from what little he knew of pregnancy—mostly gleaned from those hospital pamphlets, rather than paying attention to his sister's own pregnancy, since he'd been considerably less interested in that side of the female body's workings back then—it wouldn't be long before she really started to round out.

He wondered if she'd still be in Rumbelow then. If he'd get to feel the weight of her belly as it grew. See her round and glowing with her child.

Her child.

Would she come back and visit, Rowan at least, after the baby was born? Or would she expect her twin to fly out to New York to visit her, now she'd persuaded her to do it once?

Would he ever get to meet the baby Willow was carrying?

It seemed more of a possibility now she'd made a firm and final choice to raise the child alone, rather than with Ben. But still not guaranteed. He wasn't sure how he felt about never meeting the baby whose growth and wellbeing he'd been so closely involved with the last few weeks.

'Gwyn? I think the toast is burning...' Willow was suddenly beside him, reaching for the grill, until he stopped her and used the oven gloves to open it without burning either of them.

'Sorry. Lost in thought.'

'Reliving last night?' Willow guessed with a satisfied grin.

'Something like that.' He couldn't tell her the truth—that he was afraid he might be missing her before she'd even gone.

She couldn't stay. And he couldn't let himself feel the way about her that he did if she *was* staying.

He didn't have room in his life, or his broken heart and damaged psyche, to feel responsible for another person—two people, even, counting the baby. He knew himself, knew how little of the person he used to be was left after everything that had happened to those around him.

If Willow got hurt. If the *baby* was hurt—and children did get hurt, didn't they? They had accidents and broken bones and health scares. And they grew into teenagers and then young adults like Sean, and the capacity for tragedy and disaster was just all the greater.

It would break him for good if something happened to

Willow and the baby on his watch. Or, at the same time, to Abigail or Sean while he was looking out for Willow.

He knew his limits, and he was at them. Pushing them already, if he was honest, just by getting involved with Willow at all.

If he let himself love her—

'Breakfast.' He turned away from the counter, sharply cutting off his thoughts, and placed Willow's plate in front of her. She dug in with gusto and he watched with satisfaction.

'What did you want to do today?' she asked between mouthfuls. Then she caught herself and added, 'Not that I'm suggesting you have to stay and do things with me, that's not the deal. Certainly not beyond the bedroom door. But I don't have any plans, and—'

He decided to put her out of her misery. 'Today? Today I think we should spend here, preferably in bed. But tomorrow... Tomorrow is the village fete. The May fair, or whatever. We could go, if you like.'

'Together?' That was right. They hadn't talked about what this meant in public, had they.

'As friends,' he clarified.

'Friends who the whole village already think are sleeping together.' She gave him a wicked grin. 'Works for me.'

CHAPTER TEN

THE VILLAGE FETE was everything Willow imagined it should be. It had taken over every inch of Rumbelow, it seemed—from the playing field to the closed-off streets to the beach itself. There was bunting, a small carousel, homemade jam stalls, a local brass band playing and schoolchildren doing some sort of dance with ribbons in the village square. Down on the beach, there were short boat rides, freshly caught seafood to buy and a sandcastle competition.

It was perfect.

She tried to imagine what it must be like, growing up in this place as a child, and couldn't quite. It was probably lonely in the winter, right? When all the tourists had gone.

Except the town today was bustling with locals as well as visitors, and almost everyone nodded and said hi. It was hard to imagine ever being lonely in Rumbelow.

Her phone buzzed in her pocket and she ignored it. Again.

At her side, Gwyn glanced down at her pocket. He was walking close enough to her that he must have felt the vibration, but not actually holding her hand or touching her in any way in case people got the wrong—or right—idea. It felt strange not to be able to touch him, after being so intimate. But she understood. Soon, it would be Rowan here, and she didn't want the village assuming her sister was sleeping with Gwyn. No, she really, really didn't want that—even if she wasn't keen on delving into her subconscious right now to figure out why the idea made acid rise up her throat.

Probably that was just pregnancy heartburn anyway.

The phone buzzed again.

'Don't you need to answer that?' Gwyn asked mildly.

Willow shook her head. 'They're not for me. They're for Rowan.'

'How can you know that?' He frowned. 'And why are they messaging you anyway?'

With a sigh, Willow pulled out the phone to show him her notifications screen. Emails, direct messages, texts, voicemails…all technically for Willow, but not really. Not that he could really tell that about the voicemails, but the text preview on the others should make it obvious.

'They want you to design a dress?' His frown was even deeper and more confused now. 'But you don't— Oh!'

'Exactly. Rowan designed a dress for someone to wear to the gala dinner she went to the other week in New York, and once word got out who the designer was everybody wanted one. Except she's still pretending to be me, so…'

'So people think *you* designed the dress.'

'Yup.' Willow shoved her phone back into her pocket with a sigh. 'I'm forwarding them on to Rowan in batches, every hour or so.' And then *she* was ignoring them, as far as Willow could tell. Maybe they were more alike than she'd always thought.

'Come on.' She tucked her hand through Gwyn's arm.

That didn't scream relationship, did it?—totally a friendly thing to do—and led him towards the stalls by the church that seemed to be selling some delicious-looking cakes. 'I want to take a look around.'

They pottered happily around the May Fair, taking in the sights, sounds and smells—and indulging in good coffee and better sweet treats. Gwyn didn't pull her arm away from his, and for a long moment or two it almost felt real.

As if they were really there together, a happy couple, expecting their first child, with a traditional happy ever after awaiting them.

Then a cloud would pass across the sun, making her shiver, or someone Gwyn knew would greet them and she'd feel him shrink away, and she knew none of it was true. She was an imposter, pregnant with another man's child, and none of this was her future.

Her future was thousands of miles away, in a city that never slept, alone.

Even she couldn't blame herself for fantasising for a day.

But when it came down to it, was it what she really wanted? Not Gwyn, specifically—although, really, she could have and had done a hell of a lot worse—but that idyllic, movie-perfect ending?

She pondered the question as she sat on the edge of the beach, perched on the stone wall that separated the steps from the sand, swinging her legs a little as she waited for Gwyn to return with ice cream, even though it was really still a little too cold for it at the very start of May.

It was the ending that every woman was conditioned to want, wasn't it? The handsome partner, the family, the big wedding—ideally not in that order, but that boat had sailed. The happy ending.

Except…what ended, then? The woman's single life, sure, but what about her hopes and dreams, her goals, her career, her future? Getting married didn't mean saying goodbye to those things, and neither did becoming a mother. Not any more.

Surely it was really just another sort of beginning? An exciting one, if she approached it right.

Besides, if she'd wanted that traditional happy ending she'd have told Ben straight off and married him—and been miserable. So that was already out of the window.

But that didn't mean there weren't elements of this accidental charade she'd fallen into with Gwyn that she *would* want in her future. The great sex for a start.

No, focus. This wasn't about that.

Okay, it wasn't *just* about that. She wasn't going to deny that it was an important part of things.

But so was the support. The companionship. Having someone there to hold her hand in the hospital. A wider circle of family and friends to belong to. Someone to queue for ice cream. Someone to support her—and for her to support in return. To listen to. To love.

Yes. She wanted all that. She knew for a fact that Gwyn couldn't give it to her longer term—he'd been very clear about his position on that. But, regardless, he had shown her what she wanted.

She'd always be grateful to him for that.

Willow folded her hands in her lap, beside the tiny bump of her stomach that was only going to keep growing from here, and looked to see where Gwyn had got to with the ice cream. She spotted him walking back across the sand towards her and raised a hand to wave, when something else caught her eye.

A phone, raised and pointed at her.

Taking a photo.

Gwyn caught sight of the guy in his early twenties with the phone from the corner of his eye and realised the man was approaching Willow only a second or so later.

Swearing under his breath, he picked up speed—as fast as he could over the soft, dry sand and without dropping their ice creams. Willow was in broad daylight; she didn't need rescuing, but she might need backup.

'You're her, aren't you, though?' the guy was saying as Gwyn got closer. 'Willow Harper. I recognised you from the internet. My girlfriend said it couldn't be, but it is, isn't it?' He held up his phone proudly. 'This photo is going to get me so many hits!'

Willow shifted away a little further along the wall she was sitting on. 'I'm afraid you've made a mistake,' she said coldly. 'I'm *Rowan* Harper. Willow's my twin sister. I'm not a celebrity, and I'd appreciate it if you respected my privacy.'

The guy's smile only broadened. 'That's even better! You're a *recluse*. You just disappeared! Hell, people might even pay me money for a photo of you!'

And that, Gwyn realised, was why Rowan had stayed in Rumbelow so long, and only gone to New York under duress and pretending to be Willow. Here, she had the protection of the community. Yes, they all knew who she was, but they respected her privacy and nobody made a big deal about her past. She tended to avoid events like this, he remembered, a little too late, probably for this very reason.

'Here you go, sweetheart.' Gwyn pushed past the guy with the phone and handed Willow her ice cream. 'But we'd better get going now, if we want to make…that thing in time.'

'Right, yes.' She hopped down from the wall and he steadied her elbow. Her centre of gravity was changing, he realised. That, or the sand and the confrontation with camera phone guy had her off-balance. Either way, he was taking her home.

He took her arm and led her away, neither of them speaking until they were well out of earshot of the intrusive tourist.

'Well, that was close,' Gwyn murmured.

Willow shook her head, glossy blonde hair brushing his shoulder. It made him think of the night before, of her hair hanging down over his chest as she moved above him…

Focus. There'd be time for that later.

'We knew it was only a matter of time,' she said, staring out towards the horizon. He didn't think she was seeing the trappings of a small coastal village's May fair, though.

If he had to guess, he'd say she was seeing New York.

No. Not yet. He wasn't ready.

She couldn't stay, he knew that. But he wasn't ready for her to go yet either. And he knew that was a problem, but…right in that moment, he couldn't bring himself to care.

'Let's go home,' he said urgently. 'I picked up some great decaf coffee from one of the stalls—let's go try it.'

'Yeah, okay.' She turned to him with a smile and, for now at least, he knew he'd won her back. Back to him and Rumbelow and forgetting about the future and everything else that was coming down the road.

And he intended to make the most of it while it lasted.

The coffee had been spectacular—even if it was decaf. Gwyn brewed it in the shiny silver stovetop coffee pot she'd sent Rowan for Christmas a few years ago and which had clearly never been used before.

'Now you'll have no reason at all to come all the way up to my house.' Gwyn laughed as she moaned at the first sip.

She eyed him warmly. 'I can think of a few reasons.'

Now, Willow stretched out against the sheets, thinking that they really should make the effort to get up to the lifeboat station, though. She quite fancied a night in Gwyn's bed. Still, she slept well in his arms wherever they were.

So well she'd slept in. Well, they'd woken up for breakfast in bed hours ago…but that had led to other things in bed, and now it was early afternoon. She supposed there was a chance they might make it as far as Gwyn's house tonight…and besides, after yesterday's encounter she was perfectly happy to hide away and wait for the bank holiday weekend tourists to leave.

Gwyn was still fast asleep beside her, so she carefully slipped out from between the sheets and reached for his T-shirt, pulling it over her head. It barely hit her thighs, so she pulled on her own underwear in the name of decency—and out of respect for any of the day-trippers out on the boats who could see straight through Rowan's kitchen windows. Then she headed out to find more of that coffee.

She found her phone first, though, because it was buzzing so hard it almost fell off the kitchen counter. More messages for Rowan, she assumed. She picked it up, intending to switch off the vibrate function for a while, when the notifications screen caught her eye and froze her heart.

Not messages for Rowan—not all of them, anyway.

There were eight voicemails from Ben.

Eight.

That wasn't a sensible, just catching up or checking in number.

That was a something has gone wrong number.

She needed to listen to them. To find out what was happening.

Steeling herself, she pressed play—then held the phone away from her ear.

After listening to the first one, she tried to call Rowan but got no answer. So she went back to listen to the others.

Certain phrases jumped out of each one.

'I know everything.'

'Thought you could hide?'

'Try to fool me?'

'Take me for an idiot?'

'I know, I know, I know...'

But mostly it was the rage, the fury in his voice that came through in each message. Her chest tightened as if it was collapsing in around a sudden rock buried there.

She pressed delete.

Before she could call Rowan again, the phone started to vibrate once more in her hand.

Not Ben this time, she realised with relief. Rowan. Thank God.

She swiped to answer the video call.

'Rowan? What's going on?' she asked before her sister could say anything at all. 'I've got, like, eight voicemails on my phone from Ben suddenly telling me he knows everything, and then you weren't answering yours and—'

'He doesn't know about the baby,' Rowan said quickly, her eyes wide on the screen. 'He does know I'm not you.'

'How?' Had Eli told him? No, Rowan had said he wouldn't. Had the photo from that guy's camera phone hit the internet even quicker than she'd thought? But he'd believed her when she'd said she was Rowan, she was sure. So who? And how?

Rowan explained the events of her morning and Willow tried not to laugh. She was perfectly happy to ignore the Ben part of this story and focus on her sister's misadventures—it was far more fun, for a start.

'Wait, so Eli was naked in bed with you when Ben walked in? Oh, my God!' This definitely sounded more like something Willow would do than Rowan. 'When did this happen? What's the deal with the two of you? Is this a drunken hook-up or something more…?'

'It's…not a drunken hook-up.' Rowan's cheeks turned pink. No, of course it wasn't—Rowan didn't do that sort of thing.

Willow grinned. She'd *known* sending her twin to New York was a good idea.

'So it's something more.' Willow sat up a little straighter at Rowan's kitchen table and said, 'Tell me everything.'

Rowan opened her mouth, then closed it again. And

when she spoke, it wasn't the salacious and sexy gossip Willow had been hoping for. 'What's the point? I'm packing to come home right now. So, whatever it was, I just have to leave it here in New York.'

Willow's eyes widened. That was not where she'd thought this was going. 'Okay. This is clearly a conversation that needs tea. Go put the kettle on and I'll do the same, and while it's brewing you can tell me exactly what's been going on over there between the two of you.' She'd planned on coffee, but this conversation really did call for tea, somehow. Maybe it was just another way of feeling connected with her sister, across an ocean.

Willow reached for the teapot from the top shelf, tugging Gwyn's T-shirt down with the other hand and hoping that her sister didn't notice she was wearing someone else's clothes. Did she have time to go grab her jeans? Probably not without waking Gwyn up.

'I don't know where to begin,' Rowan admitted.

'Start from the beginning,' Willow advised. 'Right from the moment you arrived in New York and found him in my apartment. Because I'm pretty sure you've been leaving things out in your accounts of your Big Apple adventures, haven't you?' It made a change for her to be the one listening to *Rowan's* wild adventures. Usually, this was the other way around. But maybe she was going to have to get used to it. After all, she'd be a *mother* soon.

Rowan didn't deny it. Instead, she started talking— and once she'd started, it seemed like she couldn't stop.

'Well, it all sounds pretty much fairy tale perfect to me,' Willow said when she'd finished. 'Up until the part where my ex-boyfriend walked in. But he's *my* problem, not yours. So why aren't you happy? Why aren't you loved up and making dresses for celebrities and living your best life with Eli right now?' She should be. That was what she'd sent her to New York for.

Oh, fine. She hadn't *known* that this would happen when she'd asked Rowan to go. But she'd hoped that *something* would. Her sister deserved a little fun.

'Because...' Rowan took a breath and started again. 'When I came here, I was pretending to be you. So I lived life as if I *was* you, as best as I could. I took chances and put myself out there...all that stuff I haven't done since I walked out on you and Mum years ago. And I know... I know that was probably the idea—and don't think we're not going to have a conversation about why you decided sending me to New York was the best solution to your situation because we are, once I'm over this particular crisis.'

'I have no idea what you're talking about,' Willow said innocently. 'But go on.'

'These last few weeks...they haven't felt like real life. My real life is *there,* in Rumbelow. And the person I've been here... I can't be sure if she's real either. I miss my cottage, my home. And I miss the person I am there too, a little.'

Oh. Well, Willow knew that feeling. Being here in Rumbelow had been like a holiday for her too—an escape from reality. But she still knew she had to go back and face that reality, sooner rather than later.

But she had a feeling there was something more going on for Rowan here. So she decided to test the theory.

'So come home,' Willow said. 'Leave Eli behind as a fond memory. A holiday fling.'

'I would. Except...'

'Except you're in love with him,' Willow crowed triumphantly, almost upsetting her cup of tea as she thumped the table with one hand.

Rowan's eyes went very wide, her face white as chalk. Willow half expected her mouth to start flapping like a fish.

But finally she said, 'Oh, God, I'm in love with Eli.'

Of course she was. Willow could see that from thousands of miles away. And now Rowan could see it too. Everything was going to work out! Maybe Rowan would even move to New York and then she'd be around to be a part of her niece or nephew's life, and everything would be—

'I still can't stay here,' Rowan said, and Willow felt the daydream disappear.

'Why not?' she demanded. 'You love him, you're glowing, he makes you happy, it's the greatest city in the world, you've conquered your fears of being out there again… You *can* do this, Ro.'

'I… I feel like two people right now, Will. The old Rumbelow Rowan and the new New York one,' Rowan said, obviously trying to explain a feeling she perhaps didn't fully understand herself yet. 'I need to find a way to make those two people one, before I can really move forward with my life.'

Well, Willow supposed she could empathise with that one. The person she was here in Rumbelow didn't feel much like the woman she'd been in New York either.

'And you need to come back to Rumbelow to do that?' she asked.

'I think so. Yes,' Rowan said, firmer this time.

'Then come home.' A small noise across the room

made Willow glance up and see Gwyn standing in the doorway, arms folded across his broad, bare chest. She smiled at him, then turned back to her sister. 'You have to be sure, and you have to feel right about the decisions you're making. That's why *I* came here, after all. So come home and see if Rumbelow can work its magic on you.'

'Did it do that for you?' Rowan asked.

Willow didn't look back at Gwyn as she nodded. 'Yeah, I think it did. I'm ready to face the music now, anyway. This place has taught me what I want, and now all that's left is to make it happen.' Which meant leaving. Leaving Gwyn, specifically.

'That's good.'

'Perhaps Eli will come to Rumbelow with you,' Willow said hopefully.

Maybe Gwyn will visit New York some time.

'Perhaps,' Rowan echoed.

But she didn't sound very hopeful.

Willow knew how she felt.

CHAPTER ELEVEN

'YOU'RE LEAVING.'

He hadn't meant to say the words, they just tumbled out of him the moment Willow hung up on her call with Rowan. He bit down on the inside of his cheek to keep himself from saying more, and stayed where he stood in the doorway, even though every part of him was aching to go to her.

'Ben knows that Rowan isn't me.' She sounded tired—bone-weary—as she rubbed a hand across her forehead, tossing her phone down onto the table. 'It won't take him long to piece together where I am—especially if the guy from yesterday puts that photo up on social media.' She gave a wry smile. 'I should have let him keep believing I was Willow; one more photo of me wouldn't show up in a search. A new photo of Rowan will though. She's been AWOL for years.'

'You don't have to go running back to him, you know.' Gwyn couldn't make sense of the swirl of feelings in his gut. Of course she was going to go home to the city where she lived. And of course she was going to want to speak to the father of her child. This had been the plan all along.

So why did it feel so wrong?

Willow looked up in surprise. 'I'm not *running back*

to him. I'm just done hiding, that's all. It's time to face the music.' She took a deep breath and got to her feet. 'I'm ready.'

I'm not.

He wasn't ready to say goodbye to her. To let her walk out of his life. And suddenly…he wasn't sure he would ever be.

This was a disaster.

He'd only let himself get close to her *because* she was leaving. Because he knew he wouldn't have time to feel responsible for her—let alone the baby. To add that impossible weight to the one he already carried. To know that sooner or later he'd let her down and she'd get hurt, just like all the others.

He'd kept his distance—an emotional one, anyway, since the physical one had gone out of the window. But now, when it mattered, it didn't seem to make any difference.

He didn't want her to go.

'I should, uh, let you pack, then.'

'You don't have to—I probably won't be able to get a flight until at least tomorrow, anyway.'

They stood awkwardly with the kitchen table between them, the tension heavy. Was this goodbye? It should be. But she made him weak. And walking away…it felt impossible.

Until his phone rang.

He broke away from watching her and checked the screen instead—Abigail. He answered it without hesitation.

'Everything okay?'

He knew from her wrenching sob on the other end of

the line that it wasn't. 'They've *gone,* Gwyn. Scott and Kayla. They…they left a note.'

'Gone where?' He knew the answer, though. Every tensed muscle in his body told him before she did.

'London. They said…they said that if we wouldn't support their dreams they'd just have to chase them alone. I *knew* I should have—'

'I'll be right there.' He hung up without listening to any more and turned to Willow with an anguished feeling in his chest. 'I have to go. Sean…'

'I heard.' She gave him a reassuring smile. 'Go. See Abigail. I'm going to be packing anyway. And… If we're both heading back to London, I can sort us some transport and a hotel at the other end?'

He blinked with surprise. 'You'd…really? Is that okay?'

'Gwyn, you've helped me through my crazy time the last few weeks. I'm hardly going to leave you alone to get through yours. And besides, I'm worried about Sean and Kayla too. London at seventeen with no contacts and no money? Not a great place to be.'

That was the thought that was eating him up inside too. That if he'd helped them, supported them right, they wouldn't have gone like this. They'd have trusted him and he could have kept them safe.

Another loved one he'd let down because he was distracted with his own stuff—in this case, Willow. He was running out of people to disappoint.

Still, he hesitated a moment. Letting Willow help meant letting Willow in even further. And she had enough on her own plate right now, anyway. But he did need to get to London…

'Thanks,' he said finally.

She gave him a weak smile and shooed him away with her hands. 'Then get going!'

'I will,' he said. 'As soon as I get my shirt back...'

It took surprisingly little time to repack her life.

Her heart, however, was struggling more than her head.

Mechanically, she placed all the things she'd brought with her from New York into Rowan's battered suitcase, since her sister had taken hers, realising belatedly how few of them she'd actually used. Life in Rumbelow called for a different aesthetic, but also a different mindset. She'd found herself drifting into her sister's clothes almost without noticing—and not just for the slightly more generous cut that Rowan preferred, which gave her expanding stomach more room to grow.

Other things, too, had changed. She'd barely used her hair styling tools since she'd arrived, embracing instead the slight natural wave to her hair that seemed more suited to the seaside. She'd read the books on Rowan's shelves rather than magazines—sinking into fiction rather than trying to keep up with the world she usually inhabited. She'd eaten more lasagne in the last few weeks than in the decade before.

And she'd laughed. She'd had fun. She'd relaxed. She'd felt...like herself.

And wasn't that what she'd come to Rumbelow for in the first place?

She sat on the bed and thought, for what seemed like a very long time. But actually, the answers she was looking for came more quickly than she could have imagined.

Then she picked up her phone and started to make ar-
rangements.

Organising a private plane to fly them to the capital
took a little finesse, but Willow knew people who knew
people, so it wasn't too difficult. Securing a suite at her
favourite London hotel was even easier. As was getting a
table for dinner the following evening at the hottest new
restaurant in town. Easier, in fact, than getting a table
at the Star and Dragon for folk night because, here, nobody cared who she was. In London, they all wanted to
impress—or at least get the publicity that her showing
up for dinner at their restaurant would net them.

Last of all came the most difficult phone call. The one
she really didn't want to make.

But she looked around her at Rowan's cottage, then
moved to the window to watch the rolling waves for a
moment, and glimpsed Gwyn's converted lifeboat station
further around the cliffs, and knew it was time.

And so, drawing on everything she'd learned—about
herself, about the future, the world, what she wanted
from it, and the vision she had for her life—she pressed
the screen and called.

He didn't answer right away, of course—that would
have given her too much power. She counted the rings—
one, two, three, four, five—and then...

'Hello, Ben. It's Willow.'

She waited until they were in the hotel suite she'd booked
to tell Gwyn.

She'd meant to tell him before they left Rumbelow,
but he was with his sister most of the night, and when
he'd slipped between her sheets he'd needed her touch,

not her words. Then they'd overslept, so the morning had been a scramble, getting them out to the private airfield in time for their flight.

Then she'd meant to tell him on the plane, but he was busy explaining how Abigail had managed to talk to Sean the night before and got an address from him of a friend they were crashing with, and the hope and tension on his face had told her this wasn't the time.

She'd thought about doing it in the car from the airport, but he'd sunk into a kind of melancholia she assumed was brought on by his memories of the city they were driving through, so she'd just held his hand and let him know she was there.

But now they were at the hotel, and she really couldn't put it off any longer. Unfortunately.

'I'm going to head straight out and see if I can find this place where they're staying.' Gwyn pulled a clean shirt from the suitcase he'd dumped on the sofa in the corner of the suite and tugged his own off. Willow watched, drinking in every last glimpse of him.

'Okay. I can't come with you, I'm afraid,' she said. 'I've…got an appointment of my own this evening.'

He turned to her in surprise, still bare-chested, one eyebrow raised. 'An appointment?'

Damn, she'd made it sound medical, and now he was worried. Although the truth wasn't all that much better, she supposed.

'I'm meeting Ben for dinner.' Just tug that sticking plaster right off and hope the pain passes.

'You're…what?' He sounded more confused than angry, which made sense. Why would he be angry? She wasn't his…anything. And he had bigger problems than her ex to deal with, anyway.

'I didn't want him showing up in Rumbelow,' she explained. 'This way, I get to see him on my own terms.'

'You shouldn't have to see him at all!' Gwyn ran his hands through his hair, anguish on his face. 'I can't… I have to go find Sean. I can't come with you.' He looked so conflicted, so troubled by this that Willow almost laughed—except she was certain that would only make the situation worse.

'I wasn't asking you to,' she said lightly. Yes, she'd feel better with Gwyn by her side—somehow, she always did. But he wasn't going to be there after she went back to New York, and so she had to start getting used to doing things on her own again.

And she had to keep tamping down that tiny flame of hope that flickered on in her chest, that things could be different, somehow. The one that told her she wanted more than she was willing to admit, even to herself.

She'd forced Rowan into admitting her feelings for Eli. But she couldn't afford to do the same herself. She had to think about the future and the baby and Ben. And it wasn't fair to saddle Gwyn with any of that.

'You shouldn't go alone,' Gwyn said firmly. 'You said, when you came to Rumbelow, that you were afraid he'd steamroller over what you wanted, that he'd take control. You shouldn't see him alone. Wait until I've found Sean, then I can come with you.'

Willow shook her head. 'He wouldn't wait that long anyway. But honestly, it'll go better if I meet him alone. You don't need to worry.' She'd had plenty of time to think through exactly what she wanted to say. He wouldn't get the chance to steamroller her now.

She wasn't the same woman he'd known in New York, and she was kind of proud of that.

'But I do worry,' Gwyn replied, finally looking up to meet her gaze head-on. 'And that's a problem.'

'This is why I knew I should never have let myself get close to you.' Once again, the words tumbled out of Gwyn's mouth without him even meaning to say them— for all that they were true.

Willow blinked at him, eyes wide and her face paling. 'What do you mean?'

'The minute I let you in, that's when things started going wrong.' He was explaining himself badly, he knew, could tell from her hurt expression, but just because his choice of words was horrible didn't mean it wasn't the truth. 'I had things under control before then. Sean was safe, at home, listening to me. Abigail was happy. And that was all I needed. Then you showed up and I… I took my eye off the ball. I forgot that when I try to have more, care more, let more people in, things go wrong and people get hurt.' *People die.*

'Gwyn, if this is about Darrell…' Willow started, but he cut her off.

'Not just Darrell. Rachel. Even Abigail.' He'd never told her what had happened to his sister, he realised. He'd let her believe that she'd always been happy and healthy in Rumbelow. Never let on how hard they'd had to fight for that to be true.

'I never asked about Sean's dad,' Willow said slowly,

carefully. She was quick, and clever. He'd liked that about her right from the start.

'He was an utter bastard,' Gwyn spat, the memories still raw after all these years. 'He got Abigail pregnant right after she finished her A-levels, and then they had to get married, of course.' There shouldn't have been any 'of course' about it, but that was how things were then, and there. But it had been a terrible idea, he'd known that from the start. He'd only been a teenager—and a young one—then. No one had listened to what he thought.

'He left?' Willow guessed.

'Not soon enough.' Abigail had never admitted how bad things were in her marriage. If he'd known, maybe he wouldn't have left for London—or maybe he would. 'I went to London when Sean was six and I think it was after that when things got really bad.' And maybe that wasn't because he'd gone, or maybe it was. All he knew was he hadn't been there to look after his sister when she'd needed him.

'What happened?'

Gwyn sat heavily on the bed and sighed. 'She never let on that there was a problem while I was gone. Not even when I visited. But when I came home after Darrell's death, four years later, I found her with a broken arm, Sean looking terrified and his dad gone. We've never seen him since.'

Abigail had thrown him out, he supposed. And there were enough real men in the village to back her up and make sure she was safe.

But it should have been him.

Willow had her head tilted to the side, watching him.

'What?' he asked tetchily. He needed to get going, look for Sean. He couldn't let Abigail down again.

'I was just thinking that the last time you came to London you lost your girlfriend, an unborn baby, your best friend and bandmate *and* nearly lost your sister. No wonder you hate this place.'

'It's not the place I blame.'

'No. That much is clear.' She sat beside him on the edge of the bed, half on, half off, as if prepared to jump up again if he didn't want her there. But he *did* want her there—that was the problem. 'You know none of those things were your fault, right?'

She didn't understand.

'It doesn't matter. Maybe I could have stopped them, maybe I couldn't. The point is, I should have been there for the people I cared about. But they…there were too many of them. I couldn't be everywhere at once, and so I ended up letting them *all* down. That's why I have to keep it focused, concentrate on the only people I've got left—Abigail and Sean. It's why I can't afford to let anyone else in.'

'And why you don't want Sean in London,' she guessed. 'You're worried you won't be able to split your vigil between him here and Abigail in Rumbelow.'

He hadn't thought of it in those terms exactly, just known that if Sean came to London and got involved in the music scene, bad things might happen—like they had to Darrell. Oh, he knew his nephew was far more level-headed and less naive than his friend had been, not to mention that he had Kayla with him, who had to be a better guardian angel than Gwyn had managed to be for Darrell.

But none of that got rid of the heavy ball of fear that sat in his gut when he thought about Sean being here and Abigail being back in Cornwall, one of them always without his protection.

'It's not a vigil,' he snapped back. 'It's my family.'

'It's you martyring yourself, your whole *future,* to look after people who you think need you—but who would never want you to think this way,' she replied bluntly. 'All to make up for a series of events you couldn't have predicted or prevented wherever you were.'

He pulled away. 'You don't know what you're talking about.'

'Yes, I do,' she replied. 'Because I came to Rumbelow to hide this spring—I made no secret of that. But it means I know what hiding looks like. And while I hid out for a month or so while I figured things out, you've been hiding there for the last, what? Seven years? All because you're too scared to care for another person and risk losing them, or someone else getting hurt again.'

She said it like it was unreasonable.

'Why *shouldn't* I be there to look after my family? Isn't that what *matters* in this world?'

'Of course it is. But Gwyn, you have to ask yourself. Are you really looking after them? Are you giving them what they need—not what *you* need to feel safe? Because if you were, do you really think Sean would have run away to London without telling you first?'

Willow knew her words had hit home—hell, Gwyn practically flinched at them.

But then he shook them off, and hit back.

'What do you know about it? About family? I've been

Rowan's neighbour for *years,* and I never even met you before. You came to Rumbelow because you needed help, not because you loved your family. If you did, you wouldn't have left her alone there.'

'She wanted to be alone.' It wasn't anything she hadn't thought herself before. She knew she'd been a bad sister—and she wanted to do better. But they weren't talking about her right now. 'Gwyn, I'm not saying you've done anything wrong. I'm saying that…people have to be responsible for themselves. You can love them, support them, but you can't save them from themselves in the end. You couldn't have saved Darrell, however hard you'd tried. Abigail…you weren't responsible for her marrying that man. And she wouldn't want you to be, you know that. She'd hate the idea that you were only staying in Rumbelow because you were worried about her and Sean. That you'd given up your career, your future, your *life* for them. You know she would.'

His shoulders deflated a little at that, and she knew she'd got her point home.

'It's not like I had anything else to live for anyway,' he said softly. 'I lost all that when Rachel miscarried and left. When Darrell…'

'I know.' She put a hand on his arm, trying to convey that she really was only trying to help. 'But you could have, couldn't you? You could have a new future.'

His gaze met hers and the agony she saw there tore into her chest.

'I can't risk it,' he said. 'I can't risk falling in love with you, Willow.'

And there it was. The word neither of them had been saying—the one she'd barely even let herself *think*.

Love.

Was it love when you just *knew* that the person standing before you was the one you wanted beside you whenever life got hard? Was it love when you just *looked* at a person and felt like maybe everything was going to be all right after all?

It was probably love when you couldn't imagine a future in which you weren't with them, wasn't it?

Oh, hell.

Gwyn might not be willing to risk it, but it was already too late for her.

She was in love with him. And he was about to walk out of the door.

'I have to go and find Sean. I'm sorry.' Gwyn paused by the door. 'Will you be here when I get back?'

'I don't know,' she answered honestly. Right now, it felt like she knew nothing at all—like everything was even less certain than the day she'd arrived in Rumbelow.

He nodded, as if he'd expected nothing less, then walked out of the door.

She let him go.

CHAPTER TWELVE

LONDON DIDN'T SEEM to have changed much in the seven years he'd been gone. Oh, the skyline might look a bit different in places, and the names on the storefronts might have updated, but it still *felt* the same.

It felt grimy and dangerous and like it wanted to suck him in.

He needed to get back to Cornwall. He needed to find Sean.

He *needed* to stop thinking about Willow.

The moment he'd told her he couldn't risk falling in love with her, he'd known it was a lie. He'd already fallen.

What he couldn't risk was letting her know. Giving her hope or expectations that he could be anything other than the man he was.

A broken, desperate man holding together the tatters of his old life with clutching hands.

He knew she was right. Abigail and Sean wouldn't want him to give up his dreams, his chance at love and happiness for them. But she didn't seem to realise how close he'd come to losing *everything* all at once. How terrified he'd been that it could all have been gone in an instant, if Abigail hadn't fought back that one time, that last time, the one time it mattered.

It was because of Sean, of course. He'd stood between his father and his mother, ready to take the beating instead. At ten, he'd thought he was ready to be the man of the house, Gwyn supposed.

Abigail hadn't let her husband touch him. And she'd suffered for it—but she'd also found the strength to make sure it never happened again. That was what mattered.

Gwyn had lived with them for the first six months he'd been home, when letting them out of his sight had been cause for a minor panic attack. They'd helped him find his way back to life, after losing Darrell and Rachel and the baby.

He owed them. He loved them. And keeping them safe was the most important thing in his life.

Which was why he was trawling the back streets of a rather less salubrious area of the capital, looking for his errant nephew and his girlfriend.

He found the place they were supposed to be staying easily enough, but of course they weren't there. The friend who'd let them couch surf there the last couple of nights directed him towards a bar a few Tube stops away, where they were apparently playing that night—and possibly now rooming at, by the sound of things.

Wearily, Gwyn hoisted his backpack onto his shoulders again and went to find it.

He could have left his bag at the hotel. Should have, maybe. But he hadn't known, when he'd left, if he'd be going back. Still didn't, if he was honest. Besides, the bag wasn't *that* heavy. It only held his essentials for a night or two. Not like Willow's bulging suitcase, ready for her return to New York.

She might even be gone by now; she hadn't told him

the time of her flight, or if she had he'd not been paying enough attention to retain the information.

But no, she couldn't fly out yet. Because Ben was flying *in,* just to speak to her.

Would what had passed between them in the hotel room that afternoon change how Willow dealt with her ex? Would knowing that he'd written off any chance of a future between them make her more likely to go back to Ben?

She'd said from the start that wasn't what she wanted. But she might not want to raise the baby alone either...

He swallowed down the bile that rose in his throat at the thought of Willow and Ben together. Of that man he'd never met worming his way back into Willow's life, and making her life a misery. Worse, treating his child badly. Willow hadn't said a huge amount about Ben's behaviour and he had no reason to believe he'd ever physically hurt her, but there were other forms of abuse too. He couldn't let anything happen to her.

But how would he stop it? She'd be in New York, Abigail would be in Rumbelow and Sean... Sean would apparently be here, at the Black Crow Club, performing for drunk Londoners or tourists who didn't appreciate him.

He sighed as he looked up at the looming black bird on the sign out front, even the image a horrible reminder of his past, then pushed open the door.

It was early enough in the evening that the place was still mostly deserted; this was the kind of club that came to life in the early hours, the dead of night. Gwyn remembered places like this. It was exactly the sort of place he and Darrell would have played, back in the day.

The man behind the bar looked up with faint interest as he walked in.

'I'm looking for Sean Callaghan.'

'Wait, aren't you Gwyn...whatsisname? Used to be in that band, Blackbird? Whatever happened to you guys?' The barman looked far more interested now, just not in what Gwyn wanted him to care about.

'I'm Sean Callaghan's uncle and I'm here to take him home,' he said, more firmly. 'Where is he?'

'Uncle Gwyn?' Sean emerged from a back room, guitar slung over his back. 'What are you doing here?'

The barman, clearly sensing that he wasn't needed for this discussion, and probably didn't want to be part of it anyway, slunk off to the other end of the bar.

'I'm here to take you home,' Gwyn said. He was done with this. People just needed to do what was best to keep themselves safe, so he could sleep at night.

Kayla appeared behind Sean, looking defiant. 'We're playing a gig here tonight. We're not going anywhere.'

'You're seventeen,' Gwyn replied baldly. 'Neither of you should even *be* in here.'

'Uncle Gwyn...' Sean placed his guitar down on the nearest table and, leaving Kayla to guard it, approached him gingerly. He spoke softly, but reasonably—like an adult, Gwyn realised. He'd never thought of Sean as an adult before. 'I know you have good reasons to be afraid of me being part of the music scene here. And I know you're only here because you care about me and you want me to be safe. I talked about this a lot with Mum before I left. But the thing is, this is my future. This is the life I want to experience. And I'd really hope you could support me in that.'

Gwyn wondered if Sean had been practising that speech in the mirror. It was good—reasoned and reasonable, calmly delivered.

And it didn't make a damn bit of difference in the face of his own fears. Maybe, he realised, because *they* weren't rational at all. Because even *knowing* that didn't stop the rising acid that burned his throat, or the heat that flushed through him, or the way his hands flexed as if he wanted to *drag* Sean to safety.

He forced himself to keep his voice even, like Sean's. 'I know you think you're an adult, that you can face the world alone, but you don't know anything about this world.'

'Because you'd never tell me!' Sean shot back, some of his composure fading now. 'My whole life I've been asking you about music, about your career, and you'd never talk about any of it. And I get it, I do—what happened to you and Darrell was awful. But it's like you want to pretend that he never existed!'

Did he? Maybe. It was easier that way. But he wasn't going to admit that to Sean.

'My past isn't a story for your entertainment, Sean.'

'That's not—you *know* that's not what I meant!' Exasperated, Sean ran a hand through his hair. Kayla came to stand beside him, one hand on his arm, but stayed silent. When he spoke again, Sean sounded calmer, as if her touch alone had grounded him.

Gwyn knew how that felt. Willow had done that for him too.

'You know my dreams, Uncle Gwyn. You've known almost as long as I have that this is the life I wanted. And you...you know and understand this world better than anyone! I want you on my side for it, I want to do this *with* you, not against you. But I need you to trust me. And I have to do it, however that looks. I can't live my life in the shadow of *your* fear.'

Reality smashed over Gwyn like a soundwave, like that first crashing chord on the guitar before the song started.

'I can't live my life in the shadow of your *fear.'*

Wasn't that what he was asking everyone to do? Abigail had barely dated since her husband left and he knew at least part of that was because she knew how many questions he'd ask, how he'd hover and worry. Sean had run away to London not because Gwyn wouldn't help him, but because he was actively trying to stop him seeking his dream.

And Willow…

Willow was facing down her ex alone because he was too scared to let himself love her.

All this fear, all this trying to keep everyone safe, it had only driven them further away—and into danger.

And it was tearing him apart.

How had he not seen it?

Sean deflated a little, the longer Gwyn stayed silent.

'Look, just stay for the show tonight, yeah? See what you think. I know you've seen us play back home but it's different here, right? Stay, and listen. See if you think we've got what it takes. And if you do…'

Gwyn swallowed, and forced himself to speak. 'I'll support you. Because you're right. I… If you want to do this, I… I'd rather you do it with me than without me.'

Maybe he couldn't keep everybody he loved safe. Maybe he had to let them make their own mistakes.

But that didn't mean he couldn't support them. Cheer them on. And be there when—no, not when, *if*—if things went wrong.

He'd do that for Sean. For Abigail.

And maybe he'd even get to do it for Willow, when she was ready.

Willow chose her outfit for dinner with Ben carefully.

Attractive but not too sexy. Confident but not obnoxiously intimidating. Cut so that her stomach wouldn't strain against the fabric. Heels she could walk easily in. Hair up, and lipstick on.

It wasn't a battle. But it was a negotiation. Even if he didn't know it yet.

He was already sitting at the table she'd booked in the restaurant when she arrived. A classic power-play. He'd sat with his back to the wall so he could watch her approaching. In meetings, she knew, he liked to arrive last to show that he was the one in control. Here, though, he was probably hoping to put her on the back foot by making her feel she needed to apologise for being late, even though she wasn't.

She did not apologise.

He stood to greet her and she froze as he reached out to kiss her cheek in welcome. Pulling away, she dropped into the seat opposite him.

'Ben. Thank you for coming.' He'd already ordered wine for them, she realised, but obviously she wouldn't be drinking that. She flagged down a passing waiter and asked for a lime and soda.

'Well, when your girlfriend drops off the planet and

hires an impersonator to take her place, you kind of want to find out why,' he drawled.

She didn't point out that Rowan wasn't an impersonator, she was her twin, and that she hadn't exactly hired her. That was what he wanted—her on the defensive, arguing the smaller points so she forgot about the bigger ones.

Not this time.

'I came home to England because I needed time to think.' She folded her hands over the menu. 'Rowan needed an adventure, so I sent her to house-sit my apartment. It worked out for both of us.'

'Since she seduced my brother and sent him to take over my company, I'm guessing it worked out best for her,' Ben replied, bitterness colouring his voice.

Rowan was already on her way back to the UK—might even have already landed—Willow knew. And from the last phone call they'd shared, Willow wasn't sure things were working out at all for her twin.

Of course, they weren't working out for her yet either.

'So, are you done thinking?' Ben asked. 'Are you coming home?'

Home. He meant New York, she supposed. He meant home to *him* too.

'Ben, I didn't ask you here so we could get back together,' she said firmly. 'That's never going to happen.'

'Why the hell not?' He banged his wine glass down on the table. 'We had a good thing going, you and me, until you ran away here and screwed me over. Everything was fine until you left!'

'Everything was not fine.' She knew that now. When she'd been in it, her relationship with Ben had seemed...

functional, at least. Maybe the best she'd thought she could hope for, or deserved. After all, she had beauty, money, fame, success. Surely she couldn't ask for more—couldn't ask for someone to look past those things and love her for who she really was, not what she could give them?

But then she'd come to Rumbelow and met Gwyn. And suddenly, she'd known it *was* possible—even if he wouldn't admit it. She loved him, and she was pretty sure he loved her too—or could, if he'd let himself.

And if he never did… Well, she knew what it felt like now, being truly loved. And she wasn't going to settle for anything less. She wanted a life and a love that lit her up—not just for herself, but for her baby too.

'Ben, what we had wasn't a real relationship—it was a business arrangement.'

'One that worked very well for both of us,' he interjected.

'Well, it's not working for me any more.' She took a breath. 'Ben, I'm pregnant.'

If she'd had any doubt about whether she was doing the right thing, deciding to raise this baby apart from its father, the look of horror that melted into disgust on Ben's face ended it.

'God, why? Are you going to get rid of it?' Ben asked. 'Wait, it's not *mine*, is it?'

'Biologically? Yes. Practically…it doesn't have to be,' she said. 'I'm going to be raising this child. If you want to be involved in their life, we can talk about what that might look like. If you don't… I'm not going to ask for anything from you.'

'Wait, wait. If it *is* mine, we should get married, right?

That's the heir to the company in there. Pending a DNA test, of course.' She could see the calculations going on behind his eyes now—what a child, or at least an heir, could mean. He'd said something about his brother taking over the company. She'd always known that a large part of her value to him was making him look like a stable, responsible family man just waiting for that ring and the family to happen. Maybe he was thinking this was his way to regain that reliable standing in the eyes of the world—or at least the board of directors.

Time to shoot down that idea.

'No, Ben. It's a baby. Not the heir to anything—just its own person. It doesn't need your money, or the pressure of living up to your ideals or expectations. It just needs to be itself.' She frowned. 'And we are absolutely *not* getting married.'

'Then the kid will be a bastard. Illegitimate.' He spat it as if that was the worst thing that could happen to a child.

Willow could think of far worse.

'They'll be loved,' she countered.

Ben shook his head. 'I need to think about this.'

That was fair. She'd taken her time. He deserved some too.

She pushed her chair back from the table. She wasn't hungry any more, anyway.

'Take all the time you need,' she said. 'You know how to find me when you're ready.'

'No.' He grabbed her arm and yanked it until she had no choice but to sit back down. 'You want me to work with you on this, to find a fair way to deal with the situation?'

'It's not a situation, it's a child,' she replied. 'But yes.

I'd like it if we could discuss it like adults and come to a mutually agreeable way forward.' That wasn't so much to ask, was it?

From Ben's steely expression, it seemed that it was—or at least, that he was going to demand a steep price for it.

'You want me to work *with* you on this, and not call up my lawyer right now and set him on the case, you need to come back to New York with me. Tonight.'

CHAPTER THIRTEEN

WILLOW WASN'T IN the hotel room when he got back from the club in the early hours of the next morning—not that he'd really expected her to be.

A quick call to the receptionist confirmed that she'd checked out hours ago, while he'd been watching Sean and Kayla perform, and realigning his world view to include the fact that his nephew was potentially going to be the star he'd never quite managed to be, and that this was a *good* thing.

That wasn't the only realigning of reality he'd been mentally performing either, but without Willow there to hear it the rest seemed meaningless right now.

'She didn't leave a message for me?' he asked the receptionist, trying not to sound too desperate. But his own phone was silent, devoid of contact. Surely she wouldn't have left for New York without telling him?

Except she *had* told him. And he'd told her that he could never love her. So why on earth did he think she would stay?

'No message,' the receptionist replied pityingly.

'Right.' Gwyn hung up.

After a restless, unsettled night, he met Sean and Kayla for brunch and, between them, they hammered out a plan for getting them known, signed and famous—the right way. Gwyn held himself back from adding too many safety checks to the plan, but it was clear he was going to be spending a lot of time in London with them, if only for his own peace of mind.

'You realise at this point you're basically our manager,' Sean said, between mouthfuls of bacon.

Gwyn ignored him and carried on setting out the plan. One step at a time.

After brunch, and after setting them up in an acceptable short-term rental for the next couple of weeks, with strict instructions about their next moves, Gwyn headed for the station, and back to Cornwall.

Everything inside him was itching to race straight to the airport and grab the next flight to New York, but he made himself wait. He needed to report back to Abigail. Grab more things than just his overnight bag—and make sure that Sean and Kayla were okay in London alone, before he disappeared off across the ocean.

More than that, he needed to give Willow the time and space to do what *she* needed to do, before he barrelled into her life again with any dramatic declarations.

Which didn't mean he wasn't practising those declarations in his head, in preparation.

I'm an idiot. I love you. Of course I love you, and I can't believe I ever thought I could stop it. I want to spend the rest of my life with you and the baby. And yes, I'm still terrified, but it's going to be worth it. I'm sure of it.

When he wasn't imagining those conversations, however, darker thoughts and possibilities filled his mind.

Ones where Willow announced she was marrying Ben. Or that she never wanted to set foot in Rumbelow—or see him—again. Worse, ones where her plane crashed, or her taxi from the airport caused a pile-up, and he wasn't there to save her. Not that he knew quite what he'd do in the event of a plane crash, but still. The feelings lingered.

He shook them away and focused on everything he'd say when he got to New York and found her.

He was still planning the conversation in his head when he walked up the cliff road towards the old lifeboat station he called home, and past Rowan's cottage—and saw a willowy blonde standing in the garden.

His heart jumped in his chest, everything suddenly feeling tight and light at the same time. She raised a hand and waved and—

He realised the truth. It was Rowan. He could tell the difference now, even at this distance. And what that said about how far gone he was for Willow he didn't want to know.

He called out a greeting, and she gave him a sad smile in return. He wasn't sure exactly what had gone on with her in New York, but he was pretty sure she hadn't found her happy ending either.

Yet.

He still had hopes that his would be waiting at the other end of a transatlantic flight, if he could get the words right. It was like songwriting. Sometimes it could take a hundred drafts to find exactly the right words, ordered the right way, to say what he was trying to say.

When he had the words right, he'd go to New York.

He opened the door to his house and stepped inside, the glorious view out over the sea not captivating him for once. He was too lost in thought.

Until a voice said, 'Hello, Gwyn.'

He spun round to find her leaning against the kitchen counter. The small swell of her belly seemed to have increased overnight, emphasised, perhaps, by the loose shirt she had knotted over her jeans—one of his, he suspected.

In the rush of relief and joy at seeing her, all his carefully planned words flew from his head.

'What are you doing here? Not that I'm… I thought you'd be back in New York already.'

'That's what Ben wanted,' she replied. 'Gave me an ultimatum and everything. Fly back to New York with him or he'd make things difficult for me with the baby.'

'And you…'

'Called his bluff.' Willow gave a light shrug, a small smile on her lips. 'He wants me there to prove he's a responsible, reliable family man. An ugly custody battle or financial wrangling doesn't do that for him. He needs me a hell of a lot more than I need him, so I'll go back when I'm good and ready. I had unfinished business here.'

With him, he assumed. 'Why didn't you wait for me at the hotel?' Gwyn asked.

'Rowan called. She'd just arrived at Heathrow and… well, she needed me. I didn't know how long you'd need to be in London. So I got us a car and we travelled back here together. And she happens to have your spare key in case of emergencies, doesn't she? So I figured I'd just wait for you here.'

Thank God she had. Now, if he could just remember everything he had planned to say to her…

Willow took a deep breath. It was almost the moment of truth. The moment when she figured out what happened next—and if, just maybe, she could have everything she wanted.

But first… 'Did you find Sean? Are he and Kayla okay?'

'They're just fine,' he assured her. 'Far more mature and capable than I was at that age. And I think…with my support and guidance, they're going to be amazing.'

With his support. He was putting himself back out there at last—acting in the pursuit of dreams rather than hiding from them in fear of everything that could go wrong.

Maybe that meant he'd be able to do the same with her.

She opened her mouth to find out, but Gwyn beat her to it.

'I've been an idiot,' he said.

She looked up at him, studying his face for answers. 'You think you've been an idiot?' Hope started to float in her chest.

'Yes. I should have told you weeks ago that I was falling in love with you. I should have told you yesterday that I love you—and your baby—more than anything else in this world. That, if you'll have me, I want to spend every day of the rest of my life making you happy.' Not keeping them safe, she noted—although she was sure he'd want that too. But perhaps he understood a little better now that there was a fine line between keeping someone safe and limiting them—and himself.

Wait. Willow blinked, and focused in on the really important part of his statement. 'You love me? Us?'

'More than anything,' he repeated and stepped closer, opening his arms to let her in.

She moved into them without hesitation, resting her

head against his chest. 'Even though I'm pregnant with another man's child?'

'Did you not hear me say I love the baby too?'

'And even though people will be watching and gossiping about us? Even though they'll dredge up every awful story they can about either of us? Especially if Ben gets involved.'

'You know, I thought I was the one finding reasons this couldn't work,' he pointed out. 'I doubt you can think of any I haven't already thought of. And I don't care. You matter more to me than any of that.'

She looked up and met his gaze. 'Even if I want to go back to New York?'

That was the big one, wasn't it? Was he ready or willing to stop hiding away in Rumbelow and face the real world again?

She really hoped so.

'Then I'll come with you,' he replied. 'As long as we can come back to Rumbelow often. I'd miss my sea view.'

'So would I,' Willow replied, looking down at her bump to hide the tears she could feel pricking behind her eyes. Tears of happiness, of relief and of sheer amazement. 'And my sister. This baby is going to need all the aunts and uncles it can get.'

'I think it's going to have plenty,' Gwyn assured her. 'Abigail is going to be over the moon, for one.'

Willow hummed her agreement, then caught his gaze again. She needed to ask, even though it terrified her. 'You're sure about this? I mean, just yesterday afternoon, you said—'

'I know what I said.' And he didn't much want to relive it, by the sound of things. 'But you were right. And so was Sean. I was so scared… I was living a half-life. And I was forcing everyone else to just exist in it with me. It wasn't fair on them, on you—or on me. And it's not what I want any more.' He rested his forehead against hers. 'I'm lucky enough to still be here when Darrell isn't. I owe it to him to keep living for both of us. And if I only have this one life to live—I want to live it to the full, by being madly, passionately, irrevocably in love with you.'

'I can live with that.' A wide smile broke out across Willow's face, so wide it made her cheeks hurt. 'Did I mention I love you too?'

'You didn't,' he said, sounding amused. 'But I was hoping.'

'I do. I love you, and this baby is going to love you, and neither of us are going to have to hide from that, or any of our dreams, ever again.' Not if she had anything to do with it, anyway.

'I'm glad,' Gwyn replied. 'I'm tired of hiding. I'm ready to live again—with you.' And then he kissed her. Something she hoped he'd be doing over and over again for as long as they both drew breath.

EPILOGUE

FOLK NIGHT AT the Star and Dragon was always a big deal, but tonight it was bigger than ever. Local lights, Sean and Kayla, were back from a very successful few months in London, where they were definitely getting noticed—as Gwyn had been proudly telling anyone who'd listen—and were performing on home turf again.

Willow settled back into her seat, her oversized belly filling all the space between her chair and the plate of lasagne in front of her.

'That baby better come soon, Will,' her sister Rowan joked. 'Or you won't be able to reach your lasagne.'

'And that would be a travesty,' Rowan's fiancé Eli said, as he polished off his own plateful. 'This stuff is amazing. How can a tiny Cornish village have better lasagne than New York City?'

'Rumbelow is a pretty special place,' Willow replied. 'Look at what it's done for all of us.'

She'd gone back to New York at first, but it had been lonely without Gwyn, who'd stayed in the UK to help Sean and Kayla get settled in London. More than that, she just didn't feel like the same woman who'd fled the city in a panic, pregnant and alone and scared. She'd changed. Rumbelow—and, more importantly, Gwyn—had changed her.

By the time Ben had decided once and for all that he didn't want to be involved in the baby's life, she'd already come to the conclusion that, for the next little while at least, New York wasn't where she belonged.

She'd travelled back to Rumbelow before her doctors told her not to fly any more. She figured her plane must have passed Rowan's in mid-air, as her sister flew back to be in the city with her fiancé. They visited often though, splitting their time between America and the UK. Eventually, Willow hoped she and Gwyn would be able to do the same.

Up on the stage, Sean and Kayla finished their last song, to rapturous applause. Sean stepped up to the microphone and spoke over the clapping. 'That's it from us for now. But if you ask him nicely, I think Uncle Gwyn has a new song he'd like to play tonight.'

Willow looked at her boyfriend curiously. She'd heard him tinkering around with some new chords and melodies recently, but he hadn't said anything about a new song. But as the crowd called out, he grabbed his guitar and headed for the stage.

'Do you know anything about this?' Willow asked Abigail, sitting beside her.

Gwyn's sister just smiled.

The pub fell silent as Gwyn started to play—a tune beautiful and somehow full of hope. But it was the words that really caught at her heart.

They wouldn't mean anything to anyone else, she was sure. It probably sounded like a generic folk song. But under them, she heard everything that mattered.

He sang about fear. About hiding from love. About opening his arms to let someone in. About how life rarely gave him what he wanted, and how every knock and blow pushed him down, away from what he was meant to have.

But he also sang about how, when the moment was right, the perfect person could pull him back up.

Could help him face the world again.

And he sang about how he'd never let that person go.

Willow bit her lip as the song came to an end, and the audience went wild. But the show wasn't over just yet.

'So, how about it, Willow?' Gwyn asked into the microphone, the words echoing in the suddenly silent pub. Because he was down on one knee, a ring box in his hand. 'Want to spend the rest of our lives together officially? You, me and our baby?'

Willow felt the whole world shift into focus, exactly the way it had always meant to be, and smiled.

'Yes,' she replied. 'Starting right now.'

* * * * *

ACCIDENTALLY ENGAGED TO THE BILLIONAIRE

CARA COLTER

MILLS & BOON

This book is dedicated to all those who
still find enchantment in the written word.

CHAPTER ONE

DISASTER HAD STRUCK.

Jolie Cavaletti had been back in Canada for three whole hours, and her sense of impending doom had proved entirely correct.

She stared down into the white elegant rectangular box. It appeared to be entirely filled with pale peach-colored ruffles.

"Isn't it, literally, so beautiful?" her sister, Sabrina, breathed.

Jolie was fairly certain she heard a stifled laugh from at least two of the other members of the small gathering of the bridal party. She shot a look at Sabrina's old friends from high school, Jacqui and Gillian, or Jack and Jill as Jolie liked to refer to them.

It's only a dress, Jolie told herself. *In the course of human history, a dress can hardly rate as a disaster.*

Holding out faint hope that the bridesmaid dress her sister had chosen for her might look better out of the box, she buried her hands deep into the fluffy fabric and yanked.

The dress unfolded in all its ghastly glory. It was frilly and huge, like a peach-colored tent. The ruffles were attached to a silky under sheath, with a faint pattern on it. Snakes? Who chose a bridesmaid dress with snakes on it?

Oh, wait, on closer inspection, they weren't snakes. Vines. No sense of relief accompanied that discovery.

Jolie did feel relieved, however, when she contemplated

the fact her sister might be playing a joke on her. The feeling was short-lived. When she cast her sister a look, Sabrina was beaming at the dress with all the pride of a mother who had chosen the best outfit ever for her firstborn child entering kindergarten.

Jolie glanced again at Jack and Jill, who were choking back laughter. She shot them a warning glance, and they both straightened and regarded the dress solemnly.

Inwardly, she closed her eyes and sighed at how quickly one could be transported back to a place they thought they had left behind.

Her sister, by design, or by the simple human desire to form a community based on similarities, had always surrounded herself with friends who were astonishingly like her. Sabrina took after their mother, tiny, willowy, blonde, blue-eyed, bubbly.

Beth, Jack and Jill, all of them with their blond locks scraped back into identical ponytails, seemed barely changed in the ten years that had passed since Jolie had last seen them. They were like variations on a theme: Beth shorter, Jill blonder, Jack's eyes a different shade of blue, but any of them could have passed for Sabrina's sister.

The odd man out, the one who could not have passed for Sabrina's sister, was Jolie. She took after her Italian father and was tall and curvy, had dark brown eyes, an olive complexion and masses of unruly, dark curls.

Maybe it explained, at least in part, her and her sister's lifelong prickliness with one another, a sense of being on different teams.

"Do you like it?" Sabrina asked.

"It looks, er, a little too big."

Jolie would, in that dress, walk down the aisle and stand at the altar with the rest of the bridal party, looking like Gulliver in the land of Lilliputians.

"Well," Sabrina said, accusingly, "that's what you get for being in Italy both when I chose the dresses, and when we had the fittings."

This was said as if Jolie had opted for a frivolous vacation at an inconvenient time, when in fact she lived in Italy, going there directly after high school, attending university, earning her doctorate in anthropology and never leaving.

"It will look better on," Beth, Jolie's favorite of all Sabrina's friends, said kindly. "I didn't like mine at first, either."

"You didn't?" Sabrina said, a bit of an edge to her voice. Jolie looked at her sister more closely, and saw that premarital nerves, right below the surface, were raw.

Well, why wouldn't they be? Sabrina and Troy had been married before. A wedding that Jolie had not been invited to, not that she planned to dwell on that.

It had, according to Sabrina in way of excuse for not inviting her own sister to her nuptials, been a spur-of-the-moment thing, basically held on the front steps of city hall.

Jolie, more careful in nature than her sister, did not think a spur-of-the-moment wedding was the best idea.

Though she had not felt the least bit vindicated when things did not go well. Jolie had lived far enough away from the newly married couple that she had been spared most of the details, but her mother had reported on a year of spectacular fights before the divorce. The fights, according to Mom, who spoke of them in hushed tones that did not hide her relish in the drama, had continued, unabated, after the split.

"It reminds me of your father and me," she had confided in Jolie.

A psychiatrist could have a heyday with her sister choosing the same kind of dysfunctional relationship Jolie and Sabrina had endured throughout their childhood. Her father and mother had a volatile and unpredictable relationship, punctuated with her father's finding someone new, and her mother begging him to come back.

All that ongoing angst had made Jolie try to become invisible, hiding in books and her schoolwork, which she'd excelled at. Somehow, she had hoped she could be "good enough" to repair it all, but she never had been.

She shook off these most unwelcome thoughts. She had hoped she'd spent long enough—and been far enough— away not to be dragged back into the kind of turmoil her childhood had been immersed in.

But here Sabrina was, determined to try the marriage thing all over again, convinced that if she did the wedding entirely differently this time, the result would also be different.

A part of Jolie, which she didn't even want to acknowledge existed, might have been ever so slightly put out that her sister was having a second wedding when Jolie had not even had a first.

She had come oh-so close! If things had gone according to plan, she would be married right now. Sabrina would have been *her* bridesmaid. She could have tortured her sister with unsuitable dresses. Not that she would have. She would have picked a beautiful dress for her sister. No, better, she would have let her sister pick her own dress.

Thankfully, they had not gotten as far as the selection of wedding party dresses.

Though no one knew this, not her mother or her sister, Jolie had purchased her own wedding gown, purposely not involving her family.

Because they somehow thought she was *this* horrible peach confection.

Her wedding dress, in fact, had been the opposite of the peach-colored extravaganza she now held. It had been simplicity itself. Beautifully cut floor-length white silk, sleeveless, with a deep V at the neck that had hugged all her curves—celebrated them—before flaring out just below the knee

Even though Jolie was thousands of miles—and a few months—from Anthony's betrayal, the pain suddenly felt like a fresh cut, probably brought on by exhaustive traveling, and now being thrust into bridal activities without being the bride.

How she had loved him! In hindsight she could see that she had been like a homeless puppy, delirious with joy at finally being picked, finally having a place where she would belong. Riding high on the wave of love, she had missed every sign that Anthony might not be quite as enthused, that her outpouring of devotion was not being reciprocated.

Her breakup was three months ago, her wedding would have been in early June, if Anthony—the man she had loved so thoroughly and unconditionally, who she had planned to have children with and build a life with—had not betrayed her.

With another woman.

Something else a psychiatrist would no doubt have a heyday with given the fact she had grown up with her father's indiscretions.

And so Jolie found herself single and determined not to be sad about it. To see it as not a near miss, but an opportunity.

To refocus on her career.

To celebrate independence.

To *never* be one of those women who begged to come first. Jolie's name on her birth certificate was Jolie, not Jolene, but she had not a single doubt her mother had named her after that song.

And also she never wanted to be, again, one of those women who *yearned*, not so much for a fairy-tale ending, as for a companion to deeply share the simple moments in life with.

Coffee in the morning.

A private joke. Maybe even a laugh over a dress like this one.

A look across the table.

Someday, children, running joyous and barefoot through a mountain meadow on holiday in the Italian Alps.

Jolie tried to shake off her sudden sensation of acute distress. She made herself take a deep breath and focus on the here and now at her sister's destination wedding.

The bridal party—Jolie, Sabrina and Sabrina's other three bridesmaids—were currently having a little pre–big day preview of the facilities, which had led to this tête-à-tête in the extremely posh ballroom of a mind-blowingly upscale winery in Naramata, deep in the heart of British Columbia's Okanagan Valley.

Jolie was all too aware she was in possession of the world's ugliest dress, and that it was somehow woven into the fabric of her sister's hopes and dreams.

Unlike Jolie, sworn off love forever, Sabrina was braver. Her sister still had hopes and dreams! She was going to give love another chance.

Which kind of added up for Jolie to *Suck it up, buttercup.*

She calculated in her head. It was Wednesday already in Italy, which made it Tuesday evening here. The wedding was Saturday. She only had to get through a few days.

Anybody could do anything for a couple of days. In the course of human history, it was nothing.

"I think I'll go try it on," Jolie announced.

"Yes, immediately!" Sabrina ordered, flushed with excitement that Jolie could see the unfortunate potential for hysteria in. "You're the only one who hasn't tried on your dress."

Reluctant to actually wear the dress, but eager to get away from her sister and the bridal party, Jolie gathered up the box.

She went into a nearby washroom—as posh as the ballroom—and entered one of the oversize stalls. She stripped down to her underwear, dropped her clothes onto the floor and pulled the dress over her head. It settled around her with a whoosh and a rustle.

She opened the door of the stall and stepped out, resigned to look at it in the full-length mirror that she was quite sorry had been provided.

It was as every bit as horrible as she had thought it would be, a fairy-tale dress gone terribly wrong, with too much volume, too many ruffles and way too many snakes. *Vines.*

A lesson in fairy tales, really.

The bridesmaid dress made Jolie feel like a paper-flower-festooned float in a parade welcoming the *carnevale* season to Italy.

Her sensible bra, chosen for comfort while traveling, did not go with the off-the-shoulder design of the dress, and in one last attempt to save something, she slipped it off and let it fall to the polished marble floor.

No improvement.

She fought the urge to burst into tears. She told herself the sudden desire to cry was not related to her own broken dreams.

It was because she had been home less than a few hours, and already she was *that* person all over again. Too big. Too awkward. Too *everything* to ever fit in here.

The exact kind of person a beloved fiancé—the man she would have trusted with her very life—had stepped out on.

A tear did escape then, and she brushed it away impatiently with her fist. She was just experiencing jet lag and it wasn't exactly home, she told herself firmly. Even though she was back in Canada for the first time since she had graduated from high school, Jolie was about a million miles from the Toronto neighborhood where she had grown up.

Her scholarly side insisted on pointing out it was two thousand eight hundred and seventy-nine miles, not a million.

It was that kind of thinking that had branded her a geek in all those painful growing up years. She had skipped ahead grades, and so she had always been the youngest—and most left out—in her school days. Her senior year—shared with her sister, Sabrina, two years her senior—had been the worst.

In fact, it may have been the most painful year of all.

Not counting this one.

See? Jolie could feel all the old insecurities brewing briskly right below the surface. Who wouldn't have their insecurities bubble to the surface in a dress this unflattering?

Privately, Jolie thought maybe since it was a second marriage—albeit to the same man—Sabrina could have toned it down a bit. But toned down was not Sabrina under any circumstances, which was probably why she was so eager to have a redo of the vows spoken on the city hall steps.

And really, all Jolie wanted was her sister's love of Troy to end in happiness. One of them should have a love like that!

And a more perfect location than this one would be hard to imagine, and that was from someone who had spent plenty of time in the wine country of Tuscany.

Taking a deep breath, reminding herself of her devotion to someone in the family getting their happy ending, Jolie picked as much of the dress as she could off the floor and headed back to the bridal party and braced herself for Jack and Jill's snickers, Beth's kindly pity, and her sister's enthusiasm.

But even her sister was not able to delude herself about the dress.

As she watched Jolie make her way across the ballroom to

the little cluster of the bridal party at one end of it, her mouth opened. And then her forehead crinkled. And then she burst into tears, and wailed. "It looks as if it has snakes on it!"

CHAPTER TWO

JOLIE WAS UNCOMFORTABLY aware of the sudden silence that followed her sister's observation, and of the four sets of blue eyes regarding her critically.

"No, no," Beth finally said soothingly, "they don't look at all like snakes. Definitely vines."

"Even Chantelle can't fix that," Jack decided to weigh in.

"Chantelle?" Jolie asked baffled, noticing how the mention of the name deepened her sister's distress.

Jill rolled her eyes. "Only the most well-known photographer in the fashion world."

Jolie recalled it—vaguely—now. Sabrina had gushed in an email that her soon-to-be husband had some kind of connection to the famous Chantelle—one name was enough, apparently—and that she had agreed to do the wedding photography. When she *never* did weddings.

"You are literally going to ruin everything," Sabrina said to Jolie.

"I didn't pick the dress!"

"You didn't leave me time to fix it, either. Why couldn't you have come a week earlier, like I asked?"

After traveling halfway around the world to be here for her sister, it would be so easy to be offended, but Jolie recognized, again, that hysteria just below the surface.

"Sabrina, I have a job," Jolie said, striving for a reasonable tone. "I can't just put everything on hold because—"

"Oh! The all-important doctor!"

Jolie flinched that her accomplishment—a doctorate in anthropology—was being seen in this light, as if she was a big shot, flaunting her successes.

"And why would you put everything on hold," Sabrina continued, "for your sister who is marrying the same man again? You probably think it's doomed to failure. You're probably still mad that I didn't invite you the first time."

Jolie was aware vehement denials were only going to feed the fire Sabrina was stoking, and that there was a tiny kernel of truth in each of those accusations. They might hardly ever—make that never—see eye to eye, but sisters still knew things about each other.

"I can fix the dress," Beth said gently, as if any of this had anything to do with the dress. "Look!"

She got behind Jolie and pulled in several inches of excess fabric. Jolie felt the dress tightening around her.

Sabrina regarded her hopefully for a moment, then her whole face crumpled, and she wailed and ran from the room.

Jack and Jill scurried after her, sending Jolie accusing looks over their shoulders.

Beth let go of the dress. "She's just tired," she said, trailing out after her friends.

This to the woman who had left Rome over twenty-four hours ago, and been traveling ever since.

A waiter, very formal in a white shirt and black pants, came in with a tray of wineglasses. He looked around at the empty room, but did not allow the smallest flicker of surprise to cross his deliberately bland face.

"Wine?" he asked her smoothly. "I have our award-winning Hidden Valley prosecco or I have one glass of bubbly juice here, if you'd prefer?"

Bubbly juice? Jolie could not imagine any of those women

choosing juice. Was it a dig at her? That drunken prom night?

Of course it wasn't. That was ten years ago. She was being overly sensitive.

"Yes, to the prosecco."

He slid a look at the dress. "Take two," he suggested.

"Thank you. I will."

The waiter glanced around the empty room, "The deck is lovely at this time of the evening."

She took his suggestion, and let the dress trail along the floor since her hands were full. She moved outside. Indeed, the deck was lovely.

Relax, Jolie ordered herself. She had to look at the events that had just unfolded lightly, through the lens of human history, even.

The dress and her sister's snippiness were hardly disasters. Didn't family frictions always surface when a little stress was added to the mix?

She settled in a lounge chair, the dress surging up and around her as though it intended to swallow her. She set down one of the glasses on a table beside the chair, took a deep breath, moved a wayward ruffle away from her face and then enjoyed a long greedy drink of the prosecco.

Ahh.

From her place on the deck, she made herself focus on the good things. Her mother was not here yet to weigh in on the dress, or anything else for that matter.

And her father was not here yet, either, bringing the more inevitable friction.

Weddings, rather than being fairy-tale events, came with plenty of tension. Strain on broken vessels—which her family could certainly be considered—was usually not a good thing.

"Here's to not having a wedding of my own," Jolie said,

raising her wineglass to the glory of the evening light. She lifted her face to the last of the sun. The heat of the scorching July day was waning.

Jolie took another deep breath, and another sip of the prosecco. Well, maybe more like a gulp. She made herself focus on her surroundings rather than the troubling intricacies of her family.

The view was panoramic with lush hills, grape vines, copses of conifers and deciduous trees, a verdant green lawn stretching all the way down to the sparkling waters of a lake. Canoes bobbed gently, tied to the dock. The air had a faintly golden, sparkly quality, and a luscious sun-on-pine scent to it.

The patio was located off the ballroom and just to the side of the main entrance of the lodge. She imagined the beautiful doors thrown open for big events, people flowing seamlessly between the outside and the inside, laughter and music riding on the night air.

The main building of the Hidden Valley Winery was a sweeping, single-story log structure, at least a hundred years old and lovingly preserved. The manicured grounds only hinted at an interior that was posh beyond belief, the Swarovski crystal chandeliers and Turkish rugs inside the lobby in sharp and delightful contrast to the more rustic elements.

Jolie, to her everlasting gratitude, especially now, had found on her arrival that she had been assigned her own cabin.

I hope you don't mind, Sabrina had said. *Most of us are staying in the main lodge, but there aren't enough rooms.*

Even though Jolie was aware of already being cast on the outside of her sister's circle, she found she didn't mind at all. Especially now that she was pretty sure the tone for the wedding had been set.

Seeing her sister, with all that crowd of high school girls in the background, Jolie realized how invested she was in giving a different impression, showing them she was not that same geeky, gauche girl they might remember from their senior year.

If they remembered her at all.

A sound drifted on the summer air. Laughter. It would be unkind to think of it as cackling. Jolie recognized her sister's girlish shriek. So, Sabrina had returned to good spirits after she had dumped Jolie.

It made Jolie even more annoyed that her reintroduction to her sister's clique had gone so off the rails.

She'd barely finished exploring her little cabin when she'd been summoned. The cabin was one of a dozen or so structures scattered through the woods that surrounded the lodge. It was completely self-contained and an absolute delight, the same mix of posh and rustic that made the lodge so charming.

But the dress reveal had been called practically before she set down her bag. Her makeup had long since given out, and her hair had gone wild. Her outfit—that she had spent way too much on in anticipation of that very moment—was travel rumpled and stained from holding her exhausted seat partner's baby for half the journey.

So, even though it meant keeping the others waiting, Jolie showered and clipped her wild abundance of dark curls, holding them back to the nape of her neck. Taming the hair was something she was much better at now than she had been in high school. She had put on a dash of makeup, pleased she didn't need much as her work, which was mostly outdoors, gave her a healthy glow. Then she had carefully chosen a skirt that showed off the length of her sun-browned legs, and a crisp white top that was casual in the way only truly expensive designer clothing could be.

She had been annoyed at herself for being nervous when she stepped out of the cabin toward the people she had not seen for ten years.

Cavaletti, she had told herself sternly, *you are not a gladiator going into the games*.

The thought filled her with longing for the research her team was doing at the Colosseum.

And that helped her with perspective. In the course of human history, the encounter she had just survived was *not* a disaster. Not even close. And four days? Gladiators had lived below the Colosseum for years, trapped by their fates.

So the dress, technically, didn't qualify, either.

There. That was settled. In the course of human history, several days trapped at a family wedding was not even a blip on the radar. She vowed she would focus on all the good things, such as the incredible quality of the glasses of prosecco she had been given.

The first glass had disappeared rather quickly, but she *was* relaxed. Philosophical, even. She took a slower sip of the second one and worked on convincing herself that she no longer cared about being part of the *in* crowd. At twenty-six, she had lived abroad for ten years. She had a doctorate in anthropology. She was working on what she considered to be one of the most exciting projects in all of Italy, a project at the ruins of the Colosseum.

She could handle this reunion with aplomb.

Aplomb!

She wasn't the same girl in the high school annual with a *Most Likely To*...title put under their picture.

Some of them had been ordinary: most likely to marry Mike Mitchell; most likely to run a pet store; most likely to become a doctor.

And some had been surprisingly cute and original: most

likely to run away with gypsies; most likely to win the Iditarod; most likely to be a lifeguard on Bondi Beach.

And then there had been hers.

Most likely to enter religious life.

Her family had been Catholic, but not exactly what anyone would call practicing, with her parents divorced. She and Sabrina had not been inside a church since their first communion.

What had earned her that awful descriptor was that fact that Jolie had been a full two years younger than the rest of the grads. The suggestion she would join a convent and become a nun was a dig at her relative innocence. She was fairly certain it was meant without malice—someone's idea of being funny and original—and yet she could still feel the sting of it, even now, ten years later.

Which explained why she had splurged on a wardrobe that did not have one single item in it that would have been chosen by someone likely to enter religious life.

As she soaked up the serenity of the evening, she watched as a convertible sports car, top up, a deep and sleek gray, slid into the driveway and nosed expertly into a tight parking stall.

So there it was, just a little bit behind schedule.

Jolie was pretty sure this would qualify as a one hundred percent bona fide disaster.

Because look who was getting out of that car.

As soon as she saw him, Jolie knew she should have known better than to let her guard down, to think she could outrun the embarrassing decisions that high school annual judgment on her had caused her to make.

She should have known better than to think her maturity and successes were going to make this wedding/high school reunion a breeze.

Because that man who had just gotten out of the car was the man she least wanted to see in the entire world.

Jay Fletcher.

And that was before she factored what she was wearing into the equation!

Despite the fact she had been bracing herself to spend a week with the high school crowd she had only been reluctantly accepted into because of her popular sister, at no point had Jolie prepared herself for Jay. You would think Sabrina could have mentioned he would be here.

But no, there had not been a single mention of his name.

In high school, Jay Fletcher had been the antithesis of everything Jolie Cavaletti had been.

Popular. Athletic. Sophisticated. The high school hero.

Under his picture in the high school annual? *Most likely to succeed.* And while everyone else in the grad class had only had one *most likely* under their yearbook picture, an extra accolade had been heaped on Jay. *Most likely to take the world by storm.*

If the car—sleek, rare, expensive—was any indication, he had done just that.

And Jay looked every ounce the successful man as he paused and took in his surroundings. He stretched, hands locked briefly behind his neck, and Jolie noted he still appeared to be the athlete he had once been, long-legged, broad across the shoulders, narrow at the waist and hip, some extraordinarily appealing masculine hardness in the lines of his body.

He radiated confidence, which he had never had any shortage of. But now there was a subtle masculine power about him as well. A man who had come fully into himself.

Was he beautifully dressed, or could he have made sackcloth look worthy of a *GQ* cover shoot? Really, his clothing was ordinary, just pressed khaki shorts ending in the middle of a tanned and muscled thigh, a solid-colored navy blue golf-style shirt that didn't mold his perfect build but hinted at it, which was, oddly, even more enticing. When he stretched like that, the muscles in his arms leaped appealingly.

The evening light danced in his short neatly trimmed hair, threading the light brown through with gold. It also flattered features that needed no flattery. If anything ten years had made him even more perfect.

Jay Fletcher was simply and stunningly handsome: wide brow, high cheekbones, straight, strong nose, firm, full lips, a faint cleft in a square chin.

As Jolie watched, he lifted his sunglasses. Even though she could not see the color of his eyes from here—of course she couldn't—memory conjured up the deep, cool green of them that had always made her young heart flutter.

The gaze, she reminded herself, a little desperately, that had cut her to ribbons the last time she had seen him.

Besides, she was not the young girl she had been. Not even close. In fact, she was bitter and heartbroken enough to be immune to any man.

Up to and including Jay Fletcher.

CHAPTER THREE

AS JOLIE WATCHED, Jay lowered the sunglasses back over his eyes, moved to the back of his sleek, expensive vehicle, popped the trunk and threw a bag over his shoulder.

Jolie would like to claim she had barely spared him a thought over the past ten years, but that was not true. She *had* wondered if he had aged well. She *had* wondered if he was happy. She *had* wondered if he had ever spared her a thought after that last embarrassing moment together.

And yet, even as she had wondered, she had avoided asking her sister, knowing Sabrina might have guessed her pathetic interest and been cruelly amused by it.

And Jolie had certainly avoided looking Jay up online, because that would have felt as if she was indulging a secret longing for the impossible.

When she had heard his father died, her second year at university in Italy, she sent a card, but she had *wanted* so much more. To call him. To hear his voice. To be the one who soothed his pain, as if she knew things about him that others did not.

Which was silly! They had worked on a science project together and, having come to know him a little, she had deeply embarrassed herself at senior prom.

When she'd become engaged, all *that*—secret crushes and childish illusions—was left, finally, behind her. Her old life was in the rearview mirror.

But watching Jay Fletcher move toward her, his stride long and easy, Jolie knew she had been lying to herself. You didn't leave some things behind you.

And maybe it was because she was not engaged anymore that seeing Jay made her feel as if she was sixteen all over again.

Awkward.

Hopelessly out of her depth.

Like she wanted things she could not have.

She realized she had to get out of here. The jet lag. The sparkling wine. The dress. The old gang. Now Jay. It was all too much.

But then she realized, with a hint of panic, there would be no slipping away, not in this dress! She'd look like a barge heading off into the setting sun. It was too late to compose herself for the reunion she had not expected. At all.

The man Jolie Cavaletti least wanted to see in the entire world was already halfway up the walkway. Jay came up the wide stairs that led to the entrance of the Hidden Valley Lodge.

She held her breath.

Maybe she'd be lucky and he'd just go in those wide front doors, with barely a glance toward that side deck, dismissing the woman sipping wine alone as some kind of crazy eccentric in her peach explosion.

For a moment, as impossible as it seemed with the dress screaming, *Look at me*, it actually seemed that might be how it would play out.

He glanced her way, but didn't even change his stride. Just when she thought she could breathe again, he stopped abruptly, took a half step back and stared at her. And then he lifted his sunglasses.

She'd remembered his eyes with one hundred percent ac-

curacy, unfortunately. They were absolutely, gorgeously mes-
merizing, as luminescent and as multilayered as green jade.

A smile tickled across the unfairly sensuous wideness
of his lips.

It was a good thing she was well armed with cynicism,
otherwise she might find his attractiveness tempting.

She'd allowed herself to give in to that particular temptation once before, she reminded herself tartly. The memory
of how well that had gone should have kept her in check.

"Jolie?" he asked. "Jolie Cavaletti?"

That voice, damn him! Who had a voice like that? A
movie star voice, a bit raspy, a bit tinged with laughter, a bit
like fingertips touching the back of her neck.

Now what? Did she get up from her lounge chair and go
over to him. Offer her hand? Say in dulcet, husky tones, *Nice
to see you again, Jay. It's been a long time.*

Pretend she wasn't wearing the dress?

Instead of getting up, Jolie hunkered down deeper into
the folds of her fashion catastrophe, took a fortifying gulp of
prosecco—good grief, where had that second glass gone—
and lifted a hand. She hoped the gesture was casual—maybe
even faintly dismissive—but she feared she had only managed to look like a fainting Southern belle.

"Jay," she said.

He didn't appear to notice lack of invitation in either her
tone or her feeble hand gesture. He strode right over, and
looked down at her.

His scent—soap and, more subtly, mountain-air-scented
aftershave—whispered across the space between them.

Don't look at his eyes, she ordered herself. *You'll turn
into stone.*

But, of course, that wasn't really her worry at all. The opposite. That the light in those eyes could melt the stone she
had placed around her bruised heart.

She looked at his eyes.

They were the color of a cool pond on a hot day, sparking with light like sun dancing across a calm surface.

"How are you?" he asked.

I've had better moments.

"Peachy," she said.

It was unfair how the amused upward quirk of that sexy mouth created a dimple in his cheek and made him even more breathtaking. It was unfair to notice that his hair was the exact color of a pot of melted chocolate, and that the faintest shadow darkened his cheeks and chin.

She had a completely renegade thought: she wondered what those whiskers might feel like scraping against tender skin.

Those kinds of thoughts were not permitted in a woman newly dedicated to being independent, to creating her own happiness.

She gave the prosecco an accusing look, then couldn't decide whether to take another fortifying sip or set it down. So, she did the logical thing. She did both.

Apparently oblivious to his effect on the jet-lagged, deeply embarrassed woman in front of him, he tilted his head and looked at her more deeply.

"A peach. Picked fresh off the tree."

"Well, not picked by me," she said. She hoped for an airy tone. She sounded defensive.

The upward quirk at the corner of his lip deepened, and so did the dimple. "Of course you didn't choose that dress. So not you."

Did she have to be reminded, right out of the gate, why she had had such a crush on him? He had always seemed to see in her something that everyone else missed. Jolie was engulfed with a sense of being starstruck and tongue-tied and sixteen all over again.

Cavaletti, she told herself firmly, *stop it.*

"I've seen a lot of ugly bridesmaid dresses over the years," he decided, leaning toward her and regarding her intently, "but that one might win. Are those, er, worms?"

"I thought snakes."

"Hmm. I'm pretty sure that involved an apple, not a peach."

Really? Being with a man like this made the temptations of the garden seem all the more understandable.

"And maybe a fig leaf," she replied, "which would be a considerable improvement over this dress."

She intended the remark lightly, but for a moment something scorching hot flashed in his eyes, as if he imagined her unclothed in the garden.

Jolie could feel a blush heating her cheeks. She had intended the comment to be funny and sophisticated, to wipe memories of her sixteen-year-old self from his memory.

However, it had come across as risqué. She hoped the gathering darkness hid the blush from Jay. He would think she was still the innocent woman-child who once had a crush on him.

Less than two minutes with him, and she could feel an old flame leaping back to life. This was what he had always done. Made her aware of some age-old and primal longing inside of herself to explore every single thing it meant to be a woman.

Still, she admitted to herself that she enjoyed the heat in his eyes and the fact that, finally, she had managed to tempt him.

The last time they'd been together, he'd been convinced she needed his protection.

Protection from herself, her crush on him and the embarrassing proposition he had rejected that night.

Her worst memory of all time.

* * *

Jay was tired. It had been a long drive. He'd had a sense, though, of it being worth it as he had finally arrived at Hidden Valley Winery. The sun was setting and it drenched the land in light, almost mystical in its beauty.

His sense of being caught in something otherworldly had only deepened as he had gone toward the entrance of the winery.

At first, in the fading light, he hadn't seen the woman there.

But then he had caught a glimpse of her, peripherally, and though he was not a man given to enchantments, that had been his thought. Enchantment.

He'd been shocked that it was Jolie Cavaletti. Of course, he'd known she would be here. She was the bride's sister.

But somehow he'd been unprepared for her, and especially unprepared for her turning that hideous dress into something else altogether. A fairy, sitting in gossamer folds, bathed in the golden hues of a sun already gone down.

A fairy, but as always with Jolie, there was the tantalizing contradiction, because as he'd gotten closer he'd been aware of seeing, not fairylike innocence, but a certain understated sensuality that made him aware of her as one hundred percent fully adult woman.

This had always been her contradiction. In high school, she'd been so much younger than everyone else, and trying so hard to overcome that, to be accepted. And yet, at the same time, she had remained the earnest little scientist, with big round glasses and owl eyes. He remembered her in white lab jackets, usually with some kind of stain or burn on them. The absent-minded scholar.

But then there was the contradiction: the woman's full curves, the corkscrews of curls she was never able to tame, the delicious plumpness of her bottom lip, the cinnamon scent of her.

He found himself leaning in.

Yes, it was still there, exotic and spicy, a hint of something Mediterranean.

Her remark about the fig leaf had intensified his awareness. She wasn't an off-limits kid anymore, and that felt wildly dangerous. Maybe because the drive had left him tired, he gave in to the desire to play with the danger a tiny bit.

"Why don't you surprise Sabrina?" he suggested, deadpan. "Can you imagine her face if you came down the aisle in a fig leaf?"

He saw that look in her eyes that he'd had to fight until the very last moment he had seen her, Jolie going in the door to her house, shoulders slumped, after the senior prom.

She'd turned around that night, and touched her lips with her tongue. If it had been sensual as she intended, instead of uncertain as it had presented, they might have ended up in a different place that night.

Instead, he'd had to be haunted for years, by her despondent, small voice.

Is that your final answer?

Of course, she'd been trying to be funny. It had been a question posed by a game show that had been popular at the time. Only smart people need apply. If Jolie Cavaletti had gone on it, she would have been a billionaire long before he was. But somehow, it had not come across as funny.

If she licked her lips right now, he'd be helpless.

But she didn't.

She snickered.

In some ways it was worse than the lip-lick because it reminded him of how she had been. Shy and earnest, but with something wilder and bolder brewing right beneath the surface, that dry sense of humor that he, as an adult, now associated with keen intelligence.

Which, even then, she'd had in spades, an intellectual giant who towered over kids much older than her.

"Fig leaf down the aisle," she mused, considering. And then she said, "I will, if you will."

Just like that they were laughing together. The shared laughter did the very same thing to him that it had done ten years ago.

Made every other care in the world become nothing more than motes of dust, dissolved by the light that sparked in Jolie Cavaletti's doe dark eyes.

A waiter appeared, with two flutes of what appeared to be a sparkling wine, which would never be his first choice.

"I can't have one more drop," Jolie said. "I've got jet lag so bad it's wiping me out. I mean fig leaves really aren't something I would normally bring up."

"You don't say," he teased her.

And then she was blushing.

Blushing.

And it was as if not one day had passed since prom night and a slightly drunk sixteen-year-old Jolie Cavaletti—who had not looked sixteen in a gorgeous gown, with makeup on, and her hair, for once tamed, piled on top of her head—had leaned into him and whispered a dangerously tempting proposition in his eighteen-year-old ear.

To this day he was not sure how he had managed to put her needs ahead of his own, resist her invitation and hustle her back to her house before she found somebody who would not be able to resist her considerable temptation, who would not have given her the correct final answer.

Which was no.

The waiter had two flutes and he offered one to Jay. "Sir?"

"Oh, why not?" Jay took the proffered glass, let his bag

slide off his shoulder and settled easily into the lounge chair beside her.

In the last of the day's light, with a chilled glass in his hand and night closing in around him, with Jolie's cinnamon scent tickling her nose, and the dress making her look like a fairy in a flower, he felt…not just enchantment.

Something far, far more dangerous.

A sensation of coming home.

CHAPTER FOUR

OUT OF THE corner of his eye, Jay watched Jolie fight with the temptation of the wine for a second or two.

And then with a resigned sigh, she picked it up, twirled the stem between her fingers and took a sip.

"Don't even think about the last time I was drunk with you," she warned him.

"I wouldn't," he promised, ridiculously, since he already had. "Not that you were exactly drunk. Tipsy."

Uninhibited.

"I probably should have thanked you for that night. For you know…"

She was blushing again.

He did know. Saying no. Not taking advantage of her. He was sorry she was still embarrassed about it.

"I don't know what got into me."

"I do."

"Pardon me?"

"Some of us spiked the punch."

She glared at him as if suddenly it had happened yesterday and not ten years ago. Was she going to slap him?

"And I thought it was just your good looks and charisma that were intoxicating me!"

"I thought we weren't going to think about it," he reminded her hastily.

"If it was never mentioned again, I'd be okay with that," she said.

"Deal." He paused. "Even if you are in a dress that makes one think of a peach, ripe for the picking."

She did hit him, then. A light slug on his shoulder. He liked it. He laughed. So did she, and that awkward moment—this one, and the one that had happened ten years ago—were both gone.

For now.

With a woman like her—innately sensual, both then and now, without an awareness of that—those moments would never really be gone.

And she was no longer a child. He felt the danger of her again.

"How's your family, Jay? I'm sorry about your dad."

She had sent a card. Strange that he would remember that at all through the haze of pain. There had been a hundred cards. More, maybe. It must have been the Italian postmark, or maybe it had been her words. She had shared a memory of seeing his mom and dad walking hand in hand in their Toronto neighborhood, and said she had felt the love they had.

That she had felt it and that everyone who had ever been around them had felt it.

There was no better question than *how is your family?* to diffuse his dangerous awareness of her.

Because his perfect family had become a mess that day, and they still hadn't recovered. His mother and father had had one of the greatest loves he'd ever seen.

He'd been in university when his father had been diagnosed with cancer.

He had died with stunning swiftness. Jay's mother had never recovered. Her hero was gone. It was as if his illness had betrayed her in a way she could never get over. She was simply unprepared to deal with life alone, without her soulmate.

And so Jay had been left with the terrible lesson, that love, the thing he'd grown up believing was the strongest and greatest of all forces, was also a destroyer.

His mom, to this day, lived in the family home, but she had let the flower beds go, and watched too much television, and couldn't seem to muster any interest in life.

After the death of his father, there had been no choice. He had left college and gone home to look after the family his mother, swamped by grief for his father, abandoned. One minute, he'd been involved in football and frat parties, the next he'd been trying to cook dinners and check homework, and tell his sister, Kelly, that no, she could not wear that to school.

Out of all the people who had surrounded him during those sparkling days of high school and college, only Troy, his neighbor and best friend since he was four, had remained when Jay's world had been shattered.

Always there. Showing up with pizza for the whole Fletcher crowd. Dropping by with movies and popcorn, taking the kids to the amusement park so Jay could have a break from the sudden dump of responsibility.

Of course, Jay would accept the invitation to be best man—for the second time—for the man who had been there for him, always, even as his own mother had not.

She had been like a ghost during that time, which caused a confusion of feelings: sympathy, worry, anger, resentment, powerlessness.

Mom, snap out of it. The kids need you. I need you.

But nothing he had said could snap her out of it. Love had destroyed her, and she would not allow love—not even the love of her children—to repair her.

His two brothers, Jim and Mike, thankfully, were on their

career paths, and Kelly, the youngest—the one who accused
him of being commitment phobic—was just out of university. She had a newly minted degree in clinical psychology
and a certain frightening enthusiasm for saving the world's
damaged people.

Of which she considered Jay to be one.

Was it so hard to see all that responsibility had exhausted
him?

He returned to Jolie's question. How was his family? It
was a complicated question. He answered it as he always did.

"Fine. Everybody's doing fine." He turned the question
away from himself before she probed any further, because
she was gazing at him with eyes that threatened to see things
others did not. "I heard you're a doctor. Should I call you
that? Dr. Cavaletti?"

"Good grief, no. As soon as people hear that, they feel
compelled to unburden not so interesting medical stories
and conditions on me."

"Actually, I have this lump—"

He was rewarded with another thump on his shoulder.
For someone who had become so wary of all the things associated with home, he wondered why it felt kind of good
to feel at home with Jolie.

Jolie was way too aware of the nearness of Jay, of the wideness of his shoulders, the hard muscle of his thigh beneath
the fabric of his shorts, the long length of his legs as he
stretched out comfortably on the lounge chair. His scent,
mountain fresh and masculine, as intoxicating as the wine,
danced on the air in the space between them.

Jolie knew she absolutely did not need another glass of
prosecco, but the waiter had set it down on the table beside
her and whisked away the empty glasses.

Not even one more sip, she had told herself.

But, somehow, she picked up that glass, twirled it between her fingers and lifted it to her lips almost as if she had no control over herself.

And that was the only thing she needed to remember about Jay Fletcher.

That when a woman most needed control, around a man like him, it might be as impossible to achieve as resisting one more sip of wine.

"You haven't changed a bit," Jay decided.

"Well, except, hopefully, for the dress."

"We've already established you would never pick a dress like that."

She wondered if feeling like kissing a man could simply be interpreted as gratitude for being *seen*?

"Thank you," she said simply.

"Not then, not now. The absent-minded genius. Inside-out shirts. Chemical stains on your lab jacket."

If she'd been absent-minded around him, it hadn't been because she was a scholar. She was not at all surprised by his memory of the inside-out shirt. That reflected, exactly, how he had made her feel. Inside-out. She hadn't been able to think straight around him, her normally logical brain completely scattered.

"You would have set a dress like that on fire on the Bunsen burner."

"On purpose."

They were laughing again.

"Do you love Italy?" he asked her, after a moment.

"Love. I finally found a place where I fit."

She hadn't meant to blurt *that* out. Of course, how much of fitting in had to do with being welcomed into the folds of Anthony's large and boisterous family, the kind of family she had always dreamed of?

She thought of his *nonna* always cooking, always laughing, always bouncing babies and shooing children, and giving her the one thing she'd never had, a sense of belonging.

Like this, Nonna had said, then watched Jolie approvingly as she stretched the pizza dough. That pinch on the cheek.

If she was honest, she missed all that much more than she missed Anthony.

He regarded her thoughtfully. "You didn't really fit."

"And still don't," she said with a sigh.

"It's what I liked best about you."

That took her by surprise. Until that embarrassing night of the grad prom, she was pretty sure, that she had barely been a blip on Jay's radar.

He'd liked something about her?

His lips quirked upward. "Remember that science project?"

She pretended to be thinking about it, scanning the banks of her memory for something elusive.

"We extracted DNA from a strawberry?"

He remembered that stupid experiment. What she remembered was her stomach jumping at his closeness, the scent of him filling her nose, liking his laughter, the excuses to brush against him, touch his hand with hers...

"Did we?" she asked.

"When the teacher first assigned you as my partner, I was so disappointed."

"Don't hold back," she said.

"Not because of *you*. I wanted Mitch Ryerson. I thought he was the smartest person in the class and that he could drag my sorry ass through it. And then I found out you were the smartest person in the class. Possibly in the whole world."

"That's an exaggeration," she said.

He cocked his head at her. "How many grades had you skipped by then?"

"Two," she said, "And I don't remember you having a sorry ass."

Though she remembered his ass—and coveting it—with embarrassing clarity.

Do not blush, she ordered herself. "So, what's your connection to the wedding party?" she asked, which was so much more cosmopolitan than *what are you doing here?*

"I'm the best man."

Of course he was. Most likely to be the best man.

"I was the best man at their first wedding, too," he said, and something flitted through his eyes. "Troy and I were next-door neighbors since we were four."

"Oh, really? I don't even remember Troy in high school. I thought Sabrina said she met him at one of the neighborhood pubs."

If she had known they were such good friends she might have been better prepared for this meeting.

"He never went to our school. He went to private school. We're kind of like family, always there for each other."

Family. Always there for each other. Maybe he could send a memo to Sabrina.

"I wasn't able to get back in time," she said, which allowed her a little more dignity than *I wasn't invited. To my own sister's wedding.*

"Yeah, it seemed very, er, spontaneous. Just four of us, at city hall at high noon."

"I think Sabrina always regretted that. That she didn't have the traditional wedding. I think she wants everything to be different this time."

Everything. Especially the result.

He didn't say anything, and she felt compelled to rush into the conversational lull.

"So, what have you been doing with yourself?" she asked. And then wished she hadn't. The whole wedding party was going to be here until next Sunday morning. There would be lots of time to find out what he was doing with himself.

Or maybe not.

Maybe this would be her only opportunity to be alone with him.

Please, God.

But she was aware of the ambiguity of the prayer. *Please, God, no more opportunities to be alone with Jay Fletcher,* or *please, God, lots more opportunities to be alone with Jay Fletcher?*

"I started a little sporting goods company. It's done okay."

She couldn't resist glancing over at the car. That was a pretty expensive bag draped over his shoulder, too. She suspected he had done quite a bit better than okay.

She frowned. Another sports car was pulling in, way too fast. The sudden screeching of tires was incongruous to the deep evening quiet settling over wine country. They both focused toward the parking lot.

This car was also a convertible, candy apple red, with the top down, spraying gravel in a show of the vehicle's great power. It flew into a parking spot, nearly careening into the car beside it. The driver did not correct the awkward angle, but shut off the car.

Jolie actually felt terror as she glimpsed, over the back headrest, the bright blond hair shining like an orb against the pitch black of the completely fallen night.

Please don't be him, she thought.

Jay Fletcher moved down one notch in the list of people she least wanted to see in the entire world as she watched the vehicle, her heart thudding in her throat.

She stared, with disbelief, as disaster struck, this time for real. Not the least debatable on the disaster scale.

She wasn't aware she had made a sound, until Jay touched her arm. "Are you okay?"

"Only if you have an invisibility cloak," she managed to say, and then wished she hadn't, because despite her distress over Anthony's appearance, that was a particularly nerdy thing to say.

What could her ex-fiancé possibly be doing here, in a popular tourist region in Canada that was nonetheless hard to reach. It was *not* a coincidence.

She got up out of the chair, looking for an escape route. There was none. Still, she felt everything in her try to shrink, to disappear—as if that would ever be possible in this dress—as her former fiancé, Anthony Carmichael, got out of the vehicle. He didn't open the car door. He leaped over it.

In the range of chance, what were the possibilities that she would have to face the two men she wanted to see the least in the entire world in the very same instant?

And here came Anthony, charging up the steps, all that energy snapping in the very air around him.

He was stunningly handsome, but in a totally different way than Jay Fletcher was handsome. He looked like a man in those old paintings, posing, one hand tucked inside a brocade waistcoat, a certain arrogance stamped across perfect, fine features.

Stunned, Jolie realized Anthony did not look anything like his boisterous Italian relatives. He looked something like her mother. And her sister. And every other member of the wedding party.

Considering how Italy had made her feel like she fit in for practically the first time in her life, how was it she had gravitated toward him?

Another heyday for a psychiatrist!

CHAPTER FIVE

FOR A HOPEFUL moment Jolie thought that, just like the other man she had least wanted to see, Anthony's endless energy would propel him right on by her.

Of course, she was not that lucky. He stopped in his tracks when he saw her. He took her in, changed course, bearing down on her with frightening singleness of focus. Finally, he stopped. Too close. In her space.

Good grief. It looked as if he intended to take her hand, kiss it and bow. She tucked her hands behind her.

"Jo," he said. "You are like something out of my dreams. That dress!"

Having been deprived of her hand, he kissed his own fingers then flicked the kiss to the wind.

Had he always been so affected?

Of course he had. She had been so in the throes of love she had been blind to every flaw. Except the last one.

She was suddenly aware of Jay getting up from his lounge chair and coming to stand beside her. She glanced at him, and he slid her a questioning look out of the corner of his eye. Something changed in his stance. He inserted himself, ever so subtly, between her and Anthony.

"Anthony, what are you doing here?" she stammered to her former fiancé.

Anthony, ever jealous, shot Jay an appraising look. She could sense Jay grow in stature, a quiet intake of breath, a subtle broadening of already broad shoulders. When she glanced at him again, he was returning Anthony's look with a flinty steadiness. Anthony looked away first, focusing on her with that familiar intensity.

"Your sister invited me," he said. "She knows the truth!"

Jolie registered Sabrina's betrayal like a blow. "The truth?"

"We belong together," Anthony exclaimed, switching to Italian. Anthony was an expat, like her. He'd grown up in Detroit, Michigan. He'd gone to Italy in search of roots almost forgotten by his family. He had found them, on his mother's side, and been instantly welcomed into the fold. As had she, when she started dating him.

Still, Anthony's Italian wasn't perfect, but it served him to switch languages in order to lock Jay out of the conversation.

Jay shot her a look. She felt as if her pathetic love for this man who had betrayed her was an open book. Jay inserted himself more firmly between her and her ex-fiancé.

Jolie could probably count the impulsive things she had done in her life on one hand. The most regrettable involved the man, not in front of her, but beside her.

Maybe what happened next could have been Jay's fault, just like him spiking the punch on that long-ago night. Maybe he coaxed out her impulsiveness. Or maybe her need for self-protection trumped common sense at the moment.

More likely, it was way too much prosecco, an empty stomach and jet lag. And maybe the dress could even be thrown in for good measure.

But, whatever the reason, she stepped more closely into him, and then firmly took Jay's hand in her own.

She wasn't expecting the fit to be quite so comfortable. She wasn't expecting to feel his strength surging into her.

She wasn't expecting—given the awkward discomfort of the circumstances—to be so *aware*.

"You and I don't belong together, Anthony," she said. Her voice reflected the strength she was gaining, through osmosis, from Jay.

"We do!" Anthony insisted, still in Italian.

"We don't." She spoke English, her voice clear and certain. "This is my fiancé, Jay Fletcher."

Jolie felt Jay's shock ripple through him. She braced herself in case he dropped her hand. But instead, his grip tightened on hers. She glanced, once again, quickly, at his face. He did not look stunned at all. In fact, he smiled at her with just the right touch of possessiveness.

On the other hand, Anthony looked, unsurprisingly, completely stunned. For a blissful moment, she almost believed he would accept defeat.

But then Anthony's brow furrowed. He looked between the two of them suspiciously.

"This isn't even possible," he declared, as if he was in charge of all the possibilities in the world. "You are just trying to discourage me. It happened too fast."

He spoke English this time, to make sure they both understood him.

It had been three months since her breakup with Anthony.

"It's not fast," Jay said firmly. "Jolie and I have known each other forever. Haven't we, honey?"

Honey. Under other circumstances she would have certainly savored that sweetly old-fashioned endearment coming off his lips.

"Forever," she agreed.

For a moment, Anthony looked uncharacteristically flummoxed. But that look lasted only a moment before his customary confidence returned.

Only with Jay standing beside her, she felt as if she was redefining confidence. Anthony's posture had something faintly off-putting about it, the posture of a man who swaggered.

Why hadn't she seen it before?

Blinded by love, that's why! A good reminder of what love did to people, especially with her hand nestled so comfortably in Jay's, as if it belonged there, as if it had always belonged there.

"You don't have a ring!" Anthony pointed out, triumphant.

"We decided we didn't want to take away from Sabrina and Troy's big event," Jolie said smoothly, shocked at how easily the lie slid off her lips. "We're going to announce our engagement after the wedding."

Anthony glared at her. He gave Jay a distinctly pugnacious look, as if he might be planning on inviting him to a duel.

In Italian, she said to him, "Please, just go. You are going to make things awkward. You'll ruin the wedding."

If the dress doesn't do it first.

"Your sister invited me," he reminded her.

She would be having a talk with Sabrina about *that*.

"She doesn't know about Jay and me As I said before, we didn't want to take away from her big day."

"I'm not leaving," he answered in Italian. "I'm winning you back."

"You can't win me back. As you can see, I've moved on. You cheated on me." She was glad that humiliating detail was revealed in Italian.

He lifted a shoulder. "I've apologized. I have promised to change. For you."

As if he was willing to put himself out, *for her.*

"It's too late," she said firmly. How could she have ever fallen for him? The thing was, despite what Jay had said about her being the smartest person in the world, she was not.

In some areas, she was downright dumb.

Needy.

Naive, even.

Look at the way she felt about the hand in hers, despite her near-miss with Anthony!

Her former fiancé looked narrowly at her, and then at Jay.

"He's not for you," he proclaimed, still in Italian. "What's he got that I haven't?"

Since they were speaking in Italian, and since Anthony was determined not to get the message, she felt as if she had no choice but to be a tiny little bit cruel.

"He's got quite a bit that you don't have," she said with a coy smile.

Anthony's mouth fell open. His whole face reddened. And then he said huffily, "It doesn't matter what you have. It matters how you use it."

Jolie felt increasingly desperate to get her message across. That she had moved on. That it was well and truly over and that Anthony had absolutely no chance of winning her back. Ever.

Words, obviously, were not enough.

She turned into Jay.

He'd been a good sport so far.

Please don't step back, she pleaded silently as she stepped right into him.

Full contact. She could feel his heat radiating out from under his shirt. She could feel the strength of him. She could feel the hard, steady beat of his heart.

She looked up at him, looked deeply into the amazing green of his eyes, touched her lips, tentatively, with her tongue.

Then, she committed. Jolie wrapped her hands around his neck, and she drew his lips down to her own.

She kissed him.

And she kissed him hard.

As soon as her lips met his it felt as if she had been waiting for this very moment since she was sixteen.

And that it was worth a ten-year wait.

Everything else, including Anthony, faded away.

If Jay Fletcher was going to pick his top ten most unexpected moments, Jolie Cavaletti claiming his mouth with her own would certainly be up there.

Her lips were soft, and he found the invitation of them irresistible. She tasted of wine and night and the stars.

The kiss quickly moved into the number one position of his life's unexpected moments, just nudging out his other surprising encounter with Jolie, which had held the number one position for ten years.

He remembered this study in contrasts. How could someone be sweet and on fire at the very same time?

How could a kiss that was staged—a pretense—feel like the most real thing that had ever happened to him?

"He's gone," he said against her mouth, looking over her shoulder.

She broke away from him abruptly. Her lips looked puffy, and her cheeks had spots of color in them. Her eyes sparked with the fire he had tasted.

"Wow," he said softly, "you look like a princess in a fairy tale."

"It's the dress," she said, sharply. "Don't let it fool you. I don't believe in fairy tales, and I certainly don't need a prince to wake me up."

It was a rather shocking lack of gratitude given how gamely he had played along with her ruse when her spurned lover had showed up.

Maybe she was just covering her embarrassment, or maybe she didn't want him to know that she had found that as delightfully unexpected as he had.

But she was definitely trying to cover something, looking avidly and hopefully toward the parking lot, as if she was totally focused on the *goal* of that kiss and not the un-expected treasure discovered.

"He went the other way. To check in, I assume."

She swore in Italian.

They both came from the same heavily Italian neighbor-hood in Toronto, but Jay was Italian on his mother's side, and she had been blue-eyed and fair, as were many of the people from Cremona where his maternal grandparents hailed from.

It seemed duplicitous not to tell Jolie, right now, that he spoke Italian. In fact he spoke it far better than her ex-friend. On the other hand, he was feeling a bit annoyed with her.

"That was kind of a déjà vu moment," he said, unkindly.

"I thought we agreed not to talk about that."

"Not talking about it doesn't make it go away. There are some things a man doesn't forget. Strawberry DNA, a pretty girl offering her lips."

She'd actually offered quite a bit more than her lips, but her blush was already deepening, so he was pretty sure she did not have to be reminded of the details.

"I was young and stupid."

Ouch. Why did that sting?

"That's the difference, all right," he said softly. "You're all grown-up."

In fact, her lips on his had let him know just how grown-up.

That night, years ago, it had been so evident that she was the farthest thing from all grown-up.

She cast a glance at the doors of the lodge. "He went in there? Really? Like he's staying?"

"I think you've got yourself a determined fan there," he said.

"More like a stalker. How could my sister do this to me? Her and my mother met him in Italy. They couldn't stop gushing about how he was the perfect man. He's here because they don't feel I can do any better. And that's even knowing—"

She bit her lip.

He didn't say anything because he wasn't supposed to speak Italian and therefore know that pompous creep had fooled around on her.

But it said so much about how her family saw her.

Maybe how everybody had always seen her. He, himself, had seen her that way once.

Awkward. Geeky.

But then he'd worked on that science project with her.

And found out she was formidably intelligent, but also surprisingly funny, charming and original.

He'd liked her, in the hands-off sort of way that an older guy liked a too young girl. But that moment at prom she had tried to change all the rules.

Jolie had offered herself to him.

That same way, leading with those luscious lips.

And when he hadn't even fully recovered from the shock that the awkward, geeky girl was shockingly sexy, Jolie had announced, a little drunk—from punch he was suddenly ashamed that he had helped spike—that she had decided to lose her virginity that night. And she had chosen him.

He'd hustled her out of there, into his car and home—her home—as fast as he could. He'd dumped her on the door-step with a stern lecture and watched from the car to make sure she went in the house.

Chivalrous.

He'd done the right thing, even though he knew he'd hurt her by doing it.

And now, here they were. Did you ever really outrun anything in life, or did it always catch up to you?

CHAPTER SIX

"Do you think you could do me the most enormous favor?" Jolie asked him.

"I thought I just did," Jay returned dryly. And his kindness had been repaid with a reminder he was no prince.

"Could you pretend? That you are? My fiancé? Just until I figure out how to get rid of him?"

He considered that. It seemed a path rife with danger. And excitement. In other words, irresistible.

"Just until he gets it," she said hastily. "And gives up. What do you think?"

He thought it was insane was what he thought. So no one was more shocked than him to hear him answering her, his tone casual.

"Oh, sure. Why not? Nothing like adding an accidental engagement to your résumé."

"It'll help me with the mean girls, too."

"Oh, for Pete's sake. Haven't they grown up at all?"

"Maybe *mean* is too strong."

He doubted it. As a high school boy he hadn't known what to do about that—the constant digs the girls took at her, the put-downs. He felt he should have done more, but the girl world then—and probably now—was baffling to him.

"The problem is probably mine. Dragging along old baggage from high school. I wasn't expecting to be right back *there*. Feeling like I don't quite measure up somehow."

So it was an easy yes to help her out. Like making amends for not coming to her defense sooner. For spiking the punch that night.

"You know why, don't you?" he asked her, softly, even as he warned himself, *Stay out of it. Human relations are a topic you know nothing about.*

"Why what?"

"They treat you like that?"

"I don't actually."

"You know how photocopied pictures look when the printer is running out of ink? Faded and indistinct?"

She nodded uncertainly.

"That's what they were next to you. You were more than them. Prettier. Smarter. Infinitely funnier. And they never wanted you to know. They wanted to keep you down. Like Cinderella and her ugly stepsisters."

"Oh, for heaven's sake. I told you I don't believe in fairy tales."

It was her Dr. Cavaletti tone for sure. Nonetheless, she looked pleased.

"I'll pretend to be your fiancé," he said, "but only on one condition. That you act as if you're worthy of a man who loves you deeply and unconditionally."

There, he told himself. He'd agreed to this crazy plan for one reason and one reason only. Out of pure altruism. To show Jolie Cavaletti who she really was.

But was he going to be able to handle it when she found out?

"I'll make it worth your while," she decided.

He wagged his eyebrows at her wickedly, even as something in him sighed at how thoroughly she didn't get it.

It was okay to let people help you out. You didn't have to pay them back.

"Not like that." There was that smack on his shoulder again. It was a strange thing to like. He liked it.

"Like what, then?"

"I haven't decided. Maybe my firstborn."

"You have a firstborn?"

"Of course not!"

"Oh, but the possibilities," he said. "We could make a firstborn. That could be how you repay. The making. Not the firstborn."

"Maybe a puppy," she said.

"I don't want a puppy," he said. "My worst nightmare."

"How can a puppy be anyone's worst nightmare?"

"Do you have one?"

"No. But I'd like to someday."

"Well, I wouldn't. I've had my fill of looking after things."

He was shocked he had let that slip out.

She regarded him thoughtfully for a minute. He remembered this look, a certain intensity in it, a stripping away of anything that wasn't real.

"Did it all fall on you, after your dad died?"

He nodded, not trusting himself to speak at how quickly and clearly she had seen it.

"And yet, here you are, looking after me," she said softly.

"Temporarily," he reminded her. "You better make sure there's some fun involved."

She looked at him again, as if she saw it all. The late nights, and the two jobs, and trying to keep the house, his siblings and his mother together.

It looked as if Jolie saw the worrying. The constant worrying.

"I will," she promised.

And he wondered, again, just what he was letting himself in for.

"We have a deal," she said, and stuck out her hand, as if she planned to shake on it.

"Oh," he said, "I think we're way beyond that."

And he kissed her with deliberate lightness on her lips.

"Maybe we need to set some, er, perimeters," she said.

"Like setting up a scientific method?" he asked her dryly.

She didn't get that he was being funny. "Exactly."

"Well, he's watching us out the window of the lobby, so what's your method going to be for dealing with that?"

She took his hand. "Will you walk me to my cabin?"

"Of course," he said.

The cabin was nestled back in the trees, with a sign over the door. Jay glanced up at it.

Lovers' Retreat.

Good grief. It was his turn to blush. There was an awkward moment when he wasn't sure what to do with his new fiancée in such close proximity to that sign.

She solved it. "Thank you," she said brightly. "Good night."

And then, Jolie Cavaletti, his fiancée, stepped inside her cabin and firmly shut the door in his face.

He traced his steps back to the lodge. The lobby was clear so he stepped in to check in. The receptionist assigned him a room in the main building. From somewhere, he could hear girlish laughter from women he knew were not girls.

He wondered why Jolie wasn't in the main building. Were they that mean-spirited that they would deliberately exclude her?

The laughter suddenly came closer and Jacqui and Gillian—whom he knew Jolie hilariously referred to as Jack and Jill—burst into the lobby.

"Jay!" they shrieked together, as if it had been a long time since he saw them, when in fact they had all been at some kind of prewedding planning session three weeks ago. It had been extraordinarily boring, and he and Troy had entertained themselves by taking turns sending each other emoji faces on their phones as Sabrina rolled out the plans. Wedding music, rolled eyes; bridesmaid dresses, green nausea face; groomsmen attire, laugh-out-loud; cake, licked lips. Terribly juvenile and the only part of the evening he'd enjoyed.

Jack and Jill had taken him hostage and filled him in on Chantelle, the photographer Troy had lined up because she was his mom's best friend's daughter or something. Both of them had done bit modeling, even in high school. Ad campaigns for local shops, some catalog stuff. They had hinted in the past they would be great choices for his sporting goods line, but he had never taken the bait.

Chantelle, they had informed him, beside themselves with excitement and letting him know the opportunity he had missed, was well-known for discovering the next big name in the modeling world. They both seemed to think they were going to be that discovery, though he was not sure how many models were discovered at their age, which was the same as his, twenty-eight.

Jay was never quite sure how his friend, earthy, honest, brilliant, loyal, had ended up with Sabrina. Her inevitable entourage, alone, would have made Jay hesitate.

But Troy loved Sabrina. He'd been a mess when the marriage hadn't worked out the first time—another cautionary tale about love, really. Still, Troy's personality seemed to balance that of his more mercurial wife. And also wife-to-be.

His friend had a kind of affectionate acceptance of the oft quirky Sabrina that was enviable.

Still, the truth was if Jay did not feel as if he owed Troy big-time, he would not even be here.

Jill and Jacqui left in a flurry of giggles and wagging fingers, and Jay slid the key back over the counter. "Have you got another cabin? Something close to…ah… Lovers' Retreat?"

The receptionist consulted her bookings. "How about Heart's Refuge?"

Who came up with these names? A thirteen-year-old reading romance novels? And at the same time, he leaned into it. He wanted to believe there were refuges for bruised hearts.

"Sure," he said.

He found his way to the cabin—next to Jolie's—her lights were on, but he took his heart into the promised refuge without giving in to the temptation to go visit with her for a while. See what she was reading. And if her hair was wrapped in a towel. If she wore pajamas with kittens on them, or silk.

Being engaged to her was going to be way more complicated than he wanted.

If he let it, he decided firmly. He was doing a friend— were they even that?—a favor. Somebody maybe he owed something to, for never standing up for her, for spiking the punch that night.

It would be best, except for when they were "on" to set the perimeters as she had suggested earlier. He would avoid her entirely, except for official wedding activities.

The next morning, his perimeters were challenged almost instantly.

Because he walked into the winery restaurant for breakfast to find The Four, as he liked to call Sabrina and her pals, clustered around a table snickering.

They looked, with their tangled hair and smudged eyes, yoga pants and T-shirts, as if they had survived a late-night pajama party that involved booze. Actually, Sabrina looked clear-eyed. The other three didn't.

When he moved closer, he could clearly see they had a pile of clothing on the table, and on top of it was a bra.

That definitely did not belong to any of them, members of the Gwyneth Paltrow lookalike club.

"Oh, my God," Jill said, "over-the-shoulder-boulder-holder."

He was stunned by his level of fury. This is what these girls had subjected Jolie to all through high school: the constant scorn, the behind-her-back snickering, the snide judgments. He reached in over Gillian's shoulder and took the bra.

"What is wrong with you?" he said to them all, and shoved the bra into his pocket. "Grow up!"

Sabrina widened her eyes at him. "Jay! I didn't know you were here."

He could tell no one had expected to see him, as fingers ran through blond locks and clothing was adjusted.

"You should give that back to me," Sabrina said. "It belongs to Jolie. She left it on the bathroom floor last night."

Making it sound as if she had been partying along with them, and maybe even been the worst of them.

They were, of course, unaware he had already seen Jolie last night.

"I know exactly who it belongs to," he said tersely.

There was silence for a moment, and then Beth said, tentatively, "But how would you know that?"

Jolie picked that moment to walk in.

In contrast to them, she looked stunning. Her dark hair was still wet from the shower, wildly curling, but clipped back. She was wearing a lemon-yellow pencil line skirt that showed off the length of her legs and a crisp white blouse that showed off the understated sensuality of her.

She had on just a hint of makeup, a smudge around her eyes that made them look soft and brown, like the doe deer he had startled off the road on the way here. She had so much natural color, unlike the ghostly four, that she did not need blush on her cheeks. She had a touch of gloss on her lips that drew his eye there.

She hesitated when she saw The Four, and Jay watched as she shrank before his eyes, hunching her shoulders ever so slightly, shoving her hands into the pockets of that skirt. She obviously suddenly felt overdressed, as if she had tried too hard. It was all in her face: the insecurity, the fear of being made fun of.

And the jackals gathered around her bra, now in his possession, made her fear justified. It made him feel so protective that Jolie had no idea who she was. And neither did The Four.

"Ew...yellow," Gillian said under her breath.

Jolie glanced down at her skirt, and smoothed a hand over it.

"I like it," he snapped. "I like it a lot."

It was their turn to shrink, eyeing him warily.

But it was exactly as he had told her last night, and that skirt made it apparent. She was full color to their faded sepia. She was a brilliant original and they were copies.

At that moment, he committed.

To showing Jolie who she really was.

Jay strode over to her, put his arms around her and kissed her full on the lips.

It filled him with the oddest yearning that this was real. That he really got to say good morning to a woman like this, in this way.

He broke off the kiss, took her hand and led her back to the circle of women. He had to tug her slightly, she was so reluctant.

He tucked his arm around her waist.

He was quite pleased that he had, from the looks on their faces, managed to completely stun The Four.

Hopefully into silence.

"Jolie and I have been in contact," he said. Just in time, he remembered she had told Anthony they would hold off on a formal announcement until after Sabrina's wedding. As tempting as it was to cut the legs out from under the mean-spirited bride, he didn't.

"We're finding we have quite a lot in common."

He had hoped somehow to build Jolie up with that. Instead, he found he hated it, that the looks on every one of those woman's faces changed, not because of Jolie, but because of his acceptance of her.

His status, no doubt, had gone up steadily in their eyes as his star had risen. He couldn't even say how tired he was of *that*, of people adjusting their opinions about him based on his financial assets.

It was infuriating that they could be so shallow and so smugly unaware of it.

Really? In this day and age, a woman's value could be decided by her choice of a relationship? By a man choosing her?

No wonder she had stayed in Italy all these years. He glanced at her. It occurred to him his rise in the North American business world, while big news with the old high school crowd, was not such big news in Europe and had probably not reached Jolie.

He was pretty sure she had no idea he was a billionaire, and he had a sudden hope of keeping it that way.

Sabrina looked between them, quickly masking how she was appraising her very accomplished sister in a new light because of the billionaire thing.

"Jolie," she said, "I've decided the bridesmaid dress is a disaster. It can't be fixed. You'll have to find another one. There's a city not far from here. Penticton. I'll text you pictures of the other dresses. The essential part is the color. It's important for the photos."

"Color essential," Jolie repeated dutifully.

"Oh, and you left your clothes on the bathroom floor last night. For some reason Jay has taken possession of your bra. Weird. But…" she cast them a sly look "…weirder things have happened."

Queen Bee, buzzing, taking control, Jay thought unkindly. He refrained from saying that a good man like his friend Troy ending up with her would end up very high on his list of those weird, unexplainable things.

A smart, bright, vibrant person like Jolie being Sabrina's sister being another of those things.

He felt more determined than ever to show Jolie—and everyone around her—who she really was.

"Take Jay with you," Sabrina said, her tone dripping acid. "He's cranky this morning and who needs that kind of *energy*."

Completely blind, as those people so often were, to her own toxic energy.

"Yes," he said, "let's grab breakfast in town."

He couldn't wait to get away from them. He took Jolie's elbow and guided her outside. He didn't realize she'd been holding her breath until she started breathing again.

He fished her bra out of his pocket and she snatched it from him and put it in an oversize bag.

"You don't have to come dress shopping," she said.

It was true, it was not how he'd expected to spend the day. He'd thought maybe a bit of waterskiing with Troy when his friend arrived later today.

On the other hand, he hadn't expected to end up accidentally engaged, either.

There was something about the unexpected occurring in his generally well-ordered life that intrigued him, and that he was not going to say no to.

Even if it did mean spending part of a day looking for a

bridesmaid dress, of all things. Though, come to think of it, maybe that was going to be the most fun he'd ever had on a shopping trip.

Because look what he was trying to accomplish and look what he had to work with.

CHAPTER SEVEN

JAY HELD OPEN the door of his car for Jolie.

"Is this part of your award-winning acting skill?" she asked. It seemed to her Jay was doing a stellar job of pretending he was her romantic interest.

"Afraid not. Small courtesies drummed into me by my dad. Do you mind? It's a new world. I'm never quite sure if someone's going to find it offensive. I did have a lady snap at me once when I opened our office building door for her that she was quite capable of doing it herself."

"Witch," she said.

He grinned. That little dimple popped out in his cheek when he did that. He was wearing a moss green shirt this morning.

The color did wicked things to his eyes.

"That's what I thought, too," Jay said, lightly, "I didn't say it out loud, though."

"But you still open doors, even after that," she said, and something within her sighed with delight at his old-fashioned manners.

"I gauge the recipient," he admitted.

"Well, you gauged this recipient just right," she assured him.

Jolie didn't feel as if she started breathing again until she had settled beside Jay in the passenger seat. How could the very air around her sister and her friends feel so stifling?

She shot him a look.

"What?" he asked her.

"*Are* you cranky this morning?"

"I might have been if you told me you could open your own door," he said, that easy grin deepening his dimple.

This morning's outing—the impossible assignment of finding a dress aside—was as unexpected to her as a prisoner suddenly finding herself escaped from the cell. It seemed as if he was having the same reaction to it.

She sighed with relief. "What a beautiful day. What a beautiful car."

"Thanks, I enjoy it for the few months of the year it's usable in Canada. Top up or down?" he asked her. "We have to choose now. It's not like James Bond. It's not recommended you do it on the fly."

"Down," she said without hesitation.

It was like something out of a dream, whisking along roads that twisted through vineyards and clung to the edge of cliffs that overlooked the sparkling waters of the lake. Jolie was so aware of Jay's complete comfort and confidence behind the wheel. Despite his denial, he could have been James Bond! There was something very sexy about a man who handled a powerful car well, without feeling any need to show off.

After a bit, she took the band out of her hair and let the wind take it. She saw Jay glance over and grin.

"Thatta girl."

"Thank you for suggesting breakfast in town. It minimized the chances of an encounter with Anthony this morning."

"Ha! I can't wait to see the look on The Four's faces when they see two men floundering at your feet."

She hadn't thought of it like that. The wind, as well as being loud, was wreaking havoc on her hair, and with a touch of a button, Jay put the windows up. It helped marginally with the wind, but not at all with the loudness.

"Let's have fun with it," he suggested, and turned on some music. Loud.

"How'd you do that?" she shouted when she recognized music from their high school era.

"Never moved on," he said. "Stuck there. Musically, anyway."

No need to let him know fun did not come naturally to her. She had a sudden sense of being able to be whoever she wanted to be for the next little while.

"And look," he said, "the fun begins right here."

A sign welcomed them to Penticton, the Peach City. They both burst out laughing. She made Jay stop and she deliberately waited for him to come open her door. He did so with flourish and then they stood together under the sign. She took a selfie and sent it to Sabrina.

Should have no problem finding the right shade here.

Penticton, located between two lakes, reminded Jolie a bit of Italy with its dry hills, interspersed with vibrant green terraces of vineyards and orchards. It was a smaller city and the quaint downtown was already thronged with early morning tourists trying to beat the heat of the afternoon.

They found a cute little sidewalk café for breakfast, and sat down. Jolie pulled her hair clip from her pocket, but when she tried to scrape her now really wild hair back to retie it, she noticed Jay was looking at her.

"You should leave it," he said softly.

And so she did.

Jolie looked around and marveled at the unexpected turn her life had taken this morning. She watched the couples, young and old, strolling the streets, the families on vacation.

There was a distinctive feeling of summer holiday happiness in the air.

She had heard if you wanted to know who someone really was, to watch how they treated a server in a restaurant.

When the young woman brought coffee, she introduced herself. She apologized for the slow service and confided that one of the waitresses had not come to work.

"Susan, I've been watching you handle things," Jay told her. "You're doing an amazing job."

He said it casually, with just a glance up from the menu, and a quick smile, but to Jolie, as she watched the young woman take on her challenges with new confidence, it told her a great deal about Jay.

A few minutes later they watched Susan rush by with a whipped-cream-and-strawberry-covered waffle that filled the whole plate.

"I wonder if those come in smaller sizes," Jolie said.

"For simplicity's sake, why don't we just share one?"

While they waited for their order to come, Jay read the back of the menu out loud.

"Penticton," he informed her, "was named by the Interior Salish people, and translates to *a place to stay forever.*"

Jolie realized that was exactly what she felt right now, as if she would like to stay in this simple place—coffee and sunshine, people watching and an appealing companion—forever. She liked the feeling of nothing to prove and nothing to accomplish. She liked her hair being wild around her face, and she liked sitting in the sunshine, being perceived as a couple by others, and feeling like a couple, even though they weren't really.

When their waffle came, it hadn't been divided, and the feeling of being part of a couple deepened as Jolie found herself sitting very close to Jay, eating off the same plate. It seemed to her the moment was infused with an intimacy that was not quite like anything she had ever felt before. Considering she had been engaged for nearly a year, that was very telling of her relationship.

Again, she had that sense of just wanting to stay in this moment, forever, to deepen her connection with him.

"I never met your mom and dad, officially," she told him, "but I often watched them stroll through the neighborhood hand in hand."

"Their evening walk," he said. "It was their ritual. Almost sacred to them. It didn't matter if it was thirty below zero and the wind was blowing, off they went. Every day until he was too sick to do it. You mentioned seeing them walk in the card you sent. I appreciated that."

He remembered something she had written in a card years ago. It didn't necessarily mean anything. He had great people skills. She had just seen that with the young waitress.

"I have another memory of them," she said. "There was a little flower bed in front of your house, between the fence and the sidewalk."

"Mom's flower bed. Her pride and joy," he said, remembering.

"I was on the other side of the street, and I saw her out kneeling in front of it, pulling weeds. And your dad came up behind her and tapped her on the shoulder."

She remembered with absolute clarity, the light that had come on in Millie Fletcher's face when she saw who had tapped her on the shoulder. She had gotten to her feet and wiped her hands on her slacks.

"He had something hidden behind his back," Jolie continued, "and he gave it to her. It was a little bedraggled marigold in a plastic pot, the kind you get for ninety-nine cents at the grocery store. I could hear him say he'd rescued it. Your mother took that pot from him and you would have thought he'd given her a diamond.

"They knelt down side by side and put it in the flower bed right away. It didn't go with a single other thing that was in that bed. But every day, I'd walk by it and see it front and center. I don't know that much about flowers, but the next year, it had thrown seeds or volunteered or whatever it is flowers do, and there were more of them."

She realized at some point Jay had dropped his sunglasses over his eyes. He was looking away from her, and didn't say anything when she finished the story. She realized, horrified, that she had hurt him.

"I'm sorry," she said. "I've said something wrong."

"No, not at all," he said. "That's just exactly what they were like."

He lifted the glasses and squeezed the bridge of his nose.

She remembered, then seeing it so clearly last night, after he'd rescued her from Anthony. That it had all fallen on him.

"Jay?" she asked softly. "Why don't you tell me about it?"

He hesitated, taking a sip of his coffee. Then he lifted a shoulder.

"My mom never recovered," he said in a low voice, studying his plate. "She's lost without him. I was nearly grown-up, but I had younger siblings still at home. It didn't matter. Nothing mattered. She's like a shell. That flower bed you mentioned? She hasn't touched it for years now. It's a mess. Like the whole family."

"You held it all together, didn't you?"

He was still looking at their plate. "As much as I was able."

"You're a good man, Jay Fletcher." That came from the bottom of her heart.

He lifted his eyes and looked at her for a moment. She felt the deepest of connections shiver along her spine.

But then he dropped his sunglasses, and smiled.

"I don't want to be a pig," Jay said, eager to change the subject, "but I'd like another one. How about you?"

"I wouldn't normally say yes, but *pig* rhymes with *fig*, so I think it would be fine."

They both laughed, and it seemed they had moved on from the intensity of the moment when he had confided in her about his family, but she was aware of the connection remaining in some subtle, lovely way.

Sharing a second waffle with him proved as impossible to say no to as the prosecco had been last night.

They had just finished the second waffle, when her phone notified her with Sabrina's distinctive ping.

The feeling of intimacy she had been enjoying dissolved as reality intruded.

"Duty calls," she said, wagging her phone at Jay.

He grimaced.

"Ah, yes, dress instructions," she said.

"I was hoping to hold out for the fig leaf."

"Only if they come in peach," she told him sternly.

"Pigs are not peaches," he informed her, just as sternly. "Sorry, I meant figs."

She giggled. She had never really been *that* girl. The one who giggled. She was surprised by how much she liked it.

She glanced at the photos Sabrina had sent of Beth and Jack and Jill in their dresses. Like the bridesmaids themselves—except for her—the dresses were variations on a theme. The continuity factor was the peach color.

She showed the photo to Jay.

He wrinkled his nose. "Horrible color."

"Probably devilishly difficult to find."

"We could buy some construction paper," he said with a snap of his fingers, "and make it. Peach-colored fig leaves. One for me. Three for you."

She smacked him on the arm, and he pretended he was gravely wounded. She noticed an older woman smiling at them indulgently.

Assuming they were a couple.

Maybe that assumption was part of what made it so easy to reach for his hand as they navigated the busy streets on their quest for peach dresses. Or maybe it was the lingering effect of him trusting her with his broken heart.

They tried shop after shop. She couldn't help but notice how Jay treated people, with a kind of friendly respect that they responded to. Of course, a few of those women in those shops were just responding to his green eyes and dimpled grin!

Still, the search for the dress proved both exhausting and fruitless. There was apparently, not a peach dress to be found in the entire Peach City.

"I'm going to single-handedly ruin my sister's wedding photos," she told Jay.

"I think we should sue Penticton for false advertising."

"But the stay forever part is true," she said, and heard the wistfulness in her own voice.

He looked at her long and hard. "Yes," he finally said, "that part is true."

"Why don't you try a bridal shop?" the clerk in one of the stores suggested. "We have three."

She marked all three of them on a map for Jay and Jolie.

"If this doesn't work out," Jolie said, "I could try online. Sometimes delivery is shockingly fast."

"It's always good to have a backup plan," Jay agreed, as they found the first of the bridal stores.

He stepped in the door first. "Every man's worst nightmare. I think a fairy tale exploded in here. I'm drowning in unrealistic romantic dreams."

She saw the remark in a completely different way since he had shared his family tragedy with her. He was running away from the thing that had brought his family pain—love. And who could blame him?

"It's pretty estrogen rich," Jolie agreed, keeping it light.

She explained her mission to the clerk, who shook her head. No peach dresses. The second and third shops were also strikeouts.

But before they left, Jay squinted at a rack. "I'm no expert on colors, but I could swear that dress over there is the same shade you had on last night."

"Oh, that's not a dress," the clerk said, "It's an underslip."

"It looks like a dress to me," Jay said, moving over to the rack. He pulled out the slip on its hanger and held it out for Jolie's inspection.

"It's not a dress," she told him firmly. "It goes under a dress. Like a petticoat."

"I know what a slip is," he said wryly.

Of course he did! A man like this was likely quite familiar with what women wore under their clothes.

"It looks pretty sheer," Jolie said, doubtfully.

"Oh," he said pleased, "the next best thing to a fig leaf."

In some way, the item he was holding up reminded her of her wedding gown, probably because of its cut and pure simplicity. It was also silk.

"Put it back," she said. She thought she probably shouldn't try that on, but she heard the lack of conviction in her voice. For some reason it was like having more prosecco and another waffle. Irresistible.

"I think you should at least try it. You know, in the interest of having fun. And a backup plan."

Plus, it made her feel as if she would appear to be stiff and uptight if she refused. Oh, who was she kidding? She *was* stiff and up tight. But not today.

Today, she was a carefree woman who had wind-tangled hair and a handsome man at her side, and the whole world felt completely different than it had twenty-four hours ago.

CHAPTER EIGHT

"FINE," JOLIE CAPITULATED. "I'll try it on and you can see for yourself how inappropriate it would be."

"Oh," Jay said, wagging a wicked eyebrow at her, "I do love me some inappropriate."

She snatched the fabric out of his hands, and marched to the change room. What would it hurt?

She took off her clothes, and slid the silky chemise over her head. Just like last night, her underwear did nothing for it. The fabric was unforgiving of every line. She hesitated then took off her underwear and put the sheath back on.

It floated over her naked skin as sensual as a touch.

She turned and looked at herself in the mirror. She was stunned by the woman who looked back at her: bold and playful and daring. The slip hugged her in places, but it skimmed in others, hinting at what lay beneath.

She had to admit Jay had an eye. The slip was astonishing. Unlike the monstrosity of a dress last night, she looked absolutely gorgeous in it.

Taking a deep breath, encouraging the newer bolder "fun" girl to come out to play, she opened the change room door and stepped out.

Jay went stock-still. The only thing that moved was his Adam's apple, which bobbed in his throat when he swallowed.

"See?" she said, doing a twirl. "It's way too—"

"You," he croaked.

The saleslady came and looked at her. Her eyes widened with appreciation.

"You know, not everyone could pull that off, but you can. Slip dresses look like this one, cut on the bias, with spaghetti straps. They are actually very vogue right now."

"It's almost see-through," Jolie protested.

Jay grinned wickedly. "Fig leafs here we come."

"If I quickly stitched another slip inside of it, it would be absolutely perfect," the sales associate suggested, "but it will still cling a bit, so it depends how comfortable you are going without underwear."

"Commando," Jay filled in helpfully.

"Commando?" Jolie asked.

"That's what it's called. Going without underwear."

"You're a surprising expert on the topic," Jolie teased him, aware of how nice it felt to tease a man.

"Stick with me. I'm full of surprises."

For a woman who had avoided surprises, at all costs, for almost her entire life, she was not sure why that sounded quite so enticing.

"Just take it off," the saleslady suggested, "put on that housecoat behind the door and let me see what I can do with it."

Jolie looked back in the mirror. The chemise was just way too sexy. It was way too bold. Still, it was one hundred and fifty percent better than the other dress.

"Okay," she agreed, part reluctance and part hope. She retreated back to the change room, came out in an oversize fluffy white housecoat and handed the scrap of fabric to the clerk, who whisked it away to another room.

Now she was standing in a bridal shop, in a housecoat with not a stitch on underneath it. She was not sure why that felt even more intimate than standing before Jay in the crazy dress that wasn't really a dress but underwear, but it did.

Jay stared at Jolie. He felt absolutely terrified. It felt as if his mission—to show her who she really was—was going completely off the rails and leading him into dark overgrown forests where it was possible dragons lurked.

It had started when he had encouraged her to leave her hair down.

And then sharing that waffle with her had been strangely erotic.

But the worst thing of all had been telling her about his destroyed family. He'd never unburdened to anyone before.

He was aware that it should have felt like a weakness revealing that kind of information to someone who realistically was a stranger to him.

Except she didn't feel like a stranger.

He *knew* her. He'd known her since she was a kid.

Maybe it had just felt safe to confide in Jolie because their reacquaintance promised to be a short one. She would go back to Italy. He would go back to the blessed distractions of working too much.

The underwear dress she had been wearing was the epitome of what the mission was all about. To show her how bold and sexy she was. To make her not afraid of that.

But maybe he was the one who was going to have to be afraid.

Because all these things felt as if he was uncovering, subtly and slowly, layers that hid the real her.

But this—Jolie standing in front of him in a housecoat—felt as if everything had been stripped away, and what remained was purely her.

How could the housecoat—the white thick terry cloth

kind that you got in upscale hotels—be even more revealing than the underslip had been?

This was the stunning truth: she was beautiful, she was brilliant and she was kind. He could feel himself leaning toward the softness he had seen in her eyes when he had revealed the truth about his family like a sailor looking for refuge from a storm-tossed sea.

The thing about *her*—with her wild hair and her cheeky smile, and the way she could rock lingerie as if it was a dress, but especially her, standing before him in a simple white housecoat—was that he could picture her in his future.

In his kitchen.

The morning after.

In his life for a lot of morning afters.

Maybe it was because of the backdrop of row after row of pure white wedding dresses that he could hear the word *forever* in his mind as if it had been spoken out loud.

Everything was getting all mixed up inside his head. He was trying to show her who she really was.

But he had known from the beginning that there was a danger of him not being able to handle that.

Of him finding out who he really was instead.

And it was, terrifyingly, someone who still wanted to believe in what he saw shining in her eyes.

Despite the fact Jay had plenty of evidence to the contrary, something about Jolie seemed to overshadow that evidence.

That tomorrow would be okay, after all.

He was aware that he had to put the brakes on, right now, before he drove them both over a cliff.

The clerk returned with the peach-colored scrap of fabric. She had transformed it into a dress with another slip stitched expertly to the inside of the original.

When Jolie came out the second time, it felt as if the wind was knocked from him, like when he played hockey and suddenly found himself on the ice, staring at the ceiling, unable to breathe, wondering what the heck had happened.

He deliberately kept his features bland, even though he had to fight the guy who wanted to flounder at her feet.

"That's the one," he said, and then glanced at his watch. "Where has the day gone? Wow, it's nearly four thirty. We've got to go. Troy was supposed to arrive this afternoon and I have some business phone calls I have to make."

It would be very late in the Eastern part of Canada to be making calls, but people were used to hearing from him at all hours.

Business, his refuge.

His sister called him a workaholic. As if that was a bad thing!

He was a workaholic for a reason! Because work was predictable, and allowed him to be in control.

Unlike family. That sister, who was so fond of calling him commitment phobic and a workaholic, had been fifteen when their father had died. She had desperately needed a mom to guide her through that time.

Instead, it had been on him. And he'd been clumsy and ill-prepared to be the one who said, *No, you're too young to date*, and *No, you can't wear your makeup like that*, and *No*—actually that one had been *Absolutely no—you can't wear that outfit.*

Begging his mom to weigh in, begging her to come back to them.

But no, it had been Troy who had been his wingman through it all. Being there when Mike had come home drunk, and Jim had gotten in the accident with the motorbike he'd acquired on the sly.

Troy had a way of *seeing* people. It was as if he could see right through their faults and foibles to their souls, Sabrina being a prime example of that.

Watching how Troy dealt with people had helped Jay come to terms with the confusion of feelings around his mom, softened him toward her.

But what had not softened was his fierce decision that he would never put his own heart in a position to be so broken by love.

A resolve he had to firm up right now!

He put the roof of the convertible up for the trip back to Hidden Valley. He was not sure, after having seen Jolie in that dress, that he could stand watching the wind blow in her hair again. It made a man want to comb through those tangles with his hands.

Which made him think of that kiss they had shared last night.

No, things were getting way, way too complicated between him and little Miss Cavaletti.

He steeled himself against her look of disappointment.

"It's too hot," he said. "Bad for the upholstery. Not to mention heatstroke. You would not believe how many people get heatstroke in convertibles, from that sun beating down on their heads."

He should have thought it through more carefully, though, about putting the top up, because now they could hear each other. He didn't want to make any more conversation with her. It felt as if she could pull his secrets from him like a magnet held above steel filings.

He didn't put the nostalgic tunes back on. He chose classical.

And blasted it.

And pretended to be oblivious to the fact his sudden withdrawal was hurting her.

Better to hurt her now than later.

Because his mother and father had shown him what the future held if you loved someone too deeply.

There it was.

Jolie Cavaletti invited a man to love deeply, to want things he had already decided it was best that he didn't have.

And he had to protect both of them from those kinds of desires.

Desire. Another complication rearing its ugly head, the element that could guarantee a man could not think straight about anything. Her hair, her lips, the way she had looked in that lingerie? He probably wasn't going to have a sensible thought until after the wedding.

Never mind his mission to show her who she was.

In that little piece of fabric that had somehow been transformed into a dress?

It would be perfectly evident to anyone who wasn't blind exactly who Jolie was.

From the moment Jolie emerged from the changing room, she sensed something was different, that she was back to being on her own. Jay was gone. She took the dress to the front counter.

"You did such a good job, thank you."

"You're welcome." The clerk waved away her credit card. "It's paid for."

Jay was outside, scrolling through his phone.

"You shouldn't have paid for the dress," she told him.

"I wanted to."

"Well, you shouldn't have. It's not the same as holding open a door for someone. You already paid for breakfast. What do I owe you?"

"Your firstborn?"

"I'm not kidding, Jay."

He looked annoyed, but he gave her the amount, and she settled up with him.

After that, Jolie could feel the chill, and it wasn't coming just from the fact that Jay, apparently worried about heat-stroke, had the air conditioner in the car going full blast.

No, he was pulling away from her. It was in the set of his shoulders and jaw, in the line of his lips, in the way he was focused so intently—too intently—on the road, as if he was driving in a Formula 1 event. She tried to think what she might have done to bring on this distressing shift in attitude, but she came up blank. Surely it wasn't about her paying her own way?

Still, there was no mistaking the fact he had gone from warm and charming to remote in the blink of an eye.

It hurt.

But it shouldn't. No! She should be grateful to him. When they had come out of the store and it had been so hot she felt like butter about to melt, she had entertained the notion that they would stop at one of the many beaches they had passed on the way to Penticton and have a swim.

She didn't have a bathing suit with her and he didn't, either, as far as she knew, so what had she been thinking might happen?

A skinny-dip at a secluded beach somewhere?

That was what happened when you just let your hair blow around willy-nilly and were persuaded to try on slips and pass them off as dresses.

That was what happened when you stood before a man with only the thinnest of silky barriers separating your nakedness from him.

Boldness could become a drug, constantly pushing you to go further and further!

She was just getting over one relationship. She certainly did not need to be falling for another guy. Standing before him in skimpy clothing, relishing the look in his eyes, entertaining ideas of skinny-dipping on a hot day.

She slid Jay a look.

Was she falling for him?

How was that even possible? Her logical mind did not like it. Their reunion was not even twenty-four hours old.

That was chemistry, for you. Or maybe it was biology. Or some powerful combination of the two. But, realistically, how much of the present was being influenced by her feelings for Jay from the past?

So, no, she was not. Falling. Falling suggested a certain lack of control, something that *happened* to you, instead of something you chose.

She was too close to her last romantic fiasco to be making the same errors all over again. If she did ever choose another relationship—a big *if*—she decided she would take a scientific approach to it. Emotions could not be trusted.

Jay had done her a favor by keeping the roof up and blasting her with cold air and his own chilliness all the way home. A huge favor.

They arrived back at Hidden Valley, and she got out of the car, not giving him a chance to open the door for her. Who needed that? New independent Jolie did not need old-fashioned shows of chivalry!

She managed, just barely, to refrain from saying, *I can open the door myself.*

"Thanks for a nice day," she said instead, a woman grateful for the huge favor that had been bestowed on her. Why did she sound faintly snippy?

She gathered up her parcel and her purse. She tossed her tangle of hair over her shoulder and *liked* the look on his face, his chilliness momentarily pierced by an ice-melting look of heat.

Or maybe that was actual heat she was feeling. Leaving the car felt as though she was entering a blast furnace. It had probably been very wise of him to leave the top of the car up.

She didn't spare him another glance. She closed the

door—technically, it might have been a slam—and then she moved away from his car and quickly toward the relative sanctuary of her cabin.

With its stupid name that conjured up all kinds of unlikely possibilities.

CHAPTER NINE

ANTHONY HAD THE exceedingly poor judgment to intercept Jolie as she aimed for the shade that surrounded her cabin. "I've been looking for you all day."

Jolie glanced around for her accidental fiancé and saw that he and Troy had met up and, towels over their shoulders, were walking down toward the lake.

Getting the swim she had wanted.

She didn't need a man to rescue her!

"Get out of my way," she snapped in Italian when Anthony looked as if he intended to block her path.

She was aware her annoyance might have had a little more to do with being iced out by Jay than Anthony showing up.

And the heat.

Italians had the good sense to have *riposa* in the midday heat.

Undeterred—maybe not reading her mood, he had never been particularly sensitive to others—Anthony matched his stride to hers.

"You've had a fight," he said with satisfaction.

So, he read more into her than she had given him credit for. Still, how dare he think she was going to confide the personal details of her life to him?

"Go away," she said, still in Italian. "Go home. You're not welcome here."

"That's not what your sister said," he replied smoothly.

She did an about-face. Despite the temptations of the shade and her little cottage nestled in those towering trees, Jolie didn't actually want Anthony trailing her all the way to her cabin. It would be better if he didn't even know which one she was in.

Lovers' Retreat. He might see that as some kind of invitation. Who named these places, anyway?

She walked back to the lodge. and stopped at the desk. "Which room is my sister in? Sabrina Cavaletti?"

At least she knew her sister wasn't having a reunion with her husband-to-be, because she had just seen him.

She knew many large hotels would never give out a room number, but there were no such problems at the cozy, smaller lodge, and they gave her Sabrina's room information. Anthony trailed in the door behind her.

"If he asks," she said in a stern undertone, "do not, under any circumstances, tell him which cabin I am in."

She could tell by the guilty look on the clerk's face that it was too late.

She turned and glared at Anthony. "Vamoose," she snapped.

He stopped, gave her a hangdog look, as if somehow he was the victim, then turned and walked away.

Jolie hammered on Sabrina's door. Her sister apparently approved of *riposa* because she was not only in, but in her housecoat.

She had some kind of terrible mud mask on her face. The mud mask looked like something from a horror film, green and dripping, at the same time as being one of those *girl* things that Jolie was excluded from. She glanced over her sister's shoulder. She was alone.

"How could you?" Jolie demanded, without preamble. "You knew I'd broken up with Anthony. Why would you invite him here?"

Sabrina gestured her in, and closed the door behind her. She regarded her for a moment.

"Your hair looks as if you've survived a tornado."

This from a woman with green slime melting off her face! So tempting to say *Jay likes it*. Tempting, childish and off topic.

"How could you?" Jolie repeated.

"He tracked me down online. He told me it was just a spat and that you were being stubborn, which I mean, literally, you *can* be stubborn, Jolie! Mom and I both liked him so much when we met him last year in Italy, and he was being so charming. I thought it was quite romantic how determined he was to be with you. Mom and I think he's perfect for you."

"You and Mom don't have any say in my life."

"Thank you. That's more than obvious since you've chosen to live about a million miles away from us."

Jolie registered that her sister sounded hurt. "Seven thousand kilometers."

Sabrina rolled her eyes. "Anyway, he's a nice guy and very good-looking and he has a job."

"Is that where you set the bar?"

"After I spoke with him, I was convinced it would be right for you to give him another chance."

"No."

"Why not? You were crazy about him. Where did that go?"

"The most correct word in there is *crazy*. I was crazy."

"But what happened?"

"He cheated on me! And that's a pattern from our childhood that I will not repeat. For goodness' sake, Mom named me after a song where a woman is *begging* another woman to quit having an affair with her man."

"That song was called 'Jolene,' and you're Jolie."

"I think we both know what she meant. By changing a

few letters she was trying to, like, have a secret code. It's pathetic. I won't ever be like that."

Her sister looked genuinely stunned. "Jolie, I'm sorry, I had no idea."

"About the song, or Anthony?"

"I hate that song. Every time it's resurrected by another singer, I want to say, *For heaven's sake, take him already.* I just never would have pictured Anthony being that kind of guy."

"Me, either," Jolie said glumly.

"Are you sure?" Sabrina asked.

"Of course, I'm sure. I saw him in the gelato shop making kissy faces over a dish of *spaghettieis.*"

"Is that the ice cream dish that looks like spaghetti and meatballs?"

Jolie nodded.

"But that's your favorite," Sabrina breathed.

"Anthony introduced me to it."

"You didn't have a clue?" Sabrina asked with a tiny bit of insulting skepticism. "You didn't see him making eyes at the servers when you went out for dinner?"

"We hadn't been out much. When I saw him with that other woman, he actually blamed me. He said I focused too much on work."

"Why, that snake!" And then, "Jolie, why didn't you tell me?"

"I just wanted to nurse my bruised dignity in private without you and Mom kicking around my misery like a football with not enough air in it."

"It's very hurtful that you have such a low opinion of Mom and me."

"How is this suddenly about you?"

Her sister sighed. "The same ice cream dish he wooed you with. That is beyond low."

"Yes, *snake* kind of implies that."

"What did you do?"

"I walked away, of course, and sent him a text. That I had seen him and that it was over. Then I blocked him."

"He would have been wearing that ice cream, if it was me. I'll tell him to leave."

"Thank you. I just told him to leave, but I don't think he's going to listen to me."

"I'm really sorry, Jolie. I wish you would have told me sooner."

There was no nice way to say you did not trust your sister with your innermost secrets.

Sabrina unfortunately proved that assessment was probably correct when she seized on the package Jolie was still carrying, and seemed ready to leave the topic of her sister's heartbreak and humiliation behind with barely a pause.

But then Sabrina surprised Jolie by pulling out her phone and scrolling through it. "Here's the messages from him." She tapped in furiously. "There! I've told him to leave. Right now."

"Thank you."

"What's going on between you and Jay?" Sabrina asked, surprising Jolie further by actually showing some interest in her life "That kiss this morning gave us all a bit of a shock."

Interest, then, or judgment? Did they not see her in Jay's league? Well, let them wonder!

"Did it?" she said smoothly.

Sabrina chewed on her lip, struggling between wanting details, and trying to make up for the fact she'd invited her sister's philandering fiancé to her wedding.

"You got a dress!" Sabrina said, wisely putting both Jay's kiss and the debacle with Anthony behind her.

"Yes, I did." She slid it from the package.

"The color! Perfect. The fabric, though. Never mind. Try it on for me," Sabrina insisted, and shoved Jolie toward the washroom.

Jolie put on the remade chemise again. Somehow, she didn't feel it was nearly as much fun as it had been modeling it for Jay.

She stepped out of the hotel room bathroom self-consciously.

Her sister stared at her. Her mouth fell open, and then she closed it. "You can't wear that," she said firmly.

"It's that obvious?" Jolie asked.

"Obvious?"

"That it's an underslip?"

Sabrina frowned, came over and took a closer look. "I would have never guessed that, actually. It looks like the cutest ever little sundress."

"But then—"

"Hey, on Saturday there is one star of the show, and that's me. If you wear that dress, all eyes will be on you. You look stunning. You should dress like that more often. Just not at my wedding."

And then her sister actually smiled at her.

"If I wear the other dress all eyes will be on me, too," Jolie pointed out.

"Sadly, true. Such a disaster. I was trying to find all different dresses with the same color. I ordered them online. I didn't even notice the worms."

"Snakes," Jolie corrected her, and Sabrina snorted back a laugh.

"I think we've discussed snakes quite enough for one day," Sabrina said.

"Maybe you can find something else online. Delivery can be mind-blowingly quick. Thanks for saying I look stunning. You've never said that to me before."

"You know what? One sister is supposed to be the smart one, and one is supposed to be the pretty one, and I'm annoyed—super annoyed, actually—that you're both."

"I always thought you were the pretty one," Jolie said. Sabrina cast herself down on the bed and Jolie joined her.

"That would depend who you asked. You were always Dad's favorite."

"And you were Mom's," she said, feeling the sadness of two sisters in divided camps.

"I was the reason him and Mom had to get married. That came up in every fight. That she *trapped* him."

"I'm sorry."

"It's got nothing to do with you," her sister said, a little too sharply. "Anyway, who knows if that's why you were his favorite. You looked like him. And then, when you were eight or something, you started speaking Italian, just out of the blue, as if it was no big deal."

If Sabrina was a tiny bit mean to her sometimes, wasn't there an explanation for it?

"I'm afraid *vamoose* is about the limit of my Italian," Sabrina confessed.

"It's Spanish, actually, from a Latin root."

"See? That's exactly what I mean! Who knows the Latin root of *vamoose*?"

"From *vadimus*."

"Or that Italy is seven thousand miles away."

"Kilometers."

"You're such a geek, Jolie. That's why I was literally so happy for you when you found Anthony. He seemed kind of normal. But maybe you should just stick to the geeks."

Which Jay most definitely did not qualify as.

"You don't have to say that as if I'm nothing without a man. It's a little too much like that song. I've decided I won't be doing the romance thing again."

"Huh. Well, that might be one area where I'm smarter than you, sis. Because you don't choose love, it chooses you. If I could choose, do you think I'd choose Troy again? But I love him."

"What happened between you? Please don't tell me he cheated."

"Troy? Never. But we just fought all the time. Then I said I wanted a baby, he said he wasn't ready. No, he said *we* weren't ready. He finally said he'd had enough, and he wasn't bringing any poor, unsuspecting kid into a war zone. It kind of blindsided me because I didn't think it was *that* bad."

"Did you consider the fact that you were comfortable with fighting because that's what you grew up with? Maybe you actually believe that's how things get solved."

"I didn't know your degree was in psychiatry, Doc."

"Our childhoods shape us, whether we like it or not. I wonder how much our childhood had to do with me picking a philanderer."

"Seriously, Jolie, a philanderer?"

Jolie realized, resigned, her sister was commenting on her vocabulary not her choice of men. If you can't beat them, join them, she thought.

Sabrina's phone quacked.

"Mom?" Jolie asked.

"How did you know?"

"I assigned her the same tone."

They laughed together. It actually felt like they might have a sisterly bond.

Sabrina looked at her phone. "She's not arriving now until the day before the wedding."

Jolie thought her sister looked relieved.

"She says Dad's coming with her."

"Together?"

"It sounds like it."

"Reconciliation," both women said together, and not happily.

"You see, if you could choose, who would choose that?" Sabrina asked.

Who indeed? Jolie thought. Her childhood peppered with her dad leaving and her mother begging him to come back.

And she still was? All these years later? Jolie hadn't known it was still going on. She felt faintly guilty about leaving her sister alone with the family drama.

"Do you have an extra one of those? The thing on your face?"

"I do. But go take off the dress first. I don't want it to get wrecked. Just in case."

They actually had a somewhat sisterly moment while Sabrina applied the mask to her face.

"Avocado. It's miraculous."

Jolie refrained from asking to see the pouch it came in so she could study the ingredients. Instead, she allowed herself to enjoy Sabrina's pampering.

"It needs to stay on for one hour," her sister instructed her, in her wheelhouse now, doing exactly the kind of girly things that Jolie had never been able to figure out the appeal of. "If you wash it off right before supper, you'll see. Magic."

Jolie was more interested in the science behind the product than the magic, but it would probably spoil the moment if she said so. Plus, her sister did have enviably fabulous skin, like porcelain.

"Ta-da." Sabrina held up a mirror and Jolie's mouth dropped open.

"I think there was a perfectly terrible movie starring this character."

"It'll be worth it, you'll see."

"You mean I have to walk through the resort looking like this?"

"Maybe Anthony will see you and be dissuaded."

It wasn't actually Anthony seeing her that she was worried about!

CHAPTER TEN

JOLIE SHARED A laugh with her sister, as if it really was Anthony she was afraid of seeing, and not Jay. She tried, without success, to remember when the last time she had laughed with her sister was.

"Remember, one hour," Sabrina called after her.

Jolie managed to get back to her cabin without anyone noticing her. She was fairly certain she left a trail of melting green globs behind her.

The heat was insufferable.

The cabin, thankfully, was in the trees, cool and dark inside.

She looked at herself in the mirror, horrified. Was she really supposed to wear this for an hour? Her skin already felt weirdly tight. She tapped the goop. Was it hardening at the edges? Would her sister ever know if she washed it off right now?

But somehow that felt like a betrayal of Sabrina's efforts, not to mention that somehow the idea of softly glowing skin, in the face of being spurned by Jay, was too appealing to resist.

Spurned was probably too strong a word. She had been imagining a naked swim for two, he had been preoccupied with business. She probably wouldn't have had the nerve, even if the opportunity had presented itself.

Anthony was all the evidence she needed that she was not good at reading the subtle signals men were sending out.

Jolie suddenly felt exhausted. She glanced at her watch. No wonder she was tired. It was the middle of the night in Italy.

She knew the wrong thing to do was to give in to jet lag. You were supposed to tough it out.

She wouldn't have a sleep, she told herself just a little *riposa*, that was all. She'd just close her eyes for a few minutes. She set the alarm on her phone.

She went and took off her skirt, slipped her bra out from under her blouse, and laid down in her bed, on her back, so she wouldn't spoil the sheets with the green goop. Her bedroom window was open and a hot breeze blew over her.

She fell asleep almost instantly.

Jolie woke up feeling disoriented. The scent of avocado was heavy in the air, it was pitch black and she had no idea where she was. It felt as if something was encasing her face. With faint panic, she reached up and encountered a hard surface.

Slowly it came back to her.

Canada.

Her sister's wedding.

Green goop hardened on her face in the interest of glowing beauty.

Jay.

The reason for her sudden interest in glowing beauty.

"He can like me the way I am or not at all," she said, glancing at her watch. Of course, if the ride home from Penticton was any indication, he had chosen not at all.

Still, a woman wanted to be at her best when she'd been rejected.

It was past midnight. What had happened to her alarm? She had missed dinner. It had been a terrible mistake to give in to that desire to rest. She would be completely turned around now. She made herself stay in bed. She clenched her eyes firmly shut, and ordered herself to slumber.

Instead, she remembered the day. In detail.

She heard a sound outside her cabin and the hair rose on the back of her neck. First, branches broke, and then there was a groaning sound.

There was a wild animal out there. She was certain it was a bear. Toronto did not have bears, but this part of the world did.

Wasn't there even a warning on the garbage cans?

She'd heard bears had very sensitive noses. She didn't have any food in the cabin, but maybe it was being drawn to the scent of avocado. If she could smell avocado—and she could—surely a bear could, too.

"Don't be so dramatic," she ordered herself. It didn't have to be bear. It could be something smaller. Like a raccoon.

Or a mountain lion.

Heart pounding, being so quiet that the night creature, whatever it was, wouldn't be able to determine there was an edible person along with the avocado in her cabin, she slid over to the window and peered out.

Her eyes slowly adjusted to the dark. The moon was out and reflected off the lake. Under different circumstances she might see it as beautiful.

Another branch snapped. And another groan came.

Was she relieved it was Anthony? She was pretty sure she would have preferred any one of the other possibilities. He was placing himself, with a singular lack of grace, on a perch amongst the tangled branches of a large lilac shrub.

She squinted at him. What was that in his hand?

Oh, please, no. It was a guitar. The instrument looked like it may have been a toy. He strummed it thoughtfully. The sound seemed amplified by the pure quiet of the night.

It was worse than a nightmare. Anthony cleared his throat, strummed again and began to sing.

He sang, badly, in Italian. When she first heard her name, she thought it was going to be the song her mother had named her after.

But no, there were, unbelievably, more awful things than that. The song was obviously of his own creation.

It was a ballad about a misunderstood man, and one little mistake. The chorus involved *spaghettieis*, heartbreak— his—and the future children that he hoped would possess Jolie's eyes.

Such was the nature of jet lag that she pictured unruly children carrying between them a bag of eyes.

The caterwauling continued, unabated. Thankfully, her cabin was fairly isolated. There was one next door, but yesterday it had not looked occupied.

Her relief at not disturbing the neighbors—not having witnesses to the serenade—was short-lived. The cabin next door was apparently occupied now, because she saw a light come on.

She took a deep breath, ducked into her bedroom and looked around for the skirt she had abandoned earlier. She was not going out there dressed in only a blouse to shock the new neighbors even further.

Just as she bent to pick it up off the floor, she heard the back door of her cabin open. She froze, realizing she hadn't locked it. Hidden Valley did not seem like the type of place where things had to be locked.

Anthony was inside!

But no, he wasn't, because the singing continued at the front of the cabin.

She peered around the door of her bedroom and discovered it was Jay who stood there.

He glanced her way. Too dark thankfully for him to see

her face, or hopefully to notice she was only in her blouse. Who was she kidding that she would have gone skinny-dipping at the first opportunity?

She was going to duck back behind the door, but what he did next paralyzed her so completely she thought maybe even her breathing had stopped.

Jay's fingers moved to the buttons of his shirt. Her mouth went dry as he dispensed them quickly and peeled off that garment.

She had seen the statue of *David* with her own eyes, and it had nothing on Jay Fletcher. Painted in moonlight, it was obvious he was as beautifully and perfectly made as that marble statue. He was one hundred percent pure man— broad shouldered, deep chested, his stomach a hard hollow.

She couldn't have moved now if she wanted to.

She got what he was doing. Jolie thought Jay's half nudity would be ample to persuade Anthony they were in the cabin together. Lovers.

At *Lovers' Retreat.*

This had to be a dream, but no, when she pinched herself Jay was still there, and it was apparent he didn't do anything by halves.

With a quick bend and a flick of his wrist, he divested himself of his shorts and Jay Fletcher was standing in her cabin, completely unself-conscious, in just his boxer briefs.

He was magnificent, so much so that the serenade outside her cabin faded in her mind.

While her gaze was glued to him, he barely spared her a glance as he strode through her small living area. Just before he threw open the French door to the balcony, he paused and tousled his hair.

Nice touch. Making it look as if he was here. With her. Unclothed. And messy-haired.

A picture *did* paint a thousand words.

Thank goodness he stepped out, because her face turned so hot she could feel the mask softening.

"Hey," he called from the balcony. "What are you doing, man?"

Anthony' voice and the guitar strumming stopped abruptly. Jolie crept to her bedroom window and watched.

"I will win her back," he cried in English. And then added in Italian, "I am the better man."

"You aren't," she called from the window in Italian. "*He* performs like a stallion."

"You're embarrassing yourself," Jay said to Anthony, almost gently.

Anthony looked to the balcony, and then to the window, and then back again. His shoulders slumped in defeat, and he dropped the guitar. It landed with a sad twang as he shuffled away.

Jolie found her skirt, pulled it on, and slipped into the bathroom. Her face looked horrible! She took a washcloth, soaked it, scrubbed.

Everything looked worse! It wasn't coming off!

"Okay in there?" he called.

"Uh, yeah." She rubbed some more. Her face was a mess, green mask slimy-looking now, but still clinging. "Thank you for the rescue. There's no need to hang around. I don't know how you happened to know I was in need, but thanks."

"I'm in the cottage next door. I heard him. I couldn't resist rescuing a damsel in distress."

Suddenly, he was standing in the hallway, looking through the ajar bathroom door at her.

His mouth fell open.

She tried to laugh it off. "You think you're getting a damsel in distress, and you get the Grinch who stole Christmas instead."

It felt as if she had planted her whole face in a newly poured sidewalk. Jay came into the bathroom and regarded her thoughtfully. He was trying not to laugh and, thankfully, he succeeded.

He took her chin in his hands and turned her face.

"What the hell have you done to yourself?"

Oh, geez, sharing her cottage with arguably the world's most attractive man, and she looked like this?

"I'm rehearsing for my part as Fiona," she told him.

He looked blank.

"*Shrek*?" One of her favorite movies, where in the end, Fiona is loved for who she is most comfortable being.

He still looked blank. She realized she'd love to curl up with him, a bowl of popcorn, and that movie.

"Sabrina and I had a little girl time when I got back from Penticton. It's an avocado mask. It's supposed to work magic on my skin."

"Your skin did not need any magic worked on it," he told her gruffly.

She sighed inwardly, and Jay reached out tentatively and touched the edge of the mask around her mouth.

His fingers brushed that vulnerable surface.

Don't swoon, she ordered herself. *Friends!*

This could only happen to her. Instead of impressing Jay with her glowing skin, she was looking like the monster from the green lagoon. And this followed being subjected to the worst serenade by a spurned lover in the history of mankind. It was too awkward for words.

Really? Why wasn't he cutting and running?

Because he had decided they could safely be friends?

CHAPTER ELEVEN

A GREEN CHUNK of her face mask peeled off beneath Jay's fingertips. He studied it as if it was a specimen in those long-ago science classes they had shared.

"Is it edible?" he asked solemnly.

"I didn't have a chance to study the ingredients, but I doubt it."

He put the piece in his mouth and crunched down on it. "Edible," he declared. "Let's face it."

She laughed at his pun and she realized that's what he'd intended. He sensed her awkwardness and was trying to put her at ease.

It was so nice. *Friendly.*

"I might not go as far as edible, it could have hydrogen peroxide in it, and chemicals from fragrances and dyes."

"Will you save me if I topple over?" he asked, seriously.

"I will," she promised, "but at the moment I may be the one needing saving. I've left it on far too long, and it's hurting my face. It was supposed to be an hour. I think it's been closer to seven."

He touched her face with his finger, and then tried to get his fingernail under the mask. He pried gently.

"Ouch."

"I don't think that's supposed to be stuck on like that. I think we better try and get it off."

"I've been trying to get if off."

"I hope we don't need a chisel."

We? Oh, geez, wasn't this just the story of her life? She imagined skinny-dipping and instead got green goo turned to cement being chiseled off her face.

"I'll deal with it. You go."

She turned away from him and scraped at her face with the wet cloth. She yelped a little when the mask resisted, stubbornly glued to her skin.

Jay had not taken his cue, merely leaning one deliciously naked shoulder against the doorframe. After watching her for a few seconds, he came up behind her and took the washcloth from her hand.

If she had thought eating waffles with him and being with him in nothing more than a housecoat had been oddly intimate, those moments were nothing compared to this, him at such close quarters in such a tiny space.

He dabbed at her face. Scraped. Rubbed. But all with an exquisite effort to be gentle.

Had pain ever felt quite so wonderful? His touch was tempered, and his brow furrowed in concentration, his tongue ever so faintly pushing out between teeth that she noticed were absolutely perfect. As was the naked chest one small fraction of an inch from her breasts.

"Not coming off," he said.

She turned away from him, and back to the mirror. She pried at her face. A paltry little piece came loose.

"I have a sudden vision of myself standing at the altar with my sister, sporting green clumps, Jack and Jill holding back laughter, and Beth and the assembled looking sympathetic."

"We'll get it off."

There was that *we* again, and all it conjured. A life of solving problems, some small and some large, some funny and some serious, with someone you could rely on.

Who would never in a million years embarrass you with a serenade outside your window, no matter how drunk he was.

Despite the spiked punch in high school, Jay had not been a drinker then, and she suspected he still was not.

"Go lie down on the couch," he said. "We'll lay a hot cloth over your face and try it again in a few minutes."

She should protest, of course, but it seemed unnecessarily surly, like women who did not allow doors to be held open for them. Maybe, just for once in her life, she could surrender to being looked after.

So Jolie did as he asked and he busied himself at the sink. A few minutes later, he came and perched on the edge of the couch, gently laid a very hot washcloth over her face. He pressed it down around her eyes and nose and mouth.

She could feel his fingertips on the other side of that hot cloth. It felt like an exotic massage and it was unfairly sensual.

"You don't have to do this," she protested, a little too late, and not too vehemently.

"Ah," he said, "what are fiancés for?"

"I'm sorry. It seems a lot to ask, even of a fiancé, particularly a fake one. It's the middle of the night. Except not in Italy."

"Speaking of Italy," he said, "I have a confession to make."

"You do?"

"I speak Italian."

With a name like Fletcher? Life was just unfair sometimes.

"My mom's side."

She could feel the mask melting again. "How well?" she croaked.

"Not well, but better than him." He said it in Italian, and she really thought it was very good. And amazingly sexy.

Twice now, she'd referred to his performance in Italian, thinking he couldn't understand her. "I'm embarrassed."

"Don't be. I should have told you sooner."

"Not just by what I said. But by him. By my choices, I guess."

"It's not your fault he cheated on you." Another thing she hadn't known he knew, because she hadn't known he spoke Italian. "You deserve better."

"My sister and I were just talking about that. Family patterns. My father was not given to faithfulness."

Why would she tell him *that*?

"Don't worry," he said, "I've figured out there's no such thing as the perfect family."

"Yours always seemed like it was," she said a little wistfully.

"Yeah," he said, and his expression hardened, "until it wasn't."

"I'm sorry," she said. "I don't know why I said that. I say the wrong thing sometimes. I wondered if I did it today at some point. You seemed, um, changed on the way home."

"Did I?"

"Was it about me paying for the dress?"

"No, I'm just kind of used to picking up the tab when I'm with a woman."

"If it's a date!"

"We're engaged," he reminded her. "Ask Anthony."

He obviously had not really given the payment of the dress another thought.

"So why were you so different on the way home?"

He didn't answer right away. Then he sighed.

"You make me feel things I don't want to feel," he told her softly. "You saw the perfect family. I grew up feeling it was the perfect family. I never had a doubt. Then my dad died and she fell apart. Love failed spectacularly. She became a zombie. The love of her kids and for her kids wasn't enough to bring her back."

Jolie heard, not bitterness in his voice, but excruciating pain. It made her ache for him.

"Anyway," he said gruffly, "I saw what love did to my mom. I'm not going there. Not ever."

Jolie's heart felt paralyzed again. Jay Fletcher had seen the potential for love between them?

Okay, he'd very sensibly rejected the possibility, but still...

"I'm not going there again, either," she said, firmly. "Look at the mess it brought me last time. I haven't even finished cleaning that up yet. Obviously."

"Really?" Jay said, quietly. "Two people burned by love. We should be the safest two people in the world to be friends."

Jolie's poor face was a mess, Jay thought. The mask had hardened just like the concrete that it resembled and it did not want to let go.

Plan B—the hot cloth—softened it, somewhat, but it still took a long time for Jay to peel it off, trying so hard to be careful and not hurt her. Even with his best efforts, there was the occasional wince and whimper.

He was so aware of her nearness, her scent and her skin beneath his fingers that his whole body was tingling.

Given that they should have been the two safest people in the whole world to be friends, it was funny how this didn't feel safe at all.

Of course, he had known it wasn't safe. That's why he'd been such a jerk on the way home from Penticton, the Peach City, where he had learned to his astonishment that peach was just about his favorite color in the whole world.

Or at least when Jolie modeled it.

He wasn't sure he was ever going to be able to bite into a peach again without thinking about her.

Danger was not red, after all.

He was still a little surprised about her vehemence about paying for the dress. This was part of his world now. He had a lot of money and most people knew it. There was an expectation, particularly when he was with a woman, that he would pick up the tab.

He liked it that she didn't know. He liked it very much that she was self-reliant, but not in the way where she wouldn't let a man open the door for her.

Unless she was mad.

At the same time, he would have liked to have purchased that dress for her. After their paths were parted, maybe she would think of him when she wore it.

Would their paths part? Or would they keep in touch? His desire for self-preservation thought a separation of paths would be best.

Still, he'd made one attempt at self-preservation today, and he'd hurt her feelings doing it.

The man he had looked up to most in the entire world—his dad—would not be proud of him.

So, in the interest of being the man his father had always thought he was, Jay decided he could suck it up for a couple of days.

"You missed dinner," he told Jolie as he plucked away at her face. She'd closed her eyes. That should have been better than those brown eyes fastened on his, but with her eyes closed, he noticed the sweep of her lashes.

The curl of her hair.

The fullness of lips that he had tasted.

"Sabrina has some planned activities for tomorrow. Horseback riding."

He thought planned activities were probably very safe. The comfort of the crowd, the perimeters of the activity.

"It's so hot. I can't imagine that would be very much fun for the people or the horses," Jolie said a little dubiously.

"Fun doesn't seem to be the goal. She said it was team building." He kept his tone deliberately neutral.

"Who needs team building for a wedding?"

So glad she had said it.

"She probably organized that before she knew my parents had delayed their arrival. You know, keep everybody occupied, try to keep the friction at a minimum."

So she expected friction between her parents. Well, there was always lots of friction between Troy and Sabrina, too.

Despite the sword hidden in it at the end, had the love of his family been a gift? He hadn't allowed himself to think of it like that, but seeing what Jolie was up against, he wished she could experience what he'd had.

Instead, he thought wryly, he seemed to be experiencing what she had. Friction. As much as he thought team building was a terrible idea for a wedding, he did think a structured environment might help keep those fractious levels of awareness down.

"Are you just about done?" she asked.

He was done. He looked down at her face. It looked awful, with painful red splotches all over it.

"How does it look?"

He didn't want to be the bearer of the truth, so he went to the bathroom, found a hand mirror and held it out to her. Jolie sat up and looked at herself.

"Oh, no," she said.

He saw all her insecurities pass over her face. He remembered how her shoulders had hunched when she'd gone into the breakfast room this morning. He remembered the snide *yellow* comment. He could imagine The Four snickering at her face tomorrow. Or maybe behind her back, since he had chastised them.

He had probably not succeeded at stopping the meanness, just driving it underground.

He knew why they were mean to Jolie, totally threatened by someone who eclipsed them in every single area. With the exception of self-confidence.

He remembered his original mission, before it had gotten waylaid by a peach dress.

Hold that mirror up to her until she could see who she really was.

Be the better man, he told himself.

Which would mean what exactly?

He was afraid he might say a lot more than *grow up* to those mean girls this time. Because despite all his efforts at distance, this evening after rescuing her from Anthony and the mask, he felt closer to her than ever.

Protective.

Of her. Because he certainly couldn't protect himself and her at the same time. He was leaving himself wide-open in the way he least liked being wide-open.

Vulnerable.

Suck it up, he ordered himself again.

"What would you think if we took a miss on team building?"

Her whole damaged face lit up.

See? Vulnerable. A man could live for that look.

"The lodge has some canoes they sign out to guests. I could pack us some breakfast things and come get you first thing in the morning, before the team builders assemble for their outing. I'll send them a text just before we leave saying we've opted out. I bet an hour or two in the fresh air and those marks will completely disappear."

Plus, it wouldn't be anything like sharing the close confines of the car with her, watching the wind tangle with her hair. It wouldn't be anything like sharing a waffle with her.

It wouldn't be anything like watching her try on that little slip of fabric yesterday.

It wouldn't be a hands-on encounter like tonight had unexpectedly turned into.

"Have you ever been in a canoe?" she asked him.

It was a sport his company was not involved in. He was pretty sure it involved about six feet between paddlers. It was definitely a no-contact activity. His view would be of her back for the few hours that they would be on the lake.

"No," he said, making a note to himself to take a quick internet lesson on canoeing after he left here. "But how hard can it be?"

As it turned out, it could be quite hard. Even with Jay having prepared himself with a slew of internet tutorials, he was not sure anything could ready a person for the shocking instability of a canoe.

He was suddenly glad for the life jackets for two reasons: their lifesaving capabilities might come in handy; more importantly, Jolie encased in the puffy orange marshmallow looked nothing like she had in that dress yesterday.

Her hair was sensibly tamed, clipped at her neck. Her poor welted face was in the shadow of a ball cap. Her legs looked long and lean and sun-browned, but once she was seated, he wouldn't have to look at that particular temptation for the rest of the outing.

But even getting seated was not simple.

The canoes were tied along both sides of the dock, and he had been assigned a red one. For a no-contact sport, Jay noticed her hands were pretty tight on his as he stood on the dock and tried to keep her and the canoe steady at the same time as she lowered herself into it.

The boat rocked alarmingly as she found the seat behind her. When it had steadied, Jay handed her the breakfast things to tuck in, and for a moment it seemed all would be lost as the vessel dipped hard toward him as she reached for the items.

She laughed and the morning took on all kinds of dangers that seemed more immediate than a capsized canoe. After she'd gotten the breakfast items organized, he dared to hand her a paddle, and there was more rocking when she reached out to take it.

Finally, he released the vessel—which he already pretty thoroughly hated—from its mooring, and used his paddle to balance on the gunnels to take his place at the back of the canoe, or the stern, as the videos had called it.

He experimentally used his paddle to push off from the dock, then dipped it into the water and pulled it back.

The canoe shockingly obeyed and they moved away from the dock.

"I'll paddle this side, and you paddle that side," he called to her.

Really, once they were moving forward it seemed pretty simple as long as they sat ramrod straight on the extremely uncomfortable seats, and didn't make any sudden movements.

"Talk about team building," he muttered, as they headed out and tried to coordinate their paddles.

"Oh, but this is so romantic."

He grunted disapprovingly.

"I mean," she caught herself, "the *romance* is of the activity, not us. Look how quiet it is, the glide through the water, the morning light on the vineyards. It's wonderful."

It wasn't really. It was hard work to paddle, impossible to steer, and even breathing the wrong way made the vessel sway threateningly to and fro in the water.

He felt overly responsible for Jolie's safety. When a motorboat roared by, they nearly capsized in the wake it left behind it.

But, despite the challenges, they both got the hang of it, and were soon skimming the water and enjoying the novel view of the shoreline. At first there were houses and small businesses, a yacht club and another resort.

The road that serviced those must have ended, because soon they left development—or civilization, depending how you looked at it—behind. The lake was even more beautiful then, with its deep forested shorelines, rocky, steep outcrops, secret coves and sandy isolated beaches.

Jay relaxed. It was a bit of a workout, but it was a great way to see the shoreline. After an hour or so, they stopped in a tiny cove, resting their paddles on the gunnels and enjoying the gentle swaying of the canoe and the silence broken only by the screech of a hawk nearby. A single rustic cabin, cedar shakes grayed from weather, perched on the edge of a steep embankment. It must have only been accessible by water.

Reaching for the breakfast bun she passed him seemed treacherous as it set the temperamental vessel to rocking.

"Chew on both sides of your mouth," he warned her, "or I think we'll tip this thing right over."

"That might feel good right about now," Jolie said, a bit wistfully.

They had worked up quite a bit of a sweat paddling. Added to that, Jay noticed a sudden stifling quality to the air, the life jacket trapping heat against his body.

But he was not about to try either beaching the canoe or trying to swim off of it. He was pretty sure, from the videos he'd watched, getting back in it would be well beyond either of their skill sets.

Besides, he had not come prepared to swim, and he was pretty sure she hadn't, either.

Skinny-dipping was out of the question.

Though once a man had allowed a thought like that into his head, it could be difficult to get rid of it.

CHAPTER TWELVE

"LET'S HEAD BACK," Jay suggested, after they had finished the buns.

Jolie did not want to go back. Even though her arms and shoulders ached from the unfamiliar exertion of paddling, she was not sure she had ever had an experience as perfect as this one.

Early morning on the lake, stillness, the sharp scent of a man in the air, her and Jay totally in sync with each other.

Team building.

"We'll be really ready for a dip when we get back to Hidden Valley," he suggested.

The promise of a different experience made leaving this one a little easier!

They paddled back out to the mouth of the cove. Even before they got entirely back to the main body of the lake, it was obvious something had changed.

While in the cove, protected, they had missed the fact the wind had risen on the main body of water.

Where it had been smooth as glass less than half an hour ago, now the water was moody, and had a distinctive chop on it. In the distance, back the way they had come, toward Hidden Valley, dark clouds boiled up.

"It's unusual to see a thunderstorm this early in the day," Jay said. She heard something in his voice and glanced back at him.

She realized right away that the calm note in his voice was for her benefit. His mouth was set in a straight, determined line. Tentatively, they pushed out into the main body of the lake.

It was quickly apparent that even the most skilled canoeist would be challenged by trying to go into the wind. The water was getting rougher, the chop was pushing back on the canoe. She was soon exhausted, discouraged by their lack of headway and starting to feel scared.

When she glanced back, Jay was a picture of pure resolve. That strength she had glimpsed in his honed body last night made up for his lack of experience. The look on his face was a look a woman could hang on to.

It was the look of a man who rose to what circumstances gave him and dug deep into his reserves of courage and fortitude.

It was the look of a man who did not allow bad things to happen on his watch.

It was the look of a man who would lay down his own life to protect others.

But even Jay's willpower was no match for the mounting storm. The rough water began to form whitecaps. The lake was rolling. A rogue wave broke over the bow, soaking Jolie, but worse, sloshing water into the boat.

"There's a can there," Jay said. "Bail."

Though his tone remained calm, there was no missing the note of urgency.

She rested her paddle on the gunnels and reached back for the can. Unfortunately, in her eagerness to save the canoe from sinking, when Jolie reached for the can—rolling just out of her reach in the center of the wallowing canoe—she overbalanced the vessel. It tipped alarmingly in the stormy waters.

Horrified, she watched her paddle slip off the gunnels

and into the lake. Her every instinct was to make a grab for it, but Jay's voice stopped her.

"Leave it," he commanded, wisely, since grabbing the paddle bobbing tantalizingly just out of reach would further destabilize them.

Trying to be mindful of balance, she made one more desperate effort to get to the bailing can. Her fingertips closed around the lip, and she could have cried with relief.

But there was no time for something as self-indulgent as crying.

"Bail," he yelled over the storm, and she frantically began to empty water out of the canoe. The can did not feel nearly big enough, like trying to empty a bathtub with a teaspoon, but she could see it was making a marginal difference, and redoubled her efforts.

"I'm turning back to the cove."

It was the only reasonable thing to do, particularly now that they were down to one paddle.

There was a precarious moment when the canoe was broadside to the waves.

More water sloshed in, and over her, but she ignored it, working as fast as she could to empty it back out.

Jay turned the canoe around. Obviously the paddling was easier now that they were being driven by the waves instead of against them. Still, with only one person paddling, it seemed as if it took forever to find that mouth again.

Finally, with one last powerful heave from Jay, the canoe nosed into the calmer waters of the cove, though even inside the cove the water now had a chop on it.

But the wind was broken somewhat, and Jolie was able to make some headway on the water inside the boat as no more was sloshing in over the side.

Jay, his chest heaving, his breathing hard, took a much-needed break. She could see him casting a look out onto the lake and at the sky, weighing options.

"We're going to have to wait it out, and maybe not on the water."

"You had me at not on the water," she called back to him. "I can't get onto dry land fast enough."

The first big fat drop of rain fell on them. Jay paddled them toward shore. Though she thought she'd probably had the easier of the two jobs, she was nearly limp with exhaustion.

Despite that, he called encouragement. "Nearly there. Hang in there. Good job on the bailing. Everything's okay."

She needed to look at him. It seemed to be taking a long time to get to shore. It was as if the water, itself, was trying to stop them. Despite her trepidation about doing anything to disturb the balance of the canoe, she twisted in her seat and looked at Jay.

Despite his encouraging tone, she saw the worry in his eyes. Still, he was calling the strength from her, expecting her best, and she found herself digging deep for her reserves.

The water in the cove was getting more storm-tossed by the second. The temperature seemed to be dropping rapidly. The sky had turned a menacing shade of gray.

Another fat raindrop fell. Jolie had heard the expression *the sky opened up* but she was not sure she had ever experienced it as thoroughly as in that moment. The rain poured down. They were already wet from the water sloshing in the canoe, but this was a brand-new kind of drenched.

It soaked through her ball cap and the life jacket. Her hair was wet to her scalp. Her clothes clung to her as if they were suddenly made of cold, slimy mud.

She let out a cry of pure relief when the canoe finally hit shore with a terrible grinding clatter that sounded as if it was tearing the bottom out of the vessel. She scrambled to get out. Even at this last moment, the canoe threatened to capsize. Jay leaned hard the other way to balance it, and she was finally, gratefully and gleefully, free of the canoe.

She was up to her thighs in water. But it didn't matter. Her feet were on solid ground, and it was not possible to get any wetter.

Jay vaulted out, too. He patted his shirt pocket making sure his phone was there. A lifeline. A way to let the others in the wedding party know they were okay.

He came to the front of the canoe, and jerked it from the water, scraping it across the rocky beach. She rushed to help him, but she was shaking so badly she wasn't sure she helped at all.

Finally, panting with exertion and adrenaline, they pulled the canoe well up out of the water, which was now pounding on the shoreline. They overturned it.

She looked out toward the mouth of the cove. It was barely visible through the sheets of rain that fell.

It sank in.

They were safe. Jay had saved them both.

CHAPTER THIRTEEN

THOUGH JOLIE WAS cold and wet and shaking with exhaustion and shock, she was experiencing something far more powerful than relief.

A beautiful euphoria enveloped her.

She felt so alive. She could feel the beat of her own heart, the blood moving through her veins.

She tilted her head and took in Jay: his hair plastered to his head, the raindrops cascading down the gorgeous lines of his face, his cheekbones, his nose, his jaw.

His lips.

She had seen people, on the news and in movies, kiss the ground in relief when they had gotten off a bad flight, or been snatched from the jaws of danger and finally found themselves on safe ground.

As much as an overreaction as that might have been, she had a wild desire to do that. But watching the rain sluice down his lips made her think, why kiss the ground, when she could kiss the man who had used every ounce of his strength and intelligence, his discipline and his never-quit attitude to get them back to a place where they were safe?

He looked every inch the warrior as he stood there, his gaze fastened on the lake that had nearly taken them.

Suddenly, with clarity she had rarely experienced in her life, Jolie knew exactly what she wanted.

Shockingly, it had not changed much since she was sixteen.

She wanted Jay's lips on her lips and his hands on her body. She wanted their skin together, she wanted to know him completely, for every barrier between them to come down.

She stepped into him.

He thought she wanted only comfort, and he pulled her close—or as close as the puffy life jackets would allow.

And then he kissed the top of her head—as if she was still that innocent sixteen-year-old child—and broke the embrace.

She didn't realize how cold she was until Jay's hand closed around hers, warm, strong, solid.

"Good job," he told her.

He practically had to pull her up a steep embankment to the cottage. The front of it was on stilts, built into the sheer drop off of the cliff. But there was a well-worn path around it, and they followed that to the front entry.

An old sign hung there, so weathered they could barely make out what it said.

Soul's Rest.

"What's with the names?" Jay asked.

But she felt that *exactly*, after the punch of adrenaline fighting the lake had given her, the sturdy little structure whispered of safety and sanctuary.

And something more.

A place for her and Jay to explore every single thing it meant to be a man and a woman. Alone. Together.

Her sense of delicious elation deepened. Maybe it was from escaping the jaws of death, and maybe it was because of the lovely coincidence that they found themselves in a place with a shelter as the storm broke.

But no.

Those elements played into her bliss, certainly.

But the major cause was knowing what she wanted.

And she wanted Jay Fletcher.

A tingling sense of anticipation filled her as he tried the handle. The door wasn't locked. In fact, the latch opened easily and the door sprang open to reveal a small alcove. They finally took off the dripping life jackets.

Again, with Jay's sodden clothes clinging to him, Jolie was taken with the sense of him being pure warrior, all hard edges and honed muscle.

Except for his mouth, the place that looked soft and inviting, the place where she would draw his innate kindness and his warmth to the surface.

Didn't every woman dream of being the one that the warrior laid down his weapons for? That he took off his armor for?

The one that he showed the vulnerabilities of his heart to?

Jay seemed as totally unaware of her as she was totally engrossed in him, taking in the interior of their shelter with the assessing eyes of a warrior/rescuer.

She took it in, too. Despite the fact that it had looked abandoned from the lake, the interior of the cottage looked as if someone enjoyed the space immensely.

It was rudimentary, but cozy. There was a small main room with a faded couch and a patched easy chair, an openshelved kitchen with a small table in it. A miniature potbellied woodstove with a crooked pipe was in the center of the room. Bookshelves held well-worn paperbacks and jigsaw puzzles and games.

The whole lake-facing wall was windows, now being rattled by the storm, raindrops sliding down the panes.

"Supplies," Jay said, going over and perusing the open shelves. "Hot chocolate. Tea. Some canned stuff."

Here she was admiring the surprising ambience of the

little space—and plotting the conquer of his lips—and he was focusing on banal things.

Survival.

This was why men and women belonged together. They balanced each other.

"We won't be here long I'm sure," Jay said, "but I'll replace anything we use. You look like you need something hot. And to get out of those wet things."

Disrobing felt like the best idea, *ever*, for a woman who had just decided men and women belonged together. Needed each other. Should celebrate their differences.

"Jay," Jolie said softly, "thank you."

He looked up from the hot chocolate supplies, surprised. "For what?"

"Getting us safely off the water."

"Huh. Well, let's not forget it was my idea to be on the water in the first place."

"That's not the point," she said stubbornly. "I lost my paddle. One wrong move and that canoe could have gone over."

"We had life jackets on," he said with a lift of his shoulder. "Instead of looking at all the things that could have happened, I think we should focus on how well we worked as a team to get off the water."

She was so taken with his way of seeing it, not seeing her as weaker than him, in need of his rescue, but rather as part of the team. Equals.

"You are a great person to be with in an emergency."

He gave her a grin. "You, too."

She should have been frozen, but she felt warmed through to her soul by that casual remark.

"You should get out of those wet things now."

Somehow, she had always imagined Jay asking her to get undressed would be slightly different than this.

Had she imagined a request like that?

Only about a hundred times.

Or maybe a thousand.

Or maybe more.

When she'd been a teenager addled by thoughts of romance. She was mature now. She had life experiences.

And it didn't seem to matter.

When it came to Jay, she felt the same weakness of wanting that she had always felt. The storm hadn't caused it.

It had exposed how raw and real that wanting still was in her.

"That looks like a bedroom through that door. Maybe go see what's in there that you could change into temporarily."

Jolie told herself sternly that she had lost command of her senses. Was she seriously plotting the seduction of Jay Fletcher?

Their close call had obviously put her into a bit of shock.

Jay had already busied himself with the business of survival. He was crumpling paper into the woodstove.

It was a good idea to get away from him for a minute, to try and gather her thoughts. She went into the side room and closed the door. It turned out to be a bedroom, the mattress rolled up on top of a double bed.

There was a dresser but when she checked it, the drawers were empty. She went and pulled the string that bound the mattress and it unrolled. The bedding was inside of it.

It was a relief to pull the soggy clothing off. She toweled off with a rough blanket, and squeezed the water from her hair.

She waited for her tumultuous thoughts to calm as feeling returned to her body. But they didn't.

When she was done, she tucked the white sheet around herself, toga style. The fabric felt like a glorious torture on skin that was singing with awareness.

Anticipation.

She opened the door and stepped out into the main room. She felt exquisitely as if she had stepped back in time. A maiden offering herself to her warrior.

Jay was crouched in front of the woodstove. He already had a pot of water on top of it. Focused intently, he fed sticks into it. He had taken off his wet shirt. The reflection of the steadily growing flame gilded his perfect skin in gold.

It only added to the sensation of a steadily growing flame inside of her.

"There's a bit of a cell phone signal," he said, without looking up from what he was doing. "I was able to send a text saying we're okay, that we've got a safe place to ride out the storm."

She said nothing.

Jay turned his head slightly and looked at her.

It was a look every woman would hope to see in the man she had chosen to be her lover. The warrior lowered his shield.

He got up slowly, straightened, took her in.

And she saw clearly in his eyes that he had, as every warrior did, a weakness.

And that it was her.

She saw in his eyes that he acknowledged he was a man, and she was a woman, and that with the slightest nudge he would allow his power to resist to be overtaken by her power to tempt.

The sensation that enveloped her was heady.

He wanted her. And she knew it. And she loved knowing it.

She knew she had been waiting for this moment for ten years, ever since he had rejected her.

"You better get out of your wet things, too," she said.

Her voice sounded soft and husky, an obvious invitation. Jay looked at her, *that* look in his eyes—masculine appreciation, surrender.

And then he seemed to catch himself. He cast his gaze wildly about the room, as if an escape route would be revealed to him if he looked hard enough. He actually looked as if he was considering the canoe and the storm!

She frowned.

A little less fight, please!

"Go get out of those wet pants," she said, again.

CHAPTER FOURTEEN

JAY GOT OUT of that small room with Jolie as fast as he could. He went into the bedroom and shut the door, resisting, just barely, an inclination to lean on it as if some force was trying to push it back open.

The door seemed like a flimsy barrier against that force.

And it was. Because the force—his foe—was not out there. She was not the foe. The enemy was inside himself.

He was in a bad spot now. She obviously had some kind of misguided hero-worship thing going on, believing he had rescued her from certain death.

And she looked astonishing with that sheet wrapped around herself, that wild tangle of wet hair cascading around her, her shoulders naked and slender and perfect. Jolie Cavaletti was like a goddess.

A goddess who had just, more or less, ordered him out of his clothes.

Ten years ago, he had said no to her. He had recognized how vulnerable she was, and that she was not ready for what she had asked him for.

Everything was changed.

They were both adults now. Jolie was a woman who knew her own mind.

And yet somethings remained the same. She was vulnerable. She'd recently lost a relationship. And then today, both of them were coming off a bad shock, a close call.

On the other hand, Jay felt as if he had used up all his strength out there on the lake. He had none left for resistance.

There was a certain euphoric feeling—being alive, having partnered with her to accomplish that—that might make it easy to accept life tempting him with its glory.

Keep a lid on it, he ordered himself.

It would be easy for things to get out of hand. He wasn't just fighting her, but the residue of elation from having cheated the lake and the storm.

And despite the fact he had minimized the danger they had just faced, the complete truth was something else. It was not uncommon to see headlines in Canada, this land of rugged extremes, that served as reminders that Mother Nature, while magnificent, also had an unforgiving and cruel side.

Just like love.

Jay sucked in a deep, steadying breath, reminding himself he had started today with a mission to be a better man.

This storm—with all its multifaceted dimensions—would pass. Anybody, including someone who had used all his strength, could muster a bit more for a short period of time. He went over to the window and looked out.

Despite the fact it looked as if it intended to rain furiously for a week—please, no—these summer storms tended to come and go very quickly.

He formulated a plan. They would dry off. They would hang their clothes by the fire. They would probably barely have time to finish the hot chocolate and it would be time to leave, to get back in that canoe and make their way down the lake.

One thing was for sure, he was not going out there wrapped in a sheet.

He looked under the bed. To his immense relief there was a trunk, and when he opened it, it had men's clothing in it.

He yanked off his pants and dried himself, deliberately

not allowing himself to focus on how his skin stung, making him feel extraordinary, as if every single cell of his being was singing.

Because he knew if he focused on that, he would know the singing was only partially because of the exhilaration of getting off the lake.

Only partially because of the rough blanket drying his pebbled skin.

Almost entirely because of her. Jolie. The goddess who awaited him in the other room. He pulled on the dry clothes, jeans and a faded T-shirt, and took one more deep breath.

He felt more like a protector than he had felt even when he was trying to get that canoe off the water.

He made the mistake of looking at the floor, and their puddled clothing that needed to be hung up by the fire.

Her sodden underwear was on top.

He picked up his own things, and left hers there. Hopefully, when he strung the clothesline she would get the hint.

A man could only test his strength so far.

"Oh," Jolie said, when he came back into the main room. "You found clothes."

Did she sound disappointed?

She had pulled a kitchen chair close to the fire and was running her fingers through her tangled hair.

He wanted to run his fingers through her hair.

She looked as if she knew exactly what she was doing.

"Under the bed," he said with unnecessary terseness. "I think there are things there that would fit you."

"I'm quite comfortable, thank you."

She would be. He needed to remember that. Self-defense strategy number one: Jolie was quite comfortable tormenting a man.

He rifled through some kitchen drawers until he found

some twine. He focused intently on getting a clothesline hung close to the stove.

She got up and moved over to the window. Out of the corner of his eye, as he draped his soaked clothes over the line, he noticed her studying the shelves, running her fingers over some of the games there.

"Have you ever played this?" she asked, plucking a slender box from the shelf and showing it to him.

"Probably a million times, growing up. Friday was always game night. My mom loved it so much. You would have thought she was getting ready for the event of the century every week. I think she started planning what treats she was going to serve and which game we were going to play on Monday."

He had not allowed himself these kinds of memories since his dad had died. He didn't want to talk about it anymore. It felt as if he couldn't stop himself.

"Sometimes it was just our family. To be honest, I don't think my dad was a game guy. I think he enjoyed it because she enjoyed it. But lots of times there were tons of people there, my parents' friends, our friends. Even when I got older, and it should have been lame, my friends had to be at our house for game night."

He caught a look on her face. She went from a siren to a faintly wistful little girl in the blink of an eye.

"You haven't played that game?" he asked her.

"We weren't that kind of a family," she said. She slid the box back onto the shelf.

"You didn't play any games? What about at Christmas?"

"Christmas." She made a face. "Always the worst."

Christmas? The worst? "In what way?"

Jolie looked pensive, weighing how much to tell him.

"Christmas was party time," she said finally, and he felt the weight of her trust in him. "There was way too much drinking. My father, not that inhibited to begin with, lost any inhibitions he had. He loved attention from the ladies. It seems there was always a Christmas fling. My mom would be furious at first, and they'd have these dish-shattering rows, and he'd leave. But then her fury would die down, and she'd just want him back. It always seemed as if Sabrina and I were being asked to pick a side. I was Team Dad, she was Team Mom."

"That's awful," Jay said. "I can't imagine how you dealt with that."

"I escaped into books. How grateful I was to have different worlds waiting to welcome me. All I had to do was open the cover."

He suddenly remembered how she'd been in high school, the sweet little geek, absent-minded and ethereal. She'd always had a book. He remembered sometimes other kids would say she just carried them to look smart.

War and Peace.

Moby Dick.

Les Misérables.

But even before he'd done that science project with her he'd known somehow when you were smart you didn't have to *look* smart. She probably would have done anything *not* to look so smart.

Even his totally self-centered eighteen-year-old self had known Jolie found refuge in her books and her brains.

Until now, he hadn't known what she needed refuge from.

The memory of Jolie at sixteen—wary, lacking in confidence, trying to fade into the background—diffused some of what he felt when he looked at her wrapped in that sheet.

"Sadly," she said, "sometimes those books made me long for the things I'd never experienced growing up. When Anthony came along, I convinced myself he made me so blissful. In hindsight, I adored his family that he'd found in Italy. It was loud and boisterous and big and everything I had never had. His *nonna* adored me and the feeling was mutual. I realize I did have a few tiny little doubts about him, but I just steam-rollered over them, so invested in my own happy ending."

Jay was reminded, again, of the gifts his family had given him. He could not have been given a more perfect distraction from the intensity that was leaping up between he and Jolie. Despite her admission she was—or had been—a woman in search of a happy ending, he needed to put self-protection aside.

He could be a better man. He went and took the game off the shelf.

"Go get your wet stuff," he suggested, "and hang them up on the line. I'll set up the game and get hot chocolate ready."

For a brief moment, she looked as if she had another plan, but then her gaze went to the game, and he saw that wistful little girl again. She disappeared into the bedroom without a word.

He didn't even watch her put those delicate things on the line next to his as he finished preparing their hot chocolate then set up the game. He scowled down at the board, trying to remember where everything went, and what the rules were.

A good thing to remember: what the rules were.

After she was done hanging her things, she came and settled down in a chair, and he took the one facing her.

Her whole demeanor, as he explained the game to her, took him back to her scholarly intensity in high school.

Thank goodness.

The game, called Combustion, was a combination of luck and strategy. Her brilliance was quickly apparent in how fast she caught on to the strategy part of it.

The game was one of those back-and-forth ones, where it looked as if one person was going to win but then, just before that happened, the opposing player could send them back to the beginning to start all over again.

She was intensely competitive, and so was he.

She chortled gleefully when she "killed" him and he had to start over. She cried out with outrage when he did the same to her.

Seeing her childish delight in the game initially did exactly as Jay had hoped and reduced his awareness of the fact she was certainly not sixteen anymore and she was dressed only in a sheet.

But as time went on, he noticed her hair was drying, and as it dried, these crazy corkscrew curls leaped around her.

And she threw herself more enthusiastically into the game, the sheet proved flimsy, indeed. It kept slipping and moving and she was so engrossed in the game she didn't notice.

Either that or she was so diabolically invested in winning she was distracting him on purpose with her malfunctioning wardrobe.

He looked, hopefully, out the window. The rain sluiced down, unabated.

"I win!" Jolie cried.

He saw the pure happiness on her face. Maybe he wasn't so sorry the rain wasn't stopping, after all.

"Want to go again?" she asked.

Jolie won the game three times in a row. She eyed Jay with sudden suspicion.

"Are you letting me win?"

"I'm not that chivalrous."

But she suspected that he was, indeed, that chivalrous. Suddenly, she lost interest in the game. She was with the man she had wanted to be with since she was sixteen years old. There might never be another opportunity like this one in her entire life.

"Jay," she said, "I'm not a kid anymore."

"Thanks," he said dryly, "gleeful winning of games aside, the slipping sheet already let me know that."

She glanced down. She was showing quite a bit more than she thought she was. She was going to adjust the sheet, but then decided against it.

"We were playing for a kiss," she told him.

"No, we weren't!"

"Jay," she said, "I don't know how to be any more direct."

"Look," he said, "you're just breaking up with your fiancé, and our near miss on the water seems to have left you with an exaggerated sense of my heroism."

She actually laughed at that, and he looked annoyed.

"Who told you that you got to make all the rules?" she asked him quietly. "I know you're an old-fashioned guy who likes to hold open doors and all that, but I know what I want. I think I know what you want, too."

"I doubt that," he sputtered.

"Let's find out."

And then, before she lost her nerve, she got up from her place at the table, crossed over to him and wiggled her way onto his lap.

He could have gotten up. He could have pushed her away. But he didn't.

She twined her arms around his neck. The sheet slipped a little more.

He wasn't exactly participating, but he wasn't exactly withdrawing, either.

Experimentally, she touched the puffiest part of his bottom lip with her fingertip.

"If it's not what you want," she whispered, "tell me."

He didn't say a word.

So she leaned in yet closer and touched the place on his lip where her fingertip had been with the faintest flick of her tongue.

She stopped, looked at him. He returned her gaze. He still didn't say a word.

Then Jolie caressed his bottom lip with her top lip, nuzzling, a touch as light as a butterfly wing.

It wasn't like when she had kissed him for Anthony's benefit. It wasn't like that at all. It was more like her heart had waited for this moment all these years, and it sighed in recognition as she deepened the kiss.

Everything about her said, without having to say a single word, *I know you.*

His resistance collapsed when she scraped her lips lightly, back and forth, over his. With a groan of surrender, he caught her to him, bracketed her face with his hands and returned her kiss.

With hunger.

And passion.

With curiosity.

And satisfaction.

And ultimately, with certainty.

His hands moved to her hair, catching in it, stroking it, untangling it. Somehow the sheet slipped between them, and he was balancing her with one arm and tearing off his shirt with the other.

So that they could have this.

Full contact. Full sensation. Full awareness.

Heated skin on heated skin.

His eyes dark with need, his gaze swept her own, looking for permission, for affirmation. He found both, and his head dropped over her breast.

Thunder rolled outside, and the rain slashed the window. Lightning split the sky.

The power of the storm was nothing compared to what was unfolding between them.

CHAPTER FIFTEEN

WITHOUT MOVING JOLIE from his lap, Jay stood up. She managed to free her legs from the tangle of the sheet and tuck them around the hard strength of his hips.

She marveled at the ease with which he carried her. There was no pause in his lips laying claim to hers. He tasted her neck and ears and her cheeks as he carried her through to the bedroom, the sheet caught between them, and dragging on the floor.

He dropped her gently down onto the bed, pulled the tangle of the sheet completely away from her and paused for a moment, something like reverence darkening his eyes. They looked, suddenly, more black than green.

Then Jay dispensed with his jeans in a flash faster than lightning and came onto the bed. He was poised above her, holding his weight off of her with his elbows, anointing her with kisses and flicks of his tongue.

He was extra gentle with where her face was still splotched from the mask. Still, it felt as if he might be leaving marks of his own, as he trailed fire across her skin.

Jay was an exquisite lover. He was possessive and tender, but there was also no mistaking the leashed masculine strength in every touch of his hands and his lips. He seemed determined to leave no inch of her unexplored, her belly, her breasts, her neck, the bottoms of her feet.

Without saying a single word, his breath on her skin said

hello to each muscle, each limb, each eye, each toe. His lips welcomed her and celebrated this new way of knowing each other.

She could feel need building in her, screaming along her nerve endings, but he would not give in.

He tantalized.

He took her to the edge of desire, until she was nearly sobbing with wanting him, and then inched back, began the dance of knowing her all over again.

Only when both of them were quaking with need, slick with sweat, so desperate that it felt as if death were near, did he combine conquest and surrender.

With an exquisite mix that was part the fury of the storm, and part the tenderness of souls who had retreated from each other for far, far too long, they came together.

Jolie and Jay joined in that exquisite and ancient dance that the very universe felt as if it had been born out of. They came together and then fell apart.

Like a shooting star falls apart, a projectile penetrating a dark sky and then exploding, thousands of sparks of light falling, falling, falling back to Earth.

Winking out, one at a time.

"Jolie," he whispered her name against her throat, and then even softer, "Jolie."

Jay saying her name like that, as if it was a blessing, made her seduction of him feel so right.

Her boldness rewarded.

In those moments after, had Jay shown the slightest awkwardness, had there been even a moment's regret in his eyes, she might have questioned what had just happened between them, and how it had happened.

Her pushing against his reluctance.

But there was none of that.

Instead, he propped pillows up against the headboard,

pulled that sheet up around them, invited her into the circle of his arms.

They talked. They talked about his business, and about her work. They talked about life in Rome and life in Toronto. They talked about their families and shared memories from their childhoods, some funny, some poignant.

There was a sense that they could talk forever, never run out of things to say.

And then, as quickly as the storm had come up, it was gone. The sun came out and streamed across their bodies, made them freshly aware of each other. It felt as if it was her turn, this time, to explore and celebrate every single thing that made up Jay.

After, when she lamented the lack of running water in the cabin, he laughed, and gestured to the window. "Look at our bathtub."

So, wrapped in sheets they made their way down the rocky pathway to the water's edge.

He dropped his sheet first and dove cleanly into the water.

They played. They swam and splashed, and chased each other, until they were exhausted from both laughter and exertion.

Standing up to their waists in the water, Jay pulled her to him and cupped the cold, pure lake water in his hands, and poured it over her hair, worked it through with tender fingertips. And then he did the very same to the rest of her body, until she had never felt quite so clean in her entire life.

It was her turn, and he knelt in the water, so she could easily reach his hair.

But she had hardly begun when he leaped back to his feet.

"What?"

"I hear a motor. A boat is coming."

At first she didn't hear what he did, but then there was no mistaking it. Laughing like naughty children, they rewrapped themselves in sheets and scrambled up the trail to the cabin. She was glad they had retreated, because the boat pulled into their cove and cut the engine, drifting in toward where they had been playing naked moments before.

Both of them began pulling on the clothes that hung on the line, still faintly damp, terribly crusty and uncomfortable.

"Hell. It's Troy," Jay said. "He's probably coming to check on us."

He looked around and found his phone. He wagged it at her. "They've been texting for hours. This last one says he's coming in a boat. They'll bring us back."

She realized, stunned, that their moment was over as quickly as the storm.

"I'll go tell him we'll take the canoe back."

"Oh," she said, "I'm not sure I want to. Get back in the canoe."

"I think it's like falling off a horse, Jolie. You get right back on."

"There's only one paddle," she said, desperate to not get back in that tippy little vessel with all its potential for sudden death.

"I saw some under the cabin. We'll make sure we return everything we've borrowed."

"I'm scared," she said.

He laughed. He actually threw back his head and laughed. "No, you're not, Jolie. You're the boldest, bravest woman I've ever met."

It occurred to her you could become the things that someone else believed about you.

Maybe she had done that her whole life, but in the reverse of this. Becoming less than she was, instead of more.

"The thing about fear," Jay said softly, "is that once you've let it take hold, it doesn't want to let go. It takes on a life of its own. It grows and grows."

"Okay," she said, "go tell him we'll canoe back."

After he left, she contemplated the simple courage he was asking of her, that he saw in her, and that he was calling into existence.

This is what love did, then, it made you bigger, stronger, better than you had been before.

It didn't rip you to shreds one little nip at a time.

Love?

She wasn't in love with Jay just because she had slept with him. It would be unbelievably naive to think that.

He had made it clear from the beginning that he did not trust love.

Why would she? After seeing her parents? After catching a man she had trusted with her whole heart stepping out on her?

So she would not call it love.

And yet there was no denying the feeling in her heart—even if she left it unnamed—filled her with a deep sense of bliss.

Not quite like anything else she had ever known.

They did canoe back to the lodge. It was not easy getting back in the canoe. In fact, it was terrifying.

And yet, conquering that terror filled her with a sense of her own ability to overcome adversity.

She had Jay to thank for that. The best man pulling the very best from her.

They arrived at the resort to a hero's welcome. The entire bridal party were waiting for them on the shore.

After the stillness and solitude of the cabin, this was a bit of a shock, and not in a good way.

After the intensity of their togetherness, being pulled into the center of a crowd, with everyone asking questions, and doling out hugs and backslaps, Jolie yearned to get back in the canoe, paddle through the stillness of the lake, just *be* with him.

She caught Jay's eye.

He winked at her.

And she saw the bond between them survived.

"Anthony left," her sister told her, with barely a hello.

Jolie felt a certain indifference to whether Anthony had left or not. She and Jay's lovemaking felt as if it had put a shield around her that others—even her ex—could not get through.

Sabrina took her arms and guided her up toward the resort. "And Mom and Dad have arrived."

Jolie hesitated. "How are they?"

"So worried about you!"

"That's not what I meant."

"Oh. How *are* they? Like lovebirds. He's doting on her. I should know better, but I actually wonder if they've worked it out this time."

The names of these cabins. Heart's Refuge and Lovers' Retreat. Maybe this was a magical place.

Where Troy and Sabrina were going to get it right.

Where her mother and father were going to figure it all out, finally.

And where love had touched her.

There was that word again. But why not? It seemed as if it was in the air.

"They were so worried about you, Jolie. I have to take you to them right away. And then a dress arrived that I ordered online. You should try it."

Jolie pulled away from her sister's arm. Once, she might have liked this, being at the center instead of on the outside.

But she had been canoeing since her very sexy rinse in the lake, and there had been no soap or shampoo involved in that.

Plus, she needed to gather herself before a family reunion. "I have to have a shower and change clothes."

"Okay," Sabrina said, "but could you be quick about it? Oh, my gosh, Jolie, we only have one full day left before the wedding. It suddenly feels as if there's way too much to do and not enough time to do it."

Jolie wasn't sure about the way-too-much-to-do part, but it did feel, suddenly, as if there was not enough time.

"A quick shower," she promised her sister.

She went to her cabin, stripped off her clothes and got under the hot steamy jets, lifting her face to them. Her body felt delightfully different, as if she was aware of the sensuality of being alive in ways she had never been before. The steam, the hot water hitting her body, the way the pebbled shower tray felt on her feet all held sensations Jolie had not been aware of before.

Though her eyes were closed, the air changed ever so slightly, a breath of cold air touched her.

It was the shower curtain being pulled back.

She didn't have to open her eyes to know. Her heart recognized that his presence had its own feel to it.

Wordlessly, he got in behind her, nuzzled the silky wetness of her neck, before reaching past her for the soap. She realized, as much as she had been aware of sensation before Jay had gotten into the shower with her, it had not been sensual.

This was sensual. His hands, slippery with soap, exploring her entire body, mapping it, marking it, with soap and then with kisses when the soap was rinsed free.

He replaced the soap, and reached by her, this time for the shampoo. He added some to his cupped palm, and then worked it into her hair, his fingertips strong, sure, familiar.

Still, without a word, when the shampoo had rinsed free, and he had wrung her hair out between his hands, and finger-combed the tangles, he lifted her into his arms and put her wet body on the bed.

Wet bodies, it turned out, were twice as erotic as dry bodies.

"Now I have to shower again," she told him, pretending to complain after, gazing up at him, her palm grazing his chin.

He nipped her fingers. "I know," he said. "Isn't that great? It's your turn."

And so she had her turn, soaping him, getting to know every inch of his beautiful body, her hands sliding over hard and soft surfaces, in and out of his ears, the dip at his collarbone, his belly button.

It was shockingly exciting even before the real shock of the water running cold before she was finished. Jay shoved her gently out of the cold spray, finished washing off the soap himself and then came out and they dried each other off.

And that was how the rest of the day, and the hours before the wedding the next day, unfolded.

On the surface, Jolie sailed through her bridesmaid's duties. She met with her parents, and tried on the new dress, which was neither as ugly as the first one, nor as sexy as the second one. It was a nice bland dress that could not dampen down the feeling she carried inside her.

That she had a secret.

The secret was that she was not bland.

The secret was that she was a heated lover.

Jolie and Jay stole kisses behind the arbor they had been assigned to sew flowers onto. He was waiting for her along the pathway to the lodge for the rehearsal dinner, pulled her into the trees with him and covered her with kisses.

And then they sat, one of them on one side of the groom, and one on the other side of the bride, not making eye contact, nursing their secret.

She suspected everyone had assumed their relationship was fake, designed to dissuade Anthony.

Now that nothing about what they were doing together felt fake—it felt, in fact, like the realest thing that had ever happened to her—Jolie had a desire to keep it under wraps.

To not indulge in public shows of affection, to not exchange endearments, to not convince anyone anything was going on.

Ironically, it was the reverse of what she had wanted when she had first asked Jay to pretend he was her fiancé.

Impossibly, that was only a few days ago. The changes between them made it feel as if that arrangement had happened in a separate lifetime.

What was really going on now was so new it felt fragile, like it could be easily broken by a wrong move.

She did not want it scrutinized by her sister's cynical friends.

She did not want them weighing in behind her back on the way she and Jay looked at each other and touched each other and listened to each other.

What had started out as so public now felt intensely private.

You did not put the sacred on display.

CHAPTER SIXTEEN

JOLIE DID NOT consider herself a wedding person. She had not even really felt as if she was one when she had been planning her own wedding to Anthony.

Despite her enjoyment of the gown she had chosen, planning her own wedding had felt like a duty rather than a joy, something she had to get through in order to get to the next stage of her adult life, which was supposed to have been marriage.

Most of the weddings she had been to just seemed way too much like a stage set, too much about the wedding and not enough about the marriage.

There always seemed to be quite a bit of behind-the-scenes drama with a major wedding event.

Her sister's wedding, with that initial hysteria over the dresses, had held every promise of being the same.

A hysterical bride demanding perfection from an imperfect world.

And yet, as Saturday unfolded, it was so evident her sister's wedding had been pulled back from that bad start.

Jolie gave most of the credit for this to her soon-to-be brother-in-law-for-the-second-time. Troy was just one of those decent, down-to-earth guys. He indulged a certain amount of Sabrina's histrionics, but also wasn't scared to let her know when he'd had enough, or she was going over the top.

Jolie could understand, when she saw Troy and Jay together, why they were such good friends.

They were a type.

Strong.

Reliable.

Hardworking.

And underneath all that—or maybe even because of all that—was a kind of hum of understated sexiness.

But she did have to give some credit to Sabrina as well. The destination wedding had been a good idea. The Hidden Valley setting seemed to invoke calm. The team building exercise with the horses seemed to have succeeded in deepening the relationships of everyone involved.

And though she and Jay had not been part of the team, the canoeing expedition gone so wrong had brought them into the fold and seemed to have strengthened ties within the party.

Everybody seemed aware that it could have been a much different day today if Jolie and Jay had not got off the lake.

Her parents were on their best behavior. She'd had a chance to talk to her father, and he had told her he was a new man because of a twelve-step program he'd found that dealt with sex addiction.

She hadn't really known much about it, and certainly didn't want to know that about her father. Addicted to sex? Yuck!

But, on the other hand, now that she'd had several encounters of the intimate kind with Jay, she could understand why it could be addictive. Maybe she even had to watch out for that particular weakness in herself!

She didn't really want any of the details of her father's transgressions, and he thankfully did not volunteer them.

Instead, for the first time she could ever remember, he

took responsibility for the pain he had brought to the family dynamic.

"I know I caused you all a great deal of suffering. I know I'm the reason you live in Italy," he said contritely, "as far from the chaos as you can get."

"You know, Dad, that might have been my original motivation in going there, but I genuinely love it now. I love my job. I have a sense of purpose and community. Maybe instead of seeing it as you driving me there to get away from you, you could see it as it driving me there to where I was always meant to be. Don't you think life has a way of taking us where we're meant to be?"

Would she have believed that quite so completely before her reunion with Jay?

"Ah, Jolie, always my favorite," he said in Italian.

"Don't tell Sabrina," she whispered.

"That's why I said it in Italian."

They laughed together.

"I like your new beau," he said. "I was never that taken with Anthony."

"You never said anything!"

"I felt I lost my right to comment on such things when I had hardly set an example myself."

"What things?"

"You know. His wandering eye."

"You *knew* that?"

"I only met him once. That time I came to visit you in Rome. I just noticed he always seemed to be searching beyond you."

"Why didn't you say something?"

"I didn't know how. But I like the new beau."

She blushed. "*Beau* might be a little too strong."

"Not the way he's looking at you. Now, there's a man who has eyes for only one woman."

"Don't keep talking about him as if he's a stranger. It's Jay Fletcher, from high school."

Her father looked at her quizzically. "A little more than that, wouldn't you say?"

"You mean his sporting goods company?"

His father gave her another look. "Yes," he said, "that's what I mean."

The day that unfolded just had such a nice feeling. Everyone was relaxed and getting along.

Even Jack and Jill and Beth seemed to have left their hard edges behind them. They actually said really nice things about her hair and makeup and the new dress as they all helped each other, and Sabrina, get ready for the wedding.

It felt to Jolie as if she had finally been accepted—possibly by virtue of the fact they had contemplated losing both her and Jay to that storm.

There was a bit of anxiety when the much-anticipated Chantelle was late, but she finally arrived, breathless, saying she had taken a wrong turn out of Penticton. Jolie was not sure what she had been expecting, but the famous Chantelle was tiny, dwarfed by the multitude of cameras she carried. She was wearing a somewhat dressy form of army fatigues, and peered at them all through huge glasses with colorful frames.

She managed to get a few shots of them getting ready.

"Pretend I'm not here," she said with stern annoyance to Jack and Jill when they started posing for her.

And then it was time.

To the strains of the very traditional "Wedding March" by Felix Mendelssohn, the bridesmaids exited the main lodge, one at a time, slow stepping across the lawns to where the seating and an arbor had been set up by the shores of the lake.

The lake was placid today, mirrorlike, reflecting the vineyards and orchards and the spectacular houses and humble cottages that surrounded it.

The bridesmaids moved down the outdoor aisle, past the guests, the women in their beautiful summer dresses and sandals and hats, the men in light trousers and button-up sports shirts.

The groom and his groomsmen were waiting on a slightly raised dais under the arbor. Jolie only allowed herself to look at Jay briefly.

The groomsmen were beautifully dressed, in gray slacks, crisp white shirts, suspenders and bow ties.

Everything that Jay and Jolie were to each other was reflected in the deep way that he returned her brief look, the upward quirk of that mouth she had tasted over and over again, so intimately.

He gestured subtly to her dress and shook his head, *not you.*

She did the same thing for his bow tie. Even with all these people watching and a wedding about to get under way, she was aware of how the two of them could close out the world.

She reminded herself it was her sister's day, and the looks and wordless communication she and Jay were exchanging felt as if they could steal the very sun out of the sky.

She turned her attention to Sabrina, who was coming down the grassy aisle now, one arm in her mother's and one in her father's.

Jolie realized she needn't have worried about her and Jay stealing the sun. Not today. Her sister was absolutely radiant in a summer gown, constructed of white lace and smoke and magic.

She had eyes for no one but Troy.

When Jolie glanced at Troy, she saw him—that powerful down-to-earth guy—brush a tear from his eye.

And somehow she just knew it was going to be okay this time.

Her mother and father each kissed Sabrina on a cheek and clasped hands, glanced at each other and went to their seats.

It felt as if maybe they were going to be okay, too.

In fact, here at her sister's beautiful summer wedding, with the sun shining and the birds singing, with love sparkling in the air, Jolie felt something she had rarely allowed herself to feel.

As if everything was going to be okay.

The ceremony, and the signing of the register, and the bride and groom's first kiss—extended version—proved her right. Everything went off seamlessly and she felt herself surrendering to the pure fun of the day.

Chantelle was nothing short of amazing. A few days ago, Jolie might have felt awkward posing, especially for some of the more artsy shots, but she just brought that new bolder her to it all. She noticed Jay, too, had given himself over to the day.

Making other people happy, she decided, looking at her glowing sister, was a good way to make yourself happy.

It was something that she didn't think Jack and Jill would ever learn. Instead of making the photo sensation about the bride, they vied shamelessly for Chantelle's attention.

"I think we've got a lot of good photos," Chantelle finally said, clicking through the display screen on her camera.

"If you ever want to do some modeling work," she said, and Jack and Jill nearly fell over themselves to get the card she was holding out. But she ignored them, marched passed them and handed the card to the astonished Jolie.

"Look at this photo," she said, showing it to Jolie.

Jolie looked at the woman in the photo Chantelle was showing her and almost didn't recognize herself. The woman in the photo was laughing, carefree, confident.

Jolie realized it wasn't her, so much that Chantelle had

recognized as the light that was shining from her. A woman who had come into herself, completely and passionately.

She was aware of Jack and Jill also pressed close, both looking at the photo.

"I could get you a job in the industry—" Chantelle snapped her fingers "—like that."

"What industry?" Jolie asked, baffled.

"Ad campaigns, sports magazines, runway work."

"I can't even imagine," Jolie said, diplomatic enough not to finish with, *a life that shallow and dull.*

"Oh, for heaven's sake," Jill said, clearly peeved, "she's a doctor, not a model."

"A doctor," Chantelle breathed. "That explains it. The depth in your eyes. The intelligence in your face. I think the days of the too-thin vapid blonde are done in the industry, and good riddance."

Jack gasped as though she'd been stabbed.

Jolie became aware of Jay standing with them, looking down at the photo that Chantelle was showing. She glanced up at him.

A tiny, knowing smile was tickling the gorgeous line of his lips.

"I saw you first," he murmured in her ear.

It was so true. He had *seen* her first. He had drawn to the surface every single thing that Chantelle had caught with this photo. He had made her alive, and that life force shimmered in her, in a way the camera had captured.

After photos, there was a cocktail hour on the very deck where she had first sat, enveloped in that horrid dress.

She remembered that she had imagined just this: people going in and out the doors, laughter, glasses clinking.

She and Jay finally dared to stand side by side, unnoticed in all the activity.

"As far as weddings go," Jolie told him, and could hear the contentment in her own voice, "this one has been pretty peachy." He handed her a glass of wine.

"To peaches," he said and they tapped glasses. "I actually had this idea about peaches," he said. He lowered his voice to a growl, and spoke the words into her ear only.

She reared back from him, trying not to choke on wine.

He smiled wickedly, and raised an eyebrow at her.

"Jay, I'm leaving tomorrow," she said.

"What? Why didn't you mention that before?"

"I don't know. It just never came up." Their moments had engrossed her so completely that she had not looked toward that thing that never worked out for her, anyway.

The future.

"Aren't you?" she asked him, "Leaving tomorrow?"

"That was my original plan, but I seem to have taken a detour. I could be a little flexible," he said. "Can you?"

"Maybe a teensy bit."

"I'm not ready to let you go." This was growled in her ear, the same way as his naughty suggestion with the peaches had been.

That declaration and the wedding behind them suddenly made it feel okay to be publicly a couple for the first time since Anthony had left.

His hand found hers. He led her to the deck railing, and put his arm around her. She leaned her head on his shoulder as the sun went down.

The wedding feast had been set up in that grand ballroom. Jolie and Jay had not been seated together. Jay was on the groom's side of the table, she was beside Sabrina, but even so, dinner was fabulous, as were the speeches and toasts. She and Jay came together again when the dancing began.

Finally, it felt okay to be them.

It was dark now. The tables were removed from the ballroom and the doors were thrown open between the outdoor space and the indoor one, making a huge dance floor. Thousands of fairy lights illuminated both spaces.

Sabrina danced with Troy. And then they broke away from each other, and she danced with Dad and he danced with their mom.

The formalities of the order of who everyone was supposed to be dancing with seemed to Jolie to go on endlessly.

But finally, Jolie and Jay were together, dancing for the first time since the senior prom night when she had propositioned him.

She realized she was so thankful he'd said no that night. She had not been ready. And it was possible it would have ruined *this*.

Had he said yes it was quite possible what would have happened between them would have overshadowed everything, forever. Because the things he had said to her that night were right.

She had been too young.

She had not been ready.

She had been about to get herself into trouble.

Yes might have felt good at the time, but so, so bad later. He'd only been eighteen. How had he known?

Or had he been guided by a force larger than himself? That let him know taking that opportunity that night might remove the opportunity for a future one.

It was partly because of that long-ago no, that when they danced together, his presence invited her to be herself.

That had never been an easy thing for her.

Letting go.

CHAPTER SEVENTEEN

No, LETTING GO had never come easily to Jolie. And yet right now, dancing with Jay, it felt as if it was the easiest thing in the world.

She was not sure she had felt this good since she was sixteen, drunk on a punch she had been unaware was spiked.

She'd had very little to drink tonight, but she felt intoxicated, nonetheless.

They danced until they were breathless. They danced as if there was no one else on that deck that was canopied with stars. They danced in celebration of all the ways they had come to know each other.

When their feet started to hurt, they kicked off their shoes and danced some more.

He drew from Jolie her confidence.

Her sexiness.

Her certainty in herself as a woman that she had never felt with anyone but him. Even when she was sixteen.

She never wanted this magical evening to end.

But then Jay was called away by Troy for something, he kissed Jolie regretfully and departed. Breathless, she left the deck, and stood there in the darkness drinking in the stars.

"Hey, sis."

"You startled me," Jolie said, seeing Sabrina standing there, with a wineglass in her hand, almost hidden by shrubs. "What are you doing?"

"Oh, just having a moment."

"The stars are gorgeous tonight."

"What is going on between you and Jay?" Sabrina asked. "We could both be brides! You're radiant. Chantelle certainly saw it. Those photos are probably going to be all about you."

It was said without any kind of edge at all. Completely gone was the woman who had told her there was only to be one star of this show.

Jolie lifted a shoulder, not wanting to get into it right now.

The silence was comfortable between them for a few moments, and then Sabrina broke it.

"I'm sorry. About the first night. Making such a fuss over the dress."

"It doesn't matter now. It all worked out. This one is great."

"I've been a bit temperamental lately."

"It's a big event to plan," Jolie said.

"That's not it. Nobody knows this yet, but I'm pregnant."

Jolie felt the shock of that announcement ripple through her. She glanced at the glass in her sister's hand.

"It's sparkling juice," Sabrina said.

So that first night, the juice had been for Sabrina, not her. How often, Jolie wondered, had she been overly sensitive and made it about herself when it wasn't?

"Does Troy know?"

"Of course Troy knows," Sabrina said, insulted.

"It's just that you said nobody—"

"Oh! Do you always have to be so literal?"

Her sister loved to use the expression *literally.* This was the first time in Jolie's memory she'd actually used it correctly.

"Couldn't you just say you're happy for us?" her sister snapped. Apparently, their truce was over, because Sabrina gathered up her dress and lifted her chin. "It's half an hour from midnight. Could you go to the kitchen and check that the midnight snack is on time?"

Then she marched away with her nose in the air.

Jolie realized she still hadn't congratulated her sister. It just seemed there were too many questions, and that it might not be appropriate to ask them under their current circumstances.

For instance, was it an accident? Because Sabrina had told her Troy didn't want to have a baby.

Had her sister planned it? Like a trap? Is that why she was so defensive?

If it was true, if Sabrina had trapped Troy into this second marriage, wasn't it just a variation on the theme from their childhood?

A way of begging someone to love you?

The magic seemed to be draining from the evening as Jolie made her way to the kitchen as her sister had asked.

Her sister was pregnant.

And then another thought followed on the heels of that one.

What if *she* was pregnant? She'd stopped using birth control when she and Anthony had split. Swearing off men had meant her chances of a pregnancy were zero, after all.

She'd been so swept away by Jay that she hadn't even considered that.

No, that wasn't quite true. She'd swept Jay away, not the other way around. It was so unlike her not to think things all the way through. All right, Jay also seemed to have been swept away, not asking any of the usual questions, but ultimately the responsibility felt as if it was hers.

Certainly, protecting oneself from pregnancy would be part of that equation.

Who was she to sit in judgment of her sister?

She looked at her watch. It was, as her sister had pointed

out, nearly midnight. It seemed impossible that time had gone so fast. The evening—the whole day, really—had evaporated.

But she could feel something shifting. Reality poking at the edges of her consciousness.

Wasn't this where the fairy tale ended? Where Cinderella's bubble burst? When she lost her glass slipper, the mice turned into coachmen and the coach turned into a pumpkin? She went back to her old life of being the family scapegoat?

Now, where had that thought come from, like a cloud drifting across a perfect day?

She found the long dark hallway that led to the kitchen. There was a little alcove off of it, and smoke drifted out.

And then a familiar laugh.

Jack and Jill.

Still sneaking cigarettes, as if they were teenagers hiding behind the bus garage at the high school.

Jolie went to move by the alcove when Jill's voice stopped her.

"Omg, what do you think of Jay and Jolie together?"

"Obviously, they were just pretending for Anthony."

"Well, he's gone, and they're still together."

"Are they together, or she can't let go of the pretense, and she's throwing herself at him?"

"I think Chantelle gushing over her gave her a swollen head."

"I bet she asked her to say those things. To play a little prank on us."

"Or maybe Jay did! He's been quite defensive of her from day one. He seems to want to play white knight for her."

Triumphant snickers.

Maybe slightly drunken snickers, which didn't make it any less hurtful.

"No matter what the stupid photographer said, she's punching above her weight, that's for sure."

What did that mean?

"I mean she's not the little wallflower she once was, but I don't think being a doctor and living in Italy makes her Jay Fletcher material. I mean even if one photo did give Chantelle pause, Jay is one of the richest men in the world. I heard he has a private jet waiting for him in Kelowna."

"He dated Sophia Binal for a while."

"The singer? He did not!"

"He did. I'll show you on my phone."

"Wow," Jack said a moment later.

Jay was one of the richest men in the world? What? He'd dated one of the most famous and beautiful women in the world?

She remembered her father looking at her oddly when she said Jay had a sporting goods company.

She remembered him paying for that dress as if it was nothing.

Because to him, had it been nothing?

Jolie turned hastily, determined to find a different way to the kitchen to order the evening snack.

But when she passed the bathroom where she had first tried on that peach monstrosity, she couldn't resist ducking in. It was empty, but for further privacy, she found a stall and locked the door.

She did what she had not allowed herself to do in the ten years since she had left Canada. She used her phone and she looked up Jay Fletcher on the internet.

Jay was rich, all right.

He was billionaire rich.

And Sophie Binal wasn't the only spectacularly rich and famous woman he'd had on his arm in the past ten years, either.

While she was there looking things up, she searched what *punching above your weight* meant. It might have been common in Canada, but she didn't recall ever hearing it in Italy. It was a boxing term. It meant you had entered the wrong category and were probably about to get smashed to bits by a superior opponent.

Jack and Jill had obviously meant she didn't have a hope.

Jolie got up, put away her phone and tried to compose herself.

In the kitchen, she asked for the snack, just as Sabrina had requested. When she came back out, the alcove was empty, and she sat down on an upholstered bench, even if it did smell of smoke in there.

Oddly, she did not feel diminished by the remarks she had overheard.

Jack and Jill were simply horrible people. Their opinions meant nothing to her.

She felt as if the few days of being Jay's lover had given her the truest sense of who she really was that she had ever experienced.

And so, while not diminished, Jolie still felt a need to be analytical.

It was time to put emotion—that most unreliable of forces—aside and allow herself to be guided by the facts. Which were: She had been the aggressor. She had seduced Jay.

There was new evidence that sexual addiction ran in the family. Maybe she was in the first stages of that.

She was on the rebound, as Jay had pointed out when he had tried to resist her efforts.

She had been filled with survivor's euphoria when she had made her move.

She had been bonded to the man she perceived as saving her life.

She had not taken proper precautions and there was a remote possibility of pregnancy.

And lastly, though Jay had had many opportunities, he had never revealed the full truth about himself to her.

He was the kind of man women deliberately tried to trap.

Which brought up Sabrina's news.

It all felt like too much. Sabrina's surprise pregnancy, her mother and father's reconciliation, Jolie's awareness of family patterns.

Where did her new love affair fit into all of this?

Jolie suddenly *needed* to be home. Italy was home, and there was a reason for that. It was far away from all this chaos and emotion and family drama.

She needed to ground herself, to be surrounded by her things, her books and her flowers, her cozy tiny apartment, her fulfilling, satisfying work.

She needed to be away from Jay—how could she ever think straight around him?—in order to analyze this situation correctly.

Maybe she was addicted to him, already. Because she knew if she went back out onto that deck and danced with him one more time, she would be completely under the powerful sway of the forces between them.

She would never be able to draw a logical conclusion.

Just as she had that final thought, the clock struck twelve.

It was a confirmation to her that all fairy tales come to an end. It was good to leave fantasies on a high note, before the reality set in.

Part of her insisted on pointing out the clock striking midnight was not the end of the fairy tale. There was still the part about the prince finding the glass slipper, tracking down Cinderella, making his declaration of love.

Jolie sighed.

Wasn't that what she really wanted? To know what had

transpired between her and Jay hadn't been just because she'd seduced him?

Was she hoping, like in the fairy tale, he would come find her?

Of course she was! But that was a terrible, terrible weakness, to want such a thing, to believe in such a thing.

And what if she *was* pregnant? Then what?

Jolie went back to her cabin. She was not sure why she felt like a thief in the night as she quickly changed her clothes, packed up her few things, and bolted for the parking lot and her rented car.

And she was not sure why, if this was such an analytical decision, she kept having to wipe tears out of her eyes to see the dark road in front of her.

CHAPTER EIGHTEEN

"Where's Jolie?" Jay asked Sabrina.

"I'm not sure."

Did the bride seem faintly miffed about something?

"I asked her to go organize the midnight snack, but it's here now, and she's not."

Jay frowned and scanned the gathering. The dancing had ended when the clock struck midnight, and the snack had been put out. People were milling around, eating and talking. No one seemed to want to leave. It really had been a perfect day.

And yet, when the clock had struck midnight, he'd had a funny sense shiver along his spine.

The perfect day was over.

On an impulse, he checked his phone. He stared at it, not sure he was believing what he saw.

There was a text there from Jolie. It was not even to him, personally. It was a group text, to her sister and her mom and dad and him. It thanked the bride and groom for the most perfect day ever. It said she'd had an emergency at work, and when she checked flights she'd found one that could get her back to Italy immediately.

I'll catch up with everyone later!

Breezy. Casual.

It didn't even mention him by name.

Jay felt as if he had been punched in the gut, as if the bottom was falling out of his world. Here it was, right on schedule, the sword hidden under the cloak of love.

Not that he loved her.

You didn't love a person because you'd become lovers for two days.

On the other hand, he and Jolie's history stretched back a lot longer than two days. On the other hand, he was not sure he had ever felt quite what he had felt in Jolie's arms.

Or when he was with her, setting aside the lover part.

She had a way of making him feel alive, engaged, challenged. She had a way of making life feel surprising and fun.

It hadn't felt like that for a long time, not since his father had died.

So here was the thing he needed to be grateful for: the potential for love had been there. And its forces were so powerful, so all-consuming, a man could forget the lessons love had already taught him.

Jolie had done him a big favor by pulling back.

Even the abruptness—no goodbye, a text, for God's sake—was a favor. It quashed that very real temptation to go after her, to try and catch her before she boarded that plane.

But no, now Jay could be mad, instead of sad.

Sometimes it felt as if his anger was the only thing that helped him make it through the weeks ahead, as the hot summer gave way to the cooler days of September.

"Jay!" his sister, Kelly, said. "What is wrong with you? You're acting like a bear with a sore bottom."

They had met at her favorite deli, and picked up lunch.

Unfortunately, a guy had been standing outside with a guitar and an open case. His singing—if it could be called that—had reminded Jay of Anthony outside Jolie's cabin that night.

He'd thrown five bucks inside the guitar case, but suggested the troubadour might want to think about a different career path.

Was that acting like a bear with a sore bottom?

"I did the guy a favor," he told his sister. "Like Simon on that show."

"Exactly like him!" Kelly said, triumphantly. "Grumpy old men."

He could protest that he wasn't that old, but he didn't have the energy. In fact, in the last while, since the wedding, he did feel old. Disillusioned. Okay, grumpy.

They were walking together through the old neighborhood, their deli purchases in a paper bag, bringing them to share it with their mom at their old house.

They walked by the high school, and Jay had had a sharp memory of Jolie.

His life seemed to be filled with sharp—and unwanted—memories of her.

He thought, about a thousand times a day, of sending her a quick text. Casual. *How you doing? I'm sorry we didn't have a chance to say goodbye.*

But then all that anger at her leaving like that just resurfaced.

He was pretty sure *bear with a sore bottom* didn't say the half of it. Neither did *grumpy old men.*

"Is that how you treat your clients?" Jay said, determined to deflect his sister, and remove his attention from the high school in a deft two-birds-with-one-stone conversational maneuver. "Is *what is wrong with you* your lead question? I think that's what they're paying you to find out.

"I don't treat family members like clients."

"Well, they can be thankful for that. Would *bear with a*

sore bottom be like an official diagnosis? Or *grumpy old men*? From *The Diagnostic and Statistical Manual of Mental Disorders*? I remember the name of the book, because I paid for it."

There. A not-so-subtle reminder that a little gratitude might be more appreciated than *this*.

"I would never diagnose a family member," Kelly said with a sniff.

"It seems to me you've called me both a workaholic and commitment-phobe."

"Those aren't diagnoses! Observations."

Kelly had invited him for lunch with their mom. He'd talked to his mom on the phone a couple of times since the wedding, and taken her out for lunch once, but hadn't been over to their old house.

The house—a museum to how things used to be—was depressing.

"If I didn't know you better, I'd say you're having problems with love."

He snorted derisively. "You know my feelings about love."

"Yes, I do. And that belief system could cause you real difficulties if you found someone you cared about."

Ha ha, little Miss Know-It-All, as it turns out, I wasn't the problem.

"You're wrong, you know," Kelly said softly. "About love. Mom wasn't destroyed by the loss of her great love."

"Oh, geez, a lecture from the twenty-four-year-old expert on all things."

"It's because she was so codependent that she can't recover."

He swore under his breath. "I thought you didn't diagnose family members."

"Do you know what codependency is?" his sister asked.

"Vaguely. The more apt question would have been, do I want to know what it is. To which the answer is—"

His sister cut him off, undeterred. "It's putting everyone else's needs ahead of your own all the time. It's knowing what they need, but not what you need. It's knowing what they like, but not what you like."

Jay remembered telling Jolie about his mom planning those game nights. She would start on Monday planning an event for Friday.

As if her whole life revolved around that.

"She just wanted to make us happy," he told his sister.

"Yes, but then Dad died, and we grew up, and she doesn't have a clue how to make herself happy. She used to paint. Did you know that?"

"No." He felt suddenly guilty at how little he knew about the mother who had known absolutely everything about him.

"I've signed her up for some painting lessons. I'm going to tell her over lunch. I want you to back me up."

"Okay," he said, "I will."

"I wish you would remember that when you're convincing yourself about the failure of love," Kelly said softly.

"What?"

"That we had each other's backs. You and me and Mike and Jim. Look at how you stepped up for us, Jay, after Dad died. You took on all kinds of stuff that a young guy probably really wasn't equipped to deal with. But you did deal with it. You made whatever sacrifices you had to make, you did whatever it took to make sure we had education and opportunities, and most importantly, with Mom falling apart, stability. If that isn't love, I don't know what is. You showed us how to step up for each other."

He wondered about his level of self-involvement that he hadn't made note of this before. Yes, initially, he had been the one to shoulder the responsibility when his dad died.

But now his siblings stepped up for him. Consistently. Unquestioningly.

Kelly insisted on coffee or dinner with him at least once a week. His brothers were always coming up with tickets for guy activities. They all texted back and forth. It was now his siblings that arranged family activities that included his mom.

As well as his family, hadn't his friend Troy always been there for him, too? Quietly in the background, saying without ever needing to say the words, *I got your back, bro.*

The faint animosity he'd been feeling toward Kelly evaporated. It didn't have anything to do with her, anyway.

He put his arm around her shoulder and kissed the top of her head.

"You're a good person," he said, and she beamed at him.

They came around the corner, their old family home now in sight, across the street and two doors down. Both of them stopped in their tracks.

There was a landscaping truck out front. The neglected flower bed, the one between the house and the sidewalk that Jolie had remembered, was all torn up.

The weeds were out of it, and it was filled with mounds of fresh, deep dark loam. His mother was outside, in her nightgown. She rarely got dressed anymore. She was walking up and down, shaking her head in disbelief. A landscaper was on his knees, tucking plant after plant into that rich, new soil.

Even though he was no expert on flowers, he knew exactly what they were. Marigolds.

"Did you do this?" he asked Kelly. Had it been part of her plan to bring their mom back to life? Acting out of the love that he had been so certain had failed their family?

But she shook her head. "I was about to ask you the same thing."

Of course she hadn't done it. How would she know about

the marigolds? They crossed the street together. Their mom saw them coming, and gestured them over.

"Did you two do this?"

They both shook their heads.

"It must have been Mike and Jim," she said.

Since Mike and Jim had the combined sensitivity of a rock, Jay doubted that. Very much. Also, there was the question of the marigolds.

"It's a miracle," his mom whispered.

'It's just flowers," he told her gruffly.

"No, no, it isn't. I asked for a sign this morning."

Oh, geez. Signs and portents. Well, if they gave hope did it matter what his mom wanted to believe?

Still, he asked her. "A sign of what?"

"That life could be good again. Even without your father." She looked at him, both guilty for entertaining such a thought, and hopeful.

CHAPTER NINETEEN

"OF COURSE LIFE is going to be good again," Jay told her. When had he started believing that, particularly in the face of his current misery over Jolie's abandonment?

He put his arm around his mother's thin shoulder and kissed her head, just as he had done with his sister a few minutes ago.

"Years ago, your father brought me a marigold that he'd rescued from somewhere. Sickly thing. I planted it and it seeded itself. This whole front garden ended up having marigolds in it."

"I remember."

"Do you?" she said, surprised.

Actually, he was not sure he had given it a thought until Jolie brought it up.

"That year I had done geraniums," his mother said, softly. "Red, white, red, white, it was all very orderly. I thought of it as my Canadian theme. That marigold did not go at all."

"Why'd you plant it, then?"

"To make him happy," his mother admitted. "The funny thing is, it ended up making me happy, too."

Oh, this complicated, twisted, wonderful thing called family. You couldn't really capture the dynamics of all the different kinds of love—healthy and unhealthy—with labels.

He moved away from his mother and his sister.

"Hey," he said to the landscaper, who set down an armful of the bedding plants and turned to look at him. "What are you doing?"

"Planting," he said, annoyed at being interrupted to state the obvious.

"It's just that this is my mother's house, and she didn't order any flowers. My sister and I didn't, either."

The landscaper became more garrulous. "Wrong time of year, really, and hard to find marigolds that are perennials, but if the price is right miracles can be accomplished."

Miracles.

Jay looked over at his mom. "Who ordered the work?" he asked, as if he didn't know.

"Uh, I can't say. It's confidential."

Jay could say, of course, that his mother was the home-owner, and she hadn't ordered the work and had a right to know who did, but that seemed unnecessarily querulous. And might not get him to where he needed to be.

Since the man had already let it be known miracles could be accomplished for the right price, Jay took his wallet out of his pocket and practiced his superpower with two bright red Canadian fifty-dollar bills.

The guy glanced at them, took them without hesitation, and then slid them into his pocket.

"Some doctor in Italy. Weird, eh?" And then he turned back to his work.

Jay stood there, stock-still, for a moment.

Even though he'd known, it hit him hard that Jolie was thinking of him, too.

Not him, precisely, but the thing in his life that was causing him pain, how his family dynamic had changed since the death of his father. Perhaps she, like his sister, saw that as holding him back.

From love.

Did she want him to overcome that obstacle? Is that what this gift of the garden for his mom meant?

Was it a hint?

Not exactly. He saw, suddenly, precisely what it was. It was an invitation. Not just to participate in something that had been dropped in his lap, like their accidental engagement.

But to make a choice for himself.

Choosing it was momentous.

Jolie had to know that.

But what she couldn't have known, was that her gift to his family had arrived on the same day that his mother was pleading for a sign.

That it was okay to go on living.

That life would be good again.

It struck him that he was in the middle of an energetic force that was all intertwined, and that logic could never explain. He was right in the middle of the incredible mystery that was the interconnectedness of life.

What hope did he, a mere mortal, have of fighting such a force? Even if he wanted to?

Which he didn't.

"Hey," he said to the landscaper. "Can I get an address for the doctor in Italy?"

"Oh—" the landscaper looked suddenly shifty "—that's not really my department."

But it turned out, for a price, it could be.

Jolie sat on her terrace and breathed in deeply. She had changed clothes after work, into the slip dress from the wedding. It had turned out it may not have been the perfect bridesmaid dress, but it was the perfect loungewear for hot Italian evenings, particularly now since she had removed the stitched-in second slip.

She loved evenings. Her view and this terrace made up for the tininess of her apartment.

It was breathtaking, looking over the clay-tiled rooves of Rome to the Vatican in the distance. The setting sun was painting the roof of the Basilica of Saint Peter in shades of gold.

She was appreciative of the fact she could once again end her days with a glass of wine, since she was definitely not pregnant.

She took a sip of the wine, and watched a butterfly toy with the edges of the bright begonias that spilled out of her window boxes. She felt, astonishingly, as if she could hear the air under its wings.

She'd had this amazing feeling since returning from Canada.

Not of being diminished by her time with Jay.

But rather, made alive by it, as if his kisses trailing fire down her heated skin had called sleeping senses to life. She saw things differently and deeply, she heard sounds she had never heard before, the scent of a single flower could captivate her whole body.

As she watched the butterfly, a crisp knock came on her door. It was too hot to cook, so she had ordered dinner from her favorite trattoria around the corner. It was already paid for by credit card. The delivery service could leave it, so she didn't miss the setting of the sun.

The knock came again.

Firmer.

At least she was one hundred percent certain it wasn't Anthony. He had contacted her, via new phone number since his old one was blocked, shortly after her return to announce, a trifle smugly, that he'd moved on.

There'd been a picture attached to the text.

Jolie was pretty sure that it was the same woman she'd seen him sharing *their* spaghetti and meatballs ice cream with.

Anthony asked after her engagement, but she hadn't answered, just blocked his new number. There had been no sense of vindication in blocking that number, just a sense of a clean cut, a chapter closed.

The knocking came again, even firmer, and with a resigned sigh she set down her wineglass and pushed back her chair. The woman she'd been a week ago probably would have gone and put a light wrap over her practically transparent dress, but the new her did not care what people thought.

If they thought she was sexy, good. Her time with Jay had taught her that. She *was* sexy. She liked being sexy. It was part of embracing being a woman to acknowledge that about yourself.

She went through her tiny apartment to the door. Her building was three hundred years old, well before peepholes in doors had been a thing.

Not worried it would be Anthony and expecting a question about her credit card, she pulled it open.

Nothing could have prepared her for the shock of Jay standing there.

Her newly attuned senses were flooded. Even though he must have been traveling, he smelled wonderful.

Of course, private jets would do that, keep the travails of travel to a minimum, she told herself, trying to keep some semblance of a barrier in place.

He was dressed in a casual suit, which also was not travel rumpled. She'd never seen him in a suit before. It was beautifully cut to skim his sleek masculinity. It hinted at his power, rather than bragging about it.

It was also mouthwateringly sexy.

At least as sexy as the little dress she had on.

But there was also no mistaking, not just in the cut of his

clothes, but in the way he held himself, that the man was a billionaire, just as they were portrayed on the covers of books and magazines.

He had sunglasses on. They shielded his eyes and gave him a celebrity quality. She could see her reflection in them.

She tucked a stray curl behind her ear. She needn't have bothered. It leaped right back to where it had been before.

"Hi," he said, casually.

His hair was longer than when she had first seen him getting out of his car at Hidden Valley all those months ago. But then, as now, the setting sun was adding threads of gold to the light brown strands.

He was also sporting a faintly roguish look, whiskers darkening the perfect, chiseled planes of his cheeks and chin.

"Hi?" she said, trying to hide the hard pounding of her heart. Her attuned senses were flooded with him, and it made it hard to resist the desire to fling herself at him *again.* Had she learned nothing at all from her past flingings?

Jolie folded her arms in front of herself, over the transparency of the dress. It was a small gesture against the swamping of her defenses.

"Hi," she said, "as in you were just in the neighborhood and thought you'd pop by?"

"Something like that. Don't look at me as if I'm a stalker to add to your collection of men you've spurned."

"*Spurned* seems a little strong."

He lifted the sunglasses. Oh, those eyes! A shade of green that should be criminal, since it could be used as a weapon against a weakening heart.

Too easy to remember how the color of those eyes had darkened with passion each time Jay had lowered his head to kiss her.

Actually, it seemed as if maybe they were darkening a shade now, as he took in the dress.

"Does it?" he asked, quietly.

"Does what?" she stammered, getting lost in the look in his eyes, losing the conversational thread completely.

"Does *spurned* seem like too strong an expression for what you did to me?"

"Yes!"

It was sweltering, the day's heat trapped up against her front door. Reluctantly, she stepped back, let Jay in, shut the door behind him.

His presence made her cozy space seem even tinier. She knew, no matter what happened, he would always be here now, his presence leaving an imprint.

"I like this," he said.

The man who could have and buy anything liked her apartment?

Big deal.

She wondered if he'd like the bedroom. That was the problem with letting Jay in, particularly since her senses had gone wild.

"I'm trying to understand why you left me the way you did," he said. She wanted to close her eyes and listen. Not to the words. To the tone. The faint rasp.

"Just kind of mid-dance," he continued. "No goodbye."

"Come out to the deck," she said. "We'll catch the last of the sun going down. You can see Saint Peter's from there."

So first she'd invited him in. And now they were going to the deck. And then she'd pour him a glass of wine. In fact, she grabbed a wineglass off an open shelf as they passed through her apartment, the kitchen and the living room all sharing a space.

He was edging into her life, one inch at a time.

And she was allowing it.

If the butterflies in her stomach were any indication, she was *loving* it.

"I sent a text," she said, pouring him a glass of wine. He took off the suit jacket and draped it over the back of his chair, then sat down.

He lifted an eyebrow at her as he lifted the wineglass to his lips. "Right," he said, "a text."

"Okay, maybe I should have done that differently, but you're not exactly without sin, either."

Sin.

She could think of a few she wished they were committing right this second!

CHAPTER TWENTY

"SIN," JAY SAID, with a certain amount of wicked relish. "That sounds like something from our Catholic high school."

"You are in Rome. Let he who is without sin…"

"You're keeping me in suspense. What's my sin?"

His sin? So many of them. Where to begin? Bringing out the passionate side in her, making the entire world with all its rules disappear when she was in his arms, making her believe in something she had sworn off…

"You forgot to tell me a few things about yourself," Jolie informed him.

"Such as?"

"Oh, you know, the billionaire part."

"Okay, that's a first. A woman saying that as if it's a bad thing."

"It's not the billionaire part, exactly, that's the bad thing. It's you not telling me."

"You left the wedding that night because you thought I was a billionaire?" he said skeptically.

"Aren't you?"

"Having a billion dollars in sales is not the same as being a billionaire."

"Now you're splitting hairs."

"I would have thought success would make me more attractive, not less." He pushed his hair back off his forehead. It flopped back down as if he hadn't touched it at all.

"Jolie, I didn't tell you because I wanted, just for a while, for it to be the same as it was before I achieved success. Like it was in high school, where people just liked me for me."

"You're deluded. They liked you because you were the captain of the football team. And you were good-looking. And had a great ass."

"People are that superficial?" he asked, with mock horror.

"Yes."

"The point I'm trying to make is that when you first achieve success, it's not what you think it's going to be. It's lonely. You can't take people at face value anymore. It's exhausting trying to sort out if someone's interested in you for you, or if their interest is about what you can do for them."

He was actually making her feel sorry for him. That was ridiculous!

"I saw the pictures of you at home with some of the world's most well-known celebrities," Jolie said firmly. "You didn't look exhausted."

"That's what I'm trying to tell you. When it first all hits, it feels like you need a new world. So you gravitate to people who have as much as you.

"Then you find out sometimes those people—like Sophie—have the limelight on them all the time. They're in a cage that they can't get out of. They hate the attention. They love the attention. Often, they need the attention for their careers. Lots of them regard any kind of publicity as good publicity.

"So, yes, I stuck my toes in the waters of that world. I found I couldn't live with that kind of scrutiny. If you stubbed your toe and had a scowl on your face, the day's headline was that you'd had a big fight with your lover.

"The thing is, if you get too deep into that world, you can't get back out. Things are never going to be normal for you again.

"And maybe because that's what I grew up with, that's what I crave. Normal. I had to make choices, and so I've chosen a small inner circle of people I can trust.

"My family, my sister and brothers. Old friends. No one keeps me down-to-earth quite like Troy, saying *Oh, get over yourself, you still suck at a pickup game of basketball.*

"When we first met again, it was so apparent to me that you didn't know about my success, I wanted you to be like that, too. I would have told you sooner or later, but I just wanted to be an average guy for a while. What would have changed if I would have told you?"

Jolie sighed. "Have you ever heard the expression, *punching above your weight*?"

"Sure. Hasn't everybody?"

"It doesn't translate to Italian. I heard Jack and Jill talking. That's what they said about me and you."

"Punching above your weight doesn't have to mean you're in the wrong class. It can mean you have enough confidence in yourself to try anything."

Why did he always, always seem to see her in a different light than the one she saw herself in?

"That's not how they said it," she said tightly.

"And that's why you left? Without even saying goodbye?"

She nodded, tightly.

"I don't believe that's true. Not that they didn't say it, but that anything those two witches said would affect how you felt about me."

"I looked you up online after I overheard them. The plane. Hobnobbing with the rich and famous. It was obvious to me it was true. I was punching way above my weight."

He stared at her, and then he reached across the table and took her hand in his. He squeezed.

"What's really going on, Jolie?" he asked, his voice soft. "Because after that, you planted marigolds for my mom?"

"How did you find out that was me?"

"Oh, you know, that billionaire secret weapon. My superpower."

"What's your superpower?" she asked.

"Throw some money at it."

She looked at his lips. She couldn't stop herself. She said, "That's not your superpower."

He smiled at her. "Now," he said with satisfaction, "we're getting somewhere."

She sighed. What was really going on? With his hand in hers, she felt safe telling him the full truth.

"I was embarrassed, Jay. I set up the fake engagement. And then I seduced you. I was the aggressor. And, all that time, I had no idea how far out of my league you were."

He cocked his head. "There's still something you're not telling me."

It was terrifying to be seen like this.

Terrifying, and as if she had been waiting her whole life for it at the same time.

"Sabrina told me she was pregnant."

His brow lowered. "Holy. Does Troy know?"

"I nearly got slapped for asking that."

"Well, he didn't want to have kids yet."

"So I knew that, and I was considering the super yucky possibility she'd trapped him. Using the same trap my mom used on my dad."

"Oh, Jolie," he said, "I'm sad that's how your parents got together and even sadder that you knew. Kids should not know stuff like that."

"Sabrina got it thrown in her face every time they had an argument."

"That explains a few things about Sabrina," he said.

"I know."

"As gut-wrenching as all this is, what does it all have to do with us?" he asked.

Complete confession time. They were in the Catholic capital of the world, after all.

"In the throes of passion, I didn't think about birth control," she admitted.

He went very still. "That's not totally on you. I must have been carried away myself. I can't believe it never once occurred to me." And then, quietly, "Are you?"

"No."

Did he actually look faintly disappointed?

"No, Jay, I'm not. But if I had been, wouldn't it have looked as if I set a trap for the billionaire?"

"Pretty sure I just saw that title on a book at a kiosk at the airport."

She smacked him on the shoulder. She'd missed doing that. From the look on his face, he might have missed it, too. "I don't think you've been in the public spaces in an airport for quite some time."

"Okay, I saw it at my sister's house, but she'd kill me for outing her for reading *Setting a Trap for the Billionaire*."

"You did not see a book with that title.

"Okay, maybe not *exactly* that title, but I'm still going to summarize that plot, through your point of view, which is romance writer talk."

"How would you know?"

He wagged wicked eyebrows at her. "I know lots of things. So, to summarize, you seduced me, and then thought you might be pregnant. And didn't want it to seem like you were trying to snag yourself a billionaire, so you left without saying goodbye."

"Yes, that sums it up."

"Except for the marigolds."

She was silent for a moment. Then she said, "I just wanted

your mom to know somehow, that when love leaves you, maybe it comes back in a different way."

"I don't think that's all it was, Jolie."

The look on his face made her heart go very still.

"I think it was an invitation," he told her softly.

"For what?" she squeaked

"You were right. You set up the engagement. And then you seduced me." He paused.

"But those marigolds sent me a message. You hadn't left me. You certainly hadn't left me because I was a billionaire.

"You did what a woman with dignity and self-respect—a woman who knows her own worth—would do. You invited me. You said, *You want me? We have a future? It's your turn. You make the move. You be the leader. You prove yourself worthy of me.* And that's why I traveled around the world. To accept your invitation. To make my move."

CHAPTER TWENTY-ONE

JOLIE LET THAT sink in, stunned.

Jay Fletcher had traveled halfway around the world to make a move on her, to see if they had a future together.

To see if *he* was worthy of *her*.

"So, where should we start?" he asked her.

She knew exactly where to start. She was out of her chair in a flash, on his side of the table, in his lap, twining her arms around his neck.

Kissing him.

"No," Jay said firmly, "not this time."

"I know what I want," she said, nuzzling his lips, feeling like a person dying of thirst who had just found water—

That line had worked so well last time. This time, Jay gently scooted out from under her. She found herself sitting in the chair alone, gazing up at him.

"Jolie," he said firmly. "I'm taking the lead this time."

"What does that mean?" she said, and heard a touch of sulkiness in her voice.

"I knew exactly who you were when you were sixteen," he said softly. "Do you remember what I said to you that night?"

"Almost word for word," she said, and not happily.

"I said," he reminded her softly, "that you weren't a fling kind of girl, that I could see forever in your eyes. You still aren't that kind of girl. Woman. I still see the same thing in

your eyes that I always saw. A longing for happily-ever-after.
You're the forever kind. We have to find out if I am, too."

"How?" she stammered. Jay was talking about him and
her happily-ever-after. *Forever?*

Sometimes you did not allow yourself to admit how badly
you wanted something.

And then someone spoke it out loud, and with their word
breathed life and hope into your secret dream.

"I'm going to court you, in an old-fashioned way. It means
I'm going to treat you with complete honor and respect, just
like I did the night of the senior prom."

"Well," she said, and then to hide the fact it felt like she
might be going into a good old-fashioned swoon, "that
sounds perfectly dull."

"I'm going to woo you and romance you."

"It's getting a little better," she decided. "But we're going
to kiss, right?"

He tilted his head, considering. "Occasionally," he decided, and then, dead serious, "Jolie, I'm going to be the
man my father raised me to be."

Even though she just wanted to drag him into the bedroom and seduce him all over again, she was also intrigued
by the relationship plan he was outlining.

Honored by it.

"So," he said, "if a billionaire dropped by unexpectedly
to see you in Rome, where would you suggest going out for
dinner?"

"I've ordered dinner. It should be here any minute."

"If you hadn't ordered dinner, where?"

"There's a place I walk by on my way to work at the Colosseum. It's pretty famous for its food and ambience. I've
always wanted to go there. It probably takes months to get
reservations, though."

"Ah," he said, "billionaire superpower number two. A

personal assistant named Arnold. If he can't do it, it can't be done."

And so it began, with an exquisite candlelight dinner at one of Rome's most exclusive restaurants. She was pretty sure that she caught a glimpse of Al Pacino.

When they got home the dinner she had ordered was waiting on the steps, and they ate that, too!

And that's how it unfolded.

Jay was a perfect gentleman. He spoiled her with surprise weekend drop-ins. He picked her up in his private plane and they explored Paris together. He sent the plane to get her so she could join him when he had business in New York. They explored that city as the leaves began to fall.

They toured museums and sampled wine and had box seats for sporting events and concerts.

As fall turned to winter, they went heli-skiing in the Canadian Rockies, and skating on Ottawa's Rideau Canal.

Jolie loved the glitz and glamour! Of course she did. And yet what she came to love best of all were the unexpected moments that became so special because their very simplicity allowed her to see how Jay shone in the world.

One of her favorite moments was a stop for a hamburger at a little hole-in-the-wall run by a couple who had been married for forty-five years.

Or when they walked through a park and stopping to watch a little boy and his sister making ships out of leaves and sailing them across puddles.

Her favorite things became not five-star restaurants and jaunts to exotic places in the private jet, but pizza, with hand-stretched crust like Nonna had taught her, and a movie at home.

His hand in hers on a chilly day.

The way his eyes lit up every single time he saw her.

The tenderness in his voice when he spoke to her.

The biggest surprise of all was how much she started to love going back to Toronto. In fact, it began to squeeze out their explorations of other places in the world.

When Jolie came home, she and Jay would hang out with Sabrina and Troy, watching her sister's belly grow. It was delightful to witness how excited Troy was about becoming a dad.

For the first time in her life, Jolie enjoyed being around her parents. She wasn't sure if Jay's billionaire status put them on their best behavior, but there seemed to be new rules between them.

If she was not mistaken, her mother was not begging anyone to love her anymore.

Once, when they were together, that song came on.

"My namesake," Jolie said wryly.

Her mother looked puzzled. "What? This song? You were named after my favorite auntie. She died right before you were born."

And so this, too, was a lesson in family.

What you thought about your family was one part truth, and one part myth, and all the other parts were perception.

She loved meeting Jay's mom. She radiated the sweetness of a person who gave their heart completely.

And she gave it completely to Jolie.

She talked Jolie and Jay into taking a painting class with her.

"Do you think the paint is edible?" Jay asked Jolie in an undertone, midclass, obviously getting bored.

"No, it's not edible!" she told him, but giggled, remembering the avocado mask. Was there anything in the world quite as nice as a man who would go to great lengths to make you giggle?

He ate a blob of the paint.

Just as his mother looked their way, too. His mom sighed with a pretense of long-suffering.

"He's always been like that," she told Jolie, and then to Jay's embarrassment regaled the whole art class with stories of things he had done when he was young.

Jay and Jolie spent rowdy nights watching baseball games in sports bars with his brothers. She adored his sister, Kelly, and the silliness of the game events that she held at her small apartment on Friday nights.

She loved being witness to how those people that Jay had chosen for his inner circle loved him.

And respected him.

Through it all, no matter how she tried to tempt him, and oh, she did, Jay would not break.

Hard no to hanky-panky, he'd remind her, when she'd plant a kiss on his neck, or sneak one onto his lips.

"I've been thinking about Christmas," he told her one night on the phone. "You said, growing up, it was the worst time for you."

Her heart just filled with tenderness that he always remembered these things.

"So, I thought it's time to make new memories. I want us to have the most spectacular first Christmas together. I've narrowed it down to two places. Rovaniemi, in the Lapland of Finland or Bath, in England. They both would be really unique—"

"Jay, I never thought you would hear these words from me, but I want to spend Christmas at home."

"Home. Rome?"

When had that happened? Rome didn't feel like home so much anymore. She felt like she belonged other places, now, too.

"I just can't imagine not being around your mom at Christmas. Not seeing Kelly and Mike and Jim."

He groaned. "Kelly likes to play *all* those horrible games on Christmas Eve."

"Perfect. And how could we not have Christmas with Sabrina and Troy and my mom and dad? You know, with all its potential for disaster, maybe we could look at getting everyone together."

"One big happy family?" he said skeptically.

"Something like that," she said happily.

Here's what Jay did not like about her plan. He had an engagement ring for Jolie. It had been burning a hole in his pocket for months, while he tried to figure out exactly the right time and the right words.

It had been fun romancing her.

He felt as if he'd gotten to know her and her family, but also himself and his family so much better through the process.

But the no hanky-panky thing was becoming impossible.

A man's honor could only carry him so far.

His was going to carry him and Jolie straight to the altar. After that, he planned to make up for lost time.

Finally, he had decided, Christmas would be the best time to propose even if she had said no to Finland and Bath, both with much higher potential for romance than Toronto.

He wanted it to be Christmas because he remembered her saying it was the worst time of all for her.

And he wanted to start changing that.

With a Christmas proposal.

And then once he'd proposed—once it was official that they were going to be man and wife—if they were in Toronto, he might as well use that. He'd planned prosecco and his king-size bed and a celebration she would never forget. He planned to end their courtship with the complete seduction of Jolie.

An evening with family?

Sheesh.

Could nothing ever go according to plan?

CHAPTER TWENTY-TWO

"Is EVERYTHING OKAY?" Jolie asked Jay.

"Oh, sure." *Hunky-dory*, he thought to himself. Her plane had been late, they were in the middle of a bloody snowstorm, his sister was having both of their families over for Christmas Eve, and he had to figure out how to get that ring on Jolie's finger.

Tonight.

His mother and Jolie's father were planning the traditional *la vigilia* feast. No turkey for them. The last time he'd spoken to his mother, they were planning seven courses of seafood, since meat was a no-no.

While it was good to see his mom having enthusiasm for life again, where in the seven courses did he fit in his proposal?

Certainly he had to get it in before his sister started her infernal games, and then they were all herded off to midnight mass.

He'd confided in Troy because it seemed to him maybe Troy knew a thing or two about proposals, having done it twice.

It was Troy who had suggested after dinner would be nice. It was rare for the whole family to get together, but they would be on Christmas Eve, so why not do it then?

Troy even suggested they could hide the ring in a Christmas firecracker thing that would be at each place setting.

Now that they were almost at Kelly's house, Jay could feel his feet getting cold. Did he really want to propose publicly? Did he get down on his knee in front of everyone? According to Troy, nothing would say commitment quite like that.

What if she said no?

For God's sake, she wasn't saying no. He glanced over at her. She looked back at him. There it was in her eyes. Forever.

He'd prepared his bedroom before he'd gone to the airport. Strawberries dipped in chocolate, prosecco on ice, new, crisp sheets. In the interest of his old-fashioned honor, he'd never let her stay at his place.

She stayed at her parents when she came here. What if she wanted to go there after midnight mass?

She wouldn't want to go there. They'd be newly engaged. It wasn't like she was six and had to be at their house so Santa could find her.

"Are you sure you're okay?" she asked.

"I said I was okay!"

Maybe he should hold off on the proposal? Until they were alone? That would be more romantic. When the heck were they ever going to be alone?

That was it. He wasn't proposing in front of both their families. He slipped into a parking spot in front of his sister's row house.

They were the last ones there. How had his sister's been picked? It was way too small. Oh, he'd gone along with that because he hadn't wanted them all at his place, when he was getting his own private celebration ready.

Troy gave him the secret handshake and a wink when they came in the door. Jolie, his wife-to-be, was swallowed up by both families who hadn't seen her for a while.

Geez, there was her sister. Sabrina looked as big as a house. He had to work at not saying it. Hadn't Troy said she had a month left?

"Sabrina," he said, "you're, ah, glowing."

There was too much noise and too many people, and his soon-to-be father-in-law and his mom were shouting in Italian in the kitchen. The smoke detector started wailing and his sister got under it with a dish towel, and waved with what appeared to be long practice until the smoke detector burped and quit.

This was not going to work.

He saw Troy laying down the firecrackers beside each plate. With the big wink at him as he set down a yellow one beside Jolie's place.

"Jolie," Troy yelled, "you sit here."

Jay scowled at him. Did he have to be so obvious? He felt like he couldn't breathe. He didn't think he could do this.

No, he hadn't thought it through.

A private moment, a nice restaurant, just her and him.

He reached over and slid her firecracker away from her plate and put it in his pocket. Troy raised his eyebrows and mouthed, *Chicken.*

Well, so be it.

Troy good-naturedly took another firecracker from the box and threw it at him. He set it in front of Jolie's plate.

But as it turned out, no one opened those firecrackers.

Because when Troy pulled back the chair for Sabrina, she suddenly clutched her stomach and cried out.

There was a sound like a balloon full of water hitting the floor. And then, as if it hadn't been chaotic enough, all hell really broke loose.

He found himself in the back seat of Troy's car with Sabrina's head on his lap and her terrified eyes glued to his face. Every now and then a whimper of pain would escape her.

Selfishly, he was glad he hadn't proposed. A stupid rhyme went through his head.

First comes love,
Then comes marriage,
Then comes Jolie pushing the baby carriage.

Only it wasn't Jolie, it was Sabrina, but did a man seriously ask this kind of pain of a woman if he loved her?

Troy drove. Jolie rode shotgun.

A whole convoy came behind them.

He said anything that came into his head. "You're doing great. Everything will be okay. Troy's a super driver. Hang in there. Five more minutes. We're almost there."

And then they were at the hospital in the driveway reserved for emergencies. Troy screeched to a halt.

"I can't move," Sabrina whispered.

Jay catapulted out of the car and ran around and over to the other passenger door. He flung it open. If he was not mistaken that was a baby's head. He rammed himself into the back seat.

And then, suddenly, he was holding a very slippery, very bloody baby, trying to protect its fragile body from the snow. For a terrifying moment, he thought the baby, a boy, was dead.

But then it gave an outraged cry, and squirmed in his hands.

And then he was being pushed out of the way, and the baby was taken from him, and there was a stretcher and cops—where had they come from—and nurses and people yelling in Italian.

And then that great wave of noise and chaos moved away from him and it was blessedly quiet.

He sank down on the curb. Alone.

Except that Jolie came and sat on that cold wet curb beside him. And laid her head on his shoulder.

He realized he was crying.

And so was she.

And then she said, "Best Christmas Eve ever."

And he took the crumpled firecracker out of his pocket and gave it to her. There was no way he was going home alone after this.

"I'm sorry," he said. "Under the circumstances it's the best that I can do."

She pulled both ends, and there was a little clicking sound, because of course the firecrackers never worked, but it ripped open nicely and her ring had the decency not to fall out and fall down the gutter.

She took the ring and put it on her finger.

And then laid her head back on his shoulder.

"Yes," she said. "A million times yes."

EPILOGUE

JAY COULD FEEL his eyes smarting as Jolie walked toward him.

She was wearing the most simple wedding gown he had ever seen. But it did exactly what those dresses should always do, but hardly ever did.

The simplicity of the dress allowed the bride to shine through.

Everything that she had become in the last few months was there: her confidence, her belief in herself, her generosity in love.

But it wasn't any of that that was making his eyes smart.

It was what she carried.

Instead of a bouquet, she had her hands cupped around a single bedraggled marigold in a plastic container.

To Jay, it looked like the most beautiful flower in the entire world. Love was exactly like that flower. If you nursed it, it would come back, stronger and better than it had ever been before. But more than that, when you planted it, it spread. Even when the original died out, as of course it eventually would, it left its mark on the world.

That's what his mother and father's great love had done. It had left its mark on the world. It had nourished him, and his brothers and sister, given them strength, and ultimately the ability to see that love made the world better and it made people better.

It had given him the ability to help heal someone—Jolie-who had not experienced such love in her life. It had given him the gift of seeing her come to believe.

That love could be strong and true, pure and nourishing.

Eventually the gift his mother and father's great love had given him—that he had lost sight of for a while, that he had turned his back on for a while—would give again. To his children and maybe someday grandchildren and great-grandchildren.

That's what love did.

When everything else had faded away, it remained.

And it went on and on and on.

Forever.

He saw that in Jolie's eyes as she took her place in front of him at the altar. He saw there, what he had seen since she was sixteen.

Forever looked like babies taking first steps and it looked like new puppies on wobbly legs.

It looked like gardens full of marigolds.

It looked like the old ones flying away from this earth, and the sorrow of saying goodbye divided in half by love.

It looked like unexpected challenges and heartbreaking choices and losses that were every bit as much of this amazing dance as the joys were.

Love did not protect you from any of that.

Love, that thing he thought he'd said no to, had not accepted his refusal.

He listened as Jolie said her vows, her voice so strong and so sure, her forever eyes on him.

It was not part of what they had rehearsed.

Not even close.

But when her voice fell away, after she had said "I do," he leaned his forehead on hers, and he said, "Mrs. Fletcher, is that your final answer?"

* * * * *

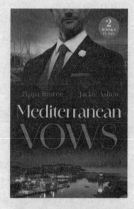

COMING SOON!

We really hope you enjoyed reading this book.
If you're looking for more romance
be sure to head to the shops when
new books are available on

Thursday 9th May

To see which titles are coming soon, please visit
millsandboon.co.uk/nextmonth

MILLS & BOON

MILLS & BOON®

Coming next month

THEIR ACCIDENTAL MARRIAGE DEAL
Nina Singh

Where had she thrown her dress? Or maybe Alden had taken it off her. That thought had heat rushing to her cheeks. She had woken up in his suite, on his mattress, curled up against his side.

All that alluded to a possibility she'd been avoiding speculating on. Had they…?

Hannah gave her head a brisk shake. She couldn't deal with that question just now.

'I have to find my dress.'

He finished throwing on a pair of gray sweatpants and glanced around the room. 'It's gotta be here somewhere.'

Hannah had to resist the urge to ask him to put a shirt on.

Luckily, Alden distracted her from that train of thought by locating her dress. It had been hiding in plain sight below the glass coffee table.

She thanked him and quickly threw it on.

'You're welcome,' he answered.

Hannah rammed a hand through her curls, her heart hammering in her chest. Between her physical discomfort and the shock flooding her system, she was sorely tempted to just crawl back into bed and forget any of this was even happening. To be oblivious again to reality, as she'd been just a few minutes earlier. When she'd been snuggled close and warm in Alden's arms.

She bit out a curse under her breath.

'What's that?' Alden asked.

Hannah gave her head a shake. 'Nothing. I was just thinking that we absolutely can't mention any of this to Max and Mandy. Or to anyone else, for that matter.'

Alden nodded once. 'Agreed. This weekend should be all about the two of them.'

'Agreed,' she repeated.

Several moments passed in awkward silence. Finally, Alden cleared his throat. 'As far as getting ready goes, I don't have to do much. I'll help you. Whatever you need.'

'I might need to take you up on that. Thank you,' she said. He could probably start with helping her uncover the mystery of exactly where her room was and how she might be able to get into it, considering there was no room key in sight.

He shrugged and smiled at her with a playful wink. For a split second, the sheer beauty that was Alden Hamid served to take her breath away and she could easily see why in an altered, uninhibited state of mind she would have pledged to marry him with eager enthusiasm.

'You're welcome. It's what any decent husband would do.'

Continue reading
THEIR ACCIDENTAL MARRIAGE DEAL
Nina Singh

Available next month
millsandboon.co.uk

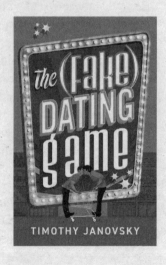

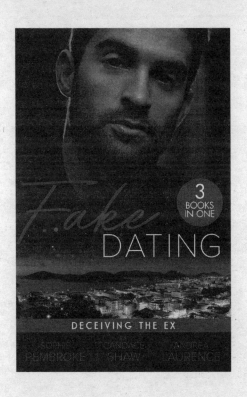

OUT NOW!

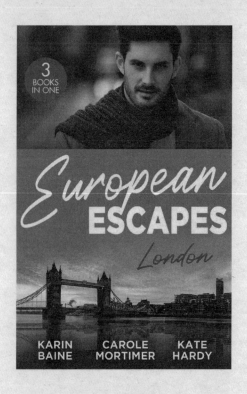

Available at
millsandboon.co.uk

MILLS & BOON

LET'S TALK

Romance

For exclusive extracts, competitions and special offers, find us online:

f MillsandBoon

X @MillsandBoon

◎ @MillsandBoonUK

♪ @MillsandBoonUK

Get in touch on 01413 063 232

MILLS & BOON

THE HEART OF ROMANCE

A ROMANCE FOR EVERY READER

MODERN

Prepare to be swept off your feet by sophisticated, sexy and seductive heroes, in some of the world's most glamourous and romantic locations, where power and passion collide.

HISTORICAL

Escape with historical heroes from time gone by. Whether your passion is for wicked Regency Rakes, muscled Vikings or rugged Highlanders, awaken the romance of the past.

MEDICAL

Set your pulse racing with dedicated, delectable doctors in the high-pressure world of medicine, where emotions run high and passion, comfort and love are the best medicine.

True Love

Celebrate true love with tender stories of heartfelt romance, from the rush of falling in love to the joy a new baby can bring, and a focus on the emotional heart of a relationship.

HEROES

The excitement of a gripping thriller, with intense romance at its heart. Resourceful, true-to-life women and strong, fearless men face danger and desire - a killer combination!

From showing up to glowing up, these characters are on the path to leading their best lives and finding romance along the way – with plenty of sizzling spice!

To see which titles are coming soon, please visit

millsandboon.co.uk/nextmonth